SLICE

LRJOHNSON

Printed in the United States of America

ISBN: 978-0692589403

Cover photo from adobe stock

Design by LR Johnson

Foreword by: Lavette Williams

MATURE_AUDIENCE_ONLY

This book is dedicated to my mother. I love you so much. You have always motivated me to push for what I want in life and never settle. You believe in me when I can't believe in myself and for that I am eternally grateful.

-LR Johnson

Pasty, white skin
Flaking lips
Stale body
Stilled fingertips
She looked well in death
But liveliness wore her better
From her '90s vintage pumps
To her button-down sweater
It broke his little heart
To see her in such dismay
But this wouldn't be his first
Lethal heartbreak
His previous lover's had left a few scars
But he'd left too many for fingers to count
His were deeper; skin-deep
With ridged marks that left him
Composed and dazed with relief
His lopsided smile
His wild eyes
The rush of their skin
Subsided by the slice of his knife
Sanity blossomed throughout his veins
When she was alive
Her lullabies, her whispers
Made it harder to say goodbye
Farewell wasn't foreign
As his father had done it before
Leather jacket in his arms
As he trekked out the door
Everything was unraveling
Into his trembling clutch
It was then that he vowed to never
Forget all the hearts she'd touched

-Lavette Williams

CHAPTER ONE

Cypress

The campus was crowded; my mom and dad had dropped me off at the new apartment reluctantly. Leaving home was something that I had decided to do without their permission. I didn't need their permission, but parents always wanted to have the last word. The breakup had torn me down in a way that I had never experienced and unfortunately my parents were no help in consoling. They adored my ex and I loathed him for more reasons that can be described. So I packed up and decided that this final year of college would not be spent in Tennessee. It would be spent in Colorado Springs, over 1000 miles from home.

There was so much to be done. I had to find a car for one. My old car had died on me during the summer break and I had some money saved up working at the local grocery store. It was not much, just 3000, which had almost been drained from this move. Thank God my parents had went ahead and gave me the money for a down payment. Their words, *spend it on a reasonable car.* So my future BMW was out of the question. My parents always helped me whenever I needed it. I was almost saddened that I had moved but I wasn't in the least bit. Moving had been a great idea, at least that is what I had convinced myself. I wanted to go somewhere I would not be known. I wanted to be unnoticed and start over. And I did just that, no social media, a new number and new beginning. It was what I needed most, after the break up that I had just been through. Phillip was the worst thing that had happened to me. My mother objected, my father objected and his parents hated me. But it was mainly because they didn't know the real Phillip. They knew the Phillip that he wanted them to know. They didn't know the guy that slung me around the room and raped me on two occasions. They knew the quarterback, churchgoing, heartthrob. I ended it.

The new college, I had enrolled in would make a difference. Colorado Springs was full of life and most importantly, it was beautiful. I felt young, free and alive just from being here one day. Hello, Colorado.

My first class was in the English department. Creative Writing 406, the teacher was an author and she graded off of your potential, not others. It was written on her door and on her teacher website for orientation, I loved writing. There was something freeing that lingered between me and the words on the page. Once my fingers started clicking to the keys there was no stopping me. All I needed was a good musician and a charged up laptop and life was better than I knew.

I sat down in the classroom, unlike the biology lab or the English 329 classroom this class was close and personal. There was no stadium of kids with a paperback notebook and a set of headphones on. There were thirty desks and they were in a circle. Then there was a blackboard. I hadn't seen one in years. I took out my notebook and wrote the date in the corner. This particular class was for the upperclassmen and one had to be accepted. It was well known among the literary world that this woman was the best in the league for crafting good writers. I put my pens on the desk and whipped out my kindle. There was always time to read, no matter where I was.

I could hear the students as they adjusted in their seats, they must have known each other because they chatted non-stop making it impossible to concentrate on my latest read The Time Keeper. I gave up and started to look at my surroundings. There were some geeky people in here. I couldn't judge. I was not exactly the most average looking person. My outfit was thrown together. Jeggings with a hole in the thigh and a tattered shirt that had Go Vols written in faded orange. Then it was the mess of curls that tried to burst from the almost broken hair tie I had found in the car.

The desk beside me went from vacant to full and I turned to meet my new neighbor. I immediately regretted not digging up that damn sundress from the bag of clothes. He was heavenly and I hadn't even seen his whole body yet. I glanced over him twice. His hair flowed past his cheek bone and draped his shoulders lightly and it was a warm brown with reddish highlights. The sun from the window beside him only accented the hints of blue in green eyes and then he spoke to me. "Hello." He whispered with a flash of his perfect teeth and dimples. He had dimples.

I melted in my seat. *Say something you dimwitted fool. Speak the words!* My hand barely rose from the desk and I could feel the rush of red heat as it flowed to my caramel cheeks. Damn it!

"Alright class! Let's get this started." Her voice rang over the small talk and chatter. "I want to hear about the summer in a short story." She turned to the blackboard with the white chalk in her hands and wrote. "I want it to be called A Summer in Paradise. 30 minutes, generate magic!"

The title was just as cheesy as she was and my summer was not paradise but I could work something. More students continued to pour in the desk beside me was no longer empty and the classroom door was closed and locked. All that was heard in the room was the clicking of pens, while the writer thought and the sound of the pages turning.

My page was only half way through when her loud hand clap snapped us away from our mental frenzy and back into reality. I closed my notebook while she ranted about her summer and she spun out the gold in her short story like it was so easy to create what she had said. I had created garbage. Pure unadulterated garbage, I had some training to do.

A Summer in Paradise   *By Cypress Tucker*
The summer started out like any other. The kids frenzied along the neighbor like they had been freed from some prison, not to simply realize they had it easy. Easy, shit my life had not been easy. I had to let Prince Charming know that I would be resigning as his Princess and the whole kingdom was bound to go into disturbia because the throne would be left unattended. Being born into that life was not what I wanted. I wanted to be free. I wanted to live without the weight of him...

I let Prince Charming down easily, but things got messy, there were tears... mainly from him. The ~~bitch and pitchmen~~... King and Queen from each fucking kingdom realized that I had tarnished the name. I was banished from kingdom they saw it as a punishment I saw it as an opportunity. I packed up a few things, leaving behind my horse and carriage and tossing in my Sketchers, Paradise was around the corner and...

I nodded my head at the grisly sight I should have been more prepared. I tried to tear it out of the notebook and a hand clasped over mine.

"It's alright, if it's tainted..." the accent was thick and beautiful.

I turned my head and met the eyes of my neighbor, god he was so beautiful and here I was still unable to formulate a decent sentence to him. "I just don't want it... to be seen."

"We'll work on it." Fuck! I looked over at my neighbor. He smiled timidly and handed me a piece of graphing paper. "Breathe, these exercises are to let you know that your worst can be a masterpiece to someone else." He smiled and his accent was overwhelming, English and perfect. He pointed to the board. Apparently I had missed the whole conversation about partnering up with the person to my left. He took my notebook and he handed me his. Lucas Elledge, my heart was about to fall on the ground. I had held onto his book and read three times before I could put it down and then started reading it again. He was published and New York Times best seller. What was he doing here?

The Last Paradise   *By: Lucas Elledge*

Was there such a thing as Paradise? I had spent my entire summer dwelling on this issue. It could not possibly be a paradise when she existed no longer. Her locks of hair, gone, her smile that healed was gone. She was gone and there with her, she took paradise.

The monster had made its grand entrance a year earlier. He attacked her in ways that she had never experienced. He weakens and he takes and never gives anything but a new pain. She suffered, more than I could bear, more than I could watch. Paradise was fucking over. There was no more laughs and giggles about the thrills of paradise and there was no more care. ~~She sat in agonizing breathtaking pain~~... and paradise left.

My mother died on a Saturday and even the skies cried for her. The drought ended and there she did too. The monster had won and my paradise was lost.

Well, damn it, I had been partnered with some literary genius, this was his quick, easy short story and it was only three paragraphs but damn it! I dropped the notebook and my face was white, was I really supposed to be in this classroom? Lucas Elledge was a fucking genius.

"I like it," He smiled. "Uhm, we have to critique each other," Lucas looked at me, his curls falling his face. "I feel like you could do better, are you nervous?"

I swallowed hard, I was embarrassed. No, it was not my best work. It was complete garbage. "Yeah, I was a little nervous."

"Well don't be, I promise it gets worst. We have to learn how to take it." Lucas nodded his head understandingly. "The teacher wants us to take criticism and understand that they are always helping not really bludgeoning us like it feels. So lightly I say your story is stuck between two worlds and you should choose one so the reader isn't lost… you started with children leaving school and then went to a kingdom… stay in the kingdom… tell it differently. My name is Lucas, what's yours?"

"Cypress," I smiled.

He continued to talk and it was hard to understand anything that he said. My mind still pondered as it tried to accurately comprehend the level of his grief, he said even the skies cried for her… he was amazing. "Okay, I understand…"

"Okay, well, what about mine?" Lucas waited as he stared at me inquisitively… he turned his head waited almost impatiently.

I looked over the writing again, it was perfect. I nodded my head, "I actually don't see anything wrong with it. It's really good." I bit my lip and handed the notebook back to him. "I mean the title doesn't sync well, but other than that it is perfect."

"There is always something that can be fixed, no one is perfect." Lucas nodded his head. "How long have you been writing?"

"I have been writing for about 12 years. I have better work, but it was unexpected."

"She does every morning that class starts. She wants people to use what they can and write, tomorrow she'll ask us to finish the short story and give it to the person on our right to be edited. Then she'll pass it to the person in front to be critiqued and then she'll grade them and send them to creative publishing class. I'm in that class, it's nice."

"So everyone will see my paper."

"We're working on it today, it's the assignment." He pointed to the board. "I'm free this afternoon around 5. I have to take my sister to her yoga class, then some other things. Can you come to the library and we can start there?"

"I can." I jotted down *5pm library* in my planner for the day and then wrote the assignment down. Luckily, there was only one more class after this and I would be done early enough to car shop. I was not fond of the bus system.

We walked out of the classroom and he stopped me in the hall, "Pardon me," He said pushing pass some students. "Cypress, you done wonderful in class. I hope that I was not a wee too harsh. Forgive me?"

"You're fine," I ran her fingers through my untamed curls and his eyes had me caught in some form of trance. Do not stare, this is just the guy who wrote the book that had made your summer better than it was going. "I really am rusty."

"Well, I would love to get together sometime and work to improve. I see real potential and I want to help. And I would like to date you, but I'm sure our love for English will be enough for now?"

"I actually would love to." She was a honey color, but her cheeks were on fire red. She crossed her legs standing and nodded her head. If she only knew what the fuck she had just gotten herself into. These American women could not resist a good accent.

"Perfect, let's just go to the library tonight and then Friday night I can take you to The Summit."

"Sounds like a perfect plan to me."

Asher

I had never put much into what the hell I was wearing, but today for some reason I put some thought into it. I grabbed my red polo and tossed it back on the ground. It was the day I finally met Lucas Elledge. There was some excitement here for me. My father had warned me to be careful and to not push him. It could be dangerous, this I knew. This research was like stepping into a lion's den knowing that there was no lifeline if I was found. But my PHD rested on this interview, or rather yet this observance if he even let me in.

Lucas Elledge was unlike any other human I had ever seen. He had successful committed almost ten murders this year alone. And no that is nothing to brag about, but there was no evidence tying him to any of the murders and those murders were just the tip of the iceberg for him. Lucas hunted like a lion. He stalked and lurked and then once he knew that they were at their most vulnerable moment he moved in to demolish whatever was in his path. I loved the thrill of it all and to the world he would be known as the one who got away, but to me he was Case Study B.

I slid on a plain black T-shirt and some black jeans. I looked at my hair in the mirror and scrambled my hands through it making sure that it was perfectly messy. I made my way out of my new apartment to my first class, this university had the worst psychology department but he had not chosen the college for the department. Lucas' had adopted parents who lived three towns over and they were crazy over the Brit. He wooed them as he had done the rest of the world, blending in perfectly even though his real home was across the globe.

I sat through class jotting down notes, but my mind was fixated on the stalk. How would I get this guy to let me in, Psychopaths were people that were good at not letting people in? He would kill me before he let me see the real him. My father said the only way to get his attention would be to call him out and let him know the cards that I held. I had sufficient enough evidence for there to be a formal investigation on him and he shouldn't kill me. That shit would not work.

I walked to my next class and ignored all the ogling eyes of the university girls that followed me. I was handsome, I knew that. My looks came from my father, he passed me the charm as well. Sex was not hard to come by, which made it even harder to find someone to marry. My mom wanted grandchildren and I had nothing to offer her. I refused to be tied down to someone that would sleep with me before they knew my last name. I had ten minutes to get to my next class and pretend to listen again.

This time in class I made strategies as to how to get close to him. He had a step brother named Mark and to be honest, I felt like he was a psychopath as well. He had no empathy. He had made three girls get abortions and then he stepped on people to get where he wanted to be, it was sickening. He had no remorse that one girl had even killed herself over him. He acted as if it never happened. He was a case study C, once I received the grant.

"Pardon me," Lucas said as he moved passed me to some girl. She was attractive and not the usual type he went for. He loved the promiscuous women who gave up easily and moved on. He wanted no emotional connection with them, he wanted everything but, four of his ex-girlfriends had gone on trips and never returned. "Cypress, you have done wonderful in class. I hope that I wasn't a wee too harsh. Forgive me?"

She looked flushed and her eyes wondered his body as if he was some kind of God. "You're fine," she ran her fingers through her curls and her eyes never left his. She was infatuated. "I really am rusty."

"Well dear, I would love to get together sometime and work to improve. I see real potential and I want to help. And I would like to date you, but I'm sure our love for English will be enough for now?"

He was so blunt. I leaned against the wall pretending to be intrigued with my phone, but I heard every word of the conversation. He had won her over without trying. I checked charming on the list.

"I actually would love to." She was a honey color, but her cheeks were on fire red. She crossed her legs standing and nodded her head. If she only knew what the fuck she had just gotten herself into. These American women could not resist a good accent.

"Perfect, let's just go to the library tonight and then Friday night I can take you to The Summit."

The Summit, it was his home and his business with his foster brother. A three story warehouse that used to be void and was nearly condemned a few years back was now the hottest place to be in town. Mark and Lucas had turned the ground floor into a club and it was thriving. People came from everywhere just to get in, I had received an invitation, but I hadn't put it down yet. Large crowds were not usually my thing. The second floor was the home of Mark. He was very private. He rarely even brought girls back there Lucas owned the third floor and liked to have guest sometimes when he wasn't busy perusing his blood lust. But the success of the club and his book ensured that he would not have to work. His book The Skies Cry had been on the top seller list for almost a year now and he refused to sell the rights for a movie. He just enjoyed the money for his work.

"Asher!" The familiar voice said from behind me.

I turned and there was an old friend. And I mean old. I had not seen her since Middle School and it was not a pleasure seeing her again. She had been obsessed. "Whitney! How are you?"

"Great, I actually work here in the Library."

"You're a librarian?"

"Yes," she blushed, from either embarrassment or nervousness, but she had grown nicely into her looks. Her brown hair cascaded down her back in ripples of curls and her eyes were still the greenest green I had ever seen. "When did you transfer in?"

"This semester," My eyes watched as Lucas walked away with his stepsister, Lydia. She was only seventeen, but she adored her older brothers more than anything in the world.

"Well, if you ever need anything, let me know, please. I would love to help you." Whitney turned on her heel.

"Dinner tonight?"

"Excuse me?" She was bright with happiness.

"Would you like to join me for dinner. I am kind of new and there are about 100 places to go here."

"Sure, I have to change, I hate wearing this vest out anywhere. What time should we meet?"

"I can pick you up around 7:30 and we can decide from there, could you write your number down?"

Lucas

Everyone has one demon or two in their closet. I have a couple of dozen and those demons like their home nestled in a tiny closet for my eyes only. The truth had never surfaced about me and I wanted to keep it that way. I lived a dual life, or at least it felt like it. I had my life for the public. My book had made it easy for me to not work, that's a good thing. My last few jobs back home in England has resulted in a death of one patron and three bosses. I was not a patient person, granted, I tried my best to make it look like I was more than patient. I hated competition and most of all I hated people with simple minds telling me what to do.

My sister continued with her playful recalling of her first day of her senior year at her school. If her mom, my adopted mother knew of her being here and not at some rehearsal Lydia had made up she would be grounded. But Lydia cared nothing for our mum's opinion. She just wanted to make sure she was in the loop with Mark and me. Mark was rarely on campus. He was so busy supervising the Summit that he almost forgot he was in school, but being as smart as he was, it was no problem, he always caught up. He always made sure that they were up to par.

"So, what do you think?"

I had listened to a small portion of whatever she was talking about and developed that she wanted to know if this guy liked her or was playing games. The simple answer was game playing. "He is more infatuated with the possibility of sex Lydia." I scrolled through my phone searching for the number of my favorite restaurant. Food was my favorite and I worked out to make sure my love for it wouldn't alter my looks.

"But he said he wanted to meet my mom."

"It still doesn't mean that he is not into shagging you, dear." I looked at their menu. They had the three bean soup as their special today and it just happened to be the best in town. "Join me for a bite to eat. They have Three Bean Soup today."

"Did you hear anything I said?"

"Lydia, I am starving, literally. I heard you unlike Mark I always hear you. I'll buy you lunch."

"Ugh, fine, call mom."

"Good, I would much rather her bust your chaps than mine." I smiled and finally we made our way to the cafe for some soup and a chat. Granted the entire chat was likely to be about Lydia and her darling Trey.

Contrary to popular belief about psychopaths we tend to have emotions. We just struggle to empathize with others. I could not and really didn't care to understand my sister's infatuation with Trey, he was a complete and utter idiot. She could do and deserved better. I knew I had to support her in her conquest, but the kid had one time to fuck up with her and he would meet the end of my blade before he could apologize. I handled most issues by hiding. Hiding and blending in. But I never forgot what a person done to me.

Cypress, she was a sweet girl. And based on the average picture of any male my age, she was what was missing. I needed a girlfriend, and up until I saw here the thought had never crossed my mind. She held my book like a bible and stared at me like her savior. And for the first time since my mom died I felt that there could be a real connection there with her. We had plans to study later and critique some work and hopefully she would want to grab some more food after we studied.

"It's your last year," Lydia said as we made our way to my car. "I'm coming here in the fall. Can I have your apartment?"

"Are you mad?" I said before thinking. Her face was pouty as if I had hurt her feelings.

"You're moving back to England aren't you?"

"I haven't even thought that far ahead Lydie. You little moocher." I laughed. I hadn't thought past Advanced Creative Writing. "We shall see. I thought maybe that I could stay in the states. I like it here and you are my family. I really only have me Nan at home and she just gardens and reads Ethan Fromm." My Nan was a character and she was boring all at the same time. I moved to find adventure and have a larger prey.

"Well, mom wants me to stay in the dorms first year."

"Why not, I did?"

"I don't want to."

"I don't want to go against mum and I don't know if I am even moving. Be normal for a change." Shit, I fucked up again. She was about to be extremely annoying and ruin my Three Bean Soup with her teenager rants. "I'm sorry. I'll think about it, okay?"

"Fine, I don't even know why you like Three Bean Soup. It's nasty."

"You have poor taste. I think they have pizza there as well. Something normal for you?"

We rode over to the Cafe and she talked about how she wanted Mark to give up being an accountant to piss her father off and how she was thinking that she would go into dance to piss him off further. In my opinion, he was a pretty good guy. He worked hard to make sure even I had food when we were younger. Our situation being a delicate one the family rarely brought up how I was brought into the family. They hated my mum and the arguments never went over well with them. So the subject was dead when it came to them.

"How do you think I should go about pursuing this new girl?"

"You are doing more than a one-night stand?"

"I'm trying. I like her. I just met her. And shut up."

"Well get to know her before you stumble head over heels. Remember your ex..."

"Oh shove off." I mumbled.

Cypress

Lucas had simply run through my mind all day. He did not exist back home. They are simply athletes or lab geeks. There was no in between. It was part of the reason I did not fit in. I preferred reading to partying and then whenever there was a free moment I was deep within the lines of a good book.

The car lot had tons of cars in the parking lot. I only had 8 grand to spend on the car. The rest of the money would have to be for living off of. I had no job yet and I doubted that I could get on the tutoring roster. I had a plan to post signs up all over the campus to tutor student for 200 a month. Five students would be good enough to cover rent and some utilities. I stared at the Black Altima. It was under my budget and the mileage was good and he was throwing in a free year unlimited warranty. Beings that I knew jack shit about cars I would have to have it.

My phone buzzed continually in my pocket. My mother was so consumed with knowing how life was it was bothersome. "Mom, I am buying a car," I said answering.

"That's great, your father and I are still around. We decided to make sure you had some groceries in the house. If you could call us when you leave with your errands we will stock, you up."

God, I loved them. That saved me 500 or so. "Yes, I am actually going to start the paperwork in about ten minutes. I looked over the car again and it rides good."

"Perfect, we will see you shortly."

I finished up with the car and swiped my card. I wanted to payment plan; I just wanted to get the car done with and start the year."

My parents were sweet and they wanted genuinely what was best for me. I was happy that they were leaving though. I wanted some alone time. I got the groceries and we ate lunch. We stocked up the empty apartment and then they left for their 7-hour drive home and there was silence.

I made my way to the library, my new story was tweaked. I had taken out the stupid parts and revamped it. Paradise was now a good start and hopefully Lucas would think the same thing. The library was huge and I had got lost walking in to three times, so I stood outside and waited for Lucas.

There he strolled with some girl, her hand intertwined in his they looked like they were perfect. I could not even think of a mean thing to say. He kissed her forehead, "Look, remember what mum said, and be home by 7. I don't want to hear her mouth, okay?"

Mum? I was lost. I thought she was dead. I twitched uncomfortably and smiled at him as he got closer. "Did you have a good afternoon?

"Perfect actually, my little sister and I went to get some soup." He chuckled and his sister pushed him playfully. "Though she hated the soup and complained the entire time."

"He read the entire time,' she had no accent. "So we'll meet here at about 630, Wednesday then?"

"Yes, and be on time. I have to do some editing for the Publisher." Lucas walked towards me as she left. "So are you ready to be creative?"

"Born to, I re-tweaked it a bit."

"I did too," We walked in the library and up to a study room. They were everywhere. I loved college already. I could lock myself up here when I didn't want to be bothered.

Lucas sat down and tossed his notebook on the table. "So this Prince Charming that you had to simply dump this year... why'd you leave him?"

"He was suffocating basically," I said simply put. "I wanted to have some time to find myself. I can't find myself while being with him."

"Nice," he jotted down some notes.

"What about your mom? How did she die?"

"Lou Gehrig's," he said. "She fought hard and that was all we could ask."

"Your story is profound, one line is circling around my head, I really can't stop it... *"Even the skies cried for her,"* I paused. "Wow," I said.

"Thanks, I thought that when she died. Usually it rains quite often in England, but the time that she was dying it was dry and it was nice. She enjoyed it and then when she took her last breath the sky started to cry and so did I. My mum was a doll. So let me see the revised copy of the Summer in Paradise."

I reached into the backpack and grabbed the notebook. "Be honest, okay."

My revision was nice; it was still garbage though. I could not find anything more than this asshole to write about anymore.

I watched him read and twiddled my fingers and rolled my eyes at the length of time he was taking. He shifted in his seat and placed the paper down. "Nice, I like it."

He was lying, I had not known him long but I could tell. "Be honest please!"

Lucas smiled. "Okay, look everyone has their summer drama and people care but readers won't. Paradise... what did you hate the utter most about him?"

I stuttered, "I, uh... I couldn't breathe."

"Okay, he was smothering." He jotted the words down and looked up. "A smothered paradise, perfect all you do is take that feeling in your gut and put it here." He slid the notebook over to me. Writing is the expression of you and this is a cliché. I don't think your cliché. Granted, I don't know you and I could be wrong, but I feel like there is nothing from here." He touched his chest. "On here," he pointed to the paper.

"Okay... well, I am not used to be prompted something to write. I just usually write and go on about my life.

"Don't think about the concept of paradise. It's fucking you up. What happened this summer?"

"I dumped him.'"

"You freed yourself." He smiled. "You were suffocating in a smoldering, smothering paradise and you freed yourself. It's all about the concept of how you think. You are happier now, correct?"

"Yes," I said. "Well, put that shit on paper." He jotted more notes down in his notebook. "I added some new things to mine. I'll let you read it and tell me some mean words to get back at me being mean to you."

I knew that my work was less than perfect. "You weren't meant to me, you were honest."

"I was and I would like to make it up you... do you have supper plans for next Friday?" Everything about him was perfect. His smile, his dimples the way he blinked was even perfect. And I had always had a weakness for men with long hair.

Next Friday? I barely knew what I was wearing the next day yet alone eating? "None at all," I said as I mentally cancelled plans to decorate my apartment.

"Perfect, we should go to this place called The Summit, I own it; I know you will like it. You can be my date if that's okay. I think the guys think I'm gay." There was a hint of humor as he smirked at me.

"Are you not?" There were so many rumors about him that floated around campus. He was like a mystery.

"Well, damn it, no." he burst into laughter. "Cypress I just asked you out. I am completely straight and completely impressed that you didn't slap the shit out of me for talking about your work. I took some writing classes under my aunt one summer and she taught me to be harsh when critiquing. It lights fires that can't easily be put out."

Every word out of his mouth was damned poem. "A date sounds like a great way to start off the year."

"Great," Lucas slid me his notebook and I read over the words. I had a date with Mr. Literary genius and then my life was getting better immediately.

CHAPTER TWO

Cypress

Colorado Springs had gone from strange to perfect in a matter of a week. I was still new and it made outings hard. I really only knew Lucas and I really didn't know him. Hopefully this trip to the Summit would change that. I had to admit it was rather weird going from Tennessee to Colorado. The mountains were hypnotic, capped with white snow and ranging in colors. It was a dream or at least it seemed like one.

I had spent a ton of time with Lucas in the past week and it was weird because after the hell I had been through it was the last thing I needed. I honestly was still reeling from the fact that he had asked me out in the first place. He was a handsome guy and not in the American way. His locks hung in his face most of the time. Even when he pulled them into a messy bun on the top of his head they still found a way to escape. His eyes were like two emeralds with hints of blue blazing through the stark green, and his smile caused my heart to skip a beat every time he flashed it. It was hard to not stare, more importantly to make a conversation worth having when he was around. Lucas made me nervous and I was afraid that the butterflies that were hidden inside would try to escape. He made me feel something new, not fear or anxious reeling.

Friday had snuck up on me quicker than expected. I had shopped for a perfect outfit to wear to The Summit, based on what my only friend and neighbor had told me, it was not a dressy place. I decided to go with a sleek cream dress and some pastel floral heels, I'd found at a thrift store. Then there was my disarray of sandy brown curls that could never be tamed. My mom had passed her curls to me and I loved them, but they made it hard to tame them. I brushed them into a bun and then put on my glasses.

Lucas was to be here in ten minutes. The apartment was cleaned; though there was barely anything in it. I didn't want to buy furniture until I knew I had a job. I tossed my backpack I the empty, guess room. And there was a knock at the door.

I knew he was prompt. Every morning he was in class like he never slept. But these final ten minutes for me were crucial. I couldn't decide on lipstick or eye shadow at the moment. I kicked off my heels and bustled over to the door. I barely busted my face on the corner of the door. Thank God for quick reflexes. I swiped down my dress and opened the front door.

"Tell me this is your outfit!" Shia, my neighbor, smiled as she walked in the apartment. She so far was my only associate in the area. I hadn't got out enough to have more than her. She was dressed up as well. Her petite stature was far different from mine. Not to mention the Brunette was first runner up for Ms. Colorado last year. It was her best feature, or so she said.

"It is," I smirked. "Should I toss on some red lipstick or perhaps this coral?" I held the two cylinder tubes up in front of her.

"No, leave it simple with the coral." She bounced into the apartment and closed the door behind her. I could smell her Chanel No. 5 clear across the room. She was drenched in money.

"Where are you going?"

"I actually got an invite to The Summit too! I got one from Mark, do you know him?"

"I've heard of him." I lied. I applied the coral lipstick and pressed my lips together. Coral was a good decision with the gold eye shadow I had laid out. I patted down my face lightly with bronze finishing powder and then spritzed some generic perfume on. Fancy was not the way around here.

"Well, he is taking me there. He said he should be over to my place in a few minutes. I came to see if I looked okay?"

My eyes rolled as I looked her over. Shia looked like she stepped out of a magazine. She knew she looked beautiful. I glanced over her long brown hair, it cascaded down her back. She didn't have a damn once of body fat on her. Unlike me who was blessed with too many curves. "You look amazing."

"Thank you Cypress! You look cute!"

Cute, I looked back in the mirror. "Perfect." I nodded as the melodic tone of the doorbell filled my apartment.

"I got it!" Shia waltzed over to the door as if her name was on the lease and posed in the jam of the door. "Hello."

"Uh… pardon me is this Cypress' apartment?" Lucas sounded confused and not the least bit amused.

It made me chuckle as I shoved my makeup in the kitchen drawer. God, I needed furniture.

"Yes, come on in, my name is Shia."

"Well actually if you are Shia my brother is across the hall waiting for you to answer your door… could we switch and I take Cypress off your hands and you take me off of his?"
He was so charming. He literally had just kicked her out of the apartment and she politely made her way out with no fuss.

I waited patiently for the door to close and then turned to him. He was dressed simple. Dark denim jeans with a pin striped black and white top that hung off of his arms. The short sleeves revealed a sleeve of tattoos that I never knew existed. But it made him all the more attractive. My eyes made their way up to his face. He was so clean shaven and neat to be so rugged. His hair was pulled into a bun and he smiled at me.

Lucas handed me the small bouquet of yellow daisies. I couldn't contain the smile on my face. "Thank you."

"You're so pretty." He paused. "Beautiful actually." He whispered. His eyes wandered over my body and he smiled a small smile. "I'm happy you said yes."

"Me too."

It was so quiet but I felt like there was something being said. He broke the silence. "I didn't know your apartment was so new I would have bought a vase."

"Yeah, I just moved down here like a week ago. My parents gave me money to buy some things for the house until they can come back out here."

"Where are you from again Cypress?"

I pulled a tall glass from the cabinet and added a small amount of water to it. "I am from Nashville." I paused.

"What brought you here? That's like 1000 miles away."

"Uhm just everything, I would rather be away from home." The truth was the past. But he didn't have to know everything. I placed the daises in the cup. "They have a temporary home."

"Well, it's a nice place you have here. Have you considered finding some furniture maybe?" The humor in his voice made me laugh.

"I have been so busy with my classes and I need to find a job. I haven't really put forth effort and I can't stay here without one."

"You could work at The Publisher on campus. I have some pull there. You just have to ask for clearance from the professor and I'll get you on."

"Okay, that's a good idea." The Publisher was something that I had not thought about since it was a campus job I just guessed it paid shit. And I needed some real money coming in. My rent was 500 and the utility bill was yet to be known. I was barely here so hopefully it would not be too much. "What does the Publisher pay?"

"It would twenty-five hours a week for fourteen an hour. It's not full time, they want you to be able to go to school and maintain a good grade point average."

"Sounds like a winner, I need to do both."

"Well, check into it. Put me down as your referral and I will work my magic."

Swoon, his magic was easily worked. I was already under his spell and the date had not yet begun. "Will do." I smiled at him and grabbed my light jacket from the bar in the kitchen.

"We should go, are you ready?"

Barely, it was hard to get my eyes unhinged from his lips. "More than."

The drive over was filled with small talk. He talked a ton about writing and how it made him a calmer person. I talked about how the pen had saved me from insanity as a child. He chuckled, but it was the truth, writing had saved me from being with my mom even when I was right in front of her. It took me places. The Summit was something different. It was dimly lit and there were cars overflowing in the Parking Lot. Lucas whipped his jeep into the vacant space that said owner.

"My brother and I started doing a Summit gathering once a week just over three years ago. People came from every school after three weeks it was packed in the school lawn, it was on a hill... The school said that we could not have them there anymore. We looked into finding a place and we stumbled upon this old building." He pointed to the three story building. The dark brick and red lighting around it made it seem eerie but I wanted to know more.

"What do you do here?"

"We dance; we sing... we eat. I have one of the best chefs in the world working for me here. We live. We are at the peak of life for us... The Summit..."

This guy was deep and he was just talking about a damn night club. I reminded myself to blink and smiled at him. "Well, I am thrilled. Did I dress okay?"

Lucas looked me up and down, then smirked. "I think you are dressed perfectly."

The crowd of people swayed to an upbeat song with too much bass and not enough words. I hadn't listened to the radio in so long I had no idea what or who it was and had no intention to care. But the up-tempo beat was catchy and he pulled me towards him with one swift movement. We were chest to chest and I felt as if I couldn't breathe. The closer I got to him the more I could smell the musk of his cologne, a deep amber with sandalwood undertones. We danced around the room our hips moved together as if we were made for one another and the final hitch of hope flared when we crossed fingers and it was magic. He was magic.

"Water, would you like some?" He whispered in my ear.

He had been talking to me apparently and I didn't hear a word while stuck in his trance. "Actually, what else do they have?"

"We have alcohol too..." he smiled. "What do you want?"

"Do you have something with Melon?"

"Melon Blitz, I think you'll like it. Entertain yourself for a while and I will be back in a few."

When he left I noticed there were eyes on me everywhere. I didn't know why and honestly would rather not know why. I looked for an empty table. Lucas was saying something to the bartender. The blond in the front of the crowd was making her way over to me and there was nowhere for me to run, so I braced myself. She wore a dress that looked like she was poured into and some heels that put her taller than everyone she passed.

"Are you here with Lucas?" she growled.

"Yes, hi, I'm Cypress." I held my hand out, but she didn't shake it. She just stared at me. I put my hand back to my side awkwardly and stared back at her. "Did you want something?"

"Did I want something? I would just like to know how you," She paused and looked me up and down as if I was not good enough, "landed Lucas?"

The smart ass in her voice had lit a fire in me that I had not felt in a while, jealously. I exhaled and remembered my manners. I had no idea what the hell her problem was but I was about to blow. "Excuse me," I turned my head to her as if I had not heard her properly. I stood from my seat gracefully and smiled. Handle it like a woman Cypress. I stepped to the side of her and she moved in front of me blocking my way. She wouldn't move.

"Pardon me, but is there an issue?" The British accent rang from behind me. He answered prayers too.

I smiled. "Hey, I was just about to look for you." I moved from in front of her and over to him. "I was wondering where you went."

"Well, I have a loft upstairs that I wanted to show you, it has an amazing view and I have the Melon Blitz that was requested."

"Perfect," I took his hand.

"Dear Persephone, is there something that I could help you with?"

"Fuck you Lucas," She stomped away like five-year-old who was told no and I felt a small piece of victory ignite in my chest.

He led the way to an older elevator that surprisingly had a key pad in it. He entered his code and we began to go up. "I apologize for her behavior. Persephone has been trying to "land" me ever since freshman year and I just prefer to date girls that the whole football team hasn't had."

I chuckled at the joke and looked around the walls of the elevator. The paintings were something I had never seen before. "Who painted these walls?"

"Mark... he owns the second floor and I own the third. We spent everything we had and built this place so we could have our own place. The frat house is only comfortable sometimes. I usually stay here."

The doors of the elevator opened and his home was something I had never seen before in my life. The windows went from the mahogany hardwood floors to the wood framed ceilings. The small lights that hung from the beams of the ceiling accented everything lightly. It was so dimly light just like the nightclub below. His furniture was dark red and black and there were fish inside of the walls. "Wow," I said.

"I know; I went overboard, but I had the means to so I did. One can only live as vicariously as he or she can afford to. In this moment ... I had no limit." He laughed. "I had them make the drinks and I took them up loft. I am going to run upstairs to my room and take this bloody shirt off. You can lose your heels if you would like."

His room had no walls the staircase floated above the loft to a small area I am sure he considered his bedroom. I could see him toss the shirt to the ground and slip his white t over his head, then drop his pants for some basketball shorts. I grabbed my Melon Blitz out of the fridge and his cold beer. I sipped the Melon blitz and all of the flavors rushed to my mouth and I knew immediately why it was called blitz. I was there in a heaven of coconut rum and melon for five brief seconds. I closed my eyes, savoring the taste and nodded my head, "Damn." I whispered.

"Exactly why it's on the menu." He watched me and opened his beer with one twist of his wrist. "How do you think your first week on campus went?"

"It went okay," I laughed. I'd gotten lost three times and had a hard time with remembering what car I drove. "I have a shit ton of work to do and not enough time to do it. Not to mention my apartment is basically a set of walls and a mattress with no cable."

"I can help with that what do you need to do for the apartment?"

"I guess the first thing to do would be to go thrifting for furniture and maybe try to find something spruce it up. Then there is the short story that's due. And I have no ending at all in mind. Then my mother wants me to go home for a weekend and I have to figure out which one so she can leave me alone..." I continued the list and I watched him watch me with amusement and pure interest. "I am rambling. I apologize."

"Please continue, I love to hear you actually speak words. I'm so used to your suppressed giggle..."

"You think I'm quiet?"

"You think I'm funny?" He questioned. Lucas flashed his smile once more and then shrugged his shoulders. "I think I make you nervous and by no means have I intended to."

"I'm nervous around you."

"Why?"

"I don't know." Because. He looked like he was chiseled by the Gods and for some strange reason he wanted me. He liked me. His gaze was intense so I broke eye contact and allowed my eyes to wander to the bookshelves and the first one I notice has his name in bold down the spine. It had to be The Skies Cry. "Is that the original copy?"

"It is the first copy of the book. I grabbed it fresh off the printers, I signed it and placed it on my own shelf."

"I know you don't want to hear from a fan, but this book brought life to a hopelessly dead summer." The nights that I clutched that book were countless. He wrote with so much emotion that I reeled from the thought.

"Thank you," He handed me the book. "I'm always pleased to hear I have helped someone better their life."

I flipped it open and looked at the words. His mother had signed the back of the book:

> *I love you for everything that you are and everything that you will become. Continue with your accomplishments and even when I'm not here, I want you to know that I love you so much and you are going to do wonderful things that this world has not even imagined yet.*   *-Luna Elledge.*

"Mum was so proud of me and for that I knew I was really talented. I try not to sound conceited. She was a writer herself. Her publishing company made my book a success."

"You love your mom so much. I admire that about you. When are you going to bring out a second one?"

"Hopefully not anytime soon, I really want to focus on finishing up these classes and defining who I am in society…"

"So who do you want to become?"

"No, Cypress… you go first? What do you aspire to be?"

"Successful," I blurted out. I bit my lip for a moment and then started back to talk. "You see a shit ton of people with aspirations, but when they get there it's not what they expected. I just want to be successful at my aspirations. I want to be a journalist for a big paper. I want to touch hearts and souls."

"A successful journalist for a major paper," He sipped his beer resting lightly on the counter. "It can be done."

"What about you?"

"Well, I am twenty-four years old. I wasted time in college and now there is this primal being inside that is craving a real woman. It's craving stability and a family. I don't want to be in my 30's dating around because I still won't settle down. I want something real and obtainable."

"Those are your career aspirations?"

"I made a ton of money… the book is still bringing in money. It's why I'm not putting forth much of an effort to be an adult. People work for money and I have all I need at the moment. I don't have any career aspirations."

"Wow, that's awesome."

"Yeah, but off to a lighter subject... I saw you looking highly uncomfortable to the music down there. What kind of music soothes your soul?"

Even his questions were beautiful, I smirked. "At the moment there is this singer named Joshua Radin that really makes me calm."

"Do you have him on your phone?"

"Yes," I pull out my iPhone and scroll through the music. The song that I'm currently addicted "The One You Knew." I don't know why, but his acoustic music is the best."

His hand gestured to the music dock. "Please, blow me away with it. I would love to be soothed."

I hooked the phone up to the dock and the music filled the entire apartment from the speakers I could not see and hadn't bothered to look for... the light picking of the guitar lulled me to close my eyes and then I found myself swaying back and forth. I had a tendency to get lost in music and this song was perfect to get lost in.

I felt his hand slip around my waist and he pulled me closer. This was comfortable and it wasn't forced. I knew what that felt like. We swayed together my head rested lightly on his chest and I fell in the moment. I could hear him inhale and exhale. I did know much of him, but I knew that there was something there already.

"I like this." Lucas whispered into my ear. His lips traced my earlobe. He swung me out gracefully and then pulled me back to him and I was Cinderella for a moment in time. We were face to face and our lips were less than an inch from touching. He gently pulled my face up to his and smiled. "Can I kiss you?"

"I would be offended if you didn't." I say quietly.

Lucas bent down and lightly kissed my lips. I could smell him even better now. My eyes were closed and breathing was slow. I didn't want his soft lips to leave mine. This was real. It wasn't forced or fake. It was sincere emotion. His hand rubbed my cheek as he kissed me again and there was a fire that ignited inside of me. I feared once it started, it would not stop. I stepped back slowly as our lips parted. "Cypress..."

"Lucas," I answered.

"I think we should change the song." He nodded. He stared at me as I spun lightly in the room.

"I like Norah Jones…" The song had lapsed over in my playlist. The light jazz piano of *Come Away with Me* bled through the speakers.

Lucas grabbed my hands and danced with me. We swayed off tempo laughing and our eyes could not leave one another. It was like a damn movie. I wanted this to be my forever and I had met him a week ago.

"Your playlist is like a walk through heaven." Lucas added. "Could I have it?"

"I could definitely make you a CD."

"Perfect, I have a road trip in the morning. I have to go a state over to see an old friend. I would love to listen to it on the trip over."

"I'll make sure I get you one before you leave. I could make it when you drop me off?"

"Perfect plan ma'am…" He sat down on the plush couch and exhaled. "Glad it's the weekend. I could do every weekend with you. Plans for next Saturday?"

"None," I looked at his couch. God, I missed the luxury of just sitting on a couch. "Well, actually I could use a partner and a good eye to couch shop with me. I like this couch and I miss my television in the living room."

"It's a date." Lucas touched my hand and pulled me closer to him.

Asher

He had really taken a liking to this girl. They had spent the entire week together and there were some real emotions pouring out of this guy that were unparalleled. She was lucky. She could be his saving grace.

Following them the entire day had become a bore. Whitney and I had plans for the evening and for once in six days I was not thinking about this irksome dissertation. I was thinking about how it would feel to have Whitney under me and screaming my name. It was destined to happen. She had invited me over to her house for dinner and a movie, but I had already eaten. So she gobbled down her spaghetti while I sipped on the wine and got lost in the Jurassic Park movie. We used to be obsessed with the movie when we were younger.

"Asher," she said from the kitchen

"Yes, ma'am, "I sat the glass down and turned towards her washing the dishes. "Why in the hell did you come here for your major?"

"Close to my Case Study." I said.

"What are you studying?"

"More like whom," I corrected her. "There are some cases here that I am following and documenting about. I have to inconspicuous. One particular case I have been studying since I was in high school. My father helped me formulate the correct research and materials."

"I never met your father," she said.

"He lives in Australia."

"Right, I forgot you were foreign," she poured her another glass of wine. "So you came here to stalk someone?"

"Study someone," I rolled my eyes. "I have been working it for so long that I could not let it finish without me."

"What's the subject?"

"The theory of real Psychopath."

"We have a serial killer here."

"No, not all serial killers are psychopaths and not all psychopaths are killer. You cannot think closed mindlessly when dealing with psychology." I had overheard Lucas saying that there was something he had to do out of town tomorrow and I had a feeling it had something to do with his ex-Summer Randy. She was a porn star now and he hated that the most. His journals, he frequently left open on the library tables displayed her name written everywhere. I couldn't decide what to do with the freedom that was before me. I could follow him and watch the kill or I could raid his apartment. Who knew when he would strike again. He waited exactly seven months to attack Summer and that must have been torture for him.

Whitney looked at me. "We'll be careful." There was no telling what she had said before. I really didn't know or care at the moment.

"I will be. I am happy I ran into you on campus Whit. You look really nice and you still can cook."

"Shut up." She chuckled.

"I am serious," I pulled her in my lap. "I remember our first kiss."

"You mean when I had my friends hold you down in the dollhouse of the backyard."

"Yes, that was amazing. Three women, one kiss. It was magical."

"Oh fuck you." She spits playfully.

"Yeah, still a little feisty. Very attractive," I rubbed her legs and she stood up. "Well, dinner was great."

"It was thanking you."

"I'm sorry... I want to fuck you." She smiled. "I have a boyfriend about three hours away and up until seeing you I was sure that I could refrain from being that girl who fucks around. And so for the sake of my blooming relationship... I have to kick you out."

I dropped my head. Shit, she was taken. "We don't have to fuck." I smiled. "Though I like that you can be filthy mouthed. Could I stay and watch Jurassic Park with a childhood friend. You can have one end of the couch and I can have the other?"

"Sure," She smiled.

This was a disaster. We watched the movie as we have done as kids. We talked to the screen, screamed like babies and all while not touching. My dick was rather disappointed and I couldn't blame him. We had plans for this night and it seemed to not be happening.

She fell asleep before the end and I took my leave. I had decided it was best to watch the kill. I kissed her lightly on the forehead and took my leave. I wanted to beat him there so he would not think he had a tail. Granted, he was so elusive with his plans and his murders there would be no reason to tail him.

Lucas

Summer. Fuck you summer. Yeah, there is some angst there, summer was a bitch and everyone seemed to love her. They dressed up for her, they changed who they were for her and waited in anticipation for her all year long. And when she finally came there was this relief that went after them like she wasn't going to make it. People planned for months in advance just to enjoy her; she was not my friend, at least not any longer. I fucking hate Summer. She was this bitch that taunted me behind the cameras and hated me, she burned me. And it was her turn to suffer, I will kill Summer.

I sound crazy, I know this already. I never say any of this out loud. People would have me bloody committed. This banter and rant continued in my head almost constantly until I was able to get rid of the issue and right now Summer was the issue. She lived out of town for the most part and at one point in our life we had been this amazing couple. The nights were filled with poems and dragon flies next to the pond by her house. They were never filled with cameras and people chasing her all around the damn place. It's why things have got to stop. Summer had to die.

The movie industry had been good to her. But it was not the movies that she had dreamed of. Real movie auditions didn't happen on a couch and yeah I understand that was how she made her money, but now she was the slut that every high school watched when his mom was gone and she was the bitch that allowed me to look stupid. I wanted to be with her more than she would ever know and now what we had is ruined by a slew of other men and that was not right. I would finish it tonight. It was not my first kill. Yeah, I know not exactly comforting. People were imbeciles that had no control over their fucking emotions.

The anticipation for a kill for me was almost better than the kill. The thought of hearing the blade slice her skin was like a high but it was not the real thing. I wanted the real thing. She was dead tonight. She was back in town for Summer, as usual. She was like a kid still coming home for mom and dad who secretly were so ashamed of her that they told everyone who didn't know she was an independent actress and she was making movies in Europe. They were damned liars.

I sat in the car a few blocks from her home. The music was graciously supplied by Cypress, though it was not my normal type of music I liked it. She was a good girl and was someone I could see myself settling down with and more importantly loving. She was different from Summer, she was pure.

Summer stretched out in her lawn beneath the last of the daylight. Her skin was already a perfect bronzed color but nothing was every good enough for her? Why was she so damned beautiful? I stared at her from my old run down car. It was good for stake outs and it was reliable. I just have an addiction. Right now it was called Summer. I never felt that I could be normal. My father said that it had happened for generations. He said that even she had to surrender to the darkness. He had started training me young and finally the first kill made me crave it more. There were forty-two people that have met the same fate that Summer was about to meet.

Summer is the first of a vindictive nature the other forty-two were personal sort of... one guy ran over my dog before Burke... he could have been personal Then there was the woman fired me for no reason and it really pissed me off. I tried not to make too many people connect back to me. I knew that Summer would be a risk. But Fuck it. I would rather see her dead.

Her hair was as red as a fire engine and her eyes were blue. Freckles lightly covered her body and she always wore a smile. I knew the difference between the real and the fake smile. She twitched her eye when she faked a smile and an orgasm. She'd done it once and it was in one of her Glorious-God awful films. It was the last one I watched. She kind of pissed me off with that one. It was when the decision was made for her. She dumped me because I cared about my education too much to satisfy her needs.

It could be easily said she was a sex addict and though some men think it would be nice... it was not. There are other things in life rather than sex. There was poetry and fiction. There was love. Forgive me, though I have my many flaws, some dangerous the others not so much... I was a sucker for romance. I just wanted to be with someone that loved me.

My cell phone vibrated lightly in my pocket.

Cypress: I hope you drove safe last night =)

I text her back quickly and I could feel the grin across my face. I liked this girl. She needed someone like me to protect her from her exes and Persephone-s of the world. I would fucking kill Persephone if it was not an obvious kill, perhaps I would visit her after the stench of college rubbed off.

I watched Summer for most of the day. She had done the same old same shit. She tweeted and text all damned day. Then finally, when she got bored she put on some clothes and left the house. They owned a cabin out in the woods, five miles out and there was where she would take her last breath.

The cabin was closed off and discreet. It was nice, still had internet connection before I had cut the lines and it would take a miracle for someone to hear the screams. She was meeting her new summer hook up there. She went there like it was a ritual by 6 every day and told her parents, she was reading at the beach. She never strolled back home until about two in the morning. Her cell phone was never answered because she was so consumed with the lust for her new hook up. He wasn't a good guy either so it made it easier for me to include him in the kill. He'd raped a girl in high school... his kill was not personal, it was well deserved.

I'd planned to take him down first, he was not a tall guy just average and he was not special in bed either. He fucked like he was a frantic virgin and was only good to her because it didn't take much to get her there. He was an asshole; she was a bitch. It was a match made in heaven.

The woods were so quiet and secluded it almost made it too good to be true. But I had left the police more to be involved in about 30 minutes out. I hid the car about a half mile from the cabin and started to make my way by foot. I wondered, would they sell the place once they found her dead in it. Most parents would, but her parents seemed a little selfish. I hid out while she greeted the dweeb with a kiss. Her foot was all in the air like she was a teenager in love. The damned slut could act. Summer was about to die.

They stumbled into the cabin barely able to keep their hands off one another and stripped down in less than a few seconds. It helped me. The less they wore, the less mess would be made. No bleeding shirts or smudging on me. No clothing would make it less of a struggle. She dropped to her knees like it was a fucking routine for her as she wrapped her lips around his dick. He threw his head back in ecstasy... in relief. Fucking Summer, I made my way through the front door and tossed their cell phones in the dishwater. There could be no distractions now. My heart was racing and there they were fucking on the floor like wild animals. I smiled as her face looked petrified to see me hold the knife so close to her beau, as if she was ever worthy enough to be called one.

She screamed, a real fear filled scream and let out a little laugh. "Summer, how are you? I whispered. My accent tended to grow thick when this piece of me came out to play.

The fucking rapist stared at me. "What the fuck are you doing?" He rolled off of her crawled away leaving her there vulnerable. This guy was not even worthy enough to be called a wanker. He was a coward. I bloody hate cowards.

I turned my head, "So you're into cowards now?" I chuckled lightly and nodded my head. "I knew that your taste had dwindled after me, but never would I see you with a coward Summer. You fucked up… God, I almost feel sorry for you." I looked at the guy huddling in the corner full of fear. "Now I am here to talk first, of course. I would like to explain first and there will be no more screaming… Summer you should have made better decisions. You hear?"

She shook her head. "Lucas…"

"Shut the fuck up, there will be no blimey begging okay?" I smiled and then turned toward the coward. "Did you know he has raped three girls in the past three years? And you have been fucking him like he is God's gift to this earth. Dumb decisions, Summer, are you comprehend now? You have to learn a lesson."

It was evident that she knew she was already dead. Her hands shook and the sobs wouldn't stop as she crawled over to the coward. He shuffled away from her quickly as he guarded himself from me with a chair. "Please, I have money. I have so much money."

"This is not about your money Summer, fuck you and fuck your money. I don't give a fuck about money. I'm a fucking published author. I have money coming out of my ass. I want you to understand that this life is not for everyone… now coward… come here and you can face your death first… I can make it quick or you can try to fight and I will fucking destroy you. Get up!!!! Move your bollocks quickly!" My voice was harsh. It almost scared me. Damn kills of passion. He left Summer by herself and tried to bolt towards the door. My foot caught him and he hit his head on the bed rail, it sent a clang sound through the room. The dummy had made things easier for me. I kicked his foot, he was out cold. It made the kill less fun. I wanted to see the life escape those eyes, it was the best part.

I shook my head and Summer walked towards me. "Baby, please…"

"I'm not your fucking baby. Sit your ass down or I'll end it quick." I warned. I pushed her on the rustic looking bed. "I'm not going to rape you… too many men have been there anyhow… I am going to tame you… Then free you. I know it'll make you happy."

The tears, I hated when they cried. The tears could not save them. The tears just made it messier for me. I hated waste and crying for life when I had made my decision was a waste. I sliced into her skin. The blood bubbled from her and spilled into a pool on the bed. The sex stained sheets were now red and she was dead. Summer was dead and my mind was quiet. For once it was quiet and there was peace. It happened every time I had a kill. The whispering in my head ceased and there was silence. And in that silence, I found peace for the first time in months.

I exhaled and finished off the coward, for him there needed to be more pain. And trust me there was. Summer was over. The coward was drained and the room smelled of blood. Sweet blood of Summer.

I really didn't understand why I loved to kill, but it was fairly common in my family. My father murdered and from what he told me his father murdered. Summer was the forty-three, or forty-something at least. I had made a vow to my father that when I reached found someone to love, I would quit. I wasn't sure if I would honor it. But with Cypress it was possible.

I never looked for companionship before her. My life was fine without it. There was a longing I couldn't hide that at least wanted to try something and perhaps Cypress could be the woman that changes me for good. I prayed she was… because there was this aching part inside of me that didn't want to kill her.

CHAPTER THREE

Cypress

The Publisher had worked in my favor. For once I had a job that was not resulting in food being sprayed on me or oil on my fingers. I tutored on Monday, Wednesday and Sunday afternoons and was required to write one article on Student life per week for the physical paper. My first article had been on the Summit, which made Lucas happy. It didn't take much to make him happy. He liked the little things in life. There was something different about him and I liked it. I had not planned to move on so fast from Phillip. I still had nightmares. I still slept with a wrench wedged under my pillow. He had done a number on me, that I had to admit. Lucas always had something to keep me busy from thinking here lately. We had done random things all week, he took me to land sites and random creaks all week. Sitting in the middle of my apartment had been the first normal thing I had done with him since our last official date, two weeks ago.

"I really like what you have done with the place." Lucas said sarcastically as he pointed to the bookshelf. Bargain shopping was my specialty. It was five dollars at a yard sale I had forced him to go to. It was perched on the wall next to the door. It wasn't much but it was something rather than emptiness. "It brings out the beige in the walls." He wiped his face and smiled playfully.

I nodded my head and pushed him lightly. "Well, if you will give me a moment to get ready, we can go shopping."

"We must go and get you something that simply screams you." He shook his head. He pulled me closer to him, his arms warm and they made me feel safe. I smiled at him and moved the hair from his face. "I think that a floral couch would match you very well."

I shook my head in agreement with him. Lucas made his way over to me a cupped my chin in ahis hand as he pecked my lips softly. He already knew me well. There was nothing that I loved more than floral. I had an obsession with flowers. "Yes, something light and festive." He held out his two hands and pulled me to my feet. "I have to change into something not so snazzy and then we can go find the world's best floral couch. I know you're excited."

"Almost overly excited," I had grown used to his sarcasm. I actually craved it, most people found it annoying, like my mom. But I found it to be comforting and actually a lot like me. "Go get casual, so I can find the Picasso of couches for you. I have a good eye for fashion." He lied. Lucas rarely anything other than the same three shirts. He tattered Pink Floyd Shirt, A Beatles shirt or just a plain black T-shirt.

I changed into a purple sundress and some Converse shoes with purple laces to add the tiniest bit of me into the recipe. Then there was my hair. The thick curls had been down all day. I applied some mousse to make the curls more defined and slid on a headband. I tossed on my glasses and some lip gloss and walked out.

"Sorry it took a tad bit longer than expected." I looked at Lucas, who could not unhinge his eyes from mine. "Are you okay?"

"You are just perfect." He said. "I like this dress and I love these glasses." He graced me with another small kiss and then waited patiently for me to get up. Lucas like to pace things, that was evident. There had not been too much intimacy since the first date and I didn't want to rush things and give him the wrong impression. I felt like I couldn't or more like shouldn't kiss him again. I lacked self-control when it came to him. We had managed small kisses and hand holding in public occasionally.

"There is a store about an hour out. We could head out there and work our way back to this area. My mother knows someone that works at this particular shop so there should be no hardship on prices." Lucas led me out of the apartment, locking the door behind him and guiding me towards his Range Rover.

"Where's the Jeep?"

"I drive this baby out of the town most of the time. I like the heated seats. The wind has started to pick up here lately. He opened the door for me and held my hand as he helped me into the SUV. He didn't look like the type that would drive one, but he did and it was so much nicer than my sedan. It screamed luxury, the damned door handles were chrome.

"I plan to spend about 500 on the living room, nothing more and nothing less."

"I understand you, dear," Lucas closed the door and sprinted to the other side of the car and hopped in.

I buckled my seat belt and scrolled through my phone to find more color schemes than what I had imagined to keep from staring at him. It was hard not to do.

"So tell me something about you that no one else knows." I blurt out. I have no idea why, but I wanted this drive to be lush with conversation.

"Something no one knows…" He started the car driving out of the apartment complex and effortlessly he pulls out into traffic. "There is the fact that I keep a mental checklist. It has minor things in it. I follow the checklist for my life."

"Like goals?"

"Like don't date a girl who drinks like a sailor, or curses like my nan." He chuckled. "Don't trust the writing teacher with your novel and make sure you don't live at home ever again. It is really a mental reminder and checklist." He paused. "Be nice people, don't stare when people or dumb or just dumb founding beautiful." Lucas winked.

"Wow, so you compartmentalize up there?" I brushed off his compliment, too timid to look at him and thank him.

"Most of the time," He continued to keep his eyes on the road. "What about you Cypress?"

There were several facts about me that no one else knew about me, but there was one that I hid but it was hilarious. I twiddled my fingers, "When I was 17 years old I tried to off myself with some vitamin E pills."

He burst into laughter, a tear rolling laughter, "My dear Cypress, not vitamins."

I burst into laughter right behind him and nodded my head. "Yeah, I was dumb, but I lived and I never took vitamin E again."

"You more than likely consumed more than you needed anyhow, I am happy that you lived though. You too much of anything can be a bad thing?" He stopped laughing for a minute. "What was so hard at 17 that you no longer wanted to live?"

"That ex that I told you about... he wasn't the best boyfriend. There were times that I would hate myself for being with him. He cheated on me firstly and then he would force me to stay with him. Everyone loved that bastard he played football and in my town that was the way you became someone, there was no other way. Fuck that writing shit, marry a football player and your life could be better." My home town was a piece of shit and that was fine. I just wanted out. "But anyhow..." I spared him the gory details and shifted in my seat.

"I hate that he treated you that way. I see no reason to find another companion when you have everything it is to offer. It is his lost and fortunately my gain."

Lucas

There are times I feel like I could implode from the inside of anxiety from not writing. It's the same kind of itch that comes with the kill only it's a less intense feeling. Dull almost, I don't think there is a way to explain it besides saying that a pen and a clean sheet of paper held infinite possibilities. It was why my book was steady success. I craved the words on the paper like nourishment. And this sensation I got with Cypress was almost better than sex.

I had continued to call Cypress every morning. Our conversations started light, but she made me think. She gave me hope that there could be a good future. Cypress was a character and she barely knew how unique she was. I was corny at jokes and I knew that they sucked but with her she laughed a whole hearted laugh every time. Even when she found them ridiculously dumb, she found the humor to make them funny. Then there was the way she carried herself. I was not one for a grand presentation and neither was she, she breathed pure simplicity in everything that she done. Her hair was always a curly mess. Even when she tried to tame it, it remained wild and free. It was my favorite thing about her. Then there were her eyes. Most women have brown eyes, statistically speaking, most human beings have brown eyes, but no one has Cypress' eyes. Her eyes were the deepest brown surrounded by tints of green that made their appearance whenever the rays of sunlight hit her eyes at just the right angle.

I had fallen for those eyes and the inquisitive look they could give while I critiqued her and strengthened her writing. I craved her touch, and by touch once again, I mean simple touch. Her hand had a tendency to trace mine whenever she handed me papers and it seemed that the smaller the touch the more intimate I felt towards her. The simple moments with her had made her the one I craved.

"There is this couch downtown that has my name on it. It's a lavender color with pastel pink floral print. It's 250 just for the love seat and there is this chair that is in a thrift shop. I want you to come with me to get them."

"I'm free tomorrow about 3pm? Would that be okay?"

"Perfect, I have some notes to revise on my short story, then the writing lab has me working with some freshman students on their paper." She glowed. I was happy she was enjoying the job. It paid well and she needed work.

"They treat you right there?" I asked. She playfully bounced on her feet, tossing the food on the paper plates. She barely had anything here.

"They are treating me great," she sat down next to me on the floor of her apartment and handed me the sandwich she had so skillfully prepared for me. "Sorry, would you shop with me too tomorrow?"

"Yeah, we could definitely go ahead and hit the grocery store. I love a good PB&J but I doubt that I can eat it three more days in a row." I watched her laugh and then bite into the sandwich. "I would love to introduce you to some of my friends besides my brother Mark of course?"

"I would love to meet them, and perhaps you could meet my mom. She keeps asking about you. I don't know what to call you." She blushes at the thought of a relationship with me.

"Well, I think the proper term is a boyfriend or something like that?" I smiled at her and watched her face turn a shade of crimson and her smile spread to her eyes. "I mean, if both parties agree."

"I agree," She smirked and chewed down into her sandwich like she hadn't eaten all day.

"I'm ecstatic." I finished off my sandwich and walked to the kitchen, it too was bare. I had to get her something, but every time I even offered to buy her a drink and she flipped out. She was the independent type and it was to be admired. I had more money than I could handle at this time though, so I had to get her things. "What about a table for this dining area Cy?"

"Dining room?" Cypress wiped her face. "One room at a time, I have some big thoughts on the living room. I have to find something to accent the flowers."

"I can buy the table for you Cypress…"

"No," she said. "And don't do it anyway. I would like to buy everything myself."

"Why?" I shrugged my shoulders.

"Because of my ex, if you buy me that table and we break up… I won't be able to function with it in the apartment. I would be reminded constantly that the table I eat my breakfast on was bought by you."

"Your ex is a bastard. I understand why you are scared, but I would never do anything to harm or hurt you physically nor emotionally Cypress. I want you and I want the best for us. So if you don't want the table I understand." I paused. "I say he is a bastard because he has royally fucked up your perception of things. I think of buying you a table and a completely different scenario runs through my head." She turned to me, her eyes glossed over and frustration written on her face. "I see a table where we share our first real home cooked meal. A table that we grow attached to so much it pains us to throw the old bloody thing away. We look at the table as our first real step the leads to the falling in love."

Her mouth gaped open, "Only you can turn a table into poetry Lucas." Cypress smiled and the world cheered. "Fine, get the table." She put no argument into it. She wanted us as badly as I did and it made it easier to exhale.

"We can pick the table and I can cook for you."

"I don't want any mash or fish and chips."

"I make the best fish and chips... have you ever had them with peas? It's like heaven on a fork."

"Dear Jesus, stop it!" She made her way to me and her hands traced my arms lightly and she placed her lips on mine barely applying pressure just lingering there and it was insatiable. I wanted nothing more than this moment to last forever. She pulled me closer to her and I leaned so she would not have to stand on her tiptoes. These were the moments that defined a couple, simple yet priceless. I could stay like this forever.

Asher

I couldn't get the vision of him as he slashed into Summer out of my head. I knew he would do it. I knew I shouldn't watch but I couldn't stop. He was a damn messy killer. My stomach had been in shambles for hours afterwards. I refused to document anything. I would go to lunch for being a damn witness. I planned to spend my life away from prison. I spent my weekend cooped up in the house in hopes that I had not been followed or watched. After long speculation, I decided to finally leave the house and went to the library. I had some more assignments to get in before the end of the day and I knew that Whitney was off today. She had made me sure that there would be no line crossing. I decided to move on. There were several women that I could seduce. I had laid off of Lucas just for the week. The love-story was becoming nauseating. I documented his behaviors and that was it. Ever since I'd witnessed him murdering those two people in the cabin I was leery of even finishing the dissertation. I couldn't change my mind, but I definitely couldn't include the murder in it. I had it in my private notes that I sent to my father.

He agreed to back off and observe as quietly as possible because he was a danger to everyone in his life. I felt bad for Cypress because she was infatuated beyond recognition and there was saving her, I hoped she could save him.

I sat at my table alone going through my notes and there she was at my table. Cypress and I could understand his infatuation with her. She was exotic. "Sorry, Could I sit here for a quick minute?"

"Definitely," I whispered. I continued to jot notes down on the notepad with just a case study as the main subject.

"Can you believe it is pouring down outside? Next is the snow. Damn Colorado."

"I can. The news said it yesterday." I sounded like an ass. But it was the truth. "Where were you coming from?"

"The English Wing, it was dreadful. I wasn't even planning on coming back to the campus, but my boyfriend reminded me that the paper was due.

They were an official a couple now. One for the books. "Yeah what's your major?"

"English... I am planning to teach it at a junior college next year if this all goes right."

"A JC around here?"

"Uhm actually I don't know just yet. If everything goes as planned, it will be somewhere near home."

"Nice, yeah I am moving to Australia with my dad after this year. I just have to tweak my dissertation."

"Wow, what are you studying?"

"Uhm, just psychology. I've grown to love it. The study of why people act like people is amazing."

"Really." She smiled and I felt the world stop. This woman was beautiful. "I know some people I would like to study and see what they were really thinking."

"There is body language of course." I smirked. "Look it up."

"Perhaps I will." She placed her books on the table and took out her pencil. "I am writing a new novel. My boyfriend said that I should I always learn something new. One day could you give me a crash lesson in some things."

"I might could."

"I hope that's a yes." She slid the card over the table and stood up. "I have to haul ass over the campus now. I hope its stopped raining for good, I doubt my hair could take another down pour like that."

"I think you and your hair will live. And I I'll call you we can set up a time and everything. I'll fill you in." I folded her card in half and placed it in my pocket.

"Good, text me. My boyfriend seems to not like me receiving calls from other guys. What's your name?"

"Asher," I smiled.

"I like that, I'm Cypress."

Her name was perfect like her. "Well, pleasure to meet you."

She left and I continued to jot away on my notebook. I could understand his obsession. She looked like heaven and it was hard to resist her. And to be honest there was nothing spectacular about her that made her more than average. Cypress was charming. "Same here...Asher..."

When she left I continued to be productive. It didn't take much. I had so much work I was drowning.

Lucas' book was published before his mother's death. Luna loved him and she made sure she lived long enough to see him be successful. It was all that she wanted. My father studied her like I am studying Lucas. Luna was not like her husband. She was very secretive and she went above and beyond to make sure her family was safe. Unlike Lucas she rarely traveled. She wanted to be near the love of her life and Lucas' father, Declan Elledge. Declan was a strong father though he was absent for a time. His family lived in Ireland and Luna rarely made an appearance because of her disease and her son. My father believed Declan's side was the dark part of Lucas' family and I hadn't had the chance to even start the research there.

The table shook again and there was no way I was going to get anything done with these constant interruptions. I looked up and there was Lucas. Maybe he had spotted me that day. I had hidden but it might not have been enough. He could have heard my gasps as he cut into Summer and her klutz of a lover.

Lucas cleared his throat and casually adjust his jacket. "How do you know Cypress?" He questioned. His eyes were piercing into me. He had wasted no time to get right down to business.

"Uh, just met her. She said she was a writer. Who the fuck are you?" Good job Asher, be an ass.

"Well uh, I'm the boyfriend. Lucas Elledge," He held his hand and with a firm grip shook my hand. "Stay away from her."

"I don't want her, she started the conversation with me." My palms had started to sweat and my heart was about rip itself free and gallop out of the library. He bled intimidation. "She just seemed cool."

"Yeah whatever, What's your name?"

"Asher," I said. I should have lied. He was a collector of names.

"Stop by the club, I own The Summit. Drinks on me all night whenever you come." He handed me the pass. It read "VIP ACCESS, per Lucas E."

I nodded my head in appreciation and partial fear. "Thanks."

"There are a shit ton of beautiful women for you to pursue and it's on me. Lose her number, okay?"

My hands shook as the vision of the river of blood flowing from her neck purged its way through my mind. I felt sick. "Okay, will do...Thanks Lucas."

He turned his head. "How the fuck do you know my name?"

My eyes skimmed the invitation once more and thank God there was his name. I held up the pass. "I read it here."

"Oh," He paused hesitantly and nodded his head. "Sorry mate, it's been an ass backward day. Come out to the club. Love to see you there." He looked through his cell phone and walked away casually. His other hand in his pocket and eyes hooked on the phone. He was like a fucking lion and I may have accidentally made his list. I grabbed my cell phone and dialed my father's number when I was sure he saw me.

"You okay?" The worry in his voice was obvious. It was three in the morning there and it was unlike me to call him at odd hours of the night.

"I don't know really. I had a conversation with Lucas. He basically told me to stay away from the girl." I chose to omit the fact that I had seen him murder two people. My father was the type to flip out and run to the authorities.

"Stay away from her. If he is forming a relationship with her. You shouldn't get in the middle. It being the first real connection since Luna's passing."

"Okay, I fucking froze up." There was a chill that ran down my spine and I couldn't stop my hand as subtly shook on the table. It was fear. His eyes had no emotion. The smile never reached them.

"You have to be tougher than you are son. He can sense and read other people's emotions better than a normal person. He won't just kill you. Call me later on. I'm exhausted."

I flipped the card over and hung up the phone. I wrote down in my journal and exhaled.

Lucas

I was never threatened by any other guy when it came to relationships because I worked to make sure that no one was in my territory. This Asher character was not a threat. If anything he was a coward. His face looked white with fear when I approached him. The invite to the club was friendly enough for him to see that I could care less about him, but he was now in my sights. He had one job to do and that was to stay the hell away from Cypress.

I sat down in my room and glanced over the letters in the box. I kept a list of them. There were now forty-four sets of initials, the lust to kill had receded. The past few weeks had been easier, but one fucking thing was liable to trigger it. I set the paper down and glanced through my plans. She wanted me to meet her mother and father in three weeks. It was a five-hundred-mile trip, eight hours in the car with her alone and we hadn't slept together yet. She was a good girl so that was fine with me. I just hoped that she wanted something. Why the fuck she was talking to this Asher character? It now irked my nerve and he would be kept in my eyesight when it regarded her. I dialed her number and she answered on the third ring.

"Hey babe!" Cypress' voice was light and chipper.

"How are you? Are you home?" Slow down Lucas. Too many questions.

"I'm actually headed back. I had to go to the writing lab and do some things and I met this psychology major named Asher. He said he would give me run through a course on personalities and behaviors for my novels. Does that sound like a good idea?"

"Yes, you can always study and get more knowledge. My minor is psychology I could help you love."

"I don't want to depend on you for everything Luke." She was climbing steps. Her breaths were short and I could hear the short tap of her feet on each step. "I want us to have balance and balance means that we have to have some free time. He seemed like a nice guy."

"I'm sure Ted Bundy was a nice guy too." The irony poured out of me covered with humor. "I guess then Cypress. Call tomorrow morning?"

"If you don't call me first babe. Don't forget to shop for furniture and food. The need is dire."

"I won't." I smiled. "Talk to you later love." I ended the call and pulled out my laptop. I typed in Asher. There were over one hundred of them in the state. And he appeared to not be from here. His accent appeared to be more West Coast.

I should have gotten his last name but possibly there would be a chance later. Most people dived at the opportunity for a VIP pass to my club. Hopefully he would too, but he looked terrified.

CHAPTER FOUR

Cypress

The Publisher, had occupied my afternoons for the past two weeks. And my job was simple. I tutored the freshmen in English. Their first papers were all about cliché topics like Summer Vacations and Comparison Papers. I flew through the sessions in a breeze and even made a few new friends in the process. Then the final hour I had to help edit the actual Publisher. I was not one for journalism. I knew nothing about the town. I couldn't write about student because I had no student life. Everything besides school and work revolved around Lucas.

"Okay, so here is the deal. We would like you to write a piece about the Summit across town." Ginger, seemed to float around the room as her she wisped through her files. Her tall, petite stature made me envious for a few extra inches. It would be easier to kiss Lucas if I wasn't so focused on reaching his lips sometimes. Though he made kissing me a habit. And it made me happy.

"Of course I could."

"Awesome, you think you could even interview Lucas?"

It was apparent that Lucas was someone important to me. They could tell by the way he smiled when he walked in the room. Then there was the fact that when he was not here he called me. He worked here sometimes when he finished his school work. It was an honor for them to have such an established author on their payroll. So he wrote occasional spotlight pieces. "I could." I grimaced.

"It's just that he doesn't really talk to any of the rest of us like he talks to you.

"Yeah Ms. Tucker, is he your boyfriend?" Brent had developed a crush on me. It was not cute to me though. He was annoying. He wanted more than the friendship that I had to offer him and unfortunately for him it was the only thing that was on the table for him.

"Just friends." It was not a lie. Lucas and I had not laid a title to our new romance. Truth be told I wasn't sure if I was ready to even step back into something. My heart was still a tad tattered from the battle of Philip.

"That's good to hear." Brent smiled his tight lip smile that made his slanted brown eyes squint together even more. He then pushed his stringy brown hair from his face and winked at me. Brent had potential to be handsome, but it would take years of molding and sculpting. "I've heard some bad things about that guy."

"Like what?"

Brent cleared his throat and turned towards me. He shrugged his shoulders almost knocking the square rimmed glasses to the ground. "For one, all of his ex-girlfriends have either gone missing or have been found dead."

I laughed at his tale. "You really are desperate aren't you."

Ginger corrected, "It was only two. They just found one of them the other week. She was killed with her boyfriend at a family estate."

"You two are ridiculous."

"Just a warning Cypress." Brent grew quiet as he stared out the front window. "Speak of the devil."

His Jeep whipped into the front parking spot by the door and he hopped out gracefully and made his way to the door. Lucas was effortlessly perfect. His white T-shirt fit tighter than normal revealing his chiseled arms and tattoos. I wasn't sure how he was surviving without a coat on. The cool breeze of autumn had set in and it was not like home where a cool breeze just meant chilly weather for two or three months. It felt like the beginning stages of winter.

"Lucas!" Ginger said. Her voice too chipper for my liking. I ignored it and continued to organize the few papers I had left on my desk.

"Ginger," He smiled. "How's everything? I'm not bothering anyone am I?"

"You're the Editor." She giggled throwing her shoulder forward. Her hands touched his chest and I exhaled.

Lucas eyes locked on mine and his face lit up with amusement. "Busy Cypress?" Lucas nodded at Ginger and dismissed her with the quick look. He made his way to my small brown desk, shifting through the disarray of desks in the middle of the room. He perched himself on my desk. "How are you?"

"Good." I said quietly.

"Are you liking it still?"

My eyes darted at Ginger who had gone back to her desk. The model everything it seemed. "Sure."

"Ignore her love, you have me blinded." His lips touched my forehead lightly. "What are your plans for today?"

It soothed me to know that he cared enough to ease a fear I hadn't fully formed yet. "I'm meeting with Asher."

His eyebrow shot up and he sighed. "The library kid?"

"The library kid, he said that he could help me with some theories."

"I bet." He smiled. "Could I borrow you after your lesson in personalities?"

"Yes." I closed my laptop. "What are we doing?"

"Watching the stars' weep."

"What?"

"The shooting stars are passing through tonight."

"I can't wait!" I shrieked unintentionally. The eyes were all on me, and I could feel the heat racing to match my mortification. "I mean awesome." I whispered.

"Perfect, and be careful with this Asher okay?"

"I promise."

Asher was not as bad as Lucas liked to think. He was smart and handsome. He even reminded me of Lucas. "So what do you study?"

"I study and major in psychology. The study of why."

I laughed. "I've never heard it put like that. I write books and it's hard to write a book when you don't know anything about the human mind."

"True. There are different types of people."

"What kind of person am I?"

"The kind of person that wants more knowledge." He said quickly. "I don't know. I have to listen and evaluate and then apply and blah. It takes too long. I really just like the studying part."

"What are you studying right now?"

"I'm currently writing my dissertation on a psychopath's decision."

"Wow, sounds scary."

"Not really. Psychopaths are closer than you know." He looked down at his work. "They blend in… they are the masters of disguise."

"Characteristics?" I asked. I stared at him. "They sound scary."

"They are humans with little emotions. To be honest, they just don't care what the world thinks and they tend to blame others for their mistakes. For example, let's say that they cheat on a test. It would not be their fault. It would Susie's fault because she didn't make an effort to cover her exam."

"Sounds like a little child."

"Could be an accurate assumption," Asher paused. "They seek out people and use and exploit them. They usually use them for their gain."

"Are they dangerous?"

"Hardly, there are some public figures that are high functioning and then there is Ted Bundy."

"A serial killer."

"Exactly, but to the world he was normal until he was exposed. Up until his death, he still stated that it was not his fault and there was something dark in him he couldn't control."

"Wow," I nodded my head. "So a serial killer with conscience and no morality meter to let him know that he is wrong. Are they rare?"

"Statistically… there is exactly one in every hundred group of people."

"Asher you love this don't you?"

"I love it more than you will know." He paused. "I have been wanting to tell you this the entire time Cypress. Watch who you get involved with around here Cypress." Asher 's voice was playful but I could sense the seriousness behind his warning.

"Are you warning me about you?" I pushed him playfully. "Are you dangerous for me Asher?"

"I'm warning you about someone else."

"Lucas?" I looked at him.

"Yeah. He fits a lot of the characteristics on the checklist."

"What checklist?"

"I'll give you a copy." He slid the thin sheet of paper across the library table. "A personality disorder that has often proved to be dangerous. I just wanted you to be cautious okay?"

My eyes glanced over the page. The Levenson-Self Report Psychopathy Scale. Psychopath. "Are you serious?"

"Yes."

"Are you trying to hit on me? Is this some kind of psychologist pick up line?" I laughed it off and folded the test in half.

"No, I have my eyes on someone, but I don't think she has her eyes on me." He chuckled. "I'm not that big of a nerd?"

"Someone else? Don't make me jealous now?" I gasped jokingly. "Who is she Asher?"

"This girl named Whitney. It's so weird, she used to stalk me in Middle School and High School and now she is all I can think of. And I don't mean to be frisky around her. I just want her."

"Make your move. You seem like a nice guy, tell me something about yourself..."

"What do you want to know?"

"Mainly what are you thinking in that big brain of yours?"

"I think geometric mean everything."

I stared at him. "Okay. So you love math?"

Asher laughed as he pulled out a small metal box from his backpack, then out with a compass. "It's not really what I meant Cypress." He sharpened the pencil and turned to a blank page of his sketch book. "Everything starts out as nothing." His hand flourished the page. "Then there is something created by some event in your life or you're just something that has to happen. It stands for the beginning." He drew a small circle on the page. "This is the beginning... of a relationship, of a job... of your life."

I smiled. "I get it."

"Let's say that this circle was created by a pebble being thrown into the lake... It sets off reactions and causes more ripples, larger ripples. Did you know that the beginning circle's circumference is equivalent to the fifth circle's radius?"

"No." I barely remembered any of these math terms.

"To me it simply means that any action you make... no matter how small in the beginning can cause a bigger problem in the end. I live by this. I live by trying to catch actions that are unjust by me and that need redeeming."

"Wow," I paused. "I didn't know that it was that much in shapes."

"It's tied to everything and people don't use it normally. There are things like infinite numbers that mean nothing to some, but everything to others."

"Like..."

"Pi and Phi... Phi is being the infinite number for the Golden Rectangle Theory."

"Do you talk to your girlfriend about this stuff?"

"She is not my girlfriend. She actually has someone."

"Oh, well don't talk about this stuff on the first date unless they are equally attuned to your thinking." I took the compass and rolled it in my hands. "What else do you like to do?"

"Yoga..."

"Yoga, like the lotus flower..."

"Definitely that position. I can meditate on it for hours. It's all about clearing the mind and knowing yourself. If you don't know yourself, you can't truly do anything successful in life. So I find my inner peace every morning. Even if it means I stay in the lotus flower for hours it helps. It calms me."

"Could you teach me?"

"It's a discipline better learned on your own. Plus, I think your boyfriend might kill me."

"So no?" I laughed.

"Right, just look it up. There are some great videos and then once you get it you will know. It starts off being the hardest thing that you have ever done and by a few weeks the sting will fade and the beauty of the quiet will take over."

"You are different Asher."

"Thanks," he paused. "I think."

"It was a compliment."

Lucas

My notebooks were scattered around me and I was lost. There was something missing from my work. I inhaled and closed my eyes, releasing my breath slow and steady. I was the nucleus and all of this shit surrounding me was my electron cloud and something was out of place. It was throwing off my element. I opened my eyes and nodded my head. Writing was best done in messiness for me. And there was an idea in my mind and it begged to be released.

The campus was flooded with freshman ready to be disobedient and get into trouble and unlike normal it was loud. I could hear every footstep and cackle from them as they passed pass my array of mess. This was a bad an idea.

"Busy?" Persephone asked.

She was persistent. I smiled. "Yes, go away."

"Why do you hate me so much?"

"I don't hate you. I find you deeply annoying. And you don't take hints well." I had told this girl to leave me alone on more than one occasion. She was persistent and consistent. That I could say."

"What are you doing?"

"I am trying to find something," My head turned to her as my eyes stared intently. Irritation had started to kick in and she didn't want to irritate me. I wasn't in the mood. I wanted to know where Cypress was and why she hadn't answered my call. "What are you doing here? Is there something that I can help you with?"

"Nope," she sat down on the patch of untouched grass next to me and opened her book. "I just want to talk."

"I'm not in the talking mood. We aren't even friends like this Persephone?"

"Where's your girlfriend?"

"She just happens to be studying. We don't have to be with each other every waking moment. It's what makes us better." It's what drives me up a damn wall. She was so comfortable not being around me it made me wonder if we were doing things too slow.

"She tell you that."

"She did," I laughed. "Persephone there are tons of other guys that would like to have a taste of whatever you are offering. I however am not one of them. Could you dismiss yourself? Like now?"

"I don't want them." she answered bluntly.

"You can't have me, seems like you have a problem. Find someone else. Get the fuck up."

"Lucas do you have to be so mean to me?" Persephone smiled and scrolled through her phone. "They are smoking at Genesis tonight, you should come. I mean ever since you have met her you just stopped coming?"

Genesis was the spot where the college weed heads gathered and I had been there several times, but it was harder for me to control myself around a bunch of weed smoking hippies. I liked to be alone when I smoked. Most importantly, when I couldn't control my urges. "They are always smoking at Genesis. It is nothing new. And stop bringing up Cypress."

"You should come."

"I actually have plans tonight. There is meteor shower passing through."

"Aw, how sweet," She mocked. "Should I come with you? Oh, I forgot, Cypress probably will be there."

"Jealousy does not look good on you."

"She looks good on him though. Asher is a nice looking guy. I hear he's hung." She pointed to Cypress. She was so perfect. Her hair bunched in the messiest ponytail I had seen yet, her curls wildly bursting from it. And then there was Asher. The kid who couldn't take a break."

"Fuck off Persephone." I moaned.

Cypress spotted me and she made a B line over to me with Asher. Persephone giggled. "Here she comes."

"Why are you so amused?"

"Why are you not? He fits her style more. He is so geeky. Look at those freaking glasses."

I cut my eyes over at her. "One more word and you are going to regret it." I stood up as they grew closer. "What are you doing here babe?"

"I actually got some good news from my new friend here. Asher this is my boyfriend Lucas."

"Pleasure," he shook my hand. "I gave her some good theories and info to use for her novel."

"Awesome," I nodded. "I was here trying to remember what exactly I wrote the other month."

"Hi Persephone," Cypress cut her eyes at her and then back at me.

"With an unwanted guest."

"Aw, how sweet of you," Persephone nodded her head. "You are the new guy aren't you?"

"I am." Asher laughed. "Who are you?"

"She is Persephone; I think you two would get along quite well." I tried to hide my smile. "Babe you wanna sit with? I was just telling Persephone about the meteor shower tonight."

"Oh yes! I can't wait. Where did you say we were going again?"

"Surprise location," I answered. She sat down with me in the array of my mess. "Welcome to my nucleus."

Cypress laughed at my nerdy remark and nestled herself in. "I am happy for the invitation."

Asher shifted uncomfortably. "Well, thank you for the chance to talk Cypress."

"You are welcome. We should link back up in a few weeks and you can tell me if you get her or not."

"I will definitely let you know."

"Good, how about you join him Persephone. I am sure you have tons of good knowledge to pass on to him about being a female." Cypress nudged my arm as my snide remark. "And Ashton it was a pleasure to meet you."

"It's Asher," Cypress nodded her head. "I'll give you a call or you can call me. Goodbye Persephone."

Persephone stood up. "You are boring anyhow."

"Thanks," Cypress opened her notebook and watched as she walked off. "What was she doing here?"

"What were you doing with Romeo?"

"I am the only person that gets to dabble in your nucleus Lucas Elledge."

"Scout's honor she was not in my nucleus." I smiled at her and pulled her closer to me.

"She better not be." She sat in my lap and wrapped her arms around my neck. "Where are we going tonight?"

"We're going to a ridge about thirty to forty minutes out. And we should get some wine and some other weird things to take up there."

"Weird like a Dark Side of the Moon CD?"

"Oh, Pink Floyd can only make this moment better. There is actually some Radiohead that could great with it. We should just make sure there is music. And make sure you have your wishes ready."

"I think my wish has already come true."

"Oh really?" I cocked my head at her. "Does it have anything to do with Captain Nerd there?" Something flickered lightly. If he didn't get the message soon enough I would have to fix it myself. Asher would not like me to fix it.

"Everything to do with you." Her lips touched mine slowly and then I placed my hands on the back of her head to pull her closer to me and crushed my lips into her.

"I'm happy to hear that."

She moved the long strands of my hair from my face. "I love your hair."

"I like it alright. I love your freckles…"

"Courtesy of my mom," she smirked. "Bet you've never seen a black chick with some."

"I have not."

"Well, another first," Cypress eyes never left mine. "You aren't going to hurt me are you?"

"I wouldn't dream of it."

"Good, because I doubt that I could take another heartbreak. I just want something normal and good. And I'm scared at how fast everything is going."

"I don't want you to fear anything. You're not supposed to fear me."

"I don't fear you, I fear what will happen after you if everything goes to hell."

"There is no after me Cypress."

"You don't know that."

"I do. I plan to do every and anything to make this work. So it doesn't matter the amount of time spent with someone. I could spend 15 years with Persephone and they would never add up to the months I spent with you. It's how you spend the time… I don't want to waste it anymore. I want to invest it in my future with you. So everything I do, every move I make is all going to add up to us being together."

"You keep taking my breath away." She whispered.

"Good I want our relationship to breathtaking and heart wrenching. So when we look back there are nothing but good memories and ones that count."

"Okay, stop before I have to steal some of your lines in my book."

"Steal away Cypress."

Cypress

I stared at my closet. Every time he wanted to take me out I ended up spending more time in this damned closet than actually getting dressed and being productive. He would be here in less than thirty minutes and my face looked drained because the steaming hot shower took away any energy I had left.

It was cool tonight. The wind had already made the day chillier than normal, so I grabbed an orange sweater and a pair of brown jeggings to make the outfit simple. My hair was a complete mess and there was no taming this beast tonight. I fixed the bun the best that I could and tossed some cold water on my face to make me feel more awake. It was a quarter till midnight and I knew that the possibility of me to doze off was high.

The ring of my cell phone echoed throughout the whole entire apartment. I ran to the living room and glanced at it. Asher? I swiped it over. "Hello?"

"Hey, I was just calling you to let you know that you left your journal with me. Did you want me to meet you somewhere tomorrow?"

"Yes, that sounds like a plan. Just bring it to the courtyard where we met Lucas at today around four. I have to work on some things after class."

"Perfect," he answered. "Um, how was your date?"

"Haven't left yet. It doesn't start until about 2 am. The showers are supposed to be beautiful though."

"Well, I wish you all the luck. And see you tomorrow."

"See you too!" I ended the call. "Great that journal had some pretty girly moments in it and I knew he read it."

The light tap at the door snapped me back into the reality that I had no shoes and an uncharged cell phone, "One moment." I slid into some boots and then opened the front door. "You are here early sir!"

"I know. I couldn't sit in the car too much longer. I would have fallen asleep."

"Are you good driving?"

"I am. I was just bored and decided to come here early. I like your outfit." He hugged me lightly and kissed my cheek.

"Thanks, I was just about to straighten my room for a minute."

"Take your time." Lucas sat down on the counter.

"What is your new book about?"

"Everything," He answered simply.

"Everything, good."

Lucas smiled at me. "I started a new book a few weeks ago. It's easy to say that you inspired me. It's not going to be a sequel. It's a standalone called "A Break in the Clouds." I haven't even told my publishers yet. It's part of the reason I can't really tell you everything about it yet."

"Wow." I walked from the bedroom as I switched off every light in my path.

"I want you to be the first to read it since you said you loved my first book so much."

"I would be honored."

"Great! Are you ready to go?"

"How far out is this place?"

"About thirty minutes."

"Okay, let's get to it."

The ridge was a phenomenal place even if the drive was a little longer than he expected. He had everything set up in the back of his jeep including blankets. I sat down and stared up at the sky.

"Have you ever seen a shooting star?"

"I try to. But every time they passed through I am passed out."

"Well, they will start in a few and then you can't sleep all the way back to the city." Lucas opened the wine and poured me a glass then poured himself a glass.

"What is the first thing you think about when you wake up?"

"Just depends, most mornings here lately, you."

"You're lying."

"I wake up every morning and send you a message. Sometimes leave you a voice mail."

Every morning like clockwork, he was right. "What do you think about me?"

"I think that I made a great decision pursuing you. You make it easier to get up, knowing that I get to see your face and touch your soft hands. I get to kiss your lips and stare at your sun kissed skin. I get to call you mine and it makes every day easier knowing only I have the privilege."

"Really?"

"God, yes," He answered.

"No one has ever said anything like that to me."

"There is a first for everything."

I look up at the sky, knowing that if I look at him there was a strong possibility tears might seep over. "Look!" I pointed at the streak of light that passed in the sky.

"They've started." He pointed at the next streak and then they all came at once. Parading the sky with streaks of light over and over. Lucas clutched my hand with his and we watched until the stars faded out and the sky started to tint with the colors of dawn.

CHAPTER FIVE

Cypress

For once in about two weeks he asked for us to get out of my apartment. We had become so accustomed to the one on one time that we had forgotten the outside world. It was perfect except we needed to have some sort of social life and what better way was it for us to have one besides going to the Summit. I had grown to the love the place as if it was my own. I was used to the back door entrance to the apartment. But tonight we entered like pedestrians and all eyes were on us. I hated the attention at first. Don't stare at us, keep dancing. But I soon realized that being on the arm of Lucas Elledge was admirable by pretty much the entire student body. He was established and everyone loved him. He wasn't even a people person. But people were drawn to him like magnets.

The decision to leave my heels at home for the night had been a good one. The warm beige sweater hugged my body, Lucas had picked it out himself. He loved to buy me things and it was something that I was not accustomed to it. But every time I tried to stop him he gave me this look and my heart melted. His emerald eyes made it hard to say no to anything.

There was strum of guitars in the air and finally there was a song on in this place that I knew. There was no one better than a good song by The Civil Wars, especially Barton Hollow. I grabbed Lucas' hand and pulled him onto the floor. We danced together like it was something we done every day. He swayed behind me seductively, making every girl in the room crave that she was me.

The Summit was not packed for the first time since I had known of it, so instead of having to yell over the crowd he simply whispered into my ear. "Who sings this?" Lucas pushed his hair away from his face and flashed his perfect smile.

It was my weakness, mainly because his smile rarely met his eyes when anyone else talked to him but with me they always touched them. They always lit up like he cared. "They are the Civil Wars; they play folk music."

"I can tell." He chuckled. He was into calmer music. I could tell by his iTunes that he was not familiar with them. He had every John Mayer CD known to mankind. I found it insanely cute that someone as rugged as him could dig Clarity and Your Body is a Wonderland.

The song ended and he scooped me up into his arms. "I have to talk to the manager about some accounting things right quickly. Would you be fine without me for a while and I should be back in about ten minutes?"

"Sure babe," Lucas leaned forward and his lips met mine. I closed my eyes and it seemed as if the world stopped for a brief moment. My hands made their way into his long brown hair, his hands gripped my waist firmly as they pulled me closer to him. "Hurry," I smiled.

"Back in a jiff," He mumbled.

I walked over to an unclaimed booth and sat down. My feet were killing me. It was a bad idea to wear heels. I melted into the plush leather seat and too out my phone. I strolled through the phone looking for someone to text to keep me entertained. There was no one. I put the phone down and the waitress cleared her throat. Rude but oh well I was thirsty. "Hi," I said.

"Hey, I am Patrice. What can I get you, sweetie?"

"I would like a Melon Bliss."

"You are one of the owner's girlfriend correct?"

"I am," I loved to say. I loved to hear it. I loved to be it.

"Well it's on the house."

"Perfect!" I sat back and watched the crowd dance to some hip hop song like it was the last dance of the night.

"Cypress," I heard a familiar voice say.

I looked up and there was Asher. He was drunk but he was so nice looking. He dressed well, his outfit was nice as usual. "How are you?"

"I am doing great actually. You called me once after that, was there anything that I could help you out with," He sat next to me. I could smell the alcohol on his breath as he swayed into the seat next to me.

"Yeah, I got everything that I needed to do out of the way."

"I wish we could have chatted more."

"Well I have Lucas for that," I smirked. "What's wrong with you Asher?"

"I have to talk to you about Lucas." He slurred his words and tossed his head back on the cushion booth seat.

"What about him?" I said.

He leaned closer and his lips formed a smile. "He is a lunatic."

"I think you are drunk," I tried to help him sit up in his seat but he was heavy. "Asher you really needed to go home, you don't look so good."

"You look great though." His hand touched my thigh and dread coursed through my veins. He was heavy and he would not back the fuck away. His lips crashed into mine and I wanted to scream. Had he not been drunk and confused I might have enjoyed it. But the taste of crown and cigarettes swirled around my mouth as his tongue crashed into my mouth and I wasn't a fan of either. I couldn't push him off of me and his hands started to make its way up my skirt. I pushed and pushed until he finally flew off of me. I didn't know I was that strong. Then I heard his voice.

"Get your bloody hands off of her!" Lucas slammed Asher onto the floor like it was nothing. The table flipped over and knocked everything to the floor.

Asher moaned. I refused to look at him. The sound of the thuds from Lucas hits were audible over the music. The guards made their way through the crowd. And they struggled as they tried to pull Lucas off of him. Once he was finally up Asher was passed out. The guards tossed him over their shoulders and moved through the crowd.

"I want him out and add him…" Lucas yelled over his shoulder. He was out of breath, "to the barred list. Get his entire name and make sure he is banned."

"Lucas" I wiped my face. There was no way to get this taste out of my mouth. I felt like I had done something wrong in having Asher kicked out. He looked like he had a bad day. It had just gone from bad to worst in a few seconds.

"Are you okay?" I shook my head quickly. My mind raced as it tried to keep up with whatever had just happened. He grabbed my hand. "Let's go."

I had never seen him so enraged. Asher had pissed him off and I felt like he blamed me. "Calm down." I said as I watched him pace around his living room. It was hard not to smile at his over usage of English slang. I barely could understand a word that flowed from his mouth.

"The bloody nerve of that wanker. Has he lost the plot? Is he off his rocker? Putting his bloody hands on you like you were fucking up for it!" Lucas pushed his fingers through his hair in frustration.

"Calm down, please?"

"You can't expect me to. Fucking Asher was sloshed and fuck!" He growled.

"I lived, he done me no harm. I really just want to snuggle up and watch a movie with you. You're angry for no reason." I tried to soothe the wound. He had a reason to be mad. This was the exact same guy he had said that he didn't want me to be around.

Lucas mumbled god knows what under his breath and continued to pace. He was erratic and it was cute but I tried not to smile. "What're you thinking?" He asked.

"I'm thinking that I would much rather you calm down before you kill him," I smirked.

There was glint of humor that touched his eyes and then it disappeared. "I don't want anyone to have what is mine. Your arse is mine."

His, I swooned inside. I could feel the heat as it traveled to my cheeks. There was no way I could hold a stern face to him now. "Babe there is nothing to worry about. I am 100 percent yours. He doesn't mean anything to me. He was just a little drunk. Now, if we could please start this movie I would be so happy."

"I'm not in the mood to watch the telly love," He nodded his head. "I should bloody kill him." He mumbled.

"Stop thinking murder. You are too young to go to jail for life."

He stared at me. "Right," he said as if he was not fazed. "Start the movie."

Lucas

I wanted to bloody kill him, I could see nothing but red. My fucked up mine had already had a plan in play. I could lure him out of the club and chop his body in tiny pieces and burn him in a fucking fire just outside of town... better yet I could take him to the morgue and crisp him alive... My heart raced at the thought, Asher to Ashes.

Cypress cleared her throat. "Please calm yourself Lucas," She smiled. She was amused and it was cute, but there was this small piece inside of me that was sincere about the threat of death to Asher. I had told this wanker once to stay the fuck away.

"I'm calm Cy," I sat on the couch and watched her but she was the last person on my mind. The hunt was now there. I wanted him dead.

Cypress hummed some Lifehouse song I could not remember the name of and slipped the DVD into the player. She bopped around my apartment and got herself wine and some fruit from the fridge. She had gotten so comfortable here. It made it easier to fall for her.

"Okay we will start with a light movie. You definitely need something to bring you down from the anger trip you just had. I have put in the best movie of all time." She poured her some wine and then handed me a beer. "You will love it. I swear."

"God Save the Queen, what is it?"

She mocked my accent playfully, "You are so bloody impatient." Cypress recited the line three times sounding more American with each attempt at the accent. "Oh Fuck it. It's Charlotte's Web. I might cry but this movie is magnificent."

"Was that movie in my stash?"

"I bought it at the thrift store we went to." She added. "And please watch the whole thing with me…"

Bloody hell, did she have to pick a cartoon, "Fine dear."

"Thanks," she kissed me on my lips and sat down next to me. "Have you ever seen it?"

"My foster mother had a copy of it. I burnt it in rebellion. During the summers when I would visit with her she would play the movie over ten times a week for my sister Lydia. Lydia loved it. I could have lived without it."

"You better keep your hands off of my copy," she mumbled and nestled herself closer to me. "I like you better when you are not on the war path Lucas… though I must admit the jealous you almost got lucky…"

"Almost got lucky?" I sat up and looked at her inquisitively. "Please tell me what steps to follow to insure that it happens next time."

"Baby," I hated when she called me that.

"Dearest," I smiled. "Are we going to watch these talking animals or are we going to call each other pet names all night?"

"We have been dating for three months now and we have yet to do anything. I'm not complaining. I am just baffled."

"Well I don't want to be rushed with you. If you want to wait it out I can wait it out." I had craved her in more ways than one over the past few months. There was something primal about my attraction to her. I wanted her raw and naked beneath me... panting and becoming incoherent with every touch of my finger.

"Well," she kissed me and ran her fingers down my chest. "I'm ready to be rushed."

Cypress

How did we end up here? I could feel my chest as it heaved in attraction. Was this really about to happen? Lucas tossed his shirt to the ground and climbed over me. Lucas Elledge was part God. I was sure of it. There was no way in hell that there could be a human alone this damn irresistible. He was careful where he put every finger. He traced the line of my hips. I was naked for him, laid out like I had known him my whole life. It certainly felt that way. My eyes closed as I relished in his touch and his playful bites to my inner thigh.

"I hope you don't mind me sampling?" He whispered.

There was so much anxiety pinned up in me I could not function. I wanted more of every and anything that he had to give. His thick finger spread through my folds separating them gently and then there was a brush of cold air and my hips bucked from the bed. It had been so long since there was someone that truly desired me I almost forgot how tantalizing it could be. He pushed me playfully back down and slid his finger completely into me rotating it and pushing it in and out. I almost lost everything I had tried to hold inside. A whimper escaped and I tried to grab his hand but he gripped my wrist above my head. "Lucas…"

"There are so many things that I want to do to you that I don't know where to start… there are these wonderful mounds of pleasure that I would like to ravage… but I can feel that you're practically starved…" His hand spread my legs and he smiled. "I want to cease your hunger first and then we can play… understood?" I felt the need to say yes sir but I simply nodded my head. "Good girl," He hovered over me and pulled my legs against his chest. He eased into me slowly, the sting was delicious as he filled me completely with one thrust. He went in a pace that slowly begun to make my body beg for more. Lucas slammed into me unyielding and it was joy, everything disappeared and I could feel my heart racing to find a release. My toes curling and it had been all of three minutes. I could barely control my taunts of satisfaction. My nails scraped down his back and were buried so deep he cried out but didn't change anything. He embraced the pain and thrust faster into me until I lost everything. I fell limp beneath him and he slowed his pace adding more kisses in with every thrust, "You're so perfect." he murmured. We were lost somewhere between ecstasy and reality and I wanted to live there forever. With his release came silence but he didn't leave my arms and it was all I needed.

Lucas

She was love. I was sure of it. There was no other way to describe her. I lay in her arms and everything that was about to surface had gone away. The monster had had left for the moment and there was just me and her. I got lost when I was inside of her and I was not sure I wanted to find my way back to reality. I lay in her arms enamored.

There were few moments in life where happiness was truly this prevalent. This was one of those few moments. I was wrapped in her scent, covered in her lust and drowning helplessly in her love. My mother had described love to me once. She simply stated it was when one changed their life for someone else. I would move mountains for her. I would slay dragons and battle giants for her. I would do anything to make sure she was mine, this way forever. This was my love. And for my love there would be no trepidations and there would be no worries, I would be sure of it. There was nothing that she could not have and there was nothing that I would not give. I fucking loved her.

"I love you," I whispered into her chest. My eyes were closed but my arms were still entangled in the mess of our bodies.

I felt her hear beat run out of her chest, "You don't mean that."

"I mean every word I said Cypress. There is no one else for me." I professed.

Her face turned my favorite shade of crimson. Though her skin was like a honey, the crimson always found a way to make a grand entrance. "Lucas, it was the sex. You can't love me."

"Why can't I?" I argued, I was still lulled by the remnants of what had just happened. "I don't need you say it back to me Cypress." Her ex was an idiot. Wasted her purity and now she was damaged. She didn't know love when she felt it. She hated gifts and she hated the fact that she could be happy. And it was his bloody fault.

"I don't know."

"Well I do. I hope that it doesn't bother you."

"You mean the world to me." She whispered as her hands went through my hair.

"You are the world to me Cypress."

We stayed like that for hours until something woke me up. My friend the monster was ready to playhouse. I tiptoed out of bed and walked down to the small office area in my loft. I sifted through the security cameras for his face and more importantly his car and license plate. I watched his every move for a while and fast forwarded the film as he harassed other females and then stumbled drunk to the car with some blond chick. There was his tag number. I jotted it down and opened the DMV site I should not have access to but didn't care. I typed in his tag number and there he was... license and all of his unpaid parking tickets.

I typed his name into some search engines and social media sites and he was known for his studies and research psychology. Why would he even be at this university? Our psychology division was horrid? He had some explaining to do and I would pry out of him. I should talk to him... soon. The monster inside would love to be drunk behind the wheel to take this fucker out.

"What are you doing in here?" Her whisper was sexy and it calmed me. Cypress made her way to the kitchen and grabbed a water bottle from the fridge.

"I couldn't sleep without knowing a few dates. I closed the laptop. "Tired?"

"I am completely drained." She drank her water.

"My mother invited us down for a small dinner. It will be just us and the parents. Can you come?"

"Sure, when?"

"At the end of October."

"I would love too."

Asher

My head pounded. I shouldn't have drink that much. I shouldn't have made that pass on Cypress and there was no telling what Lucas had formed in his head. More than likely he had already planned my upcoming death to a t. I tried to think straight but U had not yet recovered from the ass kicking and the overflow of alcohol.

My feet even ached.

"Good Morning."

My eyes opened as I tried to figure out where the fuck I was. This was not my home. This was not even my car. The room was all white. I had either been abducted by aliens or a clean
freak.

I looked up at the sandy blond guy in frustration. "Where in the fuck am I?"

"You're in my apartment. The security guards pulled your license but it had California address on it. We are not in the business of throwing people on their asses after my brother beats the shit out of you in public."

Brother? I stared. He was Mark. The foster brother of Lucas and he was the one that had the most sense about every situation. I patted down my chest in search of my glasses. "Shit."

"Exactly." Mark gulped down some of his coffee and looked at me. "I looked you up in a few databases last night. You are a genius. Especially in psychology. Why here? You got accepted into the program at Harvard?"

"Harvard is not for everyone."

"I would have taken it."

"Where are my glasses?"

"They are up until you answer my questions for a little while. I mean it won't take long." Mark's voice was calm and darker than Lucas' voice. "So, you like Cypress?"

"Actually I was drunk. I don't like her that way." I had not even considered to like her more than a friend. She was so deep into Lucas and clingy girls were not my type.

"Right." I could tell by his voice that he was not convinced. He rolled his eyes and rolled his shoulders.

"I'm serious. Let me go home. I got banned. Lucas might kill me if he even sees me here in the first place."

"He went out of town. And don't worry about him. You should actually be worried about me. You know that I found somethings in your car that you should be worried about. For example," He tossed my brown leather journal on the table in front of us and looked at me. "You are studying my brother?"

"Observing." I corrected. I swallowed hard and struggled to stop being dizzy from the oncoming hangover. "I swear it's harmless I just have b…"

"Stop lying to me!" Mark yelled. "You better be lucky that it was me that found this shit instead of Lucas. He would have killed you for thinking about following him."

"I know."

"Good then you should know that I would appreciate if you kept this information about him to yourself. I know that he is a psychopath. I know that he has a few bolts loose. But not everyone would be as open armed about it like I am. I want to know that I can trust you."

"You don't know me to trust me."

"I know that you care about your education and reporting an alleged sexual abuse charge to the Psychology head would fuck you up."

My heart pattered and I exhaled. "I won't break your trust."

"I want you to check in with me more than once a week. I want to know what you gather and you have to swear to me that you won't do anything dumb like report this to the police." He exhaled. "I think we could have a partnership. Apparently you do a better job of tracking him than I do. Could you keep it up? And I can make him answer some questions for you. Maybe it could help seal the deal on your dissertation."

"You would do that?"

"I would do that if you worked with me. I have some pull with the school. I know you just want to study and I don't have a problem with it happening."

"Deal."

"Perfect, sober your ass up and then leave. The backdoor will be open once I know you aren't driving drunk from here. The police already just want a reason to close us down."

"Alright."

"Talk to you later. I put my number in your phone."

"It was locked." I said bluntly.

"You're right, you should change the code from your birth year. It is highly predictable." Mark stood up and made his way towards the back area of the apartment.

"How'd you get my birthdate?"

"I can get anything I want. Just worry about what I said. And sober the fuck up." The door closed from the hallway and I sat down on the couch. I was either all good or fucked. I couldn't really decide which at the moment.

CHAPTER SIX

Cypress

"So what time are you leaving?" Lana was ready for me to be home. Three months was a while for us to be a part. Not to mention she had that new bundle of joy at home. Our parents were excited, but there was still the fourteen-hour drive ahead and Lucas was the driver for the trip.

"Well, Lucas has to get everything into the car and then we are on our way." Our first road trip together had me nervous. It would be uninterrupted time with him and there was nowhere for me to hide.

"Perfect, so about an hour. I can sleep and wake up and get breakfast and you should be here right?"

"Perhaps. He said that he just wanted us to hit the road first. He mentioned something about a hotel so maybe we'll drive a while and then get some rest and be there tomorrow."

"I like this guy!" Lana cleared her throat. "And please be nice to him the entire way down here."

"I will." I sat down on the couch. His loft was always so clean. I bundled in the cover and yawned. "I'll call you in the morning, okay?"

"Deal, I love you sissy!"

"I love you more Lana!" I tossed my phone to the couch and closed my eyes. I could hear him as he hopped out of the shower.

"Cypress, are you ready?"

"You're still naked Lucas." I mumbled.

"I am." He laughed. "Love, when I'm dressed we walk out the door."

"I know that babe." This I had noticed about him. He wanted me to be perfect, but he tended to take his time and be late. It was fine with me though. I could sleep the entire way there. "My sister said that she is excited about us coming."

"Excited to meet her, you talk about her all the time." He stepped out of the bathroom half dressed. His perfect hair fell in his face. A smile flickered on his lips as he caught me staring at him. "Keep ogling woman." He whispered.

"Sorry, but you're sexy."

Lucas winked and slid the black sweater over his head. "I'll run out to the car and warm her up and then we can leave," His voice was smooth and low. We weren't sure if the nap, we had taken helped us or made us groggy.

I slipped my boots on as he got the car ready and then grabbed the three blankets for me. It didn't take him long to run back inside. Mark, his older brother followed behind him. Mark was quiet and opinionated. He rarely spoke to me, but when he did, it was nothing but good and sometimes strong minded conversation. "Hey Mark!"

"Cypress," He waved. "I hope you two have a good trip." Mark was a tad bit shorter than Lucas and he dressed completely different. Lucas dressed like every day was casual day, simple t-shirt and some jeans. While Mark wore button down dress jackets and slacks continuously. He fits Shia perfectly as I fit with Lucas. I could care less about what I wore.

"Thanks," I smirked.

"Don't forget to make sure the cooks start that new dish on Mondays. I had the meeting with them, but I wasn't sure if they were actually going to do it." Lucas handed him a manila folder. "And then make sure that the hostess, doesn't drain us for overtime. Send her as home at thirty-three hours. She's killing me."

"I got it Lucas. Just give me the paperwork and leave."

"So sweet of you, Mark." Lucas grumbled.

Thankfully, he listened to Mark and we left for Tennessee soon after.

Lucas

Tennessee was nothing like Colorado. Their mountains were really only foothills. And the weather was dramatically warmer for it to be October. Coming here allowed me to see parts of Cypress that she normally hid from me.

"Do your parents like me?" I'd debated rather I should ask her or not.

"I think they do." She shrugged as she applied more mascara to her face.

"I hope they do."

"Calm down. You'll be fine. Lana likes you and that's mainly who will be around until dinner." She smirked and she pointed to the red bricked house with the brown fence that encased the yard. "Wow, mom and dad must have taken off from work to see me." She beamed.

Ace, now I would meet them in my Pink Floyd shirt and these dull sweat pants. "Are you serious?"

"More than," she said.

Her parents opened the blue door and walked out of the house. She favored her mother. They shared the same caramel complexion, freckles and even though her mother's hair was short, it was in a mess of curls. "Your mom is beautiful." I smiled.

"Thank you Lucas."

I pulled into the driveway. "Your father is a rather tall fellow." I put it lightly. He stood over her mother by a solid foot and some inches. He had no hair, but he looked friendly enough. "God, I hate meeting them looking like this."

"Breathe." She opened her door and hopped out of the car. "Mom! Dad!"

Brill. I exhaled and followed behind her. I watched her from a distance. It was easy to tell that she was missed. Her mother rocked with her and her dad kissed her forehead. It was admirable.

Cypress stepped back to me. "Meet my boyfriend, Lucas Elledge." She smiled. "Luke, this is my mom Terry and my father Nathan."

"Pleasure." I nodded. "You have a lovely home."

"Thank you Lucas." Her mom shook my hand. "We have heard nothing but good things about you." She looked me over, her eyes stopped at my tattoos. "You two look tired."

"Actually, we were going to change here. We thought you two would be at work. We drove in our night clothes." Cypress followed her mom into the house.

"We wanted to spend the entire day with you." Nathan said. "And we wanted to take you to get that couch."

"Yes!" She said. "Where is Lana?"

"On her way." Nathan added. "You two go get dressed and then we'll get something to eat and furniture shop."

Cypress was in the room across the hall from mine. I placed her bags on the floor and kissed her forehead. "I really need to change before the rest of your family thinks I'm a slouch."

"Don't worry my mom will come around."

"And your dad?"

"We'll never know." She chuckled. "Go get dressed."

I left her room and her mother was behind me. I couldn't tell what she was thinking, but for some reason I just wanted to close my door like I had no0t seen her. "Hi," I smiled.

"So, young man."

"Ma'am?"

"Perhaps we can talk downstairs while she is getting dressed."

No. I nodded my head. "Sure." The house was full of little figurines like my grandmother used to collect only black and smaller. Even the walls had shelves of them and paintings of them. I followed her downstairs and she and Nathan sat down.

"She really likes you." Nathan smiled.

"I'm grateful for that." I sat down on the brown plush couch and smirked. "She's beautiful woman."

"She's broken though." Terry added.

"I don't see that." I said. I could see it, but I don't want them to know that I see that. Everyone had a piece of them that was broken.

"She is," Terry crossed her legs. "I can see why she likes you. You're handsome and that accent is very pulling. Where are you from, England?"

"Yes, ma'am, I was born and raised in Sedburg, Cumbria and Wicklow, Ireland." The town of Cumbria was small but had produced me and shit ton of other writers. There had to be something in the water. I'm happy I had a sip.

"Wow, well how'd you get in America?" Nathan seemed like a nice guy. He hadn't hemmed me up in a corner just yet.

"My adopted mum lives here in the states."

"So, what do you do?"

"I own a restaurant and go to school."

"What kind of restaurant?"

"A place called the Summit in Colorado Springs. We serve American Cuisine."

"That's an accomplishment, how old are you?"

"Twenty-four, my birthday is right around the corner."

"Well, all that I ask is for you to treat her right. I don't know what happened with her and her ex but she can't take another heartache like the one that she had earlier this year." Nathan held his hand out. "It's a pleasure to meet you Lucas."

"Same here, sir," I smirked.

Cypress

Lana met us at the furniture store and of course she was all over Lucas. She was a sucker for a good accent and some tattoos. They clicked as well. He held my new niece Amory like he was hers and barely moved the entire time that they were in the store.

"He's okay." My mom muttered as she held up a plum colored drape. "Do you like this?"

"No, wrong color." I paused. "He's a great guy mom."

"I can see you like him."

I rolled my eyes. "Okay, so what's the problem."

"How well do you know him?"

"Well enough," I murmured I turned on my heel to Lucas holding Amory in his arms.

"I know she is so beautiful Lana." He smiled and looked up at me. "Your niece steals hearts like you."

My face burned red from happiness. "Really."

"Certainly." He winked.

Lana smiled. "He's a winner." Lana chuckled and reached for Amory.

Lucas handed her over and walked up to me. "Have you found that perfect shade of floral yet, love?"

"I don't know which one to pick." I mulled in my head. "I think pastel like floral pillows would be perfect with a beautiful light green couch and some cream drapes. What color is your mom's living room Lucas?"

"Uhm my mum here has this weird orange and tan thing going and my mum at home had a whole I like stripes vibe."

"I like stripes." The chuckle escaped my mouth.

"Well, you would have loved my old home in England. She had stripes everywhere in the house. I mean there was the couch and the striped theme bathrooms. She even painted some pictures of just strips to go in the bedrooms. She was so peculiar. I talked about those stripes every day."

"Your mom seems like she was an awesome woman. I want flowers... everywhere." I touched the plush seats of the green couch and plopped down. My mom walked ahead of us and left us alone for the moment. "It's comfortable, but ugly."

He sat down on the couch in one swift movement. His hands ran across the cushions of the couch as he swung my feet up into his lap. "This sofa is ugly... it's not you though. I see you with some Queen Ann Couch. A round back and a low sit. Something horrible to sit on while we watch Netflix."

"Yes, that is what I want. Something dreadful to watch TV on but so beautiful to the eye..."

He chuckled. "I guess it would give us a reason to travel to the bedroom." Lucas nibbled on my ear lightly.

I nudged him playfully and shook my head. "You are something else Mr. Elledge, be mindful of my six foot five dad." My eyes glanced over the room for a new couch to test out and there he was... Philip. The one person I never wanted to see again was out. "You wanna cut out of here and get something to eat?"

"Yes, darling, I want to go wherever you want to go."

"Perfect," My hands shook and the clammy feeling over took them. I folded my arms. "Great."

"Cypress!" Philip yelled. His voice brought back some wretched memories.

"Fuck," I whispered.

Lucas looked up. "Everything alright love? Do you know him?"

"Um, no, my ex-boyfriend is headed this way. Can we leave, like now?" I watched as Lana's eyes cut over to mine and she was ready to be in rescue mode.

"We can leave. But he's getting rather close." Lucas said as he noticed the strange interaction between me and Lana.

Within seconds Phillip appeared in front of us. He still looked perfect. He looked as if we never broke up, no eye aching nights and heartbreaking cries. Just normal. "Cypress, you look amazing. How is college going for you?"

I shifted uncomfortably and shrugged my shoulders. "Fine Philip, I'm actually enjoying it. What about you?"

"Good, you know. I bought a house close to your mom's house." He smiled. I knew that he and my mother still carried on like they were best friends and it irked me more than anything. She didn't realize the torture he had put me through. She would never understand. "Marley and I are expecting. Did your mom tell you?"

My mom turned and her face was pale white. "Philip, imagine seeing you here."

"She didn't." If my mom had told me that I would have freaked out. I would have died. I cut my eyes over to my mother and she nodded her head sympathetically. At least she looked like she cared. Marley was the bitch that he had cheated on me with more than once.

"Well, yeah, she's six months." Philip pointed over to her. Marley, the petite blond bobbed perfect bitch, waved and rolled her eyes in the same motion. She placed her hand back on her round stomach. I didn't respond.

"We were together six months ago Philip. Why in the fuck would I want to know that my suspicions were accurate?"

"I didn't mean to hurt you." Phillip paused and held his hands up. "I came over here to apologize actually. I joined a church group. You were heavy on my mind last week. I wanted to call you."

"Please don't." I exhaled. My whole face reddened and the sting of tears traced my eyelids. "You think I can just be happy for you after all the continued shit you put me through!" I yelled.

"Hi," Lucas touched my shoulders and squeezed them lovingly. It sent some sort of comfort through my body. "Congrats on your baby and your new home."

"Thanks." Philip's smile diminished. "Who are you exactly?"

"I'm Lucas Elledge, her boyfriend and we were just leaving. Appreciate it if you could shove the fuck off, so we can continue looking for couches too." Lucas smiled and grabbed my hand. "Dear, are you hungry? I could eat."

My dad smiled and gave Lucas a nod. "Goodbye Philip."

"Yes." I answered.

"Well, it was nice to meet you and Cypress it was good seeing you." Philip waved. "Goodbye Mr. and Mrs. Tucker."

"I can't say it was the same for her Phil... Once again, stay the fuck away." Lucas spat. We moved through the couches and his arm wrapped around my waist and I felt safe and not so incomplete. "Where can we fetch this tea?"

"The London Shoppe!" Lana said. "It's perfect there."

"Is that fine Cypress?"

"Perfect."

The London Shoppe was my mother's favorite place to get tea. We had gone there four times this week for good reason. The Vanilla tea was a real treat. The herbs mixed in with the sugar made it worth the trip across town to get it. I sipped the tea with eyes closed. "Dear God, it's amazing."

He nodded his head. "I like the plain old tea myself but I hear the Vanilla Dazzle is dazzling." Lucas' voice was calm although it was low. Lucas paused and pushed his cup in front of him. My parents and Lana had allowed us to have some alone time as they fought over which desert crepe that they wanted the most. "What did he do to you to make you feel like you should fear him?"

"I don't fear him." I lied.

"I know fear when I see it Cy," His fingers twiddled with the handle of the tea cup and he leaned forward and placed his hand on mine. "It might be the only emotion I can recognize without help."

"I..." I paused. "Our relationship was not the best of relationships. He cheated on me." I closed my eyes in frustration. "He raped me once. He was just an ass. And no I shouldn't be mad about them being together but I want something like their love..."

"Whoa, whoa." Lucas held his hand up. "You want something like that maniacal bastard? You want someone like him?"

"I meant their relationship."

"Darling, we are better than them on our worst day. He is a piece of shit and I'm happy you waited until we were away from him to tell me everything. I," he baffled with his words and clenched his fist. "I've not known you long Cy."

I felt a tingle in my stomach every time he said Cy. "I know."

"But I know you deserve more than that. You should be ashamed that you even desired a piece of shit like him. You are better than that, you know? You are perfect to me. Everything about you. And the fact that he thought he could belittle you in any form... angers me deeply."

"I know." I paused. "I appreciate it and I won't think like that anymore."

"God don't apologize to me. You were raped. You should be angry, not envious of some dumb ass bastard and his whoring girlfriend. You are so much better than you think. Give yourself credit."

"Thank you, I will."

Lucas

I couldn't fight the rage. Philip was a maniacal bastard and there was nothing that could settle the way I felt. He was prospect one. They talked and talked and I laughed occasionally. But her parents were annoying. Especially her father, though he was the one parent that liked me, he made a point to show me his football trophies. I could care less about the bludgeoning sport Americans play for sport. While the chaos surrounded, I could only think about one thing, the ex-boyfriend and how he almost fucked her up for me. I wanted to see his blood drip to the floor in a pool of blood as he begged for his life. They thirst for it had grown even more ever since Asher had decided to fondle my fucking girlfriend after I told him to stay away. I had composed a plan that consisted of the women drinking themselves into a pit and falling asleep. It was not a hard venture being that Cypress could be lit with one drink. Then, once it was all done, I would sneak out the front door for some fresh air and some fresh blood.

The dinner was actually a treat. She served some sort of mango flavored fish and some steamed cauliflower. I devoured it and Cypress chugged down wine like it was water and she and her mother became tipsy. They giggled and made goo-goo eyes at me when I spoke. An accent was a funny thing. One difference in a word or the tone of the word after a word and I was a marvel to these women. I kissed her Goodnight and let her know I would like to take a brief walk around the neighborhood. She was so tickled and drunk she knew not of what I said.

I made my way to his house. He was there. I watched him clean his beautiful house and eat his pathetic meal. I could take him out rather easily. Just go in and snap his fucking neck. The things he had done to her had made me want to kill him. It was a valid reason. I calmed myself. I had to release this damn anger that I had felt since early. If I killed him… Who would know that it was me?"

I crouched and looked around. He lived by himself. He had no one there and I had my handy black gloves. I could leave without being traced… I exhaled. I loved her and this is what happened when I loved someone… I went above and beyond to make sure that she was left with no threats… no hint of danger. He was dangerous. I teetered with the thought of him dying in my head. It was done.

I waited for the lights to turn off and crept into his house unnoticed. I snatched the phone cords from the wall and walked into the bedroom. The smell of his shower came into the hall. I turned my head and looked. He still had the picture of them on his dresser. She didn't look happy like she did when she was with me. She looked despondent and miserable. I tossed the picture to the ground and he walked out of the room.

"What in the fuck are you doing in here!" He yelled.

"Quiet," I whispered. Fucking Phillip was loud.

"I'm calling the cops." The knife slipped out of my hand and hit his leg. He screeched something terrible and ran towards me. I tripped him and pushed the knife in deeper causing him to yell. I didn't want him to bleed out. I wanted him to suffer a little. I pushed him to the floor and drug him into the bathroom. "Now be quiet. I want to introduce myself…"

"You crazy son of a bitch! I know who you are!" I stuffed a sock, dirty of course into his mouth before he could finish and avoided blood at all cost. I couldn't toss my clothes out if they were dirty…

"That new leaf that you turned over seems to have been forgotten." I growled. He was a lair too. "My name is Lucas and I am the love of Cypress' life… She doesn't know it yet. She doesn't know a lot yet." He muffled something behind the sock. "Shove off already!" I yelled. I sighed and yanked the knife from his leg. Blood spouted out like a fountain and I smiled. "It's truly a glorious sight isn't it?" My eyes stared as his blood flowed out. "Anyway Phil, is it okay for me to call you Phil?" I watched as his eyes grew wide. "Good… The reason I am here is quite simple you see. I come to you as an angel of death… you wronged her so many times it sickens me. I read her diary. She was bat shit for you and you went around shagging the entire city. How nasty and crude of you? You defiled her and I came and made her pure… So now I have to defile you, more like kill."

Whimpers escaped and the tears flowed from his eyes. "Don't cry now," I whispered. "You had a chance to love the most beautiful woman on the planet and you chose to fuck whores. And now for her hurt… I will fuck you over one final time."

There was this look of undiluted fear in his eyes and it was satisfying. He scurried back and left more blood on the floor I had to avoid. "Be still." I pushed him to the floor and smiled. "I have to unfortunately make this one quicker than usual. I wanted to make you suffer, but I guess I can be kind to you." The knife cut into his chest and I could feel his blood rushing out of his body. I snatched the knife out and stepped carefully away from the scene. I watched as his pulse stop and almost every ounce of blood flowed from his body. Then the urge receded. I could sleep now. And thank fuck's sake, I wouldn't have to come back and do this later.

Cypress

I don't know where he has been, I don't care to ask, I feel too angry to care. He's been gone for hours on foot. Where could he have been? I stared, watching him look me over. "What's the matter love?"

"Where have you been?"

"A nice walk around the city, it is truly beautiful here." He smiled. "Why do you look bothered? I just needed some fresh air. I am a bit of a night owl."

Night owl my ass, he usually slept like an angel at night. I had watched him too many times. I was not buying what he had to throw out, "Lucas, where have you been?"

"I have been out love. I don't even know anyone from this area; I just wanted some fresh air."

"Fresh air," I paused. "Why did you leave your phone?"

"Why are you giving me a third degree love? I got some air, breathe." Lucas nodded his head and slipped his shirt off. "Can I sleep?"

"Yeah, after you are honest?"

"I'm being honest Cypress." Lucas made his way up the stairs with my hand in his. "Let's get some rest."

"Ugh," I pouted, "Fine." I didn't want to sleep alone. I hadn't really slept alone since we had started to date. "Perhaps I could sleep in your room with you?"

"Your father will string me up by my toes."

"Ugh," I was moody tonight. "Fine then, I'll sleep alone." The thought in general seemed to be unbearable, I turned to go to my bedroom and smiled. "Goodnight."

"Are you mad?"

"Yes, I want to sleep with you. I sleep better when I can feel you next to me." The words sounded pathetic, but the feeling in my chest knew that they were true.

"We can sleep in here together, with the door opened." He took the pile of comforters my mother had tossed on the bed and put them on a chair. Then he laid the pillows on the floor next to the bed. "Are you coming or not?"

"I want to…" I grinned jokingly.

"Are you mad? I would like my dick to stay attached to my body love."

I snickered and realized his absurd humor was part of the reason that I was in love with him madly. I could only hope that he felt more than the same about me. "Oh my god Lucas," I blushed and climbed onto the bed with him.

"I love you, dear," he kissed me lightly on the lips.

For the first time I actually wanted to say it. "I love you more." And with that, we fell into a peaceful slumber.

CHAPTER SEVEN

Lucas

Cypress was a control freak in her own way. She always wanted to be in charge of dinner and what time the movie started and when we would visit family. I had not yet introduced her to anyone but Mark and Lydia. Lydia loved her. Mark tolerated her.

"Okay Mark, look we should make sure you get the math," she said smiling.

She didn't quite get that Mark was careless and was borderline sleep. "I don't care how you want it Cypress. I agree with you fully." He winked at her and nodded his head. "She is just like Lydia."

Lydia giggled in satisfaction. She shared some similarities to my sister, but she was totally different in the same breath. "So we have to get matching dresses."

"I like that idea. It's for your graduation party?"

"It's like ten months away." Mark mumbled.

"It's the first major event of her life."

"We don't even know if you will be here next year Cypress."

"I'm not going anywhere asshole."

God, I loved that about her. Lydia high fived her and they continued to walk through the store.

"Why in the hell did I come?" Mark mumbled.

"I was wondering the same thing."

"Asshole. She acts just like Lydia. Mom is going to love her."

"Pump your brakes."

"Brother you are head over heels for this feisty piece of work. I haven't seen Shia since that night. She was not a perfect fit."

"Mom has a bad habit of falling for someone before I can."

"I don't think you will have this problem."

"Yeah mate, I'll see."

"Are you staying for Christmas?"

"I haven't got that far, Thanksgiving is around the corner. I figure we get through that first." Thanksgiving at my parents' house was always dramatic. It was never about the actual holiday. It was about the food. Of course it was an American holiday either way. I never celebrated it.

"Exactly," I grinned. "I can't miss Nadine this year, she would fly over her and have a swing at me. Then the rest of my crazy family misses me too."

"Must be hereditary." Mark sat down on the bench in front of the store the girls had disappeared in. They had made friends with one another which was great.

"Who are you telling?" I chuckled and joined him on the cold metal bench.

Mark laughed and then leaned closer to me. "You have to be more careful brother."

"What are you talking about?"

"Did you kill Summer?" It was less of a question and more of a statement. He exhaled. "Jesus, Lucas."

"Ugh bloody hell mate, can the badgering wait?" I rolled my eyes.

"I'm telling you that a string of your ex-girlfriends being murdered is a bad look. I care for you. I want you to be wise and leave the exes alone." He leaned in. "I would look at you and think you were guilty if I was looking into them. You are the common factor."

"I understand." I said.

"You should try to find another way to funnel your anger." Mark was the only person in the world who understood me because he was more like me than anyone else knew. He was a killer that had never actually experienced the kill. He was lucky, I sometimes feared that I was unstoppable. Their lives meant shit to me, but my life, well, I kind of enjoyed it.

The news had not yet made it back to her yet. It had been a full week since he bled out the floor of his home. His heart beat completely stopped under my knife and the thrill of it still had its effects on me. I knew the moment she found out I could not be around her because I tended to look careless when people died. My mother and father were the only ones that had ever brought me to tears. And even then I tried to remain numb.

"I see what you are saying. But how in the hell do I channel it?

"Well, I thought that Cypress was a good start." He smirked.

"I'll try."

"Thank you," he sat back.

The mall had ended without anyone getting hurt and with no trunk space. Cypress bought up random items to fill her apartment. We had started working on her new project at the library. She wanted to do some psychology research and I knew what she needed to know. Thank God she hadn't mentioned Asher; he was lucky the need to kill him had dissolved once I ended her ex. She scanned through the books, writing down little things while I text my brother about some upcoming event he wanted to do.

"Hey," a too familiar voice said from above us.

We both looked up and seen Asher. Cypress did wear a shocked look on her face, she was flushed like she enjoyed seeing him again. This fucker would not disappear. "What the fuck do you want?" I whispered.

"I wanted to apologize, to you both. I had a bad day. My father gave some bad news that day and I wasn't taking it well. I usually don't act out of character." Asher stared at Cypress and the small smile appeared across her face. "I really am sorry."

"You think you can harass her and just apologize." I leaned forward and touched Cypress' hand breaking her trance to him. "Not bloody likely?"

"Calm down, he really must have been hurt." She said. Cypress looked at me with some concern. "Is everything good?"

"I don't care." I seethed.

"I just wanted to say that and I hope you don't think bad of me. You have a good day." He walked away from the table and I clenched my fist.

"You have an anger problem. He made a mistake. Most people would not have apologized at all. He didn't have to apologize. He could have just never said anything. I appreciate it Asher." She said loud enough for him to hear it.

"Okay, yes, thank you Asher for apologizing for shoving your tongue down her throat. You are a marvelous chap! Tea sometime?"

Asher walked off, nodding his head and through his hand up. Was this some kind of game to the fucker? I would ruin him. She hit my hand playfully. "Quit it damn it. You should calm down."

"I will tomorrow." I exhaled. That fucking urge had nudged its way back in. "Let's, um goes to your apartment. I have a better way to express my anger."

A smile emerged on her face. "Are you sure?"

"I have never been more certain in my life."

Asher

My research had been more than productive over the past week. I was looking out for Mark every damn second of the day. I was sure he had a tail on me. A black SUV with horrible blending skills. As far as Lucas I was more than sure that he would kill me at some point. Mark said he would not let it happen, but there was no comfort still for me. Lucas was a selfish guy and the open apology route I had just tried crashed and burned in front of me. I felt like I made him even more mad. But Cypress was okay, so maybe she could hold back the hounds. I sat down at the table and started to take more notes in notebook. Who the fuck was I kidding? She oblivious that he was even, a killer. There would be no way that she would ever care if I died.

Perhaps it would be easier for him to forgive me if he saw that I had a girlfriend, but from what I had discovered this campus crawled with women in committed relationships. Even just the thought of getting laid was a distant one. I had not gotten much sleep in the past few days. There was still so much that rambled in mind during the quiet of the night.

"Whatever you are going through could not be that bad?" Whitney's voice chimed from behind me.

"I think you are wrong this time Whit," I mumbled.

"Life sucks." She smiled. "What are you mad about or should I say what are you depressed about?"

"First, I'm a dumb ass. Second, I'm a dumbass and third, I'm a dumbass."

"You are twenty-five and you are about to have a PhD. I am sure more than one or two mistakes won't kill you. But most men are dumbasses so I won't disagree with you completely." She laughed cheerfully as she pulled a chair up to my table.

I pushed my hands through my disheveled hair. If she only knew how incredibly wrong that statement was she would hug me and tell me to get the fuck out of town. I had considered it. I had considered just moving back with my father and being his assistant, but I wanted this study to go through. "Yeah, I guess so."

"Dinner and movie tonight?"

Great, she had friend zoned me and now she wanted to do best friend shit. "I would love to." I answered, perhaps too quickly.

"Perfect," She grabbed my hand. "And perhaps something more?"

My eyebrow shot up. "Uhm... are you sure? I wouldn't want to step on any toes."

"I positive. I decided that I should follow my heart and not my mind. My mind likes to fuck shit up for my heart."

"When did you get such a potty mouth woman?"

"I don't know." Whitney shrugged and flashed her crooked smile.

"Don't lose it. I like it." I touched her hip softly. "Come on, I haven't eaten today, so what are you cooking?"

"Ordering pizza, I don't cook well when I'm tired."

"Perfect," I made sure we walked passed the table where they sat. I had no idea if it would make a difference, but I prayed it would. I waved and Lucas watched us the entire way out, and swear I heard the word fucker escape his mouth. I would stay clear now for at least a little while. My dissertation might be made up. Fuck this shit. Poor Cypress might be on her own.

We found ourselves in my apartment. I had not taken the time to tidy up the place. There were notes and crime scene photos scattered all over the place. I unlocked the door and scooped up all of the photos before she seen them.

Whitney placed the pizza on the table and grabbed her a slice. "Your place is nice. Who decorated?"

I was finally all unpacked and I agreed with her. "Thank you. I did actually. My mom registered everything at a few stores and told me to put it out. I have no sense of style. But you know that already don't you?"

"Your mom still spoils the mess out of you, huh?"

"You know it." My mom, Margot only had me. And because of that I was fortunate enough to get anything I wanted. Especially after my parents divorced. My father sent checks and she just dropped them in my account and it worked that way still. My father always sent me money because he said that as long as I continued my education I shouldn't have to work. Yes, I was spoiled and I had enough saved that I didn't have to spend with a leash. I could get what I wanted when I wanted for the most part. I grabbed the remote from the couch and smiled at her. "I only have the basic channels and Netflix babe."

"Fret not," she said. Whitney smiled at me and nodded her head. "You still are not into TV are you?"

"I have been busting my ass to make sure I get everything done for this research paper. My whole career will be judged off of it. I have some fans in the psychology department. I would love to keep it that way."

"I'm happy you are into something that you love." Whitney traced her fingers over the papers on the desk. "So this research paper means that much to you?"

"Dissertation," I corrected. "Yes, it means everything in every sense. I have to be successful. I have to go in front of the Doctoral Committee in the next month or so. They want to question me about my research."

"So, tell me about it Asher? What is this research that is so important about?"

"It's about the psychopath I told you about."

"About the killer?"

"About the subject."

"Well, I want to know about it. Tell me about it."

"He," I nodded my head. "I'd rather not. I would rather we cuddle on the couch and dive into some Sherlock. I know you like the show."

"We can do that after you tell me about him."

There was nothing that I really wanted to delve into with her. She would not understand my fascination with him or his condition. She would see him as normal people would, a killer. But there was so much in the way that he thought that could draw someone like me in. Lucas defied everything that normal people done. The most normal thing in his social life was Cypress. He was even distant with his family, but that was because he has pretty much seen himself as being alone in the world. It was not so much a lie though. His only existing family was in Europe. "Well, I can tell you that he is normal and he has not done anything dangerous. He just thinks and acts differently." She felt warm beside me. He can be intense at times. I laid off his trail a little. I just really need to document. But I don't want to talk about this all day. I would rather talk about something else." I clicked the television on. "Let's just relax..."

"Tonight a gruesome murder, the second in three months of its kind. The local police are paired with other police departments to figure if this a pattern of any kind. I have Robert Day at the scene. Robert what has happened.?"

"The news came unexpectedly to the parents of twenty-three-year-old Phillip Langford. After not hearing from him in over a week his parents and fiancé reported him missing to the local authorities. After further investigation of the home he was discovered dead in his home of knife wounds. The coroner has declared his death a murder and from the forensics report he was murdered over a week ago. We have been informed that the County Sheriff and Local police departments are questioning suspects about his murder and that they will get to the bottom of this. The camera cuts to the mother, her face red and filled with tears and her sobbing in front of the home as he was brought out of the house.

"The victim suffered two fatal wounds that lead to his death. The police do not have a suspect, but if you have any leads you are urged to contact authorities at once. There is a tip hotline number below."

My heart thudded. It was his M.O. He always let them bleed out and he had been out of town last week. I ran over to the notebook. Fuck, he killed again. My hands moved faster than I could pace.

"What are you writing?"

"Notes babe," I continued to write until my wrist pained.

"He was not behind it, was he?"

"No, sweetheart," I lied. "I was writing something down for class."

"If he was you have to tell someone. You can't allow him to murder." Whitney stared at me and I nodded my head. "Asher," she mumbled.

"I said no, Whit. Come on, let's play some games or something. This is the reason that I don't watch TV." I turned the TV off and stood up. "I have Twister."

Whitney chuckled. "Yeah, alright, be careful. I would hate to get what I wanted for forever and lose it to a document that does not mean more than your life."

"Yeah, I know babe."

Cypress

"Can you tell me about your mom?" I played in his curls. These were the moments I loved. He was all mine in his loft. And it was private, no nosy neighbors anything like that.

"My mum was a wonderful woman." He paused. "Her name was Luna; I know you know that, but it was something about the night that brought out her real self. The moon light was her friend. We sat out for hours, sometimes recanting poetry or better yet short stories. The short stories were my favorite."

"What did she look like?"

"She was remarkable. She had wavy hair like mine but it was a blond color. Her eyes were stark blue. She always wore a smile even when she wanted to kill me she was smiling." He inhaled. "Then she started crippling and not being able to do what she normally could and it was hard for me to witness. She went to school with my adopted mum. They were friends once upon a time. They made an agreement that no matter what when she started crippling I would be formally adopted by her, her name is Tracy. She's an angel and her and mum had some bad times, but she never punished me for whatever she and my mum had against each other."

"Why haven't I met Tracy?"

"Because I have never brought a woman home, and it makes me nervous," He said honestly.

"I am not just any woman Lucas."

"I never said that you were Cypress. It's hard for me to be open about anyone or anything with them."

"Okay," There was no escaping him on the couch. I flicked through the television channels. "Stop pouting. I will take you there tomorrow morning okay. You can join me for Sunday Brunch. She'll love it."

"I don't want you to take me because you have to. Forget it."

"Oh come on," He looked at me. "Are you mad?"

"You can get mad about Asher but I can't get mad over you not introducing me to your only living parents."

"Don't bring him up." He snapped. "Especially not while you are lying half naked on my couch."

"Asher, Asher, Asher. I have told you numerous times that I don't want him, but you insist on making life a living hell for him."

"Fuck that Cypress. That guy fucking had his hand up your skirt. Get mad at that shit."

"Don't curse at me." I yelled.

He growled. "Fuck!" Lucas walked away from the couch, sending a draft under the covers. "You are maddening."

I blocked him out as he paced the floor pacing like a mad man. He paced for five minutes. "Keep walking… It doesn't bother me."

Lucas picked me up from the couch scooping me in his arms. His lips crashed into mine and I fell into him as if it was a routine. Lucas walked so lightly up the stairs it felt as if I floated and tossed me into the bed. His hands made their way up my skirt and they traced the absence of my underwear. "Damn it woman, you will be the death of me."

I smiled as he pressed one finger deep into me and added another. My hips bucked off of the bed and Lucas' thumb ran over my clit in circles that drove me crazy. He was a genius with those fingers. His bed was soft and plush. The covers had swallowed me whole but he still found a way to make sure I was buckling off of the bed. I grabbed his shoulders with my hands as his mouth joined the party. I couldn't take another moment. My legs weakened and my mind numbed. I screamed and he continued driving me mad until I had to get away, I scooted forward on the bed away from him and he smiled.

"I could do that for hours."

"I would last ten minutes." a thin mist of sweat had covered my body and I was in heaven.

"Turn over." He whispered.

I turned over and I was not myself, every time I was with him I became undone. He opened a piece of me that I didn't even know existed. I was bare to him and everything I'd ever be was his. He pulled me back closer to him. My backside faced him while I sat there waiting patiently for him to start. He slapped my ass sending a delicious sting through my whole body. "Never forget whose you are..." he whispered.

"Lu..."

He slapped my ass again. "Shhhh woman." He silenced me as his fingers went into me again and he was a tad bit rougher. "You are mine... is that understood?"

I nodded my head in agreement.

"Say it!" He growled.

"I'm yours," I was exasperated.

I could feel him over me. He pushed me flat on my chest and thrust into me hard. I felt as if I might come from one more stroke. He continued at a steady pace and it drove me damn near as crazy as he pulled in and out slowly. His pace was maddening. I was unable to move at all he had me pinned and it was perfect. He drilled into me and I clawed the pillows for sanity. Lucas kissed my shoulder blades gently slowing down, allowing me to catch my breath. "I love you more than I have ever loved anyone Cypress..." He whispered. "Can you feel it as well? Or am I just driving myself mad?"

"I feel... the same." He ground himself deeper than I had ever felt anyone and the orgasm shattered me into a million pieces. My heart missed a few beats and my legs clenched together as he dove back into me. I screamed into the pillow from pleasure and he chuckled in my ear spilling himself into me. "Lucas..."

"What," he rolled off of me pulling himself out and tossing the covers to the ground.

"We have to start using condoms..."

"Why?" he said out of breath. "Can we discuss it later? You kind of ruined the moment there."

"I don't want a baby."

"I know." He mumbled. Lucas nestled into me and fell into the quickest slumber. At least he gave me the pleasure of getting off twice before he went to bed. It wasn't five minutes and I had fallen asleep myself. My body tangled in his warmth I slept better than I had in days.

We slept for three hours until the annoying vibration of my cell phone irritated us both. "Answer Cy, or I would bloody chunk it out the window."

At the moment I had agreed with his decision. The phone rung nonstop and at this point I wanted to murder my cell phone too. I reached over Lucas to the night stand and stared at the bright white screen. It was my mom. I slid the green button across the screen and nestled back into Lucas. "Mom." I answered. "I hope this important."

"It is; I've been calling you all damn day." The irritation in her voice was like music to my ears. I hadn't talked to her much since we had left.

"Sorry mom, I was tied up."

"You haven't been yet." Lucas whispered in my ear.

"Shhhh," I pushed him playfully. "What's going on?"

"Honey, it's about Phillip."

"Mom, I'm with Lucas right now can this wait?"

"No, he's dead. He was murdered. They just found his body."

The words had my world in a spiral of chaos. No, I had not had feeling for him besides hatred in the past few months, but any death of someone I knew always changed my opinion. I dropped the phone and a sob escaped my mouth. I felt as if I could not get out of the bed quick enough. My feet lead me to the steps and I slid against the wall in anguish.

"Hello Terry, I see. I'm so sorry to hear that." He paused. "Don't worry about her. I'm here for her. Yes, ma'am, I'll have her call you when she is well." I could hear his footsteps as he made his way down the steps. "Cypress..."

"Someone killed my ex."

"I know," Lucas pushed his hands through his hair. "Your mom just told me about it. Did they say what happened?"

"No," I wiped my face and I could hear my phone ringing again and again. "I have to go home."

"I can drive you. You are not in any condition to be driving love."

"I mean to my parents' house. I was close to his parents and I know his mother is in shambles about this. Plus, he had the baby on the way. And I bet they are..."

"I understand your concern. I honestly do darling. But he has a girlfriend for that. And even if you were going you couldn't go tonight." He sighed as his eyes wandered over to me. "I know you are hurt. I get it. But just not tonight, okay. There is nothing that you can do tonight. Just climb in bed and I'll be there for you and tomorrow morning when you have a clear mind and heart you can go ahead and leave. I won't stop you, but I'll worry all night if you leave now."

"Okay," the tears continued to race down my face.

"Come on back to bed."

"I didn't hate him."

"It's okay, it wasn't about you." Lucas comforted me. "I would go down there with you, but we have midterms coming up and all of that. I can tell your teachers for you and get your work."

"Okay."

"Get some shut eye and in the morning head out."

Lucas

I had not cared if she mourned or not. I guess that made me a bad person. I held her in my arms and listened to her cries. She was truly saddened by the loss of her ex-boyfriend. And she believed I cared. I went ahead and was there for her. She left an hour ago and there were some things that I wanted to get done. Number one, digging more dirt up on Asher. I had to see what the hell he was really here for; things had not linked up with him just yet. It had not eluded me that he was still here at this college when he had a resume that could impress any elite college. But there was brunch and then there was Mark. He wanted me to go over plans for the event again with him.

I got dressed. I tossed on some blue jeans and white T-shirt. I turned my hat to the back and waited for Mark to make his way up so we could go to brunch. He had insisted to ride with me.

"Hurry your ass." Mark said as he waited in the club. He leaned against the wall.

"I'm coming."

"Where's Cypress?"

"She left early, her ex died." I heard the laughter it emerged in my voice.

Mark's eye grew wide. "Shit, tell me you didn't."

"No," I scoffed. We made our way out to the truck and hopped in. I liked driving, but today I had decided to just let Mark lead the way.

"You fucking did man. Slippery slope."

"Oh fuck off."

"Yeah, fuck off," Mark nodded his head. "What did it feel like?"

"I can't explain it."

"So what about Cypress? I am sure she is hurt."

"I'm sure she will live." The words tumbled out. "She is fine."

"Are you sure?"

"He was fucking scum," The answer was simple.

CHAPTER EIGHT
Lucas

No one had ever asked me why I killed. It had always stayed below the surface, a void my mother called it. Luna said that my father had it too. This void, so to speak always danced in my eyes whenever there was nothing new. I knew that my father was a cold blooded killer and that there was no coincidence that a string of deaths related to him were scattered across England and Ireland. But no one ever touched him. His ties to the English elite and the Irish IRA had almost made him untouchable. Plus, his brothers and sister kept him close. They looked at him as the special one. It was most definitely how I was looked at by a few family members. My father taught me early that I should always have an alibi. It was the one thing that he specialized in. He always had an airtight alibi. The only person in the world besides my cousin Callum that knew of my void was my foster brother, Mark. He could give less than a fuck about what I did. He was the only person in this whole damned world that might have an inkling of what I went through and it was because I was more than sure that he had the same void. He always was my alibi. He knew when to lie and how to make sure everything he said was backed by proof. This time I would not have an alibi. This particular prey had haunted me for weeks and his name was Luther Ingram.

Luther had more than a few priors on his rap sheet. He had finally been set free from the state prison and I was in heaven. This man was a fucking ass. He raped his own fucking daughter, killed his wife and then failed at offing himself. That was a blessing for me. I needed this kill more than I needed air to breathe. Cypress here lately had been distant and I was not about to force her to make the right choice. Mark said she was grieving. Grieving was bullshit. Her ex was a parasitic ass. He was no good for her.

I clicked through my computer. Hacking the state system had not been as hard as it seemed. I could find any person that I wanted to in a matter of a few clicks. Fucking Luther was housed a Halfway Center about four to five hours away, actually it was closer to where Cypress were headed. It could serve as a problem to me. But my stealth mode just had to be perfect. He was being watched closely by more than me. The police had messed up with his arrest, most of the case was circumstantial and there was nothing that tied him down to the crime. I might should ask some questions to him before I killed the bastard. He had a kickass lawyer that had a degree is the art of creating doubt, she was next on the list. The fact that she had gotten him off was a sheer act of genius. Too bad she wasted her talent on that piece of shit.

Luther was tall and frail. He barely weighed a solid 150. His hair black and curly made him look like a predator and he was not even strong. Then he had no reason to kill. To kill without a reason irritated me. Declare a reason and make it count. If death is his art, he should have perfected it. He repulsed me. How could he get caught and be stupid? The key to commit crimes was not to get caught, it was basically the only rule I had laid out for myself. Luther did not deserve to be called a killer. But I could solve that. I scrolled back through the pages, glancing at the crimes, yes, mine was more morbid. Mine were of a greater reason. I killed to purify. This man raped and there was nothing good that came out of rape.

"Baby!" Cypress called from the shower.

Her voice had become a little annoying to me in the last few months. Maybe because I had not had any room to breathe and she was suffocating, but the Christmas Holidays were here. God Save the Queen, I was fucking saved. Her small town pleaded for her to return, and I was happy to send her there. "Yes, Cy."

"Are you sure that you have to go to Ireland?"

"Positive," I answered. Ireland had waited on me for a while. My cousin had some things that he had planned and honestly, I missed the lush green lands of one hometowns. I relished in the thought of the peace and the fact that I would be able to see my grandmother Nadine and my mum's mother whom I called Nan.

"My mom really wants you there for Christmas."

This discussion had happened more than ten times in the past few days. I know that her mom wanted me there for Christmas. I was madly in love with Cypress. She was perfect in every way. I wanted to be with her because she made me think. But I wanted this peace if only for a few weeks. "I understand that and I've told you I would try to get back in time for the latter part of the holidays."

"It's your birthday Lucas. I am going to miss our first birthday event together."

I knew my birthday was New Year's Eve. I liked the fact that I could literally start a new year of life each year. I didn't celebrate it anymore though. Why celebrate life when I was an expert at taking it? This bottomless pit I'd been dwelling in for the past twenty-five years was not a thing to celebrate. Luther's death would be a celebration as a matter of fact, I had every intention to celebrate the shit out of Luther's death. "Cypress, let's talk about it later."

"I would like to talk about it now." She stood naked in the hallway. The water dripping down her body slowly. She glistened in the light. "Please be home for your birthday and Christmas..." Cypress had become the master seductress and I was confused, seduction and charm had been my game, but now it was hers and she won every time she played it with me. She satisfied one part of me that no woman had been able to in years... my sex drive.

"Don't try to seduce me, woman." I closed my eyes in an effort to say no to her tempting body.

"I'm not." She lied as she twirled a strand of her curls on her finger.

"Get dressed," I tried not to look up at her again. I was more than certain that if she stepped one step closer or I looked one second longer I would end up fucking her on the floor of my loft. "Chivy along." My eyes clenched shut in frustration, I could feel her as she moved closer to me. She hovered over me and I could smell whatever floral scent she had doused herself in and it didn't help the fight.

She touched my chin and my eyes peered up at her. "One more time."

"Woman, what have I done to you?" I whispered.

"What have you not?"

I snatched her down to me and playfully thrown her to the couch. "I can name some things." She was slick with anticipation for me, but a part of me wanted her to wait till later. I couldn't get fucking Luther' face out of my head and she had less than ten minutes to hit the road before his journey would be completely in the dark. I kissed her cheek. "Go."

"Wow, your gonna leave hanging?"

"I have a flight Cypress. You can live a few weeks without me. As a matter of fact, use it as a challenge. I would love to see how turned on you could get for me."

"I don't want to think about it." She pouted and made her way upstairs to the bedroom. "Your acting weird Lucas Elledge."

"I'm sorry love I don't seem to think that I am."

"Yeah," she mumbled.

I continued to look at the Halfway House and the notes I had taken about their place. The layout and everything was posted here online. I could fuck him up. There were two men working the doors. They wanted to see ID and a signature every time someone left and the police were called immediately when people were late. It would have to be another daylight kill. I was not fond of the daylight. Too many risks in killing people in daylight.

"Lucas, what are you looking up?"

"Things," I replied simply.

"Who is Luther?"

Shit, she was nosy. "Why are you asking so many questions Cypress? Can I not have one moment of privacy babe?"

"I'm just wondering; you've been writing his name on sheets of paper for the past three days..."

"Well, you wonder can stop now. He's not important."

She scoffed. Her curls fell down her back. She hadn't tried to make them neat, I had not ever seen her try to tame them. "Okay, whatever," she pecked my cheek and walked towards the elevator. Her bag was tossed over her shoulder and she wore my shirt which once again drove me insane. "I'll see you next year Luke."

"I love you Cypress and stop saying that."

"I love you too." She slid her sunglasses on. "Happy Christmas." I sensed she rolled her eyes as she nodded her head at me. "Call me?"

I rolled my eyes at her dramatics. "Happy Christmas Love! And I'll call you I swear it."

She was finally gone. I had packed everything that I needed. My Nan still had clothes at her home in England and I was sure that Callum and my grandmother there had clothes for me. I hated to pack heavy to go overseas. That was all sorted out. The only thing I had to figure out was how to get the damn knife to England. This was the knife my father used on every one of his kills, or so I guessed. I was told he liked to get creative with his kills every now and then. The blade of the knife that my father had given me was short but it was sharp. Most importantly it got the job done. Declan had his name engraved on it. His father George had given it to him and he had passed it to me. I was proud of the knife even though my dad or my grandfather had never been my favorite person. The knife had become an essential part of the ritual for me.

Asher

Mark and I had met right after the death of the Phillip guy. He interrogated me like I was Lucas and there was nothing that I could tell him. I had not known that he would do a kill. He did not follow his ritual of stealth and researching like he had done for a few of the others, like his new fascination Luther. I was more than certain that Lucas was about to kill again, but I couldn't be there for it and to be honest I doubted I could bear it. He was a messy killer. His mesmerized stare at the blood from Summer's death had rested permanently behind my eyelids at night and every ounce of my body wanted to turn him in. But there was still something that told me to let it go. I did. I was happy he had found someone else to fixate on. I was out of the spotlight and it made me feel less on edge.

Christmas break had snuck up on me and Whitney had grown attached. It made me happy that for once I had a girlfriend that I didn't have to introduce to my parents. They knew her. Being childhood neighbors with her turned out to be a bonus. Holidays together, trips home and sex in the tree house. The last of which had not happened yet, but I was more than sure I could make it happen. My father had even decided that he would make an appearance. We were his only family, dating came after his work and he was honestly not that good at either.

"What time do you go before the Doctoral Committee?" Whitney sat in the passenger seat and stared at her phone.

"They told me one." I was nervous. None of my classmates had been called in this early we still had another semester to go before our approval. It even shocked me that a professor was still talking to students. Usually they were gone already. We were almost at the school and Whitney already dreaded the hour she had to wait in the car. I grabbed my research out of the backseat of the car. "It shouldn't take too long. Go shopping or something." I tossed her my wallet and my keys.

"Yeah, yeah." Whitney nodded her head. "I love you little nerd."

"Love you too babe."

I made my way to the office. I cut across the grass to make the trip shorter. The university was bare, there was not a student in sight and there were only a few cars in the parking lot. I walked into the office and smiled at the receptionist. She never looked up from her magazine as she said, "Mr. Woods will see you now."

The office smelled like old books. His collection of books on the was worth more than my car. I sat down in the chair across from him. Mr. Woods was not a bad professor granted, I knew his area of psychology better than he did. I tried to keep my smart ass remarks and sneers to myself. "Hey, Mr. Woods."

"Hello Asher," Mr. Woods smiled at me and pointed to a man I was not familiar with at all. "Asher, this is Special Agent

Tucker McMillan from the FBI. He'll take over, I don't want to ruin his introduction." Mr. Woods shook my hand. "If you two need anything I will be across the hall in the lecture hall. I have some last minute exams to get in before I leave." He nodded his head at us both and walked out of the classroom.

"Hi, Asher." Tucker was a fucking FBI agent. He adjusted his tie and perched himself at the edge of the large oak desk. I looked at him, scared shitless. What the fuck had I done? Well, there was technically a list of shit, but what the hell was he here for? "You seem nervous."

"I 'm being interviewed by a Man in Black." I chuckled pointing at is a suit.

"Indeed," he laughed. "So tell me about your research?"

"What would you like to know?"

"Well to be honest, I have read all of your research on your case study and I want to know who he is." He got straight to the point. "I don't want to hold you from going to see your mom."

How in the hell did he know where I was headed? I cleared my throat and nodded my head. This shit was about Lucas and if he went down I went down. I had witnessed too much to not get charged with anything. "Well, it's not a real case... is it?"

"We have speculations built up against the case study. He fits a classic psychopath profile. We need to know who he is and I have a clue as to who he is. So just go ahead and tell me who he is, so you go."

"Lucas Elledge." I blurted out. "But he has not done anything violent. I have been following him around for years."

McMillan nodded his head. "Don't play stupid Asher. I know that you have been following him like white on rice."

"Sir, I haven't seen him actually act out on anything." I stuttered through the sentence as my hands grew clammy and my head grew light.

"I'm not sure about that." He paused. "I know that these kind of people tend to be secretive and you seem really scared there, son."

"I follow him, everywhere Mr..."

"Agent," he cut me off. "Look, kid you are not sure who the fuck you are dealing with. I have been following him everywhere he goes too, and everywhere he goes someone gets destroyed. I've even tried to reach out to his girlfriend, but I can barely catch her away from him. Her ex-boyfriend died a few weeks ago."

"I heard about that and yes Cypress is rather attached to him."

"He was stabbed, the knife marks similar to the marks found on victims in Ireland and England. I mean all of this circumstantial, but there are some real facts that are growing here." He crossed his legs. "We just want him brought to justice and this research of yours could be the trick. Can you follow him some more and report to me with every step?"

"Why me? You are the fucking FBI. I mean you should have men on him. I have enough time just writing about him."

"You don't have to Asher. I don't want you doing anything that you don't want to. But I think that you should be warned, if we find out that you have been around him while he murdered anyone and have not turned it, we will get you for murder as well, not accessory to it... not even obstruction. You're right, we're the fucking FBI. I'll make sure you fry in a chair right next to him. I don't give a fuck about your life Asher. You have been doing it and you will continue to do it."

"Fuck," I moaned. "Okay," I stood up.

"Have you seen something?" McMillan turned his head to me. "You gave in rather quickly."

"No, I haven't. Exactly how many times are you going to ask me?" I lied. "I would love to stay and talk more, but my girlfriend is waiting in the car for me. We have a long trip ahead and I would like to start it before the daylight runs out."

Before I could stand a hand gripped my shoulder pushing me back down in the seat. "You don't understand that Lucas is dangerous. He's a psychopath, a real life freak show. This guy could kill you in a millisecond and not think twice about it."

"So can snakes, but we don't kill them if they aren't bothering us." I spat back.

"Don't make this a light situation Asher." his voice bellowed through the office.

"Fuck, look I don't know what you want from me. I said that I would keep observing him and if something happens he is yours." Great, now I was babysitting for Mark and the FBI. Way to go, Asher, fucking dumbass.

"Good," Tucker adjusted his shirt. "When you get back to town, report to this office. I've taken up an area the conference room and your teacher doesn't seem to mind. I'll know when you are back."

"Okay for fuck's sake, I'm sure you will. I'm leaving."

I could hear him chuckle as I made my way back to my Jeep. What the fuck I had I gotten myself into? For some reason I picked up my cell phone as I walked out and dialed Mark's number.

"Better be important." I could hear the female chuckle in the background.

"FBI is following your guy." I hung up and hopped in the car. Enough of this bullshit. I just wanted to enjoy my damn vacation. I turned the phone off and smiled at Whitney. "Not sleepy are you?"

"Nope."

"Good, I'm about to bore you to death with some Coldplay."

Lucas

Luther was a shit bag. He walked out of the seven-bedroom house with a smile so bright he could stop traffic. Freedom was treating him well. Bloody cock sucker, my mind raced. The kill was so near. I trailed behind the car he hopped into. My cell phone vibrated against the cup holder. I scooped it up and answered. "Lucas speaking."

"Babe, how is your trip? Are you at the airport yet?"

"It's perfect, still waiting at the airport, though." I lied. The airport was more than three hundred miles behind me. It enticed me to watch Luther. I was hours away from sheer heaven. And then it was off to Cumbria and Ireland to see my family, who annoyed me. The car he was in stopped so I pulled into a spot and watched him laugh with his buddies. *Laugh it up Luther.*

"Really," she sounded confused.

"Yes," I sat back in my seat and stared, there was nothing better than watching the last few moments of a person's life. "Still waiting to board."

The peck at my window scared the shit out of me. She stood there and her eyes were red with rage I suppose. "What the fuck? Why are you lying to me?"

I rolled my eyes. Give me time to breathe damn it. Fucking Luther got back into the car and the driver pulled back into traffic. I had lost him. Fuck it. "Why are you here?"

"No, sir, why are you here? This is twenty minutes from my home town." She turned her head and waited for my response. "Why are you over three hundred miles from where you said that you would be?"

My lip dropped and I nodded my head. This woman would be the death of me. Cypress was a detective and a fucking annoying girlfriend. Though I should have thought it out better. He only lived thirty minutes from her hometown. "Baby, you can't even let me surprise you." I lied. "We left things bad. I was going to grab lunch with you and see if I could maybe reset some things to spend more time with you."

"Why'd you park?"

"You called." I retorted.

Cypress nodded her head. "Well, I'm here. What are we going to do?"

"Why were you here in the first place? This is not where you are from?"

"My mother works in the Mayor's Office here." She pointed to the Maud building. "I was about to go see her."

"Well, we could get a room." My plan had died and went to hell might as well subdue to her demands.

"We can," her face lit up. "I'm happy you came. I'll grab my purse."

The vibrations filled the car again. The fucking phone was about to drive me mad. "Lucas speaking," I snapped.

"A cop just came by looking for you. Whatever the fuck you have planned call it off. And I suggest you stay here for the Holidays." Mark said.

"A cop?"

"Yes, a fucking cop, no you know what a FBI agent. Said he had some questions about you where you were when her ex was killed. You are getting sloppy. And it's not just you that's going down in a white fucking jumpsuit!" His nerves shattered in his voice. "You've got to stop all together."

"Fuck," he might have been right.

"Yeah, spend the holiday with her and stop what you are doing for the moment. And whatever the hell you had up your sleeve that made you leave so quickly, drop it."

"Mark," I rolled my eyes.

"I am not fucking playing with you Luke. You stop this shit right now!"

My fist slammed into the dashboard and roar escaped my chest. "FUCK!" The red heat rushed to my face. "I can't."

"Luke, are you fucking hearing me?"

"It's been months; no one understands I swear, but it's like falling off of a fucking cliff. It's a high and I'm crashing Mark."

"Crashing right into death row." He said. "I hate to even offer it, but take a hit and get the high that way. I'd rather visit you in rehab than prison."

I hadn't felt anything in months. "I don't do drugs anymore."

"I'll score them for you Luke, but fucking promise me you will call it off."

A breeze flowed into the car and Cypress tossed her purse in the back of the car, "What time is your flight?"

"Change of plans," I blurted out.

"No England?" Cypress questioned.

"Yeah, I'll have to go back and get some things at the loft." Like a bag full of shit to calm my nerves before I exploded.

"That's five hours away."

"I know that." My lips pressed together. "You can stay and I can come back." I suggested.

"I can go with," she paused. "What's wrong with you?"

"Pardon me?"

"You fucking heard me," she crossed her arms. "You look red and angry. Are you mad at me? I mean you were the person that said that you were coming to see me. I didn't ask you to come and I don't want to be around you when you have a pissy ass attitude."

"No Cypress, I've told you like ten bloody times. I am not mad at you."

"Well, drive to the loft. I don't mind going back with you. I'll tell my mom."

"Okay." I threw my hands in the air in defeat. "Fine, let's go."

Cypress

The love between Lucas and I was different from anything that I had experienced in my life. I was so used to being in second place to something or someone that the negligent behavior was normal for my past boyfriend. It was either second to sports or second to his other women he blatantly flaunted in front of me. I was the fool, but that would never be the case again.

"I wrote some chapters in my new book." Lucas said. "I want you to read it."

"I would love to." I was half asleep in the passenger side, watching the sky fade from an array of oranges and pinks to black. "I'm happy you are spending the holidays with me."

"Me too," It didn't sound sincere. I knew that his family was important to him he had talked about nothing else for the past few weeks.

"My mom is a great cook," I said

"Yes, I love her food."

"I know you wanted to spend it with your family Lucas."

"It's fine. We don't have to talk it out. I said I was fine."

"We could sleep at my apartment." I tried to ignore his attitude.

"I want to be at my loft."

"What is wrong with you? I mean you have had a piss poor attitude the entire time."

"Don't ask me again." He snapped. Lucas turned into the back driveway to the loft. "I'm tired."

"Fine, we'll sleep here. I just said my place because I don't have any clothes. They are in my car at my parents' place." He had me worried. The silent drive home almost drove me mad and every questioned was answered with a single sentence.

His fist was clenched. "I guess we can go inside and get some rest and I'll swing by in the morning for you to get clothes."

"Okay," I didn't want to argue or sleep alone. He was in a mood. I could understand it to some extent. We both gathered our things and walked towards the stairs that led three flights up to the loft.

"Lucas Elledge?" A deep voice came from behind us.

We turned and noticed the 6 foot something man holding his badge. I had seen him before. He was the detective investigating Phillip's death. I had seen him on television a few times in the background of the reporters. "Babe?"

"In the flesh," Lucas grabbed my hand and pulled me closer to him. "How can I help you?"

"Perfect, your brother said you were out of town."

"Yeah, actually we just stopped in. I left some things. I brought her back for the company, I hate a quiet ride."

"Well, I can talk to you both, could we go upstairs? It's rather chilly out here."

"We can go to the club. I have an office there." He held up his keys up. "Darling run upstairs, get comfortable and I will be right up in a few."

"What is this about?"

"I wanted to ask about where you two were the night that Phillip Langford was murdered."

I turned my head. This man was incorrigible. I've told the police department ten times that we were together that night. "Sir, I have told them several times that we were together. Why are you questioning us?"

"I know you took his death rather hard for him to be an ex." The Detective pulled out a small leather notebook. "Your mother said that Lucas went for a walk that night. Where did you walk?"

"He walked for ten minutes that night, is there something that you are trying to say?" I yelled.

Lucas arm's wrapped around me and he smiled. "Calm yourself, dear," He handed me the keys. "Go and get yourself settled while I talk to... Detective..."

"Special Agent McMillan, Federal Bureau of Investigation." He flashed his badge and the color drained from the Lucas' face.

Oh shit, he was the real deal. I thought he was a small town cop. He was from the damn FBI. I shifted uncomfortable. "I'll go upstairs."

The water from the shower had been refreshing. I slung the mass of curls into a pony tail and dressed in the Lucas' shirt. "Mark," I said, sliding shorts on. "What are you doing here?"

"I came for Luke." He smiled. They were not blood brothers, but the resemblance in the two was uncanny, "Is he here?"

"He is being interviewed by some detective downstairs."

"Fuck," He whipped out his phone and dialed Lucas' number. "Brother don't say shit. And keep that smart ass mouth under wraps... I'm headed down. Can you put this in his room for me Cy?" He gave me a black bag and I nodded my head.

"Sure," I said. "Is there something that I should know Mark?"

"No," Mark headed to the elevator and smiled at me. "Why would you think that?"

Lucas

I closed my phone and nodded my head. Mark was too late. He was already here in my office, waiting on water. If I killed this suit wearing bastard, I would be on Death Row before the blood would completely drain from his body. But his blood spilled on my white marble floor was all I could conjure. The waitress sat two glasses of water on the coasters. "Lemon Mr. McMillan?"

"No thank you," he sat stiff backed in the chair. "So let me start by saying that you are extremely successful to be twenty-six."

"Almost twenty-six," I corrected. "And thank you."

"One New York Times Best-Seller and a successful club. The campus rives for this place." His eyes searched the room.

"Thank you, what are your questions?"

"Number one, there seems to be some discrepancies with what Cypress told us." He flipped through the book. "Did you take a walk that night?"

"I did," I said.

"Where to?"

"I walked the block and then sat on the porch, the star's there are amazing."

"So how long were you out?"

"Ten minutes at the most, why?"

"Wondering." Agent Asshole moved quickly with his pen. "I looked into your past a little. What do you know about your father's death?"

"What kind of dumb question is that?" My eyes lowered. "I know my father was killed and it was rude of you to bring it up. His death has nothing to do with the death of this guy." My heart pounded against my chest.

"I think it does."

"Oh really, please tell me how? Please..."

"Well, I have a theory myself." McMillan's stupid grin was a good enough reason to knock this cock sucker down to the floor and let him bleed out slowly... covering this bright white floor with a perfect shade of crimson.

"Well, do tell," I sat back my hands behind my neck, rubbing to relieve the building pressure.

"I think you done it." He whispered. "I think you slit his throat and stabbed in where he hurt your mother the most, her heart. You done it to avenge her death."

The story he had made up in his head was complete bullshit. I loved my father no matter how asinine he acted at times. He was the man my mother loved just as much as me. "My mum loved him and he loved her. And I think you are full of shit. You probably should have been a novelist. That shit would sell millions."

"Oh, I'm thinking about it..." McMillan closed his book. "When I have you behind bars... I'm gonna write a shit ton. I want your name disgraced and everything you love to dwindle to nothing."

"I wish you the best of luck."

"I'm watching you, motherfucker." His tight grin infuriated me.

"Well, enjoy the show bitch."

He stared at me. "You don't scare me Lucas. And you don't know who I am... but I will gladly fill you in. I am your demise... remember that." His card fell on the table and he slid the glass cup of water to the floor, shattering it to pieces. "You should get your staff to clean up the place while it's still standing."

"Fuck you," I said with a grin. "The next time you come at me... I'll need notice through my lawyer and if you talk to Cypress again..." The words fell. I wanted to see him fucking dead. "Well... you seem to have a great imagination... use it and make it colorful."

"You'll need one the next time we speak Lucas. I plan to make sure you stare at white walls until they push that medicine through your veins." He nodded.

"What's up?" Mark said. "Detective McMillan, come for the steak or do you just want to continue to threaten my client with the death penalty again?"

"No, sir, it wasn't a threat. Just a direct promise." McMillan gritted his teeth, "I think you are just as fucked up as him Mark."

"Thank you, sir," Mark laughed. "Are you done here?"

"Not even close," McMillan mumbled as he walked towards the exit. "Watch your fucking steps Lucas. You know I will be. And Merry Christmas." He waved over his shoulder as he made an exit.

Fucking bastard.

"Cypress is back?" Mark questioned.

"We are leaving tomorrow for her mum's house."

"Stay out of town for some weeks. Take her to the cabin, hunt and all that shit." He whispered. "I'll bring Shia there we can just stay out of the light for a while. I think he will be relentless."

"You're still with her?" I blocked everything else he had said.

"She has great sex," Mark laughed. "See you in two weeks."

My father was a bastard, but my mum loved him with her dying breath and he loved her with his... I made sure of it. He was secretive about everything in his life and he had a tendency to put his hands on my mother. No one was allowed to hurt her, she was already in so much pain. So I handled it when she passed. I would never have killed him, but he prompted the chance and I took it.

The ride in the elevator seemed like it lasted forever. I don't know what Cypress would want to hear. I could care less. I needed something right now... anyone would do.

The doors opened and I stepped in throwing my shirt to the ground. "You showered?" I asked.

"Yeah, the all day trip threw me off." She paused. "Your brother stopped by and dropped some box off in your bedroom."

"Perfect," I sighed, relieved. "I'll shower and we can go to bed."

"What did that Agent want?"

"Well, he seems to think that I killed your ex." There was no use in hiding the truth from her. "I didn't even know the bastard."

"Stop being mean."

"He fucking raped you. And you sit here and defend him. Fuck him. Dead or not I feel no remorse for a rapist Cy."

"Where'd you go that night?"

"What the fuck do you want me to say? Is it against the law to get some air? Are you going to interrogate me like that fucking cop? I can just call him back up here and let you both just enjoy yourselves?"

"He wasn't just a cop Lucas. He was an FBI Agent? I want you to tell me where the fuck you went Lucas!" Her voice echoed through the entire loft.

"Who in the fuck are you yelling at, Cypress?" My voice was louder than I expected but she had crossed a line. She should never question me.

"I'm leaving." Her feet hit the cold floor of the apartment and lead her to the counter where she picked up her cell phone. "I'll take a bus home or call Shia. But I don't have to put up with this shit."

Before I could think I had caught up to her and pulled gently at her arm. "What is your problem? Why are you questioning me? I would never do anything to harm you love... never."

"Did you kill him?"

"I didn't." I turned her towards me, staring into her eyes, I knew that there was nothing there. My eyes never showed the world what was going on inside. "I wouldn't."

"Why would the FBI be interested in you?"

"Why would they not? I'm foreign."

"I thought you were an American citizen."

"I have dual citizenship."

"Right, where did you go that night?"

"I went walking. I was scared. I wanted your parents to like me and I have never met someone's parents so fast okay."

"You're lying."

"Yeah, you know what use your imagination since you seem to be so good at it." I turned my back towards her and walked to the shower. "I'm showering and you can stay. It's no need for you to be out without a fucking car at night. I don't want to argue with you. Stay here."

CHAPTER NINE

Cypress

The fireplace crackled in my mom's living room. My father had the turkey out and apparently had tried to teach Lucas how to marinate. Everything had found a median. He was calm now. And even though I still had some doubt I was content enough to be friendly. Christmas will be tomorrow and Lucas had successfully wooed both sets of grandparents a crazy aunt and my cousin Shera. He was gold to them.

"I'm happy you two spent the holidays with us sweetheart." My mom smiled and her eyes were lit. "He is a good one." She pointed to Lucas painting the base of the turkey. "Even your father has grown to like him."

"Good," I set my phone down. "We get to leave for Montana tomorrow afternoon. His brother and my neighbor are meeting us a town over." The trip came unexpectedly. Mark and Shia were always off and on at least from what I could see. Mark was not talkative, he was borderline mute, which was the exact opposite of Shia, the party animal. I had no clue what made them a couple. I'd rather not know.

"I hate you're leaving on Christmas. But Denver from what I hear is a perfect place. And I know you said you wanted to travel."

"I know. I didn't know too much about it until earlier this week. Lucas is good at surprises."   "That's great." My mom peeled back the snap peas and continued to watch some Hallmark movie as usual. She was addicted to the cheesiest movies, but we watched them every year. But it made the holidays the holidays. The sound of the bells and flutes in every song reminded me of my childhood.

"Cypress, I was about to go ahead and turn in for the night. You want to come with?" His accent wooed my mother with every syllable, but not me. I had grown annoyed at the seductive accent at the moment. Lucas and I had three major fights and they had all been about this lie. Why would he lie? He had been gone more than ten minutes. I waited for him over an hour that night and I had foolishly backed his story up in front of that agent. I wanted to know the truth, but there was no chance in hell he was giving it to me.

"I'm going to talk to mom for a minute and then I'll be in there."

"Alright, Goodnight Nathan and Terry. The lesson in culinary arts was quite delightful."

"I enjoyed teaching you." My dad chuckled and placed the turkey in the oven.

Lucas disappeared around the corner and pulled the cover over me. "So everyone will be here tomorrow? I'm surprised that we're not going to grandma's house."

"She wanted to get out of the house this year, but you know she can't travel far." My mom watched me and then laughed. "It's good to know that I'm not the only one who gets the cold shoulder when you are mad."

"Excuse me?" I sipped my hot chocolate.

"You heard me girl." She tossed more peas into the bowl. "What did he do? Why are you mad at him?"

"Mom, he is annoying sometimes."

"So is your father, but those are things that you get over. It's easy to tell that you are mad at him." She turned her head to me and I saw so much of myself in her. It was scary.

"Well, whatever it is you should just let it blow over. It's Christmas Eve and you can't be mad on Christmas Eve. It's like some cardinal rule. Isn't that right Nathan?"

I was sure that my father had not heard any of the conversation, but he agreed with her. "Right."

"Men have to be molded, slowly but surely into a masterpiece. Lucas is intelligent and charming. He's handsome and most importantly, he is in love with you. So you should just let whatever it is brewing between you two out. Tell him what you feel and be with him. He'll get it eventually."

"Yeah, I guess you may be right." I mumbled.

"Your mom is always right." She added.

"Mom, I am going to turn in for the night." I kissed her cheek and walked into the kitchen with my father. "Goodnight daddy."

"She has some points. Talk it over." He pecked my cheek. "I love you baby girl."

"Love you too." I pulled my plush blanket from the couch and walked to my bedroom. Not much had changed from when I had last lived here. The lights were off. I looked up and could see Lucas was standing in the corner.

"You're still up?" I made my way over to the bed.

"I'm sorry for being a pain in your bollocks."

"Are you really?"

"I'm truly sorry. I have been the biggest dick to you and you don't deserve that okay?"

"Alright," my lips formed a tight line and the lights went out.

"Can we dance?"

"Dance?"

The strums of the guitar started to fill the room and his hands clasped mine taking me closer to him. "I want to dance. I owe it to you to make our first ever holiday special."

"We had Thanksgiving," I joked.

"It's not really an international holiday. But that is true."

Lucas turned to lock the door and then faced me. I could actually almost feel then sexual tension that was built up between us. He made his way over to me and his lips traced the nape of my neck. My knees buckled as his hand pushed into my underwear. "My parents..." I whispered.

"Will not hear us I swear to it..." He bit my lip and I fell onto the bed. He tossed my underwear to the ground. "I owe it to you... But you can't make a sound. I'll be quick and you'll be quiet." He flipped me over on my stomach and with one swift tug he stripped me of my panties.

I heard the sound of his zipper and within in seconds he filled me. There was no foreplay, licking, sucking or kissing. He just went into me with punishing strokes. I purred under him, my hips writhing for more. His dick stretched me making every thrust have the sweetest pain. "Say you'll never leave me..." he whispered.   There were no words coming from my mouth, just the short pants of pleasure as his thrusts began to get quicker and quicker... Cypress... say you won't fucking leave me..."

"I'll never leave..." I gasped at the feel of my oncoming orgasm. Lucas lifted my ass up and went harder into me covering my mouth with his hand. I dived head first into pleasure. My toes tingled and my legs weakened as they fell onto the bed and he kept going into me.

"Don't ever think about it... understood..."

I had no clue what the hell he had done to me, but there was no way in hell that I could leave him. I was so enthralled I only wanted to see how much closer I could get. We lay there silent, his arms straddled most of my body and his heat was keeping me comfortable in chilly room.

"He brought up my father." The whisper filled room.

"Your father, your real father?" My fingers twirled in his hair.

"Yeah, he was murdered in England a few years back, close to my mum's death. That agent is fucking with me and I don't know why."

"Why would he bring that up?"

"He said I'm a murderer and he plans to watch me fall. He accused me of killing my father." His voice broke. "No, I won't lie and say that we were close. But my father was my father you know?"

"Why would he say that?"

"My father was a dodgy character."

"How was he dodgy?" I turned to face him in the bed. I perched my elbow up.

"I mean it was in the worst way Cypress. He led a double life and that was fine you know. I loved my father, granted, I hated him too. He was so damn secretive about everything. I didn't know or care to know what he was doing. I just wanted to take care of my mom. I wanted to be there for her like he never was, I wanted to make sure she didn't die alone."

"Wow," I paused. "So he suspects that you killed him. What about England?"

"Who knows? I didn't do it. My father was a piece of shit, but he didn't deserve what he got. Cattle didn't deserve what he got. Whoever the bastard was slit his throat and stabbed him in the heart... he bled out in minutes. Then they burnt the place to a bloody crisp. We couldn't even recognize him."

"That's horrible." I could feel him growing hot, so I stripped the covers from us.

"I was left with the rest of my family. My cousin was always there for me. I have a shite load of them. Then there was my mom, when she died, I gravitated more towards my dad's side of the family and I hate that I won't get to see them this year. I promised I would come."

"Well, perhaps we can go visit her next year?"

"Yes," His arms encircled me and I laid my head on his chest. "Go to sleep..."

Lucas

My phone had not stopped ringing for the past hour. Tracy was on my last nerve with her back to back phone calls and anxious texts. I swiped the green key. "Bloody hell mum! What?"

"Well, Merry Christmas to you too!" Tracy said. "I've called you about ten times Lucas Elledge."

"Happy Christmas Mum. What's up they are cutting the turkey over here." I cut my eyes over at her father who had placed the feast out.

"I wanted you to come here tomorrow before the trip. Please, I really want to see you."

"Mum, I can't." I said simply. "I've already made plans this year and it's like an hour drive."

"I missed you Thanksgiving this year Lucas and now Christmas. Can I have just a moment of your time before next year? I demand it. It is not a request. Let me speak to Cypress."

"Mum," I tried to talk over her, but she continued to rant nonstop in my ear. "God Save the Queen talk to my mum before I kill her." I spat through clenched teeth as I handed the phone to Cypress.

"Hello," Cypress said full of the holiday cheer or whatever people were filled of during this time of the year. She looked amazing. Red suited her, as did the golden eyeshadow.

I nodded my head at her, she talked for five minutes, guaranteed her that we would stop by before next year and that she would talk to me. It infuriated me, women got whatever the fuck they wanted. She gave me the phone back. "Breathe, we'll go there tomorrow. It's not a big deal."

"So where are you from?" Her cousin's high pitch voice shot through the Christmas Music. Shera was actually likeable and there were several similarities shared between her and Cypress.

"I'm from Cumbria, England." I smiled.

"Wow, and why are you here?" Shera added.

"Uhm, my adopted parents live here and my mum and pa died so I came to be with family. My adopted family is here."

"He's the author of that book Cypress was in love with this summer." Her Aunt Tonya, was a treat. She was young and she knew that Cypress had fallen hard. It was mutual when I wasn't seeing red.

"I should hit you for making her cry." another aunt said from behind me.

"Apologies," I laughed. "You must have missed out on the times that she made me cry."

Cypress pushed me playfully. "Those happen more often, huh?" She smirked and kissed my lips.

"Cypress have you called Bridgette? I know she is having a hard time after Phillip."

I peered over at the aunt, her hair in a bun and the red lipstick went horribly with her green eyeshadow and overly Christmas themed outfit. She was not my favorite so far.

"Aunt Mae, I haven't had the chance, but I figured I would stop by there here soon." She shifted uncomfortably in her seat. "She is gonna be fine."

"They said that they have a suspect in custody. Some homeless man from the city over. The neighbor said that they saw him snooping around the house at about 4 in the morning." This Aunt Mae continued to talk about the damned death and I could feel my eyes as they rolled in annoyance.

"That's good to hear." I sipped my tea.

"Did you ever meet him?" Mae asked.

"I had the pleasure once. I think it was about four months ago Cypress and I had just started dating." I answered truthfully.

"He was a good guy." Aunt Mae just would not back the fuck off.

"I honestly have to say that is your opinion. I know what happened with Cypress and him. He wasn't a good guy he was a dick. I don't approve of his behavior towards her and I won't start now that he's dead. So yeah." I shrugged my shoulders.

"What do you mean what he done to her?"

"If you don't know then it's none of your concern."

"Aunt Mae, we get it." Cypress voice was uncomfortable as she rested her hand on my shoulder and rubbed the tension out. "I would like to spend Christmas focusing on family. I hate that he died, but he is dead. I cried. I shed my tears and I would like to have a good day. So now if we could talk about something light. Let's sing some carols."

"It hasn't been long since you and he ended things." She said. "You should be feeling more."

"Mae!" Nathan's voice boomed from the kitchen. "That's enough."

Her father was a hero because Aunt Mae was close to meeting the blade.

"I'm sorry." Mae said. "Too much egg nog I guess." She rolled her eyes at me and made her way to the kitchen,

Cypress walked to the bedroom and I followed her. "I can't do it."

"Do what?"

"I can't pretend like I don't have my thoughts about this whole situation. If you are hiding something, then please just tell me." She paused and held her hands out. "Tell me... please."

"I promise there is nothing to tell love."

"Are you sure?" Her voice broke. "I feel like the deeper I fall the more I'm blinded by you. My Aunt thinks you done it. She all but said it last night and she still has her thoughts about it right now. She thinks that you are a killer. Are you?"

"Your aunt, oh come on she just met me. How can you believe her speculations and she doesn't know one thing about me Cy? You know me, I love you more than anything. I would never hurt you."

"I've seen you angry."

The drugs had made this easier, because she did know my anger. Normal circumstances Aunt Mae would have been sobbing outside the house or bleeding out on the floor. The drugs gave me some relief, I felt numb. And I must say having nothing to feel, no urges or pressure was magnificent. I had no blood-lust or rage. "Cypress..." I sang her name and her face lit up. "Happy Christmas okay. Are we really about let this whole ordeal ruin our first international holiday together?"

She rolled her eyes, "We had Thanksgiving."

"That's purely American." I snickered. "Your gift is under the tree. I am gonna go run and get it." I prayed that maybe this gift would make her fell okay again. Maybe it would make everything back to how it was before the fiasco with Phillip. I nodded at her family as I grabbed the small box from underneath the white Christmas tree and headed back to the room. I closed the door behind me and sat down on the bed next to her. "I bought this for you, three days after we met." This ring was special, or least I hoped in some way that it would be for her. I picked it out a month or so after we met. The pearl sat in the middle of diamond incrusted petals, my promise ring that I would try not to fuck up. I opened the box and handed it to her.

Her face brightened and there was a smile that sent a tingle down my spine, weird for me and I knew she appreciated it. I felt happy that she was happy. "Lucas..."

"Is it okay?" I whispered.

"It's perfect..." her voice barely traveled the short distance between us.

"It's my version of a promise ring. I know everything between us is so new. I know that there are times that you contemplate why the fuck am I with this gash? But baby I know I have never felt this for anyone else."

"Gash?"

"Slang...wanker..." I laughed. "Bloody hell woman, I'm an idiot sometimes. I know this. I know that I am not the easiest person to be with or tolerate. But I love you and this is my ring to promise you that no matter what we go through I will be here."

She stared at the ring. "I bought you some perfume."

"Really...can I see it? You know cologne is my favorite."

"I feel bad because I didn't get anything this nice...I thought about it but I couldn't really afford to do this much."

Cypress wanted to do everything on her own and that was admirable. But I had already covered her bill three or four times for her rent and she didn't know it. It was best to let her think that she was broke. "Darling, I have you," I paused. "And you are more to me than a ring or some random perfume that I will wear every day. You are the woman I plan to build forever with." The speech poured from my mouth and for once there was something genuine about what I had said. I meant it. I was sure she was the woman that I would spend the rest of my life with. She was my Luna... and I her Declan.

"Are you serious?"

"I couldn't be more serious. I love you." I smiled. "Now go get my cologne woman."

"Okay," Cypress' tears breached the walls as they cascaded down her face. "I'm so in love with you Lucas and it scares me."

"There's nothing to fear," though there was definitely something for her to fear. "I don't want to scare you."

"You make me see things differently than before."

"I hope that is a good thing."

"I'm blinded hopelessly by you," she smirked.

"Darling..."

"It's true, I care so much about you that no matter what the hell we go through or you put me through I just walk into it willingly." Cypress closed the box. "Did you have anything to do with Philips death? Answer me truthfully and I swear I am done... I just want to know."

"Honestly Cy, no. I don't know what you want me to tell you. I hate feeling like I'm being accused of something."

"Okay," Cypress opened the ring box and nodded her head. "Thank you."

Cypress

There was something about Colorado that made it feel like another country entirely. The mists of snow gently fell onto the jeep as we curved up the mountain to the cabin and all I could think about was getting him alone. Lucas' eyes were glued to the road and mine were glued to him.

"I can feel you staring." He smiled.

"I love it here already."

"Yes, my mum bought this place for us last year. We haven't bought food in a year and the housekeeping she has here had no clue what they are getting into."

"Well, we have some groceries and I hope Shia brings some."

"Mark and Shia have been here for a full day."

"What does this place look like?"

"Let your mind wander... I'm sure it's not what you are expecting," Lucas continued to stare at the road.

"We'll be here an entire week."

"Yes, alone."

"Well, almost alone..."

"I want to spend this time exploring you..." His voice made me clench my legs together and instinctively he gripped my thigh firmly.

"Don't talk like that." I purred.

"There is something that I am wondering. And I hope this doesn't scare you."

"Shoot." I said anxiously.

He removed his hand from my thigh snapped his fingers, "I was wondering if you were open to drugs?"

"Drugs?"

"Weed?"

"I smoked once." I lied.

"Cocaine?"

"No," I said quickly. "Are you?"

"I dabble every now and then, It's not a habit... acid?"

"Acid?" I flinched. "Are you serious Lucas? Are you a fucking hippie?"

"No, I like the sensation. Will you try it with me?"

"So you have used crack?"

"No cocaine... It's totally different things Cy..."

"What's the difference?"

"I don't really feel like explaining. I just want you to try acid with me..." His hands clasp mine and he smiles. "I promise if you don't like it... I will never bring it up again... but it's something that I think every once should try once."

"I don't know what to say Lucas." My mind raced. The answer should have immediately been no. There should have been no thinking, just no. Who was I dating and why the hell did I have to continue to ask these questions over and over? "I'm not for drugs."

"You sound like a child Cy. You are 25. Just one time with me. I will keep you safe."

"What is Acid?"

"LSD... Lucy in the Sky with Diamonds..." He smiled. "You could be my Lucy."

"One time..." I crossed my arms and he was truly happy for the first time since forever.

"One time..." The smiled emerged and he kissed my hand. "I think you will love it. You will feel everything completely for the first time. "But I want to smoke weed too."

"You can do whatever you want." The car grew closer to a monstrous house... but it was a glorious monster. The yellow lights were bright in the dark of the highway and there were two stories. The second floor appeared to be held by the giant wooden beams. It looked unreal, it wasn't a cabin it was a mansion. "Holy fuck," I whispered.

"The top floor is ours. The bottom floor beside the kitchen and the living area is Mark's and Shia's. I know we'll be together a lot... we even have a hunt planned later on this week. Shia wants you to learn how to crochet. I told her it would be dumb, but she brought a shit ton of damned yarn." The car pulled under the awning an older man stepped towards the car and opened the door.

"Mr. Elledge?"

"Murphy, did you enjoy your holiday mate?"

"I did, sir." The butler extended his hand. "Ma'am, may I show you inside?"

"Sure," I swooped up my purse and cell phone and took his hand.

"Mr. Aday is in the living area."

Every ounce of my oxygen escaped my lungs when the tall wooden doors of the home were opened. The chocolate brown couches stood out in the light wooden room. They sat around the stone fireplace with pictures of the family placed in the center.

"Dear Jesus," I whispered. The warmth of the home made me feel at ease, a great contrast to the freezing weather I had just stepped in from.

Lucas' embraced me. "Welcome to a little piece of paradise. Murphy could you put our bags in the room?"

"Certainly, sir," He disappeared into the curved staircase upstairs with our bags.

"Wow, Lucas this is incredible."

"I like to think I have good taste." Mark smiled toting Shia on his back. "You two enjoy the ride here?"

Shia's legs were wrapped around his waist and he was swinging back and forth. "These mountains are amazing."

"Yes, the ride was nice." I said.

"Well, sit down!" Shia hopped down from his back. "What did the Grinch get you for Christmas?"

I held out my hand for her. "Promise Ring..."

"Good," She smirked. She was high. Her eyes dilated and her words slurred. "I missed you Cy-Cypress."

"I missed you too."

"Woman, you are smothering her." Mark flopped on the couch and he took Shia with him.

"What are you two smoking?" Lucas said seriously.

Mark wiped his nose. "Nothing," He smirked.

Lucas shook his head, "Let's leave these animals be."

The bedroom was bigger than my apartment. My eyes wandered up to the high ceilings, "Wow, your parents know how to go all out." I mumbled.

"They do." Lucas shuts the huge door and dimmed the lights. "I am beat." He hopped on the bed and smiled at me. "There is a lake behind the cabin."

"This is not a cabin, Lucas."

"House whatever," He exhaled. "It's away from people. It makes me feel at ease for once."

"You feel at ease?"

"Yes," he rubbed the nape of his neck. "Even when I am at home there is a club below me...I can feel people around me."

"I thought you loved people."

"I love you. I hate people. People are dumb. I have generally found my assumption to be true eighty-seven percent of the time. I just like the calm... the quiet."

"You could move?"

"Not until I graduate. And when I do... I hear New York screaming my name. My publisher is there and I could open another club."

"New York?"

"Yes, we could have a house like this a few miles out of the city. You could work wherever... I could guarantee you that and we could be happy."

"New York, has more people."

"I would have you."

"Are we going to try it?" My hands tapped lightly against my leg.

"We can... It'll keep you up for hours though? Are you tired?"

"No, I'm wired."

"Perfect, be back in a jiff."

I waited impatiently for him. What would it be like to trip acid. I hated the term. I always thought it was a death sentence. Here's to hopeful wishing that I was incorrect. I stripped down my clothes searching through the smallest suitcase I have for my night clothes. I chose the pink tank top with the matching shorts. I wrapped my curls in a high bun and relaxed on the bed.

"Alright," Lucas returned drenched in sex appeal. "I have them." He extended his hand and there sat two small sugar cubes.

"I am freaking out."

"Wait, don't freak out."

"Yes," My hand was unsteady. "Am I gonna live?"

"Calm your nerve woman," he held my hand steady and placed the sugar cube on it. "You will be with me..."

The sugar cube was sweet as it dissolved on my tongue. I closed my eyes and lay on the bed. "How long does it take?"

"About 25 minutes," He laid next to me and grabbed my hand. "You will be fine."

There had never been a red so vibrant in my life. The color popping from the comforter and I could feel it engulfing me. Everything around Lucas was red. Every fiber of the comfort touched my body and everything was clear.

"Cypress..." his voice lulled me towards him... my hands grazed his face. "Cypress..." Lucas whispered. "Kiss me."

"No..." my tone playful. I ran my hands down the comforter. "Every fiber of this comforter... is heaven..."

"Every ounce of you is heaven..."

My mind would not stop raving about the texture of the comforter. Then suddenly a bright yellow light came from the top of the room. "It's so yellow."

"It's beautiful."

"I'm beautiful." I stared at my reflection in the mirror. Every curve of my face smiled with happiness.

"You are..." I could feel my hair tumbling down my back as Lucas pulled the bun down. "Have you ever thought about death..."

"Death... no." I touched him on his chest and could feel every thump of his heart struggling to break free.

"It's beautiful." he whispered.

"How beautiful?"

"Every person has a fucking light, but me... and watching it go out..." He laughed softly, "is the best feeling for me."

"You have a light..." I pull his face towards mine, his startling blue eyes pierced into me.

"I do?"

"Yes," I kissed him and I could feel everything. The warmth of his lips and touch of his tongue as he kissed me hard.

"Where?"

"Here..." I touched his chest once more and my hand slid into his underwear. "And here..." I snorted in laughter. He was larger than life there. "I want your light inside of me..."

"Not so fast... what the fuck is that over there?"

"Nothing is over there."

"It is..." Lucas smiled. "Mark! Bloody hell..."

"What the fuck is wrong with you two?" Mark stood at the door.

"What the fuck is wrong with you?" My smile conquered the world. "I was asking your brother..."

"What?" Mark leaned against the door.

"I don't know... but your brother has a light. He thinks he is light-less." I giggled. "I'm his light." My hands touched my chest and I felt my own heart as it thudded recklessly against the walls of my chest.

"I don't think you're wrong." Mark threw his head back in laughter. "Are you two on Acid?"

"What then is Acid?" Lucas fell off of the bed and a chuckle erupted from my chest. "Baby!"

"I'm alive," he laughed and I fell onto the floor playfully with him.

"Tell me you love me again..."

"I love you Cypress!"

"I love you LUCAS!" The room spun as my heels hit the floor at full speed. Though I knew I was moving fast everything still moved slow. My hand appeared to have seven fingers and a fell onto the floor once more, landing on the cold hardwood floor with my knees.

"Is this what it's like to be happy Mark?"

"It is." Mark nodded his head. "Please don't kill one another..." He laughed. "I'll be downstairs if you need me."

He touched my hand and I moved towards him. His curls lingered perfect in front of his round face. "Say it again..." He whispered.

"I love you." I smiled.

"Good."

This must be what it feels like to have someone totally entranced with you. His eyes never left mine and I felt like if they did I would explode. This was real love and I was grateful for every single heartache I went through to get here.

CHAPTER TEN

Cypress

My apartment for once, was cleaned and my work was done. The second semester had hit me hard. The teachers threw out assignments like Halloween Candy and I was expected to know how doing everything instantly. Lucas had stopped creative writing and now it was just me and Ginger and I had my fill of her. She was nice, but I missed being able to see Lucas at work.

I had decided to cook for everyone. I was not the best cook. I had already burned the sautéed onions and mushrooms and I was three seconds away from making everyone eat sandwiches. Shia was helping because she hadn't seen Mark since the cabin, almost two weeks had passed and he had not called her or anything, he was not like Lucas.

"So I think that I scared away Mark."

"How?" I mixed up the batter for the pork chops. The sweet and spicy aroma tingled my nose.

"Well number one, we spent way too much time over the weekend with one another."

"That's what couples do. It's hard for me and Lucas to even have some time apart these days."

"Lucas is weird."

"And how is that Shia?"

"Well number one, he stares."

"I like when he stares at me." I smiled. "But he gets annoyed easily and he has a hard time hiding his facial expressions. So to tame them, he stares. I know this already."

"I meant he stares at anyone. It's like he has something brewing up there that no one in the entire world knows about and it's creepy."

"You date Mr. Creepy. It took him a whole month for him to acknowledge me. His sister even said that Mark is creepy." I rolled my eyes.

"He is just quiet," she justified. "Mark just keeps everything to himself. But your guy doesn't bite his tongue at all."

"Just because Lucas lacks self-control doesn't mean that he is weird. He simply states what everyone else is more than likely thinking. He is a good guy."

"I've heard some things about Lucas." Shia mumbled. "I think you should stay away from him."

"Like what have you heard that could be so devastating that I should break up with the first guy that treats me like a woman is supposed to be treated?"

"What do you mean? You can snag anyone. I know that Lucas is handsome. I know that he has everything together, but there are some guys out there that can treat you way better than him. You are just in the infatuation phase. I pray it wears off."

I'd had just about my limit with Shia. Friend or no friend she had just about pushed me over the edge. "What have you heard Shia while you're playing around with this bullshit?"

"Well, several things that ring alarm. You know there is the fact that he doesn't get along great with exes and some have come up missing or dead. I mean it's the rumor around campus. It was why he was single for so long."

"Shut up Shia," I laughed. "Are you saying that Lucas killed his ex-girlfriends? God, literally shut the fuck up talking to me."

"No, I'm serious. A girl named Summer came up dead a few months back. They dated when she went here and she cheated on him. He took the break up well and then she came up missing, I mean it was weird. They even pulled him in for questions, but there was no proof that he had done anything."

"Exactly, there was no proof. You are pumping rumors from a dry well." I placed the batter down and started to wash the meat. "How long ago was it that they dated?"

"Three years ago."

"Wow, you are really trying to throw things together. Lucas is the sweetest person I know. Yeah, when he gets mad he is mad, but who isn't?"

"I wanted you to know. People are scared for you. I'm not because I know if push comes to shove, I will fuck him up after you."

"Well, I appreciate your concern and theirs, but you can tell those people who fed you this bullshit to go fuck themselves. I am fine with him, to be honest, I have never felt safer than how I feel around him. And I don't believe any of the garbage that is being thrown at me."

"Are you offended? I was trying to help as a friend and feel you in on everything that was going on."

"No, I'm not mad about shit Shia. I'm just tired of having to defend him when I know that he has done nothing. There are people coming at me at every angle and there is only so much more bullshit I can take."

"Just be careful." Shia nodded. "Where is the wine?"

"No wine for you."

"Girl, don't make me walk across the hallway."

"In the cabinet," I said.

The front door opened and Lucas strolled through. "It smells like heaven in here."

"It is heaven in here." Mark said as his eyes met Shia's. "You look so stunning…"

Shia knocked back her wine and stared at him. "Don't come at me with all that romantic shit. Why have you not called me?"

"Law School is not easy." He said simply. "And I told you this last week. I couldn't be talking to you every day of the week. I have so much to do."

"Save your bullshit!" She yelled.

Lucas pulled me closer to him. "Can we let these two talk?" His lips touched mine and I nodded in agreement. "Could you two watch the food while you bicker?"

We stepped into the bedroom our eyes locked on one another as if we had not seen each other in days. "You look lovely."

"You think?" I pointed to the flour on my black shirt. "Are they okay in there?"

"I don't care honestly." he answered. Lucas locked the door and sat on the bed next to me. "How was your day?"

"Ridiculously long."

"I can make it better." His seductive fingers pulled at my bra strap and I pushed him away. "What baby?"

"They are in there." I answered quickly.

"I don't care." He growled.

"No sir," I tossed my apron at him and walked to the door. His arms circled around me as he playfully laid me on the bed.

"They're gonna hear me."

"No, they won't." He stood in front of me and smiled. "I'm just addicted to you Cypress. And to be honest, I think you have been holding out on me…"

"Well, I can do something for you."

"Yes, you actually can." He nodded his head. "Strip… the flour is nice, but I'd rather see you naked."

I stared up at him. "No, they are in there."

"Please?"

"I will never be able to look at them straight. I sound like a cat in heat when I'm with you. I was surprised my mother didn't say anything."

"Fine, I can wait." He pouted.

"Thank you." I made my way to the door and I could feel him behind me. His hands traced up my skirt and he pushed me gently against the door. He spread my legs and his index finger pushed into me with sharp movement. A gasp escaped as I threw my head back in a brief moment of ecstasy. "Luke…"

He moaned softly in my ear. "I could wait but you feel so fucking good." Lucas added another finger to the mix and my head fell back on his chest. "Say yes," He chuckled and his lips traced my neck. His rough fingers circled my clit and I turned around to face him. "Please."

"Yes."

"Good," He fell back on the bed and pulled me on top of him. "Lead the way..."

"Alright." His fingers slipped out of me and I unbuckled his difficult belt tossing it to the floor. I pulled his shirt over his head and my lips pecked his chest, he flinched back in pain for a second then I realized it was a new tattoo. My name etched into his perfect chest. I sat up and stared. "Is that my name?"

"Could be... or I could really love trees." Lucas paused. "Is it a problem?"

"Oh my God," I smiled. "When did you get this?"

"I got it a week ago. I haven't had the chance to strip down for you. You have been holed up in this apartment since forever."

"It's amazing and no, it's not a problem. Now everyone in the world will know you're mine."

"Thank you." He slapped my ass playfully sending a much needed sting through my body. "Fuck me." He whispered, "Now."

I smiled as he kicked off his pants and I lifted my dress over my head. "I don't like being on top."

"It's because you are spoiled." He chuckled. "Ride me until you can't feel your legs."

It was easier said than done. I stared at his dick. It was huge and I had ridden him before, but it was my least favorite position. I mounted myself onto him slowly and his eyes never left mine as I tried to find some sort of rhythm. I rocked back and forth slowly pleasuring myself with the friction of him constantly rubbing against my clit. He arched his back, sending himself deeper with every motion I had. I moaned and increased my speed. Then he began to thrust harder into me. He gripped my waist and dug his fingers into my hips. My teeth pierced into my lip as his hand slapped my ass again. I planted my hands into his chest to get a better position on him. I slowed Lucas down from the insanely fast pace he had been gone by a slow wind with my hips and my fingers pinched his nipple. He moaned as I bounced up and down on him. And finally I felt like I had it. A stream of profanity came from his mouth as I slowed down to an unbearable slow pace, even for me. My legs were weak, but I wanted him to come from me. "You like that?" I teased.

"Fuck yes," he hissed. His dick twitched inside of me and it almost sent me over the edge. I ground against him once more and smiled. "I like this you're bloody wild..."

"You do," there was a smile in his eyes.

In one smooth motion, he flipped me over on my back and pushed my legs back. "My turn."

Lucas slid back into me slowly and then pulled me up to sit on his legs. He pulled me down further and his rhythm was punishing me. He didn't stop when my whole body turned into a boneless mess on top of him. He just chuckled and pounded into me relentlessly until I gushed out onto him. My legs shook and clenched him closer and he came instantly. He let out a melodic note in my ear and collapsed on top of me.

"I could get used to that."

"You could," he rolled off of me and nodded his head. "I want it every morning for the rest of my life." He said bluntly.

I had thought about long term for a while with Lucas. He was always two steps ahead of me. He was probably envisioning the second stage of marriage and I had not even got down the aisle yet. "I have to finish the dinner." I slipped the dress back over my head. Mark and Shia probably think we are rude."

He slipped his boxers and pants on and followed me out into the empty living room. "Looks like they left." Lucas sat down on the couch and turned on the television. "The apartment looks nice."

"I cleaned it." My hair looked a hot mess, I frowned at the mirror over the table as I tried to make some sense over what had just happened to my hair. "We need to talk about birth control Luke. We never use any. I'm thinking about getting on the pill."

"You can if you would like." He clicked on the television.

"Are you unbothered by the fact that we could be getting knocked up right now?"

"Children with you would not be horrible." Lucas was in a playful mood. I was the polar opposite.

"I'm serious!" I yelled.

"Dear God, what do you want me to do? Do you want me to rewind time to before we fucked and slide a condom on?

Shit, it's happened. The next time we are about to fuck slip it on yourself. You are never concerned until afterwards. What can I do about afterwards Cypress?"

"Nothing, absolutely nothing." I nodded my head and added black pepper to the batter before I threw in the first two pork chops.

"Bloody hell woman, let's talk. Condoms? Shall I be a condom carrier? It's fine with me although I hate them. But for you I will do anything you." The sarcastic edge to his voice irritated me for a moment but I let it slide and ignored it.

"Thank you," I said.

"Or you could get on birth control?" his voice was quiet.

"Fine." I tossed my pork chops in the pan. "But it doesn't make sense for me to change my body when you can just slip on a damn condom."

"I said I would damn it." He growled. "Must you always argue with me?"

"Must you always give me something to argue about?" I listened to the sizzle of the oil and then the smell hit me. "Are you eating here?"

"I can."

"Okay, call your brother."

"They are more than likely tied up." He stared at the television with his feet propped up on the table. I liked that he was comfortable here.

"Tell me about your exes," Shia's conversation with me had a million and one question in my head.

"What about them love? What would you like to know?"

"Why are three of them dead?"

"Because they are." He shrugged his shoulders. "I mean it is unfortunate, but people die every day."

"You know there are some people around campus that say you done it."

"I didn't do anything. I mean they were sluts, but I would not wish them dead." Lucas' eyes never left the television. "Why would you even bring this up? Did fucking Shia come over and fill your head with her gossip and shit."

"I've heard rumors about it. Shia had nothing to do with it." Shia and Lucas were not close. He tolerated her because she was the closest thing that I had to family here. And she tolerated him because she had to, so they were close but hated each other. It was evident.

"Well, forget them and don't pay them any mind. And tell Shia to keep my bloody name out of her gossip filled mouth. People always speculate when they have no real answer to it. The police don't have a suspect in any of those murders and that's their fault. They should work harder. If they wanted to truly catch the killer, they would stop investing their time in me. And you should think about making new friends."

"Were you not sad about any of their murders? Are you not sad that someone that you spent time with sexually, physically and mentally is dead?"

"I was for one. But I hadn't seen these girls in years. Why would I care? Why do you care?"

"People have told me to be careful around you and that you are bad news."

"Who? Who are these people?" Lucas stared at me from the living room as he silenced the television. "Please tell me who they are so they can say all this shit they say to you to my bloody face."

"Shia," I whispered, "some others too."

"Well, tell her to kiss my ass. I don't have shit to bloody hide. I would never hurt you and she should be worried about her crippling relationship with my brother rather than my exes and this relationship."

"Okay," I felt the need to change the subject before everything got out of hand. "What do you want for dessert?"

"I'm actually not hungry." He walked to the bedroom and returned with his shirt. "I'll be back shortly."

Asher

I hated I had to watch Lucas, but the agent had made sure that I reported to him daily. More importantly, Mark had made sure that I reported to him. I barely knew who I should report to. Lucas was highly temperamental. The only person that could calm him was Mark and he had kept his distance in the past few weeks. He only appeared when he was needed. I watched the empty loft and clicked through my phone. I had ordered a lock pic set to get into the apartment. He was gone and so was Mark. I could get in unnoticed through the back fire escape entrance. Perhaps if I got a sneak peek into his home I could get more into his mind. I walked lightly on the steps and got to the third floor where the entrance was. I wiggled the lock pick and unlocked the door. His apartment was a shit ton better than mine. The furniture screamed money and so did the stainless steel appliances.

I made my way through his books and pulled out his photo album. The large leather bound book fell in my lap and I flipped through the pages admiring his mother. Luna was a stunning woman. I snapped a picture with my cell phone. I passed a picture of a baby. M. on the bottom. I snap it and turn the page… and there is another one there. A. I snap it as well and then move to the bedroom. I sift through his drawers. There was nothing there but a small journal. I flipped open to the middle of the leather journal and scan the pages.

June, 28th

I feel like I am alone in more than one way. This need tends to grow darker and darker and every time I try to stop it…It comes back with vengeance. It's the highest point of happiness for me.

June 29th

It happened today. The urge, my father was a better man at this than me, my impulses over power my common sense, all I see is red and all I know is blood. And I feel nothing.

August 14th

I think I met my Savior and I call her Cypress.

I nodded my head, perhaps she could be his savior. I closed the book and snapped pictures of the entire apartment. The apartment was clean. It was so clean it made me wondering if he had hidden something more. I sat on his bed and closed my eyes. What the hell was I doing here? I pushed my hands through my hair and the outside door creaked.

"Lucas!"

I peered downstairs and it was Persephone. She sat down on the plush looking couch and grabbed a magazine. She looked like she had been here before. I walked down the steps. "What are you doing here?"

"Uhm waiting on Lucas? Who the hell are you?" Her head turned and the flow of loose brown curls whipped.

"I..." I paused. "Don't need you to tell him I was here."

"What were you doing here?"

"Just looking for something." I stared at her. "What are you doing here?"

"I wanted to surprise him." Persephone opened her jacket and revealed her bare chest. "I think I can talk him out of Cypress."

"Best to work him up downstairs Hun." I paused. "He could get mad with you breaking and entering."

"You were here first. I thought he was already home."

"Go downstairs and find him then lure him up." Perhaps if he denied her downstairs, she would not end up drained on the floor. She rolled her shoulders. "I don't think he will notice me."

"Well, maybe it's a blessing in disguise." I said.

"No, it's not. I've wanted him for years and he won't even look at me."

My eyes rolled accidentally. I hated redundancy more than I hated her whining. "Well, you are a looker. Maybe he's gay?"

"Maybe... but he has Cypress."

"Cypress is nice. I mean you can get anyone."

She turned her head at me. "I can't get him." She snapped. "Look leave and I won't tell anyone that you were here." She smiled.

"Perfect," I slid my phone in my pocket as I made my way to the exit. "Be careful."

"I will."

I looked over all the photos I took and paused on the kids. They were both babies. But my father never said anything about Luna having kids. There was only Lucas and he thrived off being the only one left.

I dialed my father's number and drove into town so that I wouldn't linger around his place. The feds in the cars had seen me break and enter and they had said nothing. Maybe I could go rogue and just break in everywhere.

My father answered on the third ring. "It's midnight here. I pray that you have a valid reason for calling me." He moaned.

"Yeah, what do you know about the kids that Luna had?"

"What kids?" He said puzzled. "She had Lucas."

"And two other ones, perhaps they were stillborn. I guess I can check into it."

"Why?" He snapped.

"Because it could mean something towards her feeling towards Lucas. Declan could have made her have a stillborn child. I mean... have you looked into him? I know she married three or four times before him."

"I think my angle with her has been construed. I think Declan is the killer... or was the killer."

"Why would you think that?" I knew exactly why he thought it. I had figured out more than a month ago that his father had more traits and more behavior patterns than the mother. The mother just wanted to protect her son and husband, and it didn't matter to her how she has done it.

"Because he had more of the traits pertaining to being a psychopath. She seemed normal."

"I don't know." I paused. "Could you do me a favor and see what you can pull on the kids?"

"Yeah, send me the picture."

"Awesome," I smiled. "I'll let you sleep. Call me when you get up."

"Yeah, I will. And are you being safe?"

"Yes, damn dude." I laughed. "I will talk to you later on." I ended the phone call and stared at the pictures. There had to be something more. Why would Luna keep the pictures of children that were not hers?

Lucas

The Summit had a rather large crowd for the night. There were tons that I needed to do. Mark was a madman when it came to numbers for profit and I had not yet even prepared the reports for him. His money was his obsession which was fine by me. I liked making money and the place basically ran itself with the good manager.

"Have you printed out the reports for me Kasey?"

"Not yet, there are some people crowding the bar. I was gonna help her for the moment and then bring them to you."

"Just let her be." I paused. "Bring me the papers and then could you make sure that there is another bartender on schedule for tonight. If there isn't then you should go ahead and get in getting someone else in for the night." I looked over my desk. "Bring me a Jack and Coke with the report."

She turned on her heel, "Anything else?"

"Yeah," I winked. "Smile for God's Sake... you could be flipping burgers."

"Yeah." She grimaced as she left the cold office.

I had to learn some control. I took out my pencil and a scratch piece of paper. Controlling my urge was harder than I wanted to admit. If I could learn control, then there was a possibility that I could live a more than normal life. The light tap on the door was barely audible with the music booming on the other side.

"Come in." I yelled.

The door opened and closed in seconds, sending another cold breeze towards me. "Busy?"

I looked up at Persephone. She was beautiful. Much like her namesake, her curls flourished as they ran down her back. I'd been so enticed with Cypress I forgot what she looked like. "Very, I hope whatever you want is important."

"It's very important."

I unglued my eyes from her and shrugged my shoulders. "Well then... speak woman."

She dropped her jacket and she stood before me bare. Her perfectly round breast sat up at attention, causing me to watch the curve of her hips right down to her pussy. I found myself captured. I placed my pencil down on the table and cut my eyes up to hers. "Damn..."

"I know you have Cypress..."

I nodded my head. "Yeah."

"But I can show you... that there is better out there." She swayed her hips to the beat of music from the other room. "Can I show you..."

"Put your jacket on." My tone was low.

"Lucas..."

"Now." I snapped.

"Okay..." She slid her dress on and turned towards the door.

"Let's dance." I mumbled. I moved to the door and led her out to the dance floor. The dim lights made it perfect for what I had in mind... The music was alluring... slow. I grabbed her by the hips and ground lightly against her. My hands clasped over her body and I could feel her thrusting herself on me. "What do you want from me?" I whispered.

"A chance," she said back.

"At what?"

"You..."

I slid my hand into the jacket and my fingers danced around the folds of her pussy. She was drenched. "I can give you that." I heard a moan escape her mouth as I pushed my middle finger deeper into her. She stood on her tip toes and my other a room wrapped her in security as I was working to drive her to the point of insanity. Her thighs clenched at each thrust and then I withdrew and placed my finger in her mouth. "Taste yourself..." Her tongue grazed my finger. "Good girl... Upstairs...?"

"Yes," she answered.

"Good." I grabbed her soft hands, leading her to the elevator. I pressed my pin in and watched the elevators open. "Are you sure?" I said. The doors closed and the elevator lifted from the shaft.

"Yes." She smiled.

I tossed her back against the elevator wall and hit the stop button. "When we get up here... lose the jacket and wait for me upstairs..."

"Okay." Persephone nodded her head. The excitement bled out of her eyes.

When arrived she had done as directed. Persephone walked upstairs and stripped back down to nothing. I followed her up and stared at her. "I want to do so much to you. I don't know where to start." I whispered.

"Start here..." she pushed her finger into herself and licked her lips slowly.

"That could be a good place... Don't speak again." I growled. She pretended to zip her mouth shut and tossed the key aside. My eyes wonder her body. "Good." I toss my shirt to the ground and climb in bed with her. My hands touch her stomach lightly. "You are soft." I touch her neck softly. And my eyes see the picture of Cypress and I. She turns it face down before I can think. "Let's start... Undress me."

Persephone's hands traveled up my body unzipping my pants and pulling the down. My boxers followed right after. Her eyes grew wide when I finally set free.

"Wow," she whispered.

"Hush, suck it."

She obeyed. She struggled to get all of me in her mouth, but when she did, she took me to the back of her throat. She swirled her tongue around me slowly and my eyes rolled to the back of my head. Her mouth was like wet silk. A slight moan escaped my mouth and my hands went to the back of her head, guiding her to take more of me. She was relentless as her head bobbed up and down as I could feel it coming so I pulled her up. "Damn..." She smiled.

"Lay down on your stomach and stick your ass in the air."

Persephone leaned towards to kiss me and pulled her back to my chest, pinching her nipples, making her scream out in a mixture of pain and ecstasy. "Listen to me woman." I slapped her ass as I pushed her gently to the bed, then scooped up her ass. My fingers pushed into her pussy and I reached over to the dresser. My hand grazed my knife and I grabbed the condoms, sliding one in a few seconds and I entered her slowly. I ground into her hard. I drilled into her fast barely having time to recover from how tight she was. My hands gripped her ass harder with each entry and she started to moan my name louder and louder until the moans turned into shrill screams. It was wild my hair had fell in my face blocking her from my view and all I could feel was her pussy grasping my dick with each pump.

I slowed down and slapped her ass once more just to watch her blood rush to the spot right after. My dick began to spasm as she came around me and she collapsed into bed hopelessly limp. I went into her faster and with a stream of incoherent words I pulled out of her and cum spilled all over her back. "Bloody Hell." I pushed my hair into a messy bun and fell next to her.

"That was..." Persephone didn't complete her sentence she just sighed.

"Yeah, pretty incredible." My hand made its way back over to the drawer and grabbed the knife. I climbed back on top of her. "We should talk." I smiled. I crossed my arms and revealed the knife. "I am a wee bit tired of you..."

Persephone yelped and I placed my hand over mouth.

"Shut it... or I will use this god damned knife. I am showing major self-control by not killing you. I mean major," she squirmed underneath me and my legs locked her down. "Persephone!" I yelled. "Shut your mouth now or I will spill every ounce of your blood all over these sheets. And my mum bought me these sheets. I'd rather they stay in good shape."

She exhaled and grew silent.

"Are you going to keep yourself quiet?" I watched her as she shook her head yes. "Now, I am happy with Cypress."

"Okay."

"And I would rather you disappear."

She shook uncontrollably. "Okay, I swear."

"Now, here are some rules to insure that this never happens again..." I glaze over her skin with the cold knife. "I want you to understand that I am never leaving her. And she better not find out about this."

"She won't."

"I know. Because if she does... and I find out it's from you... I will find you, Persephone. Even if that means traveling millions of miles. I will paint the walls of your home with your blood and drain you slowly while you scream for mercy... and then I will burn your body, and sprinkle your ashes in a trash can. Next stay away from me, stay away from her."

Tears flowed from her face and I could feel my anger taking over. "Don't fucking cry. You are getting off easy. I fucked you and then warn you and darling. I have done so much worst." I threatened. "I could have murdered you and done it, but I was nice. You should be grateful, as a matter of fact thank me." I applied some pressure to her neck and bit my lip. "Now."

"Thank you." she cried.

"Good, now get your jacket and leave..."

CHAPTER ELEVEN

Cypress

My bookshelf looked like a tornado had visited. All because I could not find my Stephen King book. I stared at the bookshelf in hopes that it would reveal itself and this afternoon would be saved from the hassle to relook. Of course the plan failed and I laid back on the carpet floor and groaned in frustration.

"What are you doing?" It was the first word he had said since he started to work on his book. He had seen my trouble and he just laughed and kept working three times. I wanted to slap the perfection out of him.

"Dying slowly." I moaned.

"You are over exaggerating. Are you sure you didn't let anyone borrow the book? Mark likes to read Stephen King."

"I didn't let anyone borrow anything. Did you let someone borrow it?"

"No Cypress," he continued to click on his computer. "Just buy it on your e-reader."

"I want to hold the book and read it. I can only read that thing when the lights are out."

"I can think of better things to do when the lights are out." Lucas chuckled and pecked a few more keys on his computer. "There is something that I have got to get handled out of the country in a few weeks. You are free to come with if you want to."

"No." I said. "Will Stephen King be there?"

"More than likely no," he laughed. "Are you seriously upset about this book?"

"Why are you so amused?"

"You are dying because you can't find a book. You can just buy another one. I mean, that's why author outs, no limit on how many books you can buy."

"Do you know before we met I read your book over ten times?"

"You mentioned it once." Mentioned it. He loved it.

"Well, books are therapy for me. I need them to feel alive."

"You're a hyperbole woman. You just like to read. And I understand it, baby, I love it. I love a well read, well sexed woman. Sometimes I can get lost in a book and wonder how five hours passed."

"Yeah, yeah. Somehow every conversation we have together ventures back to sex with you." I stood up and looked at him. "What are you working on over there?"

"A book," he said quickly. "My publisher asked for a sample of something new to put on my page. My audience is a little upset that there will not be a movie. So I am writing a book called *In Her Hand*. And I feel like if they read a decently written chapter they would let up."

"So that's what you are going to do when we finish college?"

"Yep, three months left for me. I'll just write and re-write and brood sometimes."

"I wish it was that easy for me. I am thinking that I will more than likely just teach English. And I really don't understand how February has passed us by already. Except for Valentine's Day. I've yet to know what the hell you have up your sleeve."

"What I have up these sleeves will never be revealed until it gets here." Lucas exhaled, "And you can write if you want to Cypress, no one ever said that writing was easy. It's actually harder because for the first time you'll let someone in your head. You can't be scared people won't accept the stupid shit that dwells up there. Just let it out. You not writing is just some nerves and laziness blending. I want you to push yourself harder than you ever have before."

"Whatever, it's Saturday and I'd rather eat and watch TV until something hits me. That's my normal process." Food had been heavy on my mind since we had been cooped up in my apartment all day. I want some pickles. You want some pickles."

"No, I do want some pea soup."

"You can get that yourself."

"You have to try it one day or better yet the..."

I finished his sentence. "Three Bean Soup." I paused. "No way, sir. That is nasty. I would really just like a sandwich with some pickles on it and maybe a side of chili cheese fries."

"Don't be fat now."

"I am not fat. I am in college, though."

"Excuses," Lucas mumbled. "The soup is really good though. I will make us some tonight."

"I have to go to your mom's house tonight. She decided that she was cooking us some kind of chicken, buffalo... something."

"Probably a casserole." he complained. "Do we have to go over there? She tends to talk too much for too long and I have a deadline."

"You can stay." I answered. "I have to change and then I need to get some rolls for the meal." I made my way to the room, stepping over half of my book collection and his large backpack.

"You are my girlfriend you know that?"

"How could I forget?"

"I don't know. You spend more time with my mum these days than me."

"You get quiet easily." I looked into the array of unorganized clothes and snatched the blue university sweatshirt from the pile and he was behind me.

"You don't like me being quiet?"

"I like you better when you talk and let me know what the hell is going on in there."

"I have some tainted thoughts in here Cy."

"Like when you said you like to see the souls leave?"

I watched as his face turned white and he turned his head at me. "When did I say that exactly?"

"Our special trip this Winter Break." I paused. "You said… I like to see the souls leave. I wish I had one. I don't know what you meant, but for once I felt like I had some insight into whatever you are thinking usually in your head."

"You really don't want to know what is going on," He answered.

"Your dark inside."

"I am?" He questioned.

"Your writing is dark Lucas and you have this look on your face most of the time that is just different. You look like you could care less about what anyone else says. Sometimes you do it to me. Sometimes you don't. I don't know."

"Well, I sincerely apologize if I make you think that I don't care. I do care about you more than you will ever know. And I didn't realize I…"

"You let me see the real you that you have been hiding for forever that day. And yes, my mind was a little off, but that was the first time that you really let me in."

"I allow you in every day."

"It's fine." I kissed his cheek. This conversation was obviously over. I had grown tired of it. At some point I needed to realize that he would never truly allow me to see the real him. "Are we leaving here soon? I hope she cooks."

"I want to finish this conversation." He snapped.

"Okay finish it. Tell me something about you that I don't know. What makes you so different from everyone else in this world? I tell you everything and you treat me like a fragile child. I will not break if you tell me something Lucas."

"I'm not normal Cy."

"I didn't think that you were." I mumbled.

"I don't think I have a soul." Lucas flashed his smile at me. "There you go. I don't think I have the capability to feel emotions."

"That is bullshit." I looked at him as he brow creased.

"So I tell you something and you are just gonna call it bullshit. I am pouring my heart out here Cypress.

"Pouring your heart out about being emotionless?"

"You asked for the truth damn it."

Lucas was humorous. "Forget it."

"Baby," He soothed me jokingly. "There is nothing to tell you. I swear to it."

"You don't feel emotions towards me?"

"I don't feel emotions towards anyone else Cypress. I just don't react the same as any normal person."

"So you are just a selfish dick?" I asked.

"Why?"

"Because like you said." He backed away towards the bed. "I tend to see things differently through my eyes. I am not compassionate and I don't care about anyone but you most of the time."

"Well, maybe you just suppress those feelings. Who did you care about before I came along? I know you love Tracy and Mark."

"I do love Tracy and Mark. But I'm not good at showing it. I would much rather banter with them." He paused as if more was to come. "I can't do this right now. I don't think telling you about me will keep you here."

"I'm not going anywhere. I'm pretty much here to stay, Lucas face it you're trapped with me."

"You will if I tell you. Hurry up and we can head on to the house. She'll start." Lucas walked out of the room holding his keys, his back turned to me.

"No, sir!" I pulled him back into the room. "What is it? What are you hiding?"

"I am not a good person. What is this a damn counseling session? I don't have shit to tell you Cypress."

"There's pretty much everything to tell. Why aren't you a good person?"

"Because I'm not. I don't have to tell you everything about. There has to be something that is left to the imagination. You are intruding on my personal feeling is annoying as shit."

"Okay, one more question." I looked at him. "Do you kill people?"

"Of course not." His eyes were bright. "Look come on."

"Are you sure? I mean these agents are hot on you. They aren't easing up. They watch the loft and they watch my place. They are tracking your every move. They feel like there is something there. I can forgive you for whatever you have done. I could help you change."

"You couldn't help me love." Lucas touched my hand. "Remember that you cannot save me and remember that I don't want you to try. And you said one more question so this never ending question has actually come to an end."

"We aren't going anywhere." I yelled. "I want to know what it is that you have tucked deep inside that is just not good enough for me to know."

"There is nothing here, Cypress!" Lucas' eyes were wild.

"Alright, well then just get out! If you can't trust me enough to tell me what is tearing, you apart, then you don't need to be with me. I open up every day and tell you every detail about me. You can't even give me a half ass effort to understanding what you have going on. So get the fuck out!"

"Oh, I'll be happy to." He tossed his hands up at me in defeat and made his way to the front door. "If you decide to stop being a pain in my ass. Give me a call."

"Goodbye," I held the door open. "And when you decide that there is something more that want to tell me… you can come back."

Lucas

I had no idea what the hell had just happened. Women were difficult creatures and I was not mentally equipped to figure out whatever the puzzle was just yet. I wanted some peace. I need some privacy and needed a kill. Someone local… someone easy. I sat in my car and banged my fist against the steering wheel in frustration. Cypress had seen a raw, unadulterated version of me that night. It wasn't supposed to slip out and I didn't want it to be seen.

I peered at my loft and then to the agents who sat in the unmarked black sedan less than a block away. I just wanted one damned night alone. Completely free to kill whoever the fuck I wanted to. I clenched my fist and freed my shoulders. I could lose them, but they would have a tail out on my car in minutes, or I could go out through the building and got it.

I hopped out of the vehicle. They were there as usual being a complete nuisance in my life. I looked at them and through up a friendly hand. I could leave America. I could visit my Nadine and Callum. A pure Irishman and cousin who knew how to have a good time in the only way that I did. I nodded my head. Just a few nights with on the streets of Dublin and he would enjoy the hunt just as much as me. There would be no Cypress, no fucking McMillan and no issues. I could be back to normal.

"What are you doing out here?"

I rolled my eyes at Mark. "It just so happens that I live here, Mark."

"Well, I'm happy you are back. There is an issue I have on my hands and you can't kill him or throw him out of any windows. I just need you to remain calm and listen to whatever the fuck he has to say."

"Who the fuck is it Mark?"

"Asher." Mark crossed his arms as if he already knew my reaction.

"Why the hell is he a problem?"

"He actually is studying you and from what I see, now the Feds are too. He is a good guy. I have done a background check and I've had him under my thumb for the past few months. I looked into him and his father. His father was studying you and your dad. And he took over and decided to study you. He is in my apartment waiting for us with everything he has on you. The only thing he wants from you is to talk one on one politely. And then he will help us get the agent off of your back."

"Absolutely not, he is supposed to be banned from the place. And what the fuck do you mean had him under your thumb? He fucking fondled my girlfriend."

"He doesn't want Cypress. He has his own girlfriend that he just so happens to be in love with. I just want you to go up there with a clear mind and promise you will not kill him."

"I won't." I snapped. Why was he studying me? And more importantly, why was he studying my family period.

"Good, because the agents over there would be mighty excited to cuff your ass." We made it upstairs rather quickly. I could feel my heart as it ripped out of my chest, I hated him.

Mark's apartment was white. Everything from the chairs, the tables and appliances. He wanted everything white. The only nonwhite items were the splashes of black arms and legs and an occasional stainless steel garnish. Asher sat in the white chair surrounded by pictures with my face and knives and items that had never left my apartment. I stared at the table. "You bloody bastard." I mumbled.

"Yeah, great way to start. Sit down." Mark snapped.

I followed his demand and stared at Asher. "You make it a habit of sneaking into my home and rummaging through things?"

"Is this what you call polite?" Asher turned to Mark.

"I'm afraid that it's as polite as he gets."

"Well, I'm here to help you Lucas." Asher opened his notebook.

"Why?"

"Because I don't like to help the feds. They are the reason that my father can't come home and I'd rather not help them."

"Your daddy issues have nothing to do with the fact you broke into my home and rummaged through my shit. Then you took pictures. Do you roll around on my sheets too?"

"Look, Lucas he wants to help. Shut up and listen to him for a moment. It could help you." Mark sat down on the couch across from me and sipped on his water. "Go ahead."

"I have been studying you and your actions for five years... maybe more." He sifted through the array of files on the desk. "I know what you are Luke."

"Are you working with them? Is this the reason that the FBI has taken it upon themselves to follow me wherever the fuck I go? You giving them shit?"

"What? Are you deaf? I just said that I wanted to help you. I really thought that you were smarter than this."

"You are a bold little fuck I see." I teetered on the edge of you my seat and cracked my knuckles. "Are you working with the feds? Have you checked him for a wire?"

Mark laughed. "Yes, you are a complete ass." Mark laughed at me and then leaned forward placing his elbows on his legs. "Can you take just a few minutes and calm your rage and listen to him? Honestly, I would have not brought him here if I didn't think he could help you. Will you listen to him?"

"No." I snapped.

"Don't make this hard." Mark threatened.

"Oh, what are you going to do to me Mark?"

"Don't little brother." I knew he was strong; without my knife he would overpower me. I only lifted weights occasionally. The gym had a room with his name on it. "Go ahead Asher."

He sat uncomfortably as he watched us too. "I believe that you are a psychopath. As a matter of a fact I know you are and no it does not excuse your behavior. But it explains so much about you that you might not understand."

"Excuse me?"

"I didn't stutter and I don't like repeating myself. You are a psychopath. You have no emotions for anyone else but yourself and maybe Cypress sometimes. It's why you kill. You do it because it doesn't hurt you to kill. You could give less than a fuck about someone else's life."

I felt uneasy. Everything he had stated was true. I stared at him. "Continue."

"You are a cold heart manipulative person and you do anything to make you feel better. They have spotted you and they know your behavior patterns. The checklist fits you like an autobiography. It's why this agent is so head strung on catching you. You are dangerous."

"Tell me something I don't know Asher."

"I can help you."

"How can you help me Asher?"

"I can teach you to control it. And no you won't be able to defeat it all the time. But you can at least control yourself while they are hunting you like a savage animal."

"Well, how sweet of you, you stalk me and then you would like to help me. How about you give me some time to think about it?" I watched as Mark grimaced and laughed.

"You should just take his help. It's really nothing to debate about, you have become reckless. I don't know what it is and I don't care either. I want you to do it. I want you to be open enough to let him help you."

"You can't tell me what to do."

"You sound like a fucking little kid Lucas!"

Asher cleared his throat. "You two stop bickering for one moment." He hands me the pictures. "I have a question about some pictures I found in your apartment."

"What pictures Asher?" My lips bared against clenched teeth. Rage seeped into my eyes. There was nothing worse in my book than rummaging through someone things. It was rude and evasive. I flipped through the pictures.

"These children, I found them on accident actually."

"Accident my ass," I mumbled.

"Your mom only had one child, right?"

"She had me and those children were the ones she kept in the orphanage with my Nan in England. Now if you would please stay out of my shit. I would hate to see you dead."

"Alright, look… just be nice."

"I'm trying as hard as I can." I gritted my teeth. "I'm actually gonna head up to my place. You take a picture of my sheets too freak."

"Okay, I'm leaving. I could have stayed home and gave all this shit to the feds. I didn't have to come here tonight. I have a girlfriend that wants me to leave everything alone, but I wanted to help. I don't have to."

"We know and we appreciate it. We can meet again soon. I want to know everything that they know so that we can know what they want."

"I'll meet with you."

"Good," I snapped. I walked towards the white elevator door and turned around. "Appreciate your help."

"Yeah, fuck off." Asher said.

"Get your pet Mark."

"What's your problem?"

"My problem? You shoved your hand up my girlfriend's skirt, you broke into my house. You are always inconveniently around."

"The only reason I even tried to test her was to get her away from you. I was scared that if she ever pissed you off, she would ever victim."

"I would never hurt her. She doesn't need you to protect her. I am the only protection that she needs Asher, remember that huh?"

"Who else is going to protect her from you Lucas? You can't even control yourself! You jump the gun too quickly. You think she loves you… do you think that she will love the real you? You know the version if you that drained Summer and her boyfriend open like cattle?"

"What did you say?"

"Oh now you're interested?" He chuckled. "Yeah, I watched you drain her and her boy toy open like cattle. Their blood poured out into the floor and you sat there and watched. You fucking smiled. You have no control. You could kill her and it would not even phase you."

"I'm controlling it right now!" The growl escaped as shoulder shook nonstop.

"Both of you shut your damn mouths. Lucas, calm down." Mark snapped, he turned to Asher. "You didn't tell me you witnessed a murder."

"I did." Asher's face was red. "I should have run to the police, but instead I found myself staring at the damned blood until I was sick. I stayed away from you afterward. I tried my best, but I had to let Cypress know to leave."

"You watched me a kill a person and you didn't turn me. You're sick too."

"Fuck you, Luke."

"We have some shit to sort out here. Okay, we can't do it if we don't work together. I want to know about the children in the photos. Why would she only keep two pictures and she worked there for most of her life? Why would you fucking, watch and not say anything and how could you allow a tail?"

"I didn't see him."

"You see, he helped you find a weakness. And now we have to make sure it never happens again by Asher teaching you how to control yourself."

"I would never hurt Cypress."

"I can tell."

"Good, so you don't ever need to defend her again. I have it all taken care of. And I'll take the pictures to Ireland with me. I am going to visit my Nadine and an old friend in Ireland next week."

"You didn't tell me that."

"I didn't know you were my mum Mark."

"Are you going alone?"

"Yeah, Cypress and I have decided to break until I can tell her what I have hidden inside."

"What do you mean?" Mark asked.

"She thinks that I am hiding something."

Asher nodded his head as if he knew already and it made me want to break his neck. "Tell her you are an addict. It's not a lie."

"Absolutely not," I paused.

"You use drugs a lot. Tell her you are addicted and you can't control yourself. It's the only way that she will ease off of you and accept you for your flaws. Women can take flawed, better than mass murderer."

"Serial killer," I corrected.

"Whatever," he mumbled.

"Do what he suggested and make sure you tell her about leaving town. We are taking a trip too."

"Who is we?" Asher asked.

"Us, we are going to further investigate some matters and make Lucas comfortable with you."

"If I step foot out of this country with him... I'm dead."

Smart kid, I chuckled. "I won't kill you."

"No, he won't. He can control himself and Asher is going to make sure that you do. He is going to be there with you every step and he is gonna give you lessons."

"Bloody hell, no."

"Will you be optimistic just this once."

"Yeah, make him stay home so he can graduate and live a full life." I walked to the doors of the elevator. "Please."

Cypress

I reorganized the bathroom four times trying to find the logic behind what Lucas said. *He was dark. He was a monster.* I just wanted him to be frank. I hated him most when he was evasive. I scrubbed the sink until the porcelain was almost dull and then tossed the gloves into the cleaning basket. I was starving and the only thing left in those cabinets would have made one horrendous dinner. I stripped down to my nice pajama shorts and his black sweater he left over from the other night.

My cell phone buzzed on the couch at the same time my front door opened. "Oh shit..."

Lucas chuckled. "I came to save the day with some food from The Summit." He held up a bag of food and a bottle of wine.

"Why are you really here Lucas?" I had a notion to just take his food and close the door. But I was afraid that would not work in my favor. I silenced my phone and watched him close the door behind him.

"I wanted to talk to you and apologize. I should have stayed and talked everything out."

"Okay..." I paused. "What do you have in the bag before we start?"

"I have some chicken strips and fries for you and some soup for me. Then there is of course cheesecake and the damn pickles I had to steal from The Summit too."

"Pickles," I smiled. "Set up the table and I will break out the wine glasses."

Lucas entered my apartment which reeked of bleach. I "You just cleaned. Why were you cleaning again?"

I cleaned whenever he pissed me off. It was my way to blow off steam when I knew I shouldn't try to be the shit out of him. "Would you mind drinking from a regular cup?" I blocked his question out as I searched through the cabinet for the wine glasses. Shia must have stolen them.

"I wouldn't." He smirked.

"Good." I pulled two Christmas coffee mug from the cabinet and I poured some wine for him and me. Then I pulled over the food over to us. I could already smell the spices of the batter. The Summit was a world class restaurant. And yes, even the Chicken Strips made me want to slap someone. They were always cooked to perfection. "Okay, what are you going to tell me?"

"Eat your food," Lucas opened his soup. He was obsessed with soup.

"Fine." The food smelled like heaven and I hadn't eaten since our fight from before. I dug into my food and waited for him to tell me everything.

"Some people aren't as lucky as you are."

"Really?" I asked.

"You grew up with a loving mother and father and you really had no issues of the outside worked corrupting you."

"Well, I did smoke once."

"God forbid tobacco." He laughed. "I know sometimes you feel as if you don't know me and that's because sometimes I don't know myself Cypress." He paused and watched me for a moment. "I know that I've always been dark Cypress and I know that people notice. I used to even do some dark things and then I met you and everything changed."

"Well Edward Cullen, what is so dark about you?"

"When I was younger, I was addicted to drugs."

This was nothing new to me. I figured by the way he casually talked about the drugs that he had some kind of prior issue with drugs.

"What kind?"

"Any kind that got me high." He joked. "Addicts don't necessarily care about the process to get to the high. It's the actual high itself."

"So what made you stop."

"A new addiction," he took another bite of his soup and tore off a piece of my chicken.

"What's the new one?"

"Wanting to be with you."

"Luc…"

"Let me talk. You wanted me to tell you what was inside and I'll tell you. Every day I used to wake up seeking a high… it didn't necessarily have to be drugs." He cleared his throat and then his hands made their way up to his face. His pinched in frustration and then he exhaled. "I'm so in love with you. It's not because I just can, it's just because I have no choice Cypress. I wake up and I want to see you every morning. I have to be around you, it's uncontrollable. You've become that something that takes me there, you're my high. And honestly, I'm happy it's you. I would rather it be you than anything else. I'm sorry that I'm closed off. I'm so sorry that I can't be that guy that tells you everything about me. I can work on it. But it's not much to see. I'm just a guy addicted to a girl that means more than anything to me."

"More than anything?"

"More than anything," He shrugged his shoulders.

CHAPTER TWELVE

Cypress

Grocery shopping, I had dreaded it for months but here I was laundering the aisle with Lucas. The aisles were packed with food that was not currently in my budget and my chaperone was someone who didn't believe in budgets. I looked at the list. Eggs, Bacon, Milk, Rice, Water. There was absolutely no way in hell I could squeeze a three-dollar jar of pickles in unless I skipped McDonalds tomorrow. "I can afford just one jar." I mumbled.

"I have told you more than once that I can buy your damned food." Lucas was emerged in his phone but it hadn't stopped him from voicing his complaints.

"I've told you that I don't want you to buy my food. I would much rather find a better job. I hardly even get to work. Had it not been for my savings account, I would be buried in debt." College sucked and bills sucked.

"Why struggle?" Lucas stopped mid step and turned his head to me. "I have told you several times that there is no reason for you to struggle."

"Don't start with me today Lucas."

"What, I am asking a general question? You struggle because of pride."

"Shut up," I rolled my eyes. The shirt he wore was loose on his chest, but his arms fit snugly. It accented them perfectly. My eyes trace down his body at the pants and how they fit him perfectly. My hormones wanted nothing more than to take him to the house and not leave for a few hours but there was no time for that. "When are you leaving for Ireland?"

"I don't know. Callum said something about coming here for a while. He was thinking about moving to New York. But I was thinking that I would like to go there for Spring Break in a few months. Maybe for summer vacation. I don't know. Why?"

"That sounds good. I was just wondering. I know that you miss your cousin and your family there."

"I miss them a ton. But I think that they can wait. Perhaps you can come with me and we could christen Ireland." Lucas wrapped his arms around me and kissed the nape of my neck. We walked through the store for a few steps and then reached for the pickle jar. "Why are you eating pickles?"

"Because I like pickles. I had three like jars last week. And then for some reason I decided that I needed some more. Pickles are like the Gods of Cucumbers."

"Gods of Cucumbers, good grief Cypress." He chuckled and stood back. "You really have a strange addiction." He stopped walking. "When was your last cycle?"

"Last cycle, Lucas, are you crazy. There is no way in hell I could be pregnant."

"Well answer my question and perhaps I could just be at ease."

"I don't know; I guess it was closer to December."

"Good grief, what in the hell do you mean closer to December. It's practically February woman." He griped. "You don't keep track of your cycle.

"I'll check and you stop fussing at me. I fussed at you for months to wear a damned condom." My heart thumped as I pushed him playfully out of the way. Shit, all the times I complained to him about condoms and now I was the one who had been so careless to lose track of my stupid period. I put the pickles back on the shelf.

"Get the damn pickles." He put them back in the buggy. "Woman, dear Jesus must you make everything difficult."

"You better watch your little snappy attitude. What is wrong with you today?"

"I can't have privacy anymore." Lucas pointed to the woman in black. It was apparent that she had followed us around the store for more than an hour. I thought she was store security. "I mean, sorry."

"Well, don't take it out on me." I put the pickles in the cart and stared at him. It was weird that he had someone from a government agency tracking him. I refused to think about it. I refused to act like I cared about it. "Are you freaking out about the test?"

"I'm not worried about the test. I am a pull out champion."

"Ugh stop talking," I rolled my eyes. "Why didn't you pull your hair up today?"

The usual man bun he rocked fit him, but the sexiness of his curls down and falling constantly in his face was overwhelming. "I don't like rocking the same style as my girlfriend all the time."

"I like it. This is sexy too."

"Thank you." He picked up a can of artichokes. "I am cooking tonight."

"What are you cooking?"

"Food, you need to eat."

"I think I'm gonna eat a frozen meal. Lasagna."

"Come on, woman. I am trying to shower you with my love and you keep pulling out a damned umbrella. I said I was cooking and you are gonna eat."

"Fine, but I don't eat artichokes. You are so bossy today."

"Beggars can't be choosers."

"Well, I'm not begging you."

"I love you." he tossed the artichokes in the cart and started dancing to whatever the random music was that blasted over the speakers. He bounced and slung his hair. "This is my song!" He danced playfully around me and I nodded my head. "Dance with me."

"No," I laughed. "You're insane."

"I'm a mad man. Have I not told you?" He sways with me and kissed my neck. The two older ladies smiled at us like we were in some kind of movie. His lips grazed my entire neck, biting occasionally and I felt my knees grow weak.

"Stop," I whispered.

"Pardon me," Lucas kissed my hand. "I forgot where we were for a moment. We should go home so I can forget we have neighbors."

"You're pardoned." I laughed and we made our way through the aisles. "And no, we've been cooped up in that house all day."

"You look better." Asher said from in front of us.

I glanced at Lucas and he didn't look like he wanted to kill him. Something had changed in their relationship and it almost weirded me out. But then again, I was just really happy that he had a friend besides Mark. "Hey Asher, how have you been?"

"Perfect," Asher looked at Lucas. "I called you yesterday."

Lucas shrugged his shoulders. "I was gonna call you back then I fell asleep and basically forgot. But I had every intention to call you back."

"Sure you did." Asher laughed. "How have you been doing Cypress?"

"Great, just ready to graduate and finally not have to worry about school."

"Aren't we all." Asher nodded at me. "Have you talked to Mark?"

"I talked to him earlier, but he disappeared last night. He does that."

"Yes, I've noticed. Well, Whitney wants to have some company over for dinner and I thought about you two. I invited Mark already and now I'm asking you. You and Cypress should join us for dinner this afternoon."

"We're cooking ourselves." Lucas held up the artichokes in an attempt to ignore the offer.

"We haven't made solid plans." I added. "I would actually like to get out for once. He keeps me locked away in that damn loft like a prisoner."

"A prisoner of love." Lucas grimaced. "What are you cooking Ash?"

"You think you two would want to try some stuffed Bell Peppers? She is cooking those and some kind of side. And I'm making dessert."

"If you swear that you're only doing dessert."

"Yes, that sounds wonderful." I pushed at Lucas.

"What is a stuffed bell pepper?" Lucas sounded disgusted.

"Dude are you gonna complain the entire time?

"Fine, tonight at what time?"

"It'll start about 8."

"Great, we will be there and we will bring a nice wine."

"A fair wine," Lucas corrected.

"Mark is coming with Shia."

"Have I missed something?" I looked at the two of them. "Why are you two all of a sudden friends and why haven't you told me?"

"Surprise your boyfriend made a new friend. Asher we will see you toni..."

"Asher! I found the perfect bell peppers. I just need some... oh sorry."

"This is Lucas and Cypress." He grabbed her hand. "This is my girlfriend Whitney."

Whitney smiled at the both of us. "I am so happy to hear about you two coming to dinner! He hasn't really had a friend here since he moved."

"I wonder why?" Lucas mumbled. "He can be a nosey bastard."

"And you can be an obnoxious dick. I guess we were made for each huh" Asher said not fazed by Lucas or his remarks. I was proud of him for some reason. He never seemed like the type actually stand for himself.

"He is a great guy. We are excited about dinner. Should I bring a dessert wine or a dinner wine?"

"Um either or, I don't know the difference." Whitney chuckled.

Lucas shifted uncomfortably. "Have you talked to Mark today?"

"Yeah, I wouldn't know he was coming if I didn't."

"He's an ass."

"Okay, so we will see you tonight around 8." Whitney said.

"My thoughts exactly." I tugged his shirt. "When did you two become friends?" I asked as we walked away. "I mean I am happy to see you have friends. It is weird to see you be nice to someone besides Mark. Mark doesn't even deserve it. I mean most of the time you two are equal dicks to one another."

"Mark is my brother. Asher is a friend. The end baby," He grabbed a cheap wine and placed it in the cart. "And you aren't drinking any until you take the test."

"Oh, hold up, it can't be like that already. I haven't even pissed on a stick yet Luke."

"Like what? Caring about my child having alcohol poisoning?"

"There will be no bossing me if I am pregnant. I want total control of the situation and I want to make sure that you understand it."

"Even if you aren't pregnant, baby, I have control. You just don't know it."

"Shut up Luke."

Asher

January had flown by and I had become friends with Lucas and Mark. More of Mark, I was sure that Mark tolerated me more than friended me. I would settle for it. It felt better now that I knew that I was not on his to kill list. It was weird that in some way I had someone to talk to when shit with sideways. I normally kept everything bottled inside.

The drive home had been awkward and quiet. Whitney did not particularly care for Lucas. I could tell by the way she slammed the pots in my sink and while she banged cabinets like it was her home. "Whit."

"What?" She said with a weird edge to her voice.

"Are you going to slam shit the entire time?"

"I am." The pots clanged in the sink once more and I made my way over to her. I snatched the light green pot from her. "Calm down. What is your problem?"

"I thought you were just going to invite Mark and his girlfriend. Now you have me cooking for the whole damn neighborhood."

"You should have said something when I asked you earlier. You said yes babe invite anyone you want to, I'm in a cooking mood." I mocked her as I imitated her voice. "If you had a problem, why not tell me before I invited someone else."

"Whatever, I'm not arguing. There is no time to argue. I still have to cook all this shit."

"I can help too Whitney. You have a shitty attitude today babe," I rolled my eyes at her and grabbed the bell peppers from the bag.

"I looked through some of your work." She blurted out.

"You did?" I hadn't decided if I was angry or excited. Besides Mark and some professors there had not been any outside eyes on it. "Why?"

"You told me about it and ever since that guy was killed a few months back it had been irking me. You know your reaction that day was... odd."

"Someone was murdered, was I supposed to act excited?"

"Asher, I mean you are acting like you knew it was about to happen."

"I did not." I thought back to the night. I jotted down notes. I made sure that I documented the date so I could observe his behavior. Lucas tended to have a ritual for the kill and after the kill. If he truly killed someone, then there would be a pattern.

"Right." Whitney batted her eyes at me and crossed her arms. "I met Lucas once, it was a few years ago. He has been going here and at one point he was the campus celebrity. His book made millions and then on top of that he was handsome, or so they said. When I met him I could feel it. He was dark and he was the guy that gave looks that scared. He just seemed," She paused. "He seemed cold."

"I mean, okay. People have different vibes. You can't punish the guy because he does not seem friendly. I've been hanging around him for a month or two and he seems nice."

"I know he is the test study you are studying." Whitney threw her hands up. "I know what psychopaths do."

"How in the hell do you think you know?"

"I just know. He is sick and you should stop going around him. It is not worth it and you can make up shit and still get your doctoral degree. You can do that and be done with him."

I pushed my hands through my hair and groaned. "You can't tell me what to do with my research and most importantly, I am not going to let you dictate who I can and cannot be friends with. There is more to this story Whitney. It's not all cut and dry like you want to believe it is."

"You mean the pictures I found of the babies in your suitcase."

"You went through my things?"

"I unpacked for you in California. I saw the pictures and I saw you in them with some woman who was not your mom."

"Stop nosing through my shit please." My father and my mother had decided that they no longer wanted to answer questions that regarded those photos. So I had done my own research and I had basically figured out that I was adopted and it opened a shit storm of a door that I wanted to get through. It was significant to me to find out who in the fuck I was in this world? If not Asher Langford, then who?

"Why are you inviting him here?"

"Because, we actually became friends. He is not a bad person." I sat the table and watched her as she grabbed the food from the bags. "It's just one dinner and he has promised to be on his best behavior."

"Great," she mumbled. "Are you worried about those pictures?"

"My parents a dodging me Whit? I should be worried. I should be mad as hell. I just want to know the truth. I want to know everything so that for once in my life I will not feel like I am leading some false state of life."

"You never told me you felt like that."

She never asked. "Well, there you go."

"Why do you want to know?"

"It's about knowing who I am in this world Whit. What if he is my brother and I can help him? You know, like I don't know. I would hate to know that there was someone else kin to me and I couldn't help."

"You doubt your mom?"

"She won't let me have my birth certificate Whit."

"For good reason may be. Maybe she didn't want you to turn out like him. He is a monster. I can see it when I look in his eyes. He has no soul and he barely smiles. He is not like you."

"I'm not perfect Whitney. I have issues too."

"Murder?"

"I never said that he murdered anyone. Just because he is a psychopath doesn't mean that he is a danger."

"Keep fooling yourself like that. I just want you safe."

"Thanks." I stared at the picture. "I don't know who I am."

"You are Asher. You are smart and caring and you don't need to waste your time here with him."

"I hear you. But you will play nice while he is here."

"Who is the other baby?" She pointed to the second picture.

"I haven't figured it out. I want to go to England and do some investigating myself. I feel like Lucas doesn't want to reveal that his mother was a liar."

"There might be more to it." Whitney walked away from me and back to the food. "The girl he is with doesn't seem like his type."

"He doesn't have a type and I actually believe that she makes him a better person."

Whitney paused. "Are you still helping the Feds?"

"I'm gonna stop. He isn't a killer, he doesn't deserve to be harassed, he just needs to be helped. And I feel like I can help him."

"Have you told them that?"

"Not yet, I have a meeting tomorrow and I plan on going ahead and telling them then."

"Whatever you do, please be careful."

"I will babe."

"Good."

Lucas

This was the absolute longest minute of my life. I paced the living room and waited for her to open the bathroom door. She had peed in front of my two million times, but the one time it was important she had slammed the door in my damned face. I leaned against the door and finally she opened it. "About bloody time."

"I'm not." She wiped her face.

"Whoa... what's wrong?"

"I kind of wanted to be."

"Dear..." My heart beat slower as she sobbed into my chest. "Come on now, we have time. I swear I will knock you up one of these days."

I doubted how good I would be at fatherhood. I was better at ending life rather than creating it, but it was fine. I rubbed her back and she shook in my arms. I say once again women are strange, strange creatures.

"I'm sorry." Cypress sniffled. "I shouldn't be acting like this you know? We just dodged a major bullet."

"It's not called dodging a bullet if it is something that want Cypress? You came out of that bathroom like you were hurt. Is this something that you want?" I asked.

"Yes." I could barely make out what she said. Her head was buried in my chest and she sobbed. I hated to see her hurt.

"All you have to do is say it. But how can we be parents if you won't even allow me to buy your food or read the damn test with you. We should work on us then work on baby. I swear."

"I don't even think I can have kids."

"You can't say things like that Cy. Why would you even assume that you couldn't have kids? It takes people years to have a baby with perfect health." I nodded my head. She talked crazy when she was upset. I hadn't even realized that she would want something more than me. We fought like cats and dogs and on our best days we were still a little cranky.

"I can't, I can feel it."

"Stop worrying your head like that." I pulled her off of my chest and looked into her eyes. "You worry too much about things that should not be an issue. If you want a baby with me... I am more than happy to have a child with you. It's not something we have ever discussed. Tell me what you want Cypress. What future do you expect from us?"

"I see us being happy and not this forced on happy. I mean like really happy with a family."

"Okay, how many kids?"

"Three, all girls." She looked at me and smiled. "After your mom… and my mom and your Nan. Then we could move to England and raise them in the country. We could leave here and have some privacy."

"You want to move?"

"I want to be wherever will make you happiest."

I kissed her forehead. "It cannot all be about me. You want the kids to know your parents and your aunties… no matter how annoying they can be. When you and I officially become a we… it'll be decisions made together for the best interest of our family. Perhaps we needed a score to know that there is something more to us. There are some things that we should consider okay?"

"Have you ever wanted children?"

"Before you?" I paused. "There was no desire… but when you fall in love with someone… your hopes become mine and your fears become mine. I want whatever you want and I want you."

I watch her walk to her bedroom and begin to get dressed. "We have to be there in a little under an hour and he lives a far way out."

"Yeah, the GPS says it's about thirty minutes out. I can't even fathom to think why he moved somewhere that far out. Asher is a strange guy sometimes."

"He seems nice enough. Is that what you are wearing?" she pointed to my white shirt and black pants.

"Absolutely."

"Put on a different shirt at least."

"Fine, for you I will."

Asher's apartment was dimly lit and the table was set for six. He and Whitney sat at the head of the table. Cypress finally wore a smile on her face and Shia was locked into Mark. "So you and Mark are brothers?"

"Yes," Mark answered. "Adopted but still brothers." Mark knocked back his drink.

"Are you from around here?" Whitney asked Mark. "Sorry to pry, I just have never seen you two anywhere else besides on campus."

"I lived a few cities over and came here for college. Really my mum is a bit too attached to us both."

"Agreed." I added. "Tracy is a doll though." I hated small talk more than I hated editing my books. It was just as tedious only a tad bit less eventful. I twiddled my fork around my plate and watched as Whitney barely made eye contact with me. It was as if she was scared of me. It didn't bother me. I just hoped that it couldn't be picked up around the table.

"Nice, what about you Shia?" She dismissed my comment and turned to Shia. Shia had apparently drowned herself in some sort of floral perfume that had started a headache for me. So it was torture just bland food and conversation.

"I have lived here my whole life. Just happened to be lucky enough to run into Mark." Shia picked through her food and Mark twitched uncomfortably at her comment. He was not all for her as she was for him. She just wanted an instant husband, which was Mark and add water. "What about you two? I have seen Asher with you a few places on campus. You two look like you're in love."

"We grew up together in California and then met back up here. It is weird actually. And as far as love, I know I love him. He is the smartest man I've ever known in this world and he is all mine." She gripped his hand and Asher nodded his head. He seemed much like Mark to me.

"You two make a good couple." I said. "What is your major Whitney?"

"I'm a librarian." She answered. "I graduated two years ago. I just decided that I really liked the campus."

"Both smart," Cypress smiled. "It feels like this school year has flown by. I was thinking that we should get out of the country and celebrate it."

"Like where?" Mark sipped his tea.

"Maybe England, huh? We have a beach, Asher you can come and bring your lovely lady here and I can show you the town. Better yet, we could go to the coast or Ireland and I could really show you a good time."

"We're actually visiting Australia this year." Asher leaned forward on the table. "They have the clearest waters I've ever seen in my life and it is past due for me to see my father. But I think we could push it back and join you if we get the dates and everything."

"I'd like to meet your father." I paused. I wanted to drain his throat. Why the fuck was into my mother and father? There was a glint in my eye, perhaps a not so friendly one, but I had made myself clear about how I felt about his father.

Asher smirked at me. "I bet you would, perhaps one day he can truly show you the ropes around there."

Whitney shifted in her seat uncomfortably. "How long have you and Cypress been together?"

"Eight months almost," Cypress could not hide her smile.

"That's awesome, you know I had never really paid attention to you on the campus until Asher brought you up one day. You've been going here a while haven't you?" She looked at me and waited for my answer.

"I've been here a while. When my book came out it made it harder to actually be a full time student so I took online courses for the book tour. Then, once the book died down and the dogs were called off, I decided to finish up. I'm a fifth year senior."

"What about you Cypress?"

Cypress scarfed down her broccoli and sipped her water. "I am a fourth year senior but I transferred from out of state to get some change in my life. My ex-boyfriend was a douche."

"So are you happy with him?" Whitney questioned and gestured towards me.

Mark's foot hit me under the table and I stared at him. Why would she not be? This bitch had crossed a line that almost made me snap her neck at the table. I watched as Asher gripped her hand tentatively. I had started to like Asher somewhat. He seemed to be open to listen to me when no one else would.

"More than, we have plans for a great future together. We were actually planning it earlier." Cypress was a time bomb for tears. She almost cried on the way up about not being pregnant. So if she made her cry, she would meet my blade tonight.

"Well, that's interesting to hear."

"I mean what couple wouldn't be?"

"Right," Whitney grimaced.

"Yeah, they are one of the happiest couples I have ever seen." Shia vouched. "And I know that he will treat her right or I will kill him."

Try it bitch, I still was not sure if I liked Shia. I didn't like her for Mark and most of the time I didn't like her around Cypress. I faked the best tight lip smile that was possible. "We are a great couple. She accepts me for everything I am and I love for it. If you can't give yourself exclusively to a person that you love... then it's quite simple you don't love them. So this food is amazing. Purely American in every sense." Bland and full of bad taste. I tried to stop my eyes as they rolled but it was hopeless.

"They don't have stuffed bell peppers in Ireland?" Asher aimed at a conversation change.

"Sometimes... I mean it's not a custom in my family. My Nadine makes a killer bangers and mash; my mum was particularly good at soups."

Whitney cleared her throat. "Tell me about your family."

"Uhm they are English and Gaelic." I peered at Asher. "Get your hound." I mouthed at him.

"Any kin living?"

"I have a whole slew of family alive. Why the fuck is it your business? And why do you have this condescending attitude towards me?"

"What condescending attitude Lucas? I have been... nice. I just wanted to know more about you? You know, like what are your hobbies? What do you like to hunt? People? Animals? Deer? Birds?"

"That's enough." Asher grumbled. "Dessert is ready if you all are ready to eat."

"Does she know about the research you done on him?"

"What research?" Cypress asked.

My eyes grew wide and I stared at Asher. "Um, nothing darling. I have done an interview for Asher and she read it more than likely. He asked me some questions about my book and all that."

"He's a psychopath." Whitney spat.

I fought the urge to slice her open with my kitchen knife. It twiddled around in my fingers and "Well... nice. She is just bloody nice." I murmured under my breath.

"What does she mean psychopath?" Cypress touched my hand.

"Does he control you?" Whitney asked. "I mean does he threaten you? Tell me please."

"Asher, I think we are done here." I tossed the knife on the table before it ended up in her throat and red blood squirted on the perfect white cloth. Just the thought had my mind in a fucked up space. I wanted this bitch to die.

"No he doesn't. Why are you even talking to us like this? He isn't a killer." Cypress voice was defensive and it was sweet but not needed.

"Whitney that is enough, you are being rude!" Asher yelled. "And no he's not Cypress. Give us one moment please." He grabbed Whitney by the arm and led her away from the table.

"Why would she say that?" Cypress asked.

"I don't know. I don't know her and honestly and I don't care to. Mark do you see this shit?"

"I see." Mark nodded. "It's not him. It's her and we can just come back another time."

"Don't bother," Whitney said as she made her way to the door. "Keep your friends. I'm leaving."

"Great meal love!" I added through a clinched lip.

"Shut up!" Cypress pushed me.

"Apologies," I snipped out.

"Well, I'm sorry guys. I can't apologize enough for her behavior." Asher had not seemed shocked that she behaved that way. Like Mark he was not fazed by how she acted. He just wanted her gone. "Can I talk to you both?"

"Sure, ladies, we will be right back." Mark and I stood from the table and we followed him out of the dining area.

Asher leads us to his den. For an apartment the place was huge and I liked the fact he had a real bookshelf in his office/den area, it was a nice room. "She thinks you are crazy and surprisingly you behaved well. She just needs to learn how to bite her tongue, no matter how much she hates you."

"It's fine." I sat down on the floor. "Had a pregnancy scare today, I've been rattled a little. So your hound dog was not much of a scare for me."

"Cypress?" They both said.

"Yeah, yeah, but it was negative and she cried. And to be completely honest, I am completely fucking confused. What the hell does she want? She complains all day that I need to wear a condom and then we have a fucking scare and she's sad."

"Women," Asher laughed. "But in this you learned that she wants a child and you don't have to wear one."

"I'm halfway convinced to start." I laughed.

"You would be a horrible father." Mark added.

"Damn, that was a little harsh, Mark" Asher laughed.

"Never said that I was a nice guy." Mark sat down on the leather couch, "What'd you want?"

"Well, when I went home I did some digging and the child in this photo is me." He handed the picture to me, my mother looked down at the baby with that beautiful smile as her blonde hair blocked half of her face.

"How would you know that?" My eyes were glued on her face. I missed her more than I would ever be able to explain.

"My mom has the same photo... only her face is cropped out."

"So what're you trying to say?" I asked.

"I don't know." Asher tossed the picture on the dresser and looked at me. "I have asked my mom several times for the birth certificate and she will not let me see it. So I am going to go and request it myself."

"You think you're my brother?"

"I do."

"Why not just test it out?" Mark asked.

"With my blood?" I sneered. It was a dumb question. "My mum was not a liar. My mum was always honest with me."

"She could have kept things from you Lucas. You don't know. I am just saying that I think that we should just."

"I said no!" I bellowed. "I will not have you questioning my mother. If you think that she is your mother, you will find out another way. I have to leave. If I stay here I will probably snap your neck." I glared at Mark. "Why are you so apt for it?"

"You can't be so close minded." Mark pushed me back. "Just. This child..." He held up the second photo. "It looks a shit ton like the one in the frame in the living room of me."

"No," I said. Though he was right. I had never made the connection and I hadn't bothered to care about a connection.

I kept those pictures to have of my mother. I "And if you touch me again, I will end you."

"Fine be stubborn." Mark moved. "But the chances of you ruining me are slim Luke. Remember that."

"Yeah, whatever…" I opened the door and walked out of the now stuffy room. "Cypress, we are leaving. Shia till next time." I slid my coat on and waited on Cypress.

"I want to see the interview." Cypress looked at Asher.

"I don't have it." Asher said.

"Yeah, you do. Don't lie to me Asher. What is a psychopath if not a killer?"

"Someone who doesn't do well with emotions." Asher provided her with a false definition.

"Do you not believe me?" I questioned. "I told you everything."

"I believe you, but why would she just snap and leave her own boyfriends house if she didn't believe herself."

"I am leaving." I grabbed my keys. "And you are coming with me."

CHAPTER THIRTEEN

Cypress

Saturday mornings had a routine about them now. I washed clothes while Lucas folded and divided the stacks. All while we tried to act like cleaning was our favorite past time. But theses moment together were the ones that defined where we were in the relationship. They defined everything. My clothes were in pile in the living room and Lucas had misplaced every sock I've ever owned. And they were gold to me because of these ice cold floors in the halls, bathroom and kitchen of my apartment.

"The other night when you said that your mother used to make soups it rang a bell with me you know?"

"What bell love?" Lucas was entranced in some television show with guns and blood. It was really all he needed to have a good Saturday. He wore an old long sleeve shirt and a pair of pajama pants. His hair was still in a perfect mess and he had on his glasses. I rarely got to see them, but when I did I was appreciative.

"You love soups because your mother used to always make them."

"You're right. They remind me of her definitely. Luna could take any old veggies we laid around the house and turn them into a masterpiece. She'd bake this bread my dad loved. It was basically a sourdough, but in her broths, it came to life and danced with the flavors she had. There is really no one that can touch my mom in soups."

"That's so sweet."

Everything grew quiet and I watched him as he zoned out. His voice soft. "The day before she died, she made a Three Bean Soup. Declan had taught her how to cook it and she made it better is what he said. She was so weak that day. But she wanted that soup. I argued with her much like I do with you, I told her not to get out of the bed. I wanted her to let me cook it. She said no of course. I gathered everything there for her," He swallowed. "The beans, black beans, pinto and kidney bean and I got her some veggies. Onions, Peppers, tomatoes and she tossed it in a pot with her blend of seasons. Then she let it cook. Me and her sat out on that porch that day and made fun of almost everyone that walked by and it was heaven. I could smell her soup and hear her laughter and for a second it was as if she was not crippled. We ate and my father came home and he ate and talked with us the entire time I just sat there relishing in the moment. It was so weird. I knew that it was over. You know how things tend to go perfect before they go to hell. Declan tucked her in the bed that night and he read to her their favorite book. I slept in the wooden chair next to the window and that next morning she was gone. It was weird. But I was envious of her Cypress."

"Luke."

"She wouldn't have to put up with this shit hole of a world. I feared that I was truly the person that was suffering and then I lost my dad and shit got bloody difficult for me."

"I'm sorry that you lost her and I'm sorry that you lost him. I can tell that you truly loved them both and maybe…"

"Maybe what?"

"We can find a love like them and I hope that our children will have as much love for us as you do them."

"We will."

I tossed the last load of clothes into the dryer. I didn't want to make the day become bleak by reminiscing so I sat down in his lap and wrapped my arms around his neck. He was so warm and smelled amazing. "We're in the middle of a Zombie Apocalypse, and you have to choose one weapon... what would it be?" It was the best question that I could conjure to change the mood.

"How'd the zombie apocalypse start?" He asked.

"I don't know. Lucas do not make this more difficult than it has to be. You can choose one weapon baby!"

"I choose to hide and just wait. What if my weapon doesn't kill them?"

"You are an over thinker." I laughed. "Favorite fictional character?"

"I don't have one. Your turn?"

"Hmm... I would have to say I am quite fond of Aragon and his sexy beard."

"Aragon and his beard? I can't even grow a bloody beard... are you kidding me?" He paused. "Fine then... Beyoncé."

"I didn't say musician."

"She's my choice." He kissed my shoulder and knocked the clothes over onto the floor. My back touched the floor and he hovered over me. "I like this view."

"I like it too..."

The knock at the door startled me and Lucas. He looked down at me. "I thought Shia had to go out of town for the day?"

"I don't know. Just answer the door and I'll get the clothes off of the floor. I would hate for someone to see this place looking like a pig sty."

"Yes, master," He kissed my cheek and made his way over to the door.

"Hello Lucas, Special Agent McMillan has instructed us to take you and Ms. Tucker down to the station for questioning. Could you please gather your things and come with us?"

"Come with you? For what?"

"I was sure she just said questioning." I heard the male agent state.

"Don't get smart fucker." Lucas growled.

"You can make it easy or you can make it hard." The statement came across as a threat.

"We'll go." I said from behind Lucas. "If you could just give us a minute to get dressed it would be appreciated."

The smell of the roasted coffee filled the air and I wanted to vomit. It was too overwhelming. I sat patiently in the lobby filled with lawyers. I was unsure if I was in need of one. I had no idea why I was here, but I would rather it be over quickly. Lucas had already been taken back to a room.

"Cypress Tucker," McMillan held a fresh cup of coffee in his hand, it steamed from the mug. "Come this way with me. I swear I will have you in and out of here in a matter of an hour." His smile made me relax. I hoped that this time would be a good meet. The last few times he had been rude and even though they were all pertaining to Lucas I felt like it was unnecessary. "You have a good weekend?"

"Yes, I caught up on some work and I got some laundry done with Lucas. So it was a good week for me. What about you?"

"Well, I have been doing some work here at the station, mainly investigating my latest serial killer. I think you know him." McMillan smiled his tight lipped smile and sat down across from me at the table.

"You think I do?"

"I do." He opened the manila file. "This is a slim version of the shit that has my desk buried in daily. I really just wanted you to get a taste of who you are with before I went ahead and dived in." He sat his coffee mug down on the table and held up a sheet of paper. "Here is a list of people we believe that he has killed."

"Oh, please spare me this bullshit." The words came out harsher than I intended.

"You believe everything he says huh?" He tossed some photos across the table. "It looks like he was with some chick name Persephone Cook about a month ago... Do you know anything about her?"

I rolled my eyes and pushed the photos back across the table. Don't even look at the photos Cypress. "Why am I here? I honestly just wanted to get some laundry done and watch a few television shows this weekend. I really didn't have time to come down here, but I did."

"You are here because I really want you to know what happens when he leaves someone. I feel like your time with him is winding down." McMillan nodded his head. "How long have you been with him?"

"I have been with him for over seven months."

"Wow, that's a big deal for him. You might be a special kill for him." He took another folder from his desk and handed them to me. The face was his and Persephone's inches from another and his hand was slipped under the green cloth she called a dress. "She is his next one I think. He always has one sitting there waiting in reserve. Is that how he says hello?"

The breaths came out uneasy and unsettled. What the hell was happening? I wiped my face. McMillan stared at me as I wiped the tears. "Why are you showing me these pictures?"

"They are all his exes. I have tried to show you this several times. But you are so in love with this man. Does he beat you?" The special agent sat on the edge of the table. "Does he threaten you? You are protected here you know that." He placed the box of tissue in front of me.

"No," I stared at the women. Her long brown hair splayed everywhere and her face was in a pool of her own blood. "He didn't do this."

"He is a charismatic killer. I can actually give some credit for that. He waits and his charms. He fucks them and then they get fucked over."

"I know Lucas."

"You know what he wants you to know."

"I know that I am done talking to you." My tears fell on the table.

The white door swung open. "I could have sworn that you had been told to stay away from her?" Mark said. He handed the folder over to the agent. "Cy, come on love."

I grabbed my bags at this point I needed to be anywhere but here.

"She is being held for questioning."

"Alright as her lawyer I demand to know why?" Mark demanded.

"You can take her. She has seen everything she needs to see." He grabbed the photos. "Take these and give them to your boy toy. Let him know we know. Mark… you behave or we will be seeing you next."

"Oh fuck you." He spat. "Come on Cy."

The drive to the apartment could not come fast enough. Mark barely said a word. He sat there staring at the steering wheel. "I'm sorry that he brought you down there."

"What should I know about Lucas?"

"There's nothing you don't know."

"Right." I nodded my head. "I'm tired of guessing the lies. He said that he had not seen Persephone, but those pictures that he showed me…"

"Are to throw you off," he completed my sentence. "They had not time stamp. They had nothing to say that they were taken when they were messing around. They are working to make you think that there is some doubt in the relationship. Do you love Lucas?"

"Yes."

"Good, fuck what they say. Take some medicine for your headache and get some sleep. If you see Shia… tell her that I will be by once I head home and sort some shit out."

"Mark, why are you two so different?"

"We aren't blood brothers… which it doesn't matter, but it kind of makes a difference when it comes as. Lucas and I are alike but different in too many ways." He paused. "Do me a favor and don't tell him about this shit just yet. I know that he has that evaluation coming up and that is important. He is meeting with some campus freak about it."

"He went to meet Asher."

"Yeah, he calls him a freak... pot and kettle." He mumbled. "Alright." He unlocked the doors as a subtle get the fuck out of my car and smiled. "I will call you later and check up on you. I know the special agent has a special way of making you think that there is something there that isn't. Stupid Fucker."

"Great," I mumbled. "I will head up."

Asher

My head spun lightly. I shouldn't have been drinking this early this morning. I should have worked on the last few touches of some assignments and finding jobs. But here I was, three bottles into a case of beers and in lazy spell. I had made the couch, my permanent spot on the couch for the moment.

The dinner with Whitney had spun out of control and she hadn't really talked to me in weeks. But there was not much to talk about. Whitney and I differed in interests and she would have to get over this one. Lucas had become tolerable even to talk to me. I reached for my phone as it buzzed across the table. Mark, it flashed in white letters.

"Yes, master," I mumbled.

"Don't be an asshole." Mark laughed. "What are you doing?"

"I was on a bender this morning. Why?"

"Well, I sent Lucas to your house. Some shit has gone down between McMillan and him. He showed Cypress some pictures of Lucas with another girl. I'm knee deep in legal shit right now and the last thing I want to hear is his soap opera shit right now."

"Oh and I do?" I could feel the favor before it came off of his tongue. "What do you want me to do Mark?"

"Don't sound so down Asher. I really would like for you just to talk to him. The FBI has sent a request for a Levenson Test."

"That's not good." I chuckled. "It's a test that determines rather a person is a Psychopath. News Flash Lucas passes the test like he is the one who wrote it."

"Well could you test him and give me the results. And hopefully we can see what we are about to face. Is this test good enough to book him?"

"No, tons of people pass the test. In a group of ten at least one has psychopathic tendencies…" I paused. "Most people don't act on them. Lucas has a low tolerance for anything he doesn't like. It's like something irks him to the point of he must fuck it up."

"Can you test him for me?"

"How far out is he?"

"Ten minutes."

That was no surprise. "Yeah, Mark."

"Have you found anything out about the pictures?"

"Nothing yet, I'm planning on going to see my mom. I'm hoping that she can shed some much needed light on everything. Why?"

"I was wondering; could you keep me updated with everything on that subject. I know Lucas doesn't care, but I do. There's some strange shit happening there."

"I can do that."

"Thanks."

The line disconnected and contemplated even the act of getting up. I knew he had passed the test I had never had the opportunity to ask him some key questions though. Perhaps this would be a success filled day.

A nervous knock on the door occurred a few minutes later. I opened it and walked to the couch. "What's up Lucas?"

"A ton of shit." He mumbled and he looked around at the dark apartment. "Bloody hell, are you going to rape me. Open the blinds."

"Chill out." I laughed. "I heard about the Feds and you. Mark said that you have to take the Levenson test."

"I do." Lucas shrugged out of his jacket and opened the blinds and sent a ray of light throughout the whole apartment. His hands went through his head. "They still had Cypress once I left. I have no idea what they are telling her."

"So you're worried that she might find out the truth?"

"I don't need a counselor or fucking therapy." He spat.

"Then why the hell are you here Lucas?"

"I haven't figured out yet."

"We can start with the test."

"I'd rather not."

"Then what can I do for you?"

"Are we not friends?"

"I guess." I mumbled. "Why do you kill?"

"Nice way to break the ice." He chuckled.

"Or when did you first want to kill?"

"I can answer that for you, the price being one beer?"

"Help yourself?" I opened the cooler next to the couch and slid it over to him.

"You have an actual cooler?"

"I'm having relationship problems."

He shook as he laughed at me. "Well, that girl of yours is a first class bitch. I mean she had no problem flipping me over to the entire table."

"Yeah, she is very head strong and most of the time she is very annoying."

"Alright, here is your answer." Lucas paused. "I grew up in Ireland and England. But my time in Ireland was tense sometimes. We only went there when Luna had spells. ALS, Lou Gehrig's Disease was a bitch to her. And we needed to be around people at all times and more importantly the hospital there was better."

"I didn't know that was what she had," I paused. "I'm sorry to hear that."

"Yeah, I know it's not the best way to die, but at least we knew what was wrong with her. So it made it easier to deal with. But anyway, there was this pussy named Seymour. He lived next door to us with this girl named Holly. Holly loved that bloody past. And Seymour was a terror. He would purposely knock over pottery and my mum's vases. That bloody pussy used to destroy everything in our yard and my mum and pa used to brush it off. I could tell it annoyed her, but she knew that Holly loved that pussy. So one day we sat on the porch of the house and Seymour knocked over her favorite vase. It was one that we had made together when I was a wee lad. And that hurt her feeling more than anything. She cried as still as the pot shattered on the wooden porch. My pa tried to console her in the best way that he knew how, he even tried to glue it back together." Lucas paused and nodded his head. "But there was no saving it and for the first time this urge I had held inside since I was born came out. I had to kill him. I had to kill him because he needed to die. Some people and animals aren't meant to live a long life Asher."

"What'd you do to him?"

"I drained him with my favorite knife. My father had given it to me when I was young. He said it was for hunting and I never knew what he meant until I was older. I hunted down Seymour and drained him like cattle and burnt his body in the woods."

"How'd you feel?" It felt cold in the room as a chill rushed over me.

"Freeing…" He whispered. "Then it became an even worse urge than before and it felt like someone constantly scratched at my eyes to be free again."

"Lucas, that started everything for you, you know that?"

"I know. I could tell after that moment that I was no longer that little boy that I had once been. I can never be that innocent again."

"Do you scare yourself? I mean you feel nothing."

"Why do you care?" He asked.

"Because there is this possibility that you are my younger brother and family cares for each other no matter how fucked up they might be."

"Good answer," He chugged down the beer.

"And because Lucas," I paused. "There has to be someone to care for you so you might can stop. There has to be someone to help you enough to stop."

"Thank you."

"You're welcome." It was unexpected, his sincere notion of gratefulness. I allowed the silence to feel the room for a few moments and then opened another beer. "The questions that they will ask you, could be vast. Some include, did you bed wet, have you ever killed an animal and how often did you start fires? These questions are called the Triad. If all three are yes, it falls in the theory that every serial killer suffered from these as a child."

"I literally have done all three." He was amused. "One huge fuck up after another."

"Well, whatever you would normally do… do the opposite for the test. They can use it as base work in their case." I answered and shook my head. "If you can do that then you will be fine."

"I can do that."

"Tell me more about how you feel about Cypress, it kind of amazes me that you feel nothing and then all of a sudden you…"

"I honestly love her endlessly and I have been hopeless ever since I met her. I stand no chance against my love for her. "She infuriates me. She understands me, even though she has no clue what I am."

"What are you?"

"I'm an anomaly..." He stated simply. "Do you think she would love me if I was to reveal everything I am? If I was exposed?"

"I don't know her well enough to know."

"Good answer," Lucas smiled as he stood and his long strides lead him to the door. "One day, I unveil everything I am to her and if she stays... I'll quit."

"You feel that strongly for her?"

"I feel everything for her."

Lucas

Good talk. Good walk. I closed the door to Asher's apartment and headed towards my car not surprised to see the two suits leaned up against them. "Can I help you?"

"Just wanted to have a word." McMillan appeared beside me like a magician. He wore his goofy smile and his hands folded neatly over the extremely pressed suit. "There might be some trouble in paradise. I showed her Persephone..."

I could feel my face drain. "You what?"

"I showed her the surveillance from Persephone. Who really must have feared you because she withdrew from all of her classes and fell off the face of the Earth. It took weeks to find her and even when we did she refused to speak to us. What did you say to her you sick fuck?"

"I said nothing." My fingers pushed through my hair. "What do you want from me man? You have jack shit tying me to any of the murders you're pursuing and yet here you are following me around the bloody campus and town. I can't shit without one of your agents handing me the toilet paper. I feel harassed honestly."

"I just missed you Luke." He chuckled and bit into his candy bar. McMillan perched up against my car as if it was his.

"Get off of my fucking car," I stammered. This fucking prick was not about to stop.

"Are you mad? Are we on your list now? You going to drain the blood from our bodies like you done Phillip?"

Actually he was at the extreme top of the list. It had been more than 3 months since I had felt blood flow under my knife and this prick was making it harder and harder to hide it.

"No, sir, and I didn't do anything. I just want to go home to my girlfriend."

"You should have seen those tears." McMillan paused. "When I showed her your latest work..."

"Tears?"

"Yes, I wanted her to see how close you and Persephone could get." McMillan shrugged his shoulders. "The pictures can be interpreted in any way. I mean her face looks like you are doing everything just right." McMillan slid the profane picture across the table. My hand pushed up her skirt and her head thrown back in ecstasy. "She really broke down once she seen that one."

"Fuck you," I snapped. "Do you know who you are dealing with, you filthy piece of shit??"

"Who am I dealing with Lucas? Shall I take you down to the station for a full confession?"

"You'll see soon enough?"

"Was that a threat?"

"Oh no, I would never threaten you McMillan, it was just a sincere promise," I unlocked the door to my jeep. Escape now or enjoy quality time in isolation on Death Row.

"I'll document that for you just in case your sincere promise serves as evidence in the future. Is it normal in England to be a killer? I'd love to see you at work, though you seem messy a little bit. Should I join you sometimes make sure there are no more messes?"

"Oh please do."

"Hey Luke!" Asher's voice rang across the parking lot. "You forgot your phone." He paced quickly across the parking lot. "Drive away." He whispered with a tense smile and a headshake.

"I am. Hopefully with one of them under my tires."

"Leave," He pushed the cell phone in my hand and backed away. "Don't forget next week!"

My hands shook the entire way home. I dialed her number and there was no answer. Ten times of repetitive calling and she had not answered. Her car was in the parking lot, parked horrendously crooked and her living room light was on.

I couldn't see straight from the hate that radiated from me. I wanted to see that man dead. His blood flowing under my blade until every ounce of the little soul, he actually had flowed uninterrupted into a pool around him.

"What are you doing here?"

The little flaws made her the perfect woman. My shirt hung from her shoulders and her shorts peeked at the nape of her ass. "I called you love."

"I didn't answer." She placed her hand in the door jam. "You fucked her Lucas. And you made me a sincere promise that you would never do that to me.:

"What?"

"Persephone," Cypress had not control over the tears that fell from her eyes. She sobbed, and shook her head at me as I stepped closer to her.

"Don't cry, I was with her for a moment."

"A moment? Why was your hand up her skirt?"

"Oh come on," I mumbled frustrated. "I told her to leave."

"Did you? Was it before or after she came from your fingers. You fucking disgust me!" She roared.

"I..."

"Make up a lie," she wiped her face. "I fucking trusted you Lucas."

"I swear it was nothing."

"What was nothing?" Her screech filled the apartment complex.

"I told her to leave." I stepped towards her and she jerked away violently.

"Did you fuck her?"

"I told her to leave."

"Before or after you fucked her?"

"After," I whispered.

"After," I could hear her heart break. "Stay the fuck away from me." The wind from the door hit my face as she disappeared behind it.

My fists hit her door. "Baby! Please open up."

"Go away!" She yelped.

"Please," My hands fell helplessly to my side. "Fuck, I'm so sorry. I swear. I meant nothing by it. I meant nothing. I couldn't bloody think..."

The door swung open and I felt clothes being tossed as they fell to the ground. "Don't bring your ass back here!"

I pushed pass the mass of clothes I had bought her mixed in with shirts I'd left here. "Sit down."

"No, no… I don't care what the detective said about you killing your exes I am not the one! I am tired of being treated like this! What did I ever do to you Luke? I loved you like no one had ever loved you. I gave you every inch of me."

"I'm still here. I fucked up I know."

"Yeah, get out."

"Let me talk." I closed the door.

"What is there to say? You didn't mean to fuck her?"

"It was never intended to get to you…"

"Wow," She stood dumbfounded. "You are a piece of work."

"I don't mean to be."

"You are. Get the fuck out." Her small hands hit my shoulders and I nodded my head.

"Stop."

"No!" Her fists collided with my chest and she started to push more forcefully. I fell onto the wall and her hand fist hit my mouth. "Get the fuck out!" Her hand was covered in my blood. "I hate you."

"You hate what I did." I felt the salty blood fall to my lip. "I am so sorry." I whispered.

"I can't forgive you."

"Then don't." My lips crushed against hers and there was no resistance as she kissed me back. I could taste my blood in with her tears as they rushed from her eyes. "Please don't leave me…"

"I can't stay with you." She wept. "I can't."

"Please," I pleaded as the desperation in my voice overcame me. "I can't…"

She pushed me back, wiping her face with my shirt and sliding it off of her perfect body. "Get out."

Asher

The pounding on my door had continued for the past thirty minutes. I was sure it was a nightmare or it could have been the alcohol. I wanted it to be the alcohol. What could Lucas want? Surely not to kill me after making this big of a scene. I opened the door and there he stood and he looked destroyed. "What is it Lucas? It's late as shit."

"I fucked up."

"What did you do?" My thoughts wandered to what 5-10 years in a white cement walled room. I was not good with jumpsuits. Maybe they would be lenient and give me the shirt and pants. "What did you do?"

"I cheated."

"On a test, what are you talking about Luke?"

"On Cypress." He pushed his way passed me and into my apartment. "I cheated."

"We must be friends now. You're banging down my door because of relationship problems?"

"I guess I don't know." He looked at me, his stare was cold but amusement danced around them. I feared whatever kind of amusement he had. "I searched for Mark he was gone. She dumped me."

"With whom?"

"What?" He looked genuinely confused as he paced the entrance to my apartment.

"Who did you cheat on her with Lucas?"

"Persephone," he grimaced.

"You get checked?"

"Asshat," he spat. "How do normal people handle this shit? Should I give her space or should I go and fucking kill that agent and Persephone? I am not trying to be rash but I swear the second one seems the most logical."

"How does it seem logical?" I shook my head and tried to stifle my laugh. "Normal people don't handle it with murder," I answered. "They usually do what you're doing. They try to confide in someone to tell them the right way to handle their situation. You actually done good by coming here." Surprisingly there was not a trail of dead bodies sprawled across Colorado Springs.

"Well, I haven't killed anyone. I won't. I fucking can't, they won't stop bloody following me. I mean they're following me everywhere. I can't piss without seeing their bloody feet in the next stall."

"Well, you brought it upon yourself Luke. You're their prime suspect. I'm just happy you haven't killed anyone. I know we drank earlier, but do you want one?" I had no idea why alcohol had become my newest friend but I seemed to drink more and more here of late.

"Put a damn shirt on will you?" Lucas said from out of nowhere.

"I thought it was my girlfriend at the door. And it is late man."

"That librarian chick?"

"Yes," I smirked. "The librarian chick hates you."

"Well, tell her to join the majority of the world. I don't know what the fuck I do to people to make them hate me."

"You don't care for one." I made my way to my bedroom and grabbed my shirt from the bed then turned to head back to the kitchen and grabbed two chilled beers. "Tell me how it feels."

"It doesn't." He said blankly. "I just don't care."

"That's not normal."

"Well, pardon me," He popped the top open. "I don't care. I just want to be alone most of the time. The only person I have tried to care about is Cypress and sometimes I don't care for her either. I mean she can be the most irksome person to deal with, like for example she brushes her teeth in front of the mirror."

"That's normal Luke."

"Why do you have to stare at yourself while cleaning your teeth? How is that normal?"

"I don't care to argue it with you but that's normal Luke. You have to learn to care what people say Luke."

"Teach me oh wise one."

"That's a lesson for another day." I paused. "You had me on your list didn't you?" I was curious how close to death I had actually come. "I mean you can tell me. I just want to know."

"I was about to slice you from ear to ear the moment you stuck your nasty hand up her skirt."

"I'm grateful you didn't."

"Lucky you," He knocked the drink back and chuckled. "I wanted you dead, so bad I had fucking migraines about it. I researched everything about you and had planned to burn you alive after I watched the blood spill onto your nice hardwood floors here."

"Dude," I stopped him with my hands up. "Please spare me the details of my impending death."

"I was destined to send you to ashes Asher." He laughed in amusement. "I'm happy I didn't though, you do have good taste in beer."

"Glad my beer choice saved my life." I mumbled.

"Oh, lighten up. I just wanted you dead. We all have to die some time, your death was just planned"

"Yeah, no big deal." I nodded my head. "As friends, let's promise to not ever bring up that one time you planned to kill me."

"I can do that for now." Lucas was quiet and his eyes looked around the room. He seemed so relaxed contrary to earlier in the day.

"You're like a lion you know that?"

"Explain," he leaned back on the couch and one of his arms draped over the back of the couch. "I mean I have never seen myself in action."

"You're graceful... you smile too often and no lie, it's creepy. You lurk and lurk until the person is vulnerable and then you pounce on them leaving no way out and they're terrified. You like to taunt them and then you slice."

"I love the feeling of slicing someone open."

"I've seen the joyous face Luke. I can tell."

"It's like it opens up a happiness that only some things can bring out. The first slice means everything in a kill."

"Why?"

"Are you studying me Asher?"

"Not at the moment." I lied. I wanted to know every detail as to why he acted the way he did. It amazed me that he talked about a kill like I talked about soccer. He truly enjoyed it. Lucas was a psychopath and he embraced it without any trepidation.

"You are too." He finished his beer.

"Well, why is it important?"

"It doesn't matter. They die and I feel better."

"You do know that when you're caught which statistically speaking it will happen... everything around you will fall."

"I won't ever get caught." He sounded one hundred percent sure of himself as he said it. He sat the beer bottle on the table. "I am never careless. I am never uncertain and even when I challenge myself to pursue outside of my normal encounters... I never do too much. I have just ventured enough to know that I can."

"I hope not. I prefer a Serta rather than a spring filled cot."

"Yeah, I prefer a tanning bed to the electric chair." Lucas burst into laughter and shook his head. "I'll never give anyone the satisfaction anyhow."

"What do you mean?"

"I will slice myself open before I allow someone to take away my final kill."

"Lucas," I paused.

"I would kill myself Einstein."

"Wow," I looked at him. "How would you know when to do it?"

"How would I not?"

CHAPTER FOURTEEN

Lucas

I'd heard of the world crumbling. My mum used it to describe Declan. He was her world and when he left her world crumbled. Her world mourned. My mind was there and it could only think about how to heal. The scar of Cypress. I would not kill her. That would destroy me more than heal me. But I could go after Persephone. I could watch her bleed out as I pushed the blade into her heart. I could mute her and tie her down to a bed make sure I saw every moment she suffered. I slapped my face and stared back at the television. I hadn't watched it since the demise of the relationship that brought me sanity.

"Are you okay?" Tracey said from the kitchen.

"I'm fine." I murmured. Visits home were normally few and far between but ever since she'd left me, I'd made it a point to be around people so the urge to kill would simmer. McMillan watched me like a hawk. So home was a safe haven even if I had to listen to Tracy gawk over her cooking shows and lavish tree houses.

"How is she?"

"Mum," I said. "Could we just watch this man slice and dice veggies?"

Slice, my heart pumped at the thought. "Sure," she handed me a glass of tea. "I don't know how you drink this sock water." She nodded her head as she handed me the warm cup of tea.

"I don't know either, my mum used to drink so it became a habit." I gulped the tea down.

"Your father was always into tea as well. He said it made him feel at home."

She hated my father. "Oh god not another tale of Declan, spare me."

"You and him are too much alike."

"I said you can spare me details. I don't want to hear it."

"What did you do?"

"I slept with another girl."

"Cypress is perfect for you."

"Tell me more mum." My eyes cut over to her as I tried to bite back my sarcasm. "Can we sit in silence? Is that too much to ask?"

"You can sit in silence at home, when you come here I want you to talk."

"Perhaps I will head home. These shows are nauseating."

"I think you should calm down. You should write her a letter, women love letters."

"Oh God Save the Queen woman," I took my keys from the sofa. "I'm leaving. Tell Mark I'm headed back to the Summit and tell Lydia that I will help her with her English paper another day."

"Sit down," Tracey whined with her hands on her hips. She rarely had them but I could tell this was about to be a mothering heart to heart that I would rather not sit through. She watched as I slouched back down on the couch. "You're stubborn like him too." She rolled her eyes.

"I don't want her to be with me if she hates me, Tracy."

"She doesn't. She's just hurt and it's no one's fault but yours. So you have to fix it and you should do it sooner rather than later."

"Please, tell me something I don't know."

Lydie made her entrance into the room crunching loudly on her cereal. "Perhaps you shouldn't have cheated on her and you wouldn't have to be over sulking around drinking tea. You could be at home with her being the normal great happy couple that you were."

"Perhaps you should shove off." I clenched my eyes shut and every time I closed my eyes I seen red, mainly towards Persephone. No, I shouldn't have fucked her. I should have just killed the bitch. I stretched and tried to hide my irritation. "Mum, I'm leaving."

"You know I'm happy you are wallowing in self-pity Lucas. You shouldn't have cheated on her." Lydie opened her water and laughed.

"I'm not talking about this."

"Yeah, exactly what all men do." It was apparent that she was in favor of Cypress over me at the moment.

"Lydie," I paused. "Leave it be."

"Leave him alone Lydia." Tracy warned.

"Well you know mom, Mark does this kind of shit. You were always the one big brother that gave me some hope. I love my boyfriend but if you can cheat I don't know if can even be hopeful anymore. You were supposed to be the one that treated her right."

"Watch your mouth," Tracy interjected.

"It was an accident Lydie! Do you think I don't love her? Do you think that every damn night I don't regret it? So yeah, bash me. I fucked up. I know this. So let me torture myself and you keep your thoughts to yourself."

"Whatever," she rolled her eyes. "She is still coming to my graduation and you will be nice. Do you understand? As a matter of fact, just stay away from her."

"Goodbye," I pecked Tracey's cheek and walked towards the door. "One more bloody moment in here and you'll witness War World III."

I hadn't thought about Luther in a few months and he was now a successful product of the Colorado Corrections Department. Rehabilitated and successful merged with normal society, it was a major feat. I wanted to personally reward him. But Mark had forbidden it. They watched my every move like a hawk. But if I could slip away from them unnoticed I could take a road trip to see my dear friend Luther and have some fun. Some much needed distraction.

The two agents parked in the front of building had nodded off. I had brought them a good cup of coffee earlier. I left the lights of my loft on and walked down the fire escape silently and took Mark's mini coop. He loved the car, now I did too. Quiet, small and black it was perfect for the kill. My chest tightened as the car drove out to the interstate, he'd move three hours out and the was just perfect. I could say I was going to visit Cy. I should really go. I clenched the steering wheel. I needed to kill. Luther was a little more important.

His lights were out. I parked a few blocks away and started my prowl. Luther was a piece of shit. He deserved it. I picked the lock and made my way in his home. It smelled of cigarettes and old beer. His clothes lay scattered all over the house.

"Who the fuck are you!" He yelled.

"Shhhh..." I smiled. Luther had startled me but it was okay. I wanted to talk to him. "It's time Luther."

"Look kid, I have to work early in the morning. I just want to get some sleep. I'm not gonna call the cops. I'd much rather they not get involved."

"Shut the fuck up." I snapped. "Sit down. I want to talk."

"Kid, don't get your British ass whooped."

"Be nice Luther," I laughed. "Sit down, please?"

Luther lunged towards me. I dodged him quickly leaning to the side and the skinny frail man landed hard on the tile floors. I took advantage of the situation. I secured his hands in a belt then his feet I tied to heavy oak table in the kitchen.

"What do you want? I don't have anything. I just got out the pen."

"I don't need anything. I can't control myself and you have been on my list of kills for years. How could you rape that little girl?" I stared at him as he lay spread out on the floor of his own home like a punished dog.

"I was found innocent."

"Oh fuck off, you raped her. Admit it, why lie when you are about to die?"

"I didn't." He cried. He pulled at the restraints and nodded his head. "I swear I went to jail for drugs." his tears began to overflow.

"Oh well, lying is not going to make it easy on you." I touched the hilt of the blade in my pocket and showed him. "This is my father's." I pushed harder on his throat. "He was a bastard. I feel like he made me like this."

"Crazy?"

"Different!" I yelled. "I prefer different Luther. Of course I'm not as fucked up as you are, I would never harm a child. I feel sorry for them. They have to grow up in world with people like you. I have a sense of morals... well kind of... I do like to see blood drain from a body. But I have to ask you something. How do you get someone to forgive you? I mean you have tons of people that have forgiven you. The state for instance?"

"Kid," He cried. "I've changed."

"I don't care. Answer my fucking question! I have to know. I don't know how to feel remorseful. I'm trying, honestly. My girlfriend," I paused. "My ex now... well I cheated on her. I only done it to make a point to a girl I used to shag. She needed to leave me alone."

"That makes no sense."

"I know that now Luther. It took her hating me to figure it out. Perhaps I should have just killed her too. But the damned feds are following me like a Map. I had to put pills in their coffee just to get to you. And I should really be going. They are probably prowling the city for me."

"Turn yourself in kid."

"Stop calling me that!" I nodded my head at him.

"Why are you here? Go hunting. Go do something not illegal kid. I won't even turn you in."

"I'm an addict dumb ass. Killing an animal doesn't do shit for me." My hands lingered in my hair. "I crave this shit. And it's worse now that she has decided that I am no good. I wanted everything to go right. I bought her a ring you know. I was about to marry her. And I fucked Persephone."

"Just kill me."

"Pardon me?"

"I don't want to hear your High School Musical Crisis. Just kill me."

"No! I want you to listen. I can't talk to anyone else. So you're gonna listen." I crouched down beside him. "You smell."

My knife cut into his leg slowly and the blood seeped to the floor. His scream filled the room and I crammed a towel from table in his mouth. "How do you get people to be remorseful for you?"

His tears stopped. Poor Luther could feel the end as it neared.

"Well, I hate that you are not going to give me any advice before you die." The terror in his eyes made me smile. His dark brown eyes closed and slid the blade across his neck. I sliced into him slowly and the blood seeped through towel. I exhaled slowly and pressed deeper into his neck feeling everything separate beneath my blade. His stifled words and I sat next to him. "Luther, thank you."

I sat there mesmerized by the pool of red that grew more and more around him. I dipped my finger in the warmth of it and made a little message for Special Agent McMillan. For my friend, McMillan. I doused my gloves with bleach in the sink. Then doused my knife as well removing any trace evidence that could led back to me. Finally, there was some peace.

Cypress

There had come a point in this process that I had decided that to leave him alone would be the best resolution. But my loneliness fought tooth and nail about it constantly. He slept with Persephone and she was someone that I could not deal with him sleeping with. She was a tramp and better yet she was a whore. He chose her over me.

"I suggest you just call him." Shia lay on the end of my bed. "He seemed genuinely sorry when I saw him."

Shia had been a comfort and good friend here lately. She was over constantly when she was not at the beck and call of Mark. She loved him and he was so tied up in law school that she knew for some reason that he was always honest.

"Yeah, he is sorry." I typed the final words of my assignment and nodded my head. "I can't, I know I love him. I will find someone else."

"Like who? You are so picky? A star has to even meet your criteria. Just yesterday you said you wouldn't date Brad Pitt because he has blonde hair."

"I don't date blondes."

"Not that the scenario is real but he is fucking Brad Pitt. He could have orange eyebrows and I would still fuck the shit out of him." Shia had her feet propped up on the loveseat. She winked. "I know you miss sex with him."

"I miss everything about him Shia. I miss the way his messy ass hair falls in his face. I miss the way he smiled whenever he was getting ready to pick me up and throw me up over his shoulder. I miss the way he stared at any guy who looked like they were interested. He hated that more than anything. He always wanted it to be about us."

"You should take him back."

"Look, I am not like you." My words came out harsh but it was true. "He fucked up and yes it has been a whole month. I have cried myself to sleep. I have skipped school and I'm losing myself in him. And he told me himself that he never wanted me to lose sight of who I am for him."

"He made you the new person that you are. You aren't losing yourself in him he is just an important piece of you. So maybe you should take a page out of my book and get the hell over it."

"He slept with that bitch."

"Have you talked to Persephone?"

"Why would I talk to that slut?"

"Because she slept with your boyfriend, you have the right to confront her. You should ask her what happened? You should ask for details and sort out every issue to see why he done it."

"I'm not." I exhaled. "I have bigger fish to fry."

"Well then you sit here and be miserable."

"I will." I snapped. "And lock the door on your way out."

"I will." She rolled her eyes. "See you tomorrow."

Shia left finally and I scrolled through my contacts. I had been here nine months and the only friend that I had besides Shia was Lucas. I should get out more. I dialed Lydia's number fort the tenth time today and waited on her to answer.

"Why are you still up?" She moaned.

"Because I'm miserable here. You think your mom would let you stay this weekend with me."

"I can't. I promised Trey that I would go out with him this weekend. He is all about some me."

"Were you sleep?"

"I was completely knocked out." She chuckled. "He misses you as much you miss him."

I felt my chest tighten. "I can't talk about him right now. But maybe one day we could get lunch?"

"Yes we should! And it will be on me!"

"I'll think on it. Well good night Lydia." I ended the call.

This grieving process was about to drive me up a wall. I was constantly lonely. I couldn't get that stupid crooked smile of Lucas' out of my head and every time I tried to insure myself that it was getting easy I saw something that reminded me of him and the cycle started all over again. I don't know if it was hard for him. But burying everything kept me strong. I clicked his name. It rang twice, my heart beat out of chest.

There was silence and then there was a sigh. "I'm sorry Cypress."

"I know." my voice choked and the tears were about to come before I could form any words. "I know that you are. Where are you?"

"Almost to my loft? Would you like to meet at The Summit? We can talk, clothes on and minds open."

"It'll take me about an hour to get presentable."

"I'll take you however you come." He whispered.

"Kay," I waited for him to speak again.

"I love you."

"I'll see you in a minute."

"Alright love."

The drive over to his place allowed me time to think. I had formulated every thought and for once I felt like I could face him and the get everything out. I pulled into the back entrance and he stood there waiting on me. His hair was pulled into a messy bun on his head.

"You look beautiful."

"Thanks." The pink pants and his sweat shirt were the only clothes that I had washed in the past three weeks. "Are they still following you?"

"They are always here." Lucas threw his hand up in amusement. "I'm thinking of moving away from here soon."

"Where?"

"I was thinking England." He paused.

"Oh," My heart broke at the answer.

"Come on inside, I know your cold. You can put on some of my sweats if you would like."

"No, I want to talk out here. I can't function without you." I spat. "And I'm pissed at you. So, I can't sleep. I can't think and I didn't do anything wrong, it's not supposed to be like this."

"I..."

"And I want you back. But every time I think of you, I see that bitch."

"Cypress," He paused. "I will never hurt you again. I can't make any other promise but that one."

"I don't know if I can forgive you. I don't know if I can even stand to look at your face but I am scared and terrified that if I don't I will fall apart."

"I know," He grimaced. "Can we please just go inside?"

"I need this time apart from you. And I need to know that you will give me time to be alone. No more appearing at my house or shit like that. Just let me be alone."

"I'll do it for you."

"Good, I'll call you tomorrow and we can try talking it out."

"See the love birds have found their way back to each other." McMillan smiled.

"Just remember what I said Lucas."

"Do you need me to drive you?" He seemed unlike himself, timid.

"No, thank you though."

"Okay, just let me know when you are at the apartment okay."

"Yes, give the station a buzz." McMillan stared at Lucas. "I have some questions for you.

Lucas

The kill had been days ago and for some reason I still felt light as a feather. The only bad news was that Luther had been found. The small white room had grown on me. I had been at the station so much these past few months I had grown fond of the bright white room that echoed every time a word was spoke. It was even better that no matter how much McMillan hated me he didn't have shit on me. I tapped the table lightly as the door opened. "McMillan, how was your weekend?"

"Let's talk about yours?"

"Spent it with my friend Asher for the most part. Then I caught up on the last few assignments before midterms. But you know that don't you. The way those vultures sit outside my apartment and school day and night. I'm sure you know everything."

"Look at this." he pushed over a picture of Luther in his glorious death. I wanted to smile but I refrained and nodded my head. "What do you think?"

My first opinion was beautiful inscription and nice handwork but that would land me in padded cell sooner that I had intended. "You pissed someone off."

"Did I piss you off Lucas? Who else am I pursuing?"

"I don't get paid to know your case load McMillan. But I do know that you have never pissed me off sir. We have a great relationship." I chuckled. "It's sad. How'd his family take the news?" Just my point they couldn't. He murdered them in cold blood.

"You think you're funny?"

"I think you are funny sir. I'd like to see my lawyer if you are implementing me on this gruesome murder."

"You played in his fucking blood!" McMillan yelled as his hand gripped a fistful of my shirt. "You're so fucking sick."

"I want a lawyer." I snatched my shirt from him and looked up at him. "Did you not fucking hear me?"

"Just admit it, you are one sick fuck you know that?"

"Oh did you not hear me? You must be deaf and dumb, not surprising but I'll say it again. I want my motherfucking lawyer."

"You think you are untouchable?"

"Are you refusing counsel?" I bantered.

"You're not under arrest."

"I still want my fucking lawyer."

"What did your girlfriend tell you?"

"Are you deaf?" I folded my arms. "I'll just wait."

McMillan's face grew red. "Just give me an alibi for where you were Last Thursday?"

"Ask your surveillance. I was there at home. Better yet ask Mark or Asher. You know him yeah?"

"You threaten to kill him too?"

"Not really my type there sir."

"Get Copeland and Marsh in here, I need to see their surveillance notes." McMillan said to the tall man who hadn't said a word during the whole interrogation.

"I will."

"How do you do it?"

"Do what?"

"Not leave any trace evidence?"

"I don't even know what that is." I lied.

"Keep playing dumb. I like it, it's going to make convicting your sorry ass so much sweeter."

"I honestly would like to see what evidence you have against me?"

"Go home, get close to that girl of yours while you can."

"I will. Are you going to give me a lift home or do I have to wait for someone to come and get me?" I smiled and something inside had awoken. It was a game and he had no idea what the rules were. And I was already several moves ahead.

"When I catch you... you are gonna fry. I hope you like heat."

"I actually do." I winked. "I live for it."

"Good," McMillan came closer to me and his face was inches from mine. "When I figure out your motive..." He pushed me into the wall hard and his cohort pulled him up with one quick move.

"I'm sorry. I don't care about your idle threats."

"You're just like your father."

"Pardon me," I clenched my teeth.

"I hope you are better than him... Because I know how his life ended."

"What did you say?" The only nerve he could hit he trampled on. I lunged at him in full force only to be tossed back in the chair by the fucking giant in the corner. "My father is none of your concern. Do you understand?"

"Oh touched a sensitive subject?" He smiled.

This fucker wanted to die. I clenched my fist. "I'd like to get you alone one day."

"Really..."

"Yes."

"Watch my blood drain and play in it?"

I wished to watch it drain slowly as his eyes begged for mercy. "Just to chat." I inhaled deeply. "Is my lawyer here?"

Mark opened the door. "What's going on here?"

"You really should change lawyers."

"Fuck you." Mark pulled at my arm. "What has been going on here?"

"Nothing." I spat. "Let's go."

Asher

Perhaps the ending to my thesis was not as bad as my father had described. I had skipped some main theories but the professor raved about it. I stared at the mountain of paper on the desk. All this damned hard work didn't mean shit if the goal was not achieved.

"Asher!"

I turned and there he stood again. Lucas sat down in the chair next to my desk and smiled at me. "This fed... has he talked to you?"

"Yeah, he knows about my research. But it's nothing." I shrugged.

"Nothing Asher? It's my life. He is toying with my life. Make it stop."

"I can't intimidate a fed. I mean what do you want me to do?"

"Give me your research." Mark said from my other side. For Lucas to be serial killer he was the scary one. He was calm and refined which seemed more dangerous than irate and angry. Mark done what Lucas could not, he controlled it. "Now."

"Here, look there is nothing there can help their investigation. I just observed behavior. That was all I wanted to do. It was all that I needed, and I'm done."

"We are friends now and I respect the fact that you have stopped. If I ever find out that you are continuing... I will burn your corpse and lay your ashes on your mother's doorstep. Do you understand?"

"Why don't you trust him?" Mark rolled his eyes. "He saw you kill Summer and he hasn't said anything." He paused. "Your behavior is getting out of control."

"Fuck you Mark."

"You're being careless! Lucas, why don't you fucking listen?" Mark snatched him towards him like a paper weight and nodded his head. "Why don't you fucking listen?"

I jumped back watching the two tussle. Lucas pushed him and stepped back. "Don't touch me Mark."

"What, you wanna kill me now? It is not about you anymore. You're being followed by people. You have friends that are risking their lives for you and you..."

"Mark, get the hell out of my face. I know."

"Do you care? Can you pretend to care?"

"Get the fuck out of my face, right now." His voice was low.

I nodded my head. "He can't pretend because he doesn't know how to care. You know I don't care what you do. I just don't want to be taken down with you."

"Oh my God. I have to get home."

"You need to get home. You need to stay home. And Asher, we need to talk. We need to sit down and formulate a good strategy. Lucas get the fuck out."

"Great, I didn't want to be here anyhow." Lucas left the apartment.

I locked the door and Mark stared at me. "Are you really trustworthy?"

"I am. I mean... I have everything to lose why wouldn't I be?"

"The feds are buzzing around him." He slid a picture down on the desk and it was Lucas' handwriting. "He wrote in his blood. He doesn't care."

"What the actual fuck?" I gasped.

"I'm worried about him. Cypress is an anchor for him. His blood lust goes down. He feels like with her everything can be normal. Then someone pisses him off or someone that he has hated for a while... Luther here... comes along and he can't resist. He can't stop himself sometimes. And that is going to be his demise."

"If he is addicted I can try to counsel him."

"One wrong word and you are dead to him."

"He trust me for some reason and I wouldn't cross him." I looked at Mark. "Teach him to be like you."

"Like me?"

"Quiet reserved...fighting... channeling it into something else."

"I channel my... whatever by a greed for money. I just want to be rich and worry free. I don't want the extra."

"Make him want money."

"He has money Asher."

"Well look I don't know what you want me to do."

"Continue to watch him." Mark whispered. "Be there and stop him."

"I have to have a life Mark. I can't just follow a grown man around hoping that he doesn't kill anyone. I can't just stop my life."

"I know." He pushed his hands through his short blond hair in frustration and I nodded my head. "This would be better if Cypress knew. But she would freak out. They got back together."

"So we leave her clues. I am sure she is wondering something already."

"No," Mark sighed. "I don't know what the hell to do. I don't know. Look Ill swing by sometime tomorrow and don't talk to the feds anymore. Is there anything that you know that they are looking for?"

"A knife."

"They said something to you about a knife?"

"Yeah, they said it is the link between London and America..."

"Cumbria?"

"Yeah whatever, the strokes of the knife are they key."

"Fuck alright, thank you. I'll talk to you later."

CHAPTER FIFTEEN

Asher

Lucas could never be simple. I asked for one simple thing from him, a blood test and of course he was dead that I was wrong. He refused and now my life was a living hell. My mom swore she wanted nothing to do with it and begged that I leave it alone, but I now understood that she was hiding something from me. I made a special trip back home to California. I missed the bright skies and liveliness of the city. The palm trees on every block and the beautiful painted homes. Our home was perfect.

I sat on my old porch and waited for her to get off from work. She was a registered nurse and she worked long hard hours. It was part of the reason my parents split. My father wanted a wife and she wanted a career. And she got what she wanted. She was the head nurse of three different wings in the hospital, but she lost a husband and basically a son in the mix.

She had the cigarette in her lips and her face was less than amused. "I can't believe you even came to see me." She closed the door and smiled at me. She was as pretty as her name. Margot's hair was a silky mixture of gray and black. Her eyes slanted like she as Asian and I looked nothing like her. "Must be important."

"Hey mom." I hugged her as she sat down on the porch in the plastic chair next to me.

"Enjoy the drive?"

"I did not." I laughed. "I'm done with my thesis. I turned it in. It's just awaiting the grade."

"My son will be a doctor. How does it feel?"

"Like a burden that I'm more than happy to have off of my shoulders." I took the cigarette from her lips. "You're a nurse. You know what those things do mom."

She took it back from my hands. "I feel like the conversation we're about to have will be worst if I don't have it. Where did you get the photos from?" Margot re-lit the cigarette and turned her head to me.

"I got it from a friend in college. Someone, I think you know already."

"Lucas Elledge," She exhaled and blew the smoke into the air. "How did you meet him?"

"Coincidence, really," I lied. I folded my arms. "Mom, I know that this little boy in this picture is me." I held it out in front of her and waited. Her shaking hand took the picture from me. "Please, just tell me."

"She was so beautiful." Margot smiled and then her eyes shifted to me. "Yeah, Asher it is you." She rolled her eyes. "I hate we are even talking about it, but I can tell you. But I don't want you to stop being my boy. You're all I have."

"You'll always be my mom. Nothing that you can say can change it."

"You say that," The silence sat between us and then she sighed. "You were born in England and you are English."

"She's my mother?"

"Luna," she smiled. "We were best friends. Tracy and Luna both went to UCLA with me. We were dorm mates and roommates after the first year in our own home. No one really expected us to be so close. But we were," She nodded her head. "Luna met Declan and she had got pregnant. He didn't want her to have it. He wanted her to give it up and I thought it was a bad idea. She loved him and he loved her. So they gave the oldest child to Tracy. His name was Marcus."

My heart raced. "Tracy, who?"

"I don't know her last name now, but at the time it was Tracey Todd. She loved the child and she made a pact with Luna that she would make sure the child knew her at least as a godmother. It was beautiful."

"Okay," I shook. "And then?"

"She got pregnant less than a year later. I had just found out that I could not have children and here she was popping them out like it was nothing. Tracy said that she had her hands full and she just couldn't. They were about to throw you into the system in England. I told her to bring you here. I told her that I would raise you, but only as my son. I didn't want her to have anything to do with you... But most importantly, I didn't want Declan around you. Declan was a bad guy. He was always a bad guy and she couldn't get it. She agreed and when she left I changed everything. I moved and hid out."

"So, Luna had me?"

"Yes and Lucas is your younger brother. He looks like Declan you know. The hair, the smile... I saw him on the back of his book. He looks just like him, especially those eyes." She paused. "You look like Luna, but your hair, this beautiful mess of chocolate brown hair, is Declan."

"Mom, why didn't you just tell me?"

"Because I didn't want you to know them. They're not good people."

"Luna died." I said. "And Declan."

"She did?"

"ALS, and I could have at least met her once. That is important to me mom. I would have never called her mom."

"She is your biological mom." She sniffled back her tears. "I just wanted you to love me only. It was selfish, but I don't regret it."

"That's selfish mom. I have a brother out there. Two of them and I haven't had the chance to know them or anything because you want..."

"Because I protected you from something that you didn't need."

"You could have let me be the judge of that." I spat back at her. "I love you." I stood up. "I am gonna go to bed. The drive killed me."

Cypress

Lydia sat on the edge of her bed reading her magazine like it was a science. "So… tell me some good positions?"

I spit out my water and stare at her. "What? Are you and Trey sleeping together?"

"We are." She blushed. Her cheeks flushed and she done her small happy dance with her fist balled and in the air. "It was amazing."

"Wow, your brothers have no clue do they?"

"Hell no," Lydia smirked. "And you won't tell them right?"

"I won't." I nodded my head. "Where were you two?"

"Valentine's night," she answered. "Picture it, the hotel was full of roses and candles and he gave me this ring. He's going to Texas AM."

"Where are you going?"

"Texas AM." She was giddy.

"Well, I wish you the best of luck!" I stared at the ceiling.

"He has been asking about you."

"I know he has, I can't even focus on him right now. I have something bigger at hand."

"And what's that?"

"Well, I haven't had a cycle in months. We tested a while back and I haven't tested again."

"You wanna take it here? We can barricade the doors for privacy and then debate on the results. We could turn this into some freaky girl's event."

"Will he show up here?"

"More than likely," she looked down at her hands. "Look, I know my brother is not the best person. He has some issues. But I know he loves you and I know you need time. I won't pressure it and I don't blame you for hating him. If Trey ever done anything like that I would be freaking out. So hate him and do what girls do. But don't make a rash decision about your life and not look at every side of the situation."

She had gained some wisdom in her few years. "Okay, well do you want to ride with me to get the test and some pickles."

"If mom sees pickles she will know something is up. So we can get the test and we will have to carry huge purses to sneak all of this into my room."

"What do you mean all of this? It's a pregnancy test and some pickles."

"I want some fat snacks and some Redbox movies. Dear we will make the day of this." She grabbed her keys. "Come on, I can't wait to see the results. If you are... make me the Godmother."

"But you are the Aunt."

"I would really like to be the Godmother." She added. "Please."

"Fine," I laughed. "Come on."

We made our way down the steps carrying huge purses down the steps. "The two lovely ladies..." Mark greeted as he bit into his apple. "Where are you going?"

"Um, we were about to run to the store."

"Can I go?"

"No," We both said.

"Mean, the both of you." He plopped onto the couch. "You should be warned that Lucas will be here later on today. I don't know where the love saga is currently. Law school has me trapped in its grasp for too long."

"We don't care that he will be here." Lydia answered for me. "You make sure he stays down here away from her and if he wants me, I can come downstairs to him." She grabbed my hand. "And you better not be plotting anything Mark. I swear it will be war."

"When did you grow a set of balls?"

"I've always had them." She pulled me out of the house towards the car. "Now we have some planning to do. Should we get some food first? We could go to a restaurant and pig out."

"I don't know... should I even go back?"

"Did you not hear my threat? We'll get pizza on our way back."

This girl day was much needed. We grabbed unnecessary items and tossed them into the shopping cart. Then of course grabbed ten pregnancy tests and made out way to the house. Lucas was there as Mark said he would be. He sat on the couch with Mark engrossed in some horror movie.

"Shit," I mumbled as we opened the door.

Lucas watched me with every step I took into the house. "Cypress..."

"Hi," I waved. My eyes welled and I stared at him.

"Um, so you two cannot have any of the pizza and do not disturb us. We have some chick flicks and some food." She pushed me passed them. It was much needed because my feet felt like they were planted there permanently.

I climbed the steps out of breath and tossed the heavy purse full of fat snacks and pregnancy test on the high bed. "Thank you."

"You two are so weird. Just talk to one another. Staring is weird." She locked her door. "Do you want to eat and watch a movie first?"

"I don't know what I want."

"I know that." Lydia turned the movie on and smiled. "You will have to say something to him one day you know that don't you?"

"I said hi."

"I mean you will have to talk to him about everything or you will never truly heal."

"Thank you Dr. Phil." I bit into the pepperoni pizza. "I guess we can start The Hunger Games."

"Good, I was hoping that would be your answer."

The movie flew by. My hormones took control every time someone died and I cried like a newborn baby most of the movie. I barely touched my food and half way through the best scene I vomited it up by the end. "I will never watch that again."

"You are pregnant."

"I am not." I paused. "I don't know."

"Well, the movie is over and you need to go ahead and fold on the test. I can't wait anymore and I think I know the results. Step in there and pee on all these sticks..."

"Do you have a cup?"

"I don't." She stood up. "I will go into the battlefield and get one if you promise to still be awake when I return?"

"Scout's honor, I will be here waiting."

She stepped out of the room and I read the instructions. My life could be about to change for the better or worst. If I was not pregnant, there was a voice screaming inside of my head that said to leave him alone. And then there was still a voice screaming if I was. I twiddled with my fingers. My eyes were glued to the door for five minutes. Did she have to make the cups or something? Finally, she returned and locked the door.

"Go piss on the stick."

"What took you so long?"

"Your ex-boyfriend wanted to come talk. I told him no. And then he cursed me and I cursed him and Mark stepped in and cursed us both. Got to love having brothers." She handed me the foam cup and shrugged her shoulders. "He said that he would be here in ten minutes rather I wanted him in here or not. So get the test over with and we can decide what we are going to do."

"Dear God," I walked into her bathroom and looked myself in the mirror. My hands shook. I peed and then washed my hands. I dipped three tests into the cup and set them down. My feet were unsteady as I walked back to the room. "I can't read the test."

"It hasn't been one minute yet."

"I know. I just want you to read them."

"Are you sure?"

"Yes," I whispered. "Everything can change in the next minute Lydia."

"I know." She hugged me. "Just breath."

There was a huge urge for me to cry. I fanned my face and then placed my hand on my head. At the moment I couldn't picture Lucas being with me. I could only see red for him and even more for Persephone. "Go check it."

"Okay, just breathe. You should know that no matter what this test says I am here for you." Lydia hugged me and smiled. "And if you aren't pregnant you still need to go down there and talk to him." She turned on her heel and walked into the bathroom. Everything around me slowed. Time, my breaths even the audio from the television seemed to drag as she grabbed the napkin that held the test. She peered up at me and nodded. Her eyes welled as a small smiled covered her face. "I'm an auntie!"

"You're lying!" I shrieked. I shot up from the bed and made my way over to her quickly.

"I am honest. Every last test says the same thing… One word PREGNANT."

My tears ran over leaking onto my shirt like someone had turned on the faucet. Lydia wrapped her arms around me. "I'm pregnant!" I yelped in a mix of emotions, fear, relief and happiness.

"Go tell him, please." She wiped her face. "You need to."

"I don't know if I can do that."

"You can." Lydia opened the door. "And you need to do it now."

How could an eighteen-year-old have more sense than me? I exhaled. The last thing I wanted to do was to look him in the face and take him back. It shouldn't be that easy for him. I took the test from her and walked down the stairs. "Luke." I said.

His eyes met mine and he paused. "Cypress."

"We should talk." I sobbed. "Like now."

He was up the stairs and in front of me before I could think. My hands shook and I was certain that my face was a complete red mess. "What's the matter?"

Mark sat uncomfortably on the edge of his seat and stared at Lydia. "What did you do?"

"I have done nothing," she moved as she wiped more tears from her face. "But you are an asshole Lucas. I've told you this so many times. But I mean it. She loves you so much and you still found a way to fuck things up."

Lucas blatantly ignored everything that she had said. His emerald eyes were locked on mine. "Cypress, what is it? What's wrong love?"

"I don't know how to say it." I placed the pregnancy test in his hand and covered my mouth to hide another sob. Everything that had been locked up for the past month wanted to escape and it had become hard to hold it back.

Lucas' eyes widened. "What is this?" He flipped the test over and then looked at Lydia. "Whose is this?"

"Why are you looking at me? You would be the last person on my mind if it were mine." Lydia snapped as she pushed passed him. "Asshole."

"Mine." I said. "It's mine."

"Oh fuck," he dropped the test and pulled me closer to him. His tatted arms wrapped around my body and it felt warm and right. It seemed as if the world had gone back to normal for a split moment. "You're pregnant?" he whispered.

"Yes. I took ten tests."

"Oh baby."

"Little sis, let's get some ice cream. And leave them to talk."

Lucas

The door closed to Lydia's bright room and she looked at me. There is so much pain in her I could barely stand to look. "I don't know where to start," I said. "I can only apologize."

"I am stuck in between happy and petrified." Cypress sniffled.

"I know."

"Can I trust you?"

"Yes, I swear to it."

"I mean about everything. I am about to bring a child in this world. And now everything looks so weird. I'm sick because I have a child growing inside of me. I am no longer one person. I will never be one person again."

"What can I do?"

"Start from the top… what happened with her?"

"Persephone?"

"Yes."

"She came to my office and she was naked. I didn't want her. But I wanted her to leave me alone."

"So you fucked her?"

"That was weakness…" I whispered. "But I fixed it. She will never be around again. I swear."

"How do you know?"

"I can't tell you."

"You better start talking." She snapped.

"I threatened her." The truth was exposed. "I told her not to come around us anymore."

"With what? What did you threaten her with?"

"A knife Cypress."

"You pulled a knife on her?"

"Yes," I paused. "I didn't know what else would work on her.

She burst into laughter. "I can't believe you did that to her. She must have been scared?"

"She was terrified. I just wanted her to go."

"You know she could have you thrown in jail for that?"

"She wouldn't. I would kill her."

"That shit scares me." She touched her forehead. "You sound so sincere when you say that you will kill someone. That is not how it is supposed to go. You have anger issues."

"I know."

"Have you ever killed anyone?"

I leaned against the wall. "Do you want the truth?"

"Tell me everything you think I should know now."

"I think about it frequently. But I have never killed anyone. If I wanted to kill someone I would just do it." It was not entirely a lie. I had learned to control myself ever since Luther. The playing in the blood thing had been an overkill. I had to lay low. Unless I wanted to really spend the rest of my life behind bars.

"Don't... look its we now. We have a baby."

"You need to set up appointments and start your vitamins."

"Don't just yet, please. Give me some time to get used to us again. We can't just hop on this ride with no ticket."

"I love you Cypress. I can't take another night alone. I have been grieving and self-medicating trying to find a way to numb it. There is nothing that can heal the pain. I am sorry. I made you suffer and you didn't deserve it. You are more than right. I will do whatever I have to do to make sure that it never happens again. But I cannot take another night away from you."

I touched her shoulder gently and she moved back "Lucas."

"I'm sorry." My voice pleaded with her. "Please I'm sorry." I pressed my hands to my face. "Love me back." I felt like there was nothing else in the world that I needed more than this. I needed her to love me back.

"Lucas."

"Try please, I can't make my love for you die. I can't. I've tried everything to try and get over you and everything I do leads me back to you. I am better with you. I am in love with you. I want you. So you have to love me back."

"I can't stop it." Cypress yelled. "Do you not think that I love you back!" Her tiny hands collided with my chest and she pushed me away from her.

"Then show me..." I slapped my face. The sting of the pain was nothing compared to what I had been through without her. A kill wasn't even enough to make losing her okay. "I've been killing myself slowly for your touch. I just want you to touch me... Please." My hands pleaded for me as the soothed her face caught her tears.

She turned her back towards me. "You cheated on me and I was there for you in every way."   "I know."

I brought her close to me and the familiar scent of her overwhelmed me. My hands explored her body, remembering how everything used to be. My eyes closed and everything returned to the state of normalcy. I touched her through her leggings. My fingers traced her labia and her head fell back onto my shoulder. I turned her around to face me. "Never again, I swear." I whispered.

"Okay," her voice was breathy and lost in whatever was about to happen. I guided her to the bed, knocking everything to the floor and she laid back. It felt like everything was new to me again. I hadn't felt her beneath me in more than a month and I wanted to savor everything about her. "You are so beautiful." I admired her smile and slid her leggings off and threw them to the ground.

"Lucas... tell me again."

"You are beautiful." I whispered. I slid my hands into her underwear, pushing a finger pass her lips into her fully. She was so tight. I sucked my finger and the taste of her was sweet. I pushed two fingers into her and look down on her as she bucked her hips off of the bed. My dick flinched at her reaction and I withdrew removing her shirt and releasing her breast. They were larger from the last time I had seen her.

"Your tits are huge." I added with a smirk.

"I know they are like two huge balloons. Be careful... They're..."

I bit down on her nipple and watched her mouth form an O as she ran her fingers through my hair. I circled my tongue around the tip of her nipple lightly and relished in the moans that escaped from her. I gripped her other one and pinched it between my fingers. A sharp sigh escaped from her as she whispered a stream of profanity. I missed her dirty mouth. I slapped her thighs playfully and made my way to her mouth. Her tongue crashed into my mouth as our mouths locked together. She gripped my hair, sending a pleasurable pain down my back. "Did you miss me?"

"More than you will ever know." She answered.

"Good." I moaned. Her hands eagerly tried to set my dick free. I unbuckled my pants and pushed them to the floor. My dick ached to be inside of her. "I'll be gentle."

"Don't be." Cypress added.

I lifted her leg up and turned my head at her. "My wish is your command." I pushed into her slowly. She was so tight there was a chance two strokes could get me there from anticipation. I relished the moment as her face went from calm to painstakingly filled with pleasure. I thrust into her slow grinding my hips deep into her. The sound of our skin slapping against each other echoed throughout the rooms and then her moans and shrieks of pleasure joined. She pulled my hair again and it added to the buildup that had started. I flipped her over so that she was on top and gripped her breast. She rotated her hips on me slowly anchoring herself in my chest and closed my eyes in pleasure. I loved the way she felt on me. She had total control, I was her slave and all she had to do was command me. Cypress had her eyes closed and her mouth open as she ground on me slowly rubbing her clit against me. I sat up with her still in my lap and placed my hands on her back. She gasped as I filled her deeper and pounded into her with no remorse.

She cloaked her arms around my neck and I couldn't stop. My strokes became longer and her pants came with each one. She was there. I could feel her whole body as it surrendered to me fully. I laid her back on the bed and anchored myself on my knees going deeper as she finally found her release and watched her come in a shrill scream as usual. A grin emerged on my face and I bit my lip. "I missed that sound." I dove into her relentlessly the sweat that grazed her body now covered mine and we were filthy and I loved every second of. My back twitched at every entry of her until the tingle made its way to my dick and finally I came inside of her. I thrust into her a few more times getting everything that was left in me, out. And she watched with a goofy smile on her face. "What?"

"We just fucked on your teenager sister's bed."
I laughed. "Yes, yes we did." I nodded in amusement.
"She is going to kill us."
"It's okay. I'll wash her sheets."
"She's gonna burn them."
"More than likely," I agreed.

CHAPTER SIXTEEN

Asher

I had never had to face with anything of this magnitude in my life. For the first time it was confirmed that I was not who I thought I was and for some reason it hadn't surprised me. I felt that I had been tossed into my life for the majority of it anyhow. But it was particularly hard because I had no one to fall on. Margot became distant. She refused to answer the phone and she had not responded to any texts in the last week. It baffled me to think that she could be mad at me. Margot acted as if she had received the news. I had reached the breaking point with her stubbornness. I just wanted my birth certificate and it was going to take an act of congress to even get that from her. So I stopped bothering her. I focused on the bigger issue around me. Whitney and I had met the end of the relationship. I feared my world would collapse.

"Are you still focused on Lucas?" Whitney was curled on the couch next to me. Her eyes focused on the television and her cold feet planted in my thigh.

"No," I paused. "I mean I have nothing more to focus on really. My paper is basically done. It just needs to be fine-tuned and then it's off to the professors.

"So is he out of your life?" She asked.

"No," I turned a few pages in my book.

"Why is it so important that you are around him and what does he have over you that makes you hooked to him and Mark for that matter?"

"What do you want me to say Whitney?" I snapped. I had a shit ton on my plate and the last thing I wanted or needed was for her to hound me all things concerning my new found family.

"I want you to say that you are done chasing crazy."

"I went to see Margot and she confirmed everything that I thought about the picture. It was me and I am his older brother and Mark coincidentally, is my older brother as well. For once I have some brothers and some family."

"You have always had family."

"I have always had someone who called me family. I have never had a real family. Margot spent so much time at that hospital and my dad spent so much time researching god knows what that I was alone. They never listened to me and they never pretended to care about what I was into. They were a filler."

"A filler? Are you insane Margot worked all of those long hours at the hospital to make sure you had food on your table and roof over your head. And you can't just drop them to be a part of a family that you barely know anything about. You have lost it."

"You haven't even taken the real time to get to know him. Lucas is not bad and neither is Mark."

"Yeah, I think it's better that we no longer talk about it. I will never see your side and I don't want to." She picked her purse up from the table. "Who are we meeting here?"

"Mark, I figured it was time to tell him about it. He is better at breaking news to Lucas than me."

"That's because they are the same kind of crazy." She snapped. "I'll leave you two to whatever you are planning."

"Thanks," I responded.

"We'll talk tonight."

Mark waved at Whitney as she turned to leave. "Hey Whitney, you look gorgeous today."

"Thanks." Whitney rolled her eyes as she made her way out of the door.

"Real ray of sunshine you have there," Mark chuckled. "What's up Asher?"

"Not much," I shook his hand and slid the picture over to him. He was cradled in Luna's arm's. Her beautiful blonde hair fell behind her ears as the tears seemed to roll in streams down her face. "That is you."

"Bullshit."

"And this is me."

"Get the hell out of her man!" Mark smirked. "This shit is ridiculous."

"Has your mom told you the story?"

"No," Mark stared at the picture. "So this means that we are indeed brothers?"

"Yes." I answered.

"And no one has told Lucas?"

"Not a soul, I kind of wanted you to tell him?"

Mark dropped the picture on the table. "Oh, you think that I should be the one to deliver that shit storm to him. I mean he seems to be in a good place. He has Cypress back and has he told you the news of the week." he laughed.

"No, ever since she took him back I've seen him like twice a day and we usually don't talk. I've started meditation with him. It seems to be working."

"You will want to hear this news yourself. I was kind of shocked, but then not really. You can come too. Because I believe we are actually the older brothers and we should ban together. This can either piss him off or make him happy."

"You think he will be happy?"

"Like I said there is no real way to know how he will act Asher; he tends to be unpredictable. But I want to know more about our parents. I don't care to know about he feels. I'm happy about this whole situation. It makes sense to me in a way as to the connection my mother had with Luna."

"Did you ever get to meet her?"

"On a few occasions, mostly when she was dropping Lucas off to be with us for a while. He had a fucked up childhood. He was bounced between three homes constantly." He touched my shoulder lightly, "Asher you aren't a bad guy and I think we'll be fine. You just worry too much."

"I hope."

"You'll be fine. How did your mom act?"

232 | *LR Johnson*

"Margot has not called me since. She won't answer the phone and she won't talk to me. I didn't think it was going to be like this. I would have just found out on my own."

"Margot," Mark nodded his head as he noticed that I didn't call her mom. "Is she mad?"

"She said that Declan was not a good guy."

"I've researched. He was an enforcer for some pretty bad guys. But it' not important about him. This is about us defining who we are in this world. And a major part of that rest on who our family is…"

"Good."

"We are going to Ireland in a few months and you should come. There is a guy named Callum there. He's Lucas' cousin, ours too apparently and he wants to meet us."

"Why us?"

"I think that was Lucas' excuse so that we could go. He doesn't want to just go with Cypress, she's pregnant and everything. He said that she has been an emotional wreck and he's not too good at being kind to her."

"So… is that the news you were hiding out? I had no idea that she was pregnant." I laughed as he covered his mouth.

"Fuck it, yep. Lucas is about to be a father and he is scared shitless. I hate to say it, but it's funny as hell."

"I can imagine."

"So are you down for Ireland? I think it will be nice to get out of the country and for once out of the hair of the feds. They have been a fucking tick for me."

"I'll go."

"Bring your ray of sunshine, I'm sure that she would love to meet the entire family."

"Fuck you Mark."

Cypress

Lucas apparently thought that being pregnant was an excuse to play driving Miss Daisy. He acted as if I was crippled. Lucas stared at me like I could break at any wrong movement. If I reached for something off the top of the refrigerator, he would scowl at me or move me entirely out of the way so that he could do it. He was overly affectionate and at first I enjoyed it, now I wanted everything to be normal. I wanted him to give me my space and for him to have his space as well. Not to mention he monitored everything that I was doing like I was constantly being babysat. I wanted to scream and punch him in the throat most days. Then there was Tracy, she demanded time with me because she said that she didn't know enough about me. Never before had she tried to put in extra effort into knowing me, but throw a baby in the mix and I was the perfect daughter-in-law.

Sunday afternoons had gone from the normal being lazy on my couch with Lucas to mixing the biscuit batter with Lydia and Tracy. Then there was the part of me that still hated Lucas for cheating on me with that bitch. Even as I sat with them cooking I wanted to beat the shit out of her.

The spell with Persephone always hung in the air when he was around me. I wanted to know why he went to her and pound a million and one questions into his head but I couldn't. "I wonder why men cheat." I mumbled aloud.

"Men are dumb." Tracy answered simply. "And everyone makes mistakes. It's just that they learn a lesson from the mistake that they make. If it happens over and over again, it is a habit. If it happens once… it can be a lesson learned and then it ends up serving a purpose."

"Never thought of it likes that."

Tracy smiled, moving the mixture to the bowl and dashing a sprinkle of salt on it. "I heard about why you two took a break."

"Yeah, it was the longest month of my life."

"I can understand why you were. I would never expect that from Lucas, but he is and men are unpredictable."

"I wish that he would tell me why."

"Have you ever considered that maybe he doesn't know why? Sometimes there isn't a reason."

"Possibly."

"There are some things about my son that I want you to know."

"Okay." I watched her as she flipped through her photo album. "You do know that we adopted him."

"I know that. He talks about his biological mom so much."

"Has he told you about his father?" Tracy asked.

"He hasn't told me much." I smiled at her. "You knew him?"

"Yes, well actually, his mother and I were best friends. She went to school over in America for a while and then when we got older we spent every waking moment together. She came to California for college and she was a free bird. My mom liked her, but she had a way of making parents think the worst. Her hair was the prettiest of strawberry blonde and she had a laugh that could light up any room. We got to the campus and the first person we met was Declan Elledge. He was English as well and she was under his spell for the moment she heard his name. He seduced her with his brown eyes and his smile. His smile was alluring. Much like Lucas'. They started to date and they had this amazing connection and honestly, it reminded me of you two. There was not much that could keep them apart."

I bit into my apple. "Yeah, I figured that it was from his father. He has charm that is just.... ridiculous."

"Right, well it is definitely genetic. Anything that we say in here stays between you and because I haven't yet told them about it." She paused and pulled a picture from her photo album. "She had Mark when she was 19 years old."

I felt my jaw drop. "Mark?"

"Mark is her oldest son. His name on the original birth certificate read Marcus Declan Elledge. When she had him she decided to go ahead and put him up for adoption. I begged her to not be that person. So I took him. I raised him as my own."

"Oh my God." I gasped and stared at her.

She placed a picture of her holding the small infant Mark in her hands. "That was when she decided to give him up. She said that her mother would have her shipped off. So she didn't claim him as hers. But she loved him none the less. I sent her pictures once she moved back to America and we stayed in contact. I met my husband and he followed the program."

"They have no idea."

"Mark can feel it. But Lucas is such a loner, again he is like his father in more than one way." I could feel the double meaning in her words. "Wow."

"One year after she had Mark, there was another child. She offered, but I couldn't take another one in. Mark was a handful and I was still pushing through school. I told her I couldn't. And I was not a fan of Declan at that moment. He had been a pain. She named him Asher Elledge. She gave him to a friend in California that could not have kids. Her name was Margot."

My mind wandered. "Asher... couldn't be his friend Asher could it?" I nodded my head. Things were coming together.

"It is." She laughed. "Margot and her husband decided it was for the best that they change his last name as I done with Mark. He looks like her side of the family as does Mark. Lucas the baby of the family has everything from his father. They had him two years later and named him Lucas and she kept him. She had finally made Declan into a man that could handle a family. She raised him until Luke turned 14 then something happened that she least expected."

"ALS?"

"Indeed, she caught it early and at first there was nothing that changed with her, but she started to make Luke attend school in different places, one year in Ireland and the then several over with us. He and Mark hung out every summer together and that was the start of a beautiful friendship. Margot cut all ties with us. She married a psychologist and she demanded that we stay away from Asher, mainly Declan. Declan was this towering gentle giant to us. He loved everyone and everyone loved him, but Lucas adored him. He saw the real version of him and it was obvious because of the type of bond that they had with one another. Declan was not the best father, though, they had their differences and Lucas and him were alike. They fought like cats and dogs because whatever Declan's job was caused him to be out of the house a lot. And whenever he left Luna was sadder. He didn't like to see his mother sad or sick. He was left to deal with his mother along. And in my opinion when he started to take care of his mother it made him a stronger man, but it also made Declan less of one. He left his family and he didn't care or at least to them it didn't seem like he did. He checked in with him and then he would playhouse when she was really sick. Then she started to send Lucas here for longer bouts of time up until she died and she knew that there was something that she had to do to make sure that he didn't suffer while she died."

"She spared him the horror of it all and sent him to be where he could be a child."

"It was our pact with one another. We would never let him be motherless. I adopted him and he has been mine just like Mark. Mark was happy and then we had Lydia as well."

"Wow, so why is Asher here?"

"His stepfather puts the crazy notion in his head that Declan was a killer. I think it was sick way to turn him off to knowing anything about him. Asher started to study Lucas and then well... you know how it goes."

"So you know all of this and you are not telling Lucas. Why?"

"Lucas is different and he is like his father. He is dark. He has secrets and I don't know what they are. I just know that he is something different."

"There are FBI agents asking questions about him. They are saying that he killed someone. He seems like he is not fazed."

"He is more than likely fazed by it, but he will not show it all. He is a quiet guy. But what I am saying is that you are so much like his mother. You are beautiful and you are giving him a real shot to have a life. Don't get involved with anything he has going. That was Luna's safety. She was blind to everything and she wanted to be blind to everything. So you need to do that."

"Okay..." My mind raced. Was he a killer? "Lucas is dangerous?"

"He is not dangerous to you."

"To anyone Tracy?"

"Yes, he has an anger problem. I don't think that he would hurt you. What have the agents been asking?"

"His ex-girlfriends have all turned up dead to missing."

"They think that he did it."

"Yes, but he has an alibi for every death. My point is that you don't have to worry about him hurting you. He loves you unconditionally."

I was not sure exactly how I was supposed to take the conversation with Tracy. Was I supposed to be happy I was not in danger or you should I be worried that other people are in danger. I mulled it around my head for a few minutes while she finished cooking the quiche.

"What's the matter love?" Lucas touched my shoulder. "Nothing babe."

"You sure? Did Tracy say something?"

"I'm just hungry Luke, calm down." I laughed. "What are we doing when we leave here?"

"I guess we are sleeping you think? You have been snoring here lately. It's hard for me to catch some shut eye if I don't doze off before you." Lucas poked me annoyingly and sat down on the stool across from me. "Tracy, how much longer?"

"Calm down. The quiche will be done when it's done. Have you looked into those master programs that I asked you to look into?"

"I looked into a few. I think I want to travel a while though. There are some parts of Northern Ireland that I have yet to see. And I would love for you to come with me. There is no way to describe to you the color of their greens."

"It sounds like a plan to me." I twiddled with my fingers. I had to get him out the house for a while and investigate him more. "I am really tired."

"Are you ready to leave love?"

"I am." I touched my stomach lightly. "The little one is begging to nap."

"Well, we can leave," he whispered. "I could get something to eat later on."

"Yeah, let's do that."

Lucas

Home felt less like home lately. She stayed over every night and the house hunting was a pain. And it was not because I didn't want her. I just didn't know how to react to someone in my space. She nestled into the couch covered with her blanket and a trash can next to the couch. Morning sickness had set it's on hours for her.

I clicked through the computer. I wanted a bigger playground. New York had so much crime that a few deaths every now and then would be expected. I wouldn't have to leave my family just to plan something to soothe desires. I had a control of them lately. It felt like relief to know that I could say no to the urge to cut into someone. It had grown easier because she was here so much. And there someone else important in the picture, my child. The feeling was new. I had created another being. The thought had never crossed my mind that I could be a father. I was so used to ending a life that being a father was foreign.

"Your mom was upset about the quiche."

"She will live." I pecked at the keys. "Would you be okay living in New York?"

"As in the state?"

"And the city," I said.

"No," She mumbled. "Can we do this when I don't feel like shit?"

"Have you been to the doctor about this?"

"I have, it's called pregnancy. They said the symptoms would continue for five more months and then a kid would pop out."

"Oh, okay." I chuckled at her sarcasm. It had become the norm here. "Are you hungry? I could go for some takeout?"

I watched her as she placed the headphones on her stomach and scrolled through the music on her iPod. "I don't want to leave. I'm tired."

"What are you making him listen to?"

"We don't know what we are having?" She reminded.

"I know it's a boy."

"I'm listening to Coldplay."

"So, you want our child to come out wining in a high pitch melody about lost love or stars?" I turned my head to her.

"What would you prefer?"

"Bach?"

"Didn't you say that you were going to get some food?" She snapped.

"I'll step out. What do you want?"

"Ooh, I could go for some pizza and an egg roll! And some pickles."

"Darling," I moaned.

"Please." Cypress begged, her bottom lip dropped and I could hear the profane thought as they raged in my head.

"Bloody hell, that's four places I have to stop and not to mention the car is out of petrol. Could you not just live with some General whatever's chicken?"

"That's spicy!" She yelled.

Cypress had turned my couch into her haven. Her books were scattered on the table in front of her with an empty jar of pickles and a giant lemonade bottle. Then there were the tons of blankets that had engulfed her. She lay perfectly on the couch with her feet propped on three pillows and her a glow about her that warmed my heart. "What all do you want?" I groaned as I grabbed the keys from the table.

"Well, go to the grocery store first and get some Turtle Chocolate Ice Cream, then grab some Kosher Pickles and some Nutella."

"What the hell?" I stared at her in frustration. "You don't need Nutella."

"You don't tell me what I need Lucas!" Cypress had turned an annoying shade of red. "I have been craving the damn Nutella for a week! Buy it!"

"Yes, your highness." I rolled my eyes.

"I want three Spring Rolls from The China Palace and some sweet and sour sauce. Then I would like a large pepperoni pizza no sauce add garlic season from Pizza Shack." She smiled and shrugged her shoulders.

"There is no way that you can eat all of that shit."

"You wanna bet?"

"I would rather not. But you are sleeping on the couch with that horrid gas."

I watched her as her eyes grew wide. "Lucas!"

"What!" I chuckled and she put her head down.

"I'm pregnant."

"This I know already." I smiled. I kissed her forehead lightly and made my way towards the door. "Anything else?"

"Could you please hurry back? I'll place the order. I just miss you already." She winked.

"I will do my best to travel all over Colorado Springs like a chicken with my head cut off to get back to you."

"I appreciate it and I love you."

"Love you too."

Spring had broken through the cold shield of winter. The cool breeze hit my face as I walked to my car, the place had never looked so beautiful. The feds sat in their car a block away and started their engines. I couldn't even piss without a friendly visit from them. My move with Luther had been a rush. Writing out his name in the blood with that smiling face. McMillan had chased his tail and finally I knew for sure that he had nothing on me at all. I was a speculation and in a few months they would demand that he pull the case back. My life would be back to normal and I would leave this place.

I threw my hand in the air with a smile. "Cheerio!"

The agents nodded their head and looked at one another. There was no telling what they were thinking. They would never take coffee from me again. I was happy I got that off of my chest. Luther was dead and now I could get on with life.

"Lucas," a voice said from behind me.

I turned my head and there was Persephone. I gritted my teeth. Her tangled ponytail lay to the side and she shielded her eyes with her glasses. "What the hell? Did you not understand?" I hissed.

"I'm sorry." She winced. "I wanted to let you know that my mom is making me finish the year but you don't have to worry. I'll go to classes and leave you alone."

"She can't make you do anything."

"She can."

"Dear Jesus. Alright, understood. Leave here before Cypress comes."

"Okay." She hopped in her car and left.

My stomach growled in frustration, skipping lunch had not been smart. The engine of my car started and I had only one thing on my mind, food.

"Want company?" Mark asked from the passenger side of the car. He unlocked the door and Asher jumped in the backseat.

"Well, certainly," I rolled my eyes. "What do you want?"

"To talk, we can ride with you, right?"

"I suppose since you both have hopped your asses in." I waited till they were settled to pull out of the parking lot. The music strummed in the background and the silence was annoying. "What do you two want?"

"We have some news?"

"What news?"

"We're brothers, all three of us." Mark gestured between us three.

I had gained more family in the past month than I could comprehend. So my mother was a liar and I had two ok guys as brothers. I sat in silence as I waited for them to say something. I was fine. I mean now I technically couldn't kill Asher and he wasn't that bad. He calmed me down with that yoga shit sometimes. "Okay."

"Okay?" Asher asked.

"I mean you two aren't the worst people in the world to be kin to I guess. This doesn't mean that we have to do dinners and all that shit all of the time. And Asher you can't borrow my clothes. I get enough of that shit from Mark. So to make it fair Mark stay out of my shit."

"That's all you have to say?" Mark burst into laughter and Asher followed soon behind him. "I'll stay out of your shit."

"Thank you. And I'm not paying for your food either, you bloody bastards."

CHAPTER
SEVENTEEN

Cypress

The only good thing about pregnancy so far had been the non-stop pampering everyone gave me. Though it had been annoying at first it was hard not to fall into the spoils of it. Mark and Asher even found a way to cater to me. Everything else had died and gone to hell. Little things that I used to enjoy now were a pain in my ass. For instance, instead of relishing college, I couldn't wait to get out of the hell hole. The long walks through the campus that I once enjoyed and lived for were now a pain in the ass. The hills of the campus were a nuisance. Then there was the snow and ice that had finally started to melt into ridiculous sludge and made me a living trip hazard. I was only four months and no I didn't have a major bump, but it was enough that I had a slight waddle.

The next issue with pregnancy had been the lack of privacy. First, there was Lucas and his constant need to know where I was and know what the hell what going on with me. He was like an alarm clock. I could basically pinpoint when he was about to call me. And if I didn't answer, he found a way to get someone around me to get to me. Then there was Lydia. I loved her like a precious sister, but it was as if I was carrying this damn baby for her. She had planned every event thus far. The first being the reveal party. They generally came when the sex was determined. Well, she had planned one for me already and she was the host. Then she had planned a baby shower for us, themes for each sex. She overwhelmed me. She wanted to talk and the only thing I wanted to do was to sleep for long periods of time in Lucas' bed.

The last issue was my mom and sister. They wanted me to move back home immediately after the baby was born. They could care less about Lucas being the father of the baby and she could care less about our relationship. Mom wanted her grandchild near her where she could protect him or her. Lana wanted my child to be able to grow up around them and she was usually pro-Lucas but she wanted him to let go. Lucas begged to differ and that was one argument I didn't any part of, they should just hash it out among themselves and leave me out of it.

The spring had started to show its head, but it was still chilly out. Lucas made sure he kept our visits to the park a minimum. Moments like this were rare. Our eyes were hooked on the mountains and the pale blue and white background the sky had provided. There was a warm pallet under our bodies as we lay on our backs entangled with one another.

"I could stay like this for forever." I murmured.

"I say you're right. Let us build a home right here. We can sleep here and dream here… fuck here." He whispered. His lips traced my ear lightly. "We could do that here."

"We could go to jail." I gestured to the people as they passed us by.

"We could do that by jaywalking, the way that I have in mind would be so much better." He kissed my forehead and pulled me closer.

"What makes you happy?"

"Moment like this." He answered. "Simple yet, they mean so much." Lucas' hand touched my stomach. The small bump emerged from the yellow shirt and he pulled me closer. He readjusted my shirt and his hand rested on my stomach. The small nudge of a foot or elbow bulged through. "Awry little chap huh?

"Wonder where he gets that from?" I smiled. We had no idea what we were having. But he was dead set on a little boy and I had grown accustom to calling him little chap like Lucas.

"I never want to let you go, you know that."

"I guessed it." I place my hand over his and for a moment I felt bliss. I had fallen into his gravitational pull and there was no escape. No matter how much something inside told me to flee, I was his and he was mine. "You wanna know what I think about constantly? I mean it literally just sits in my mind for hours."

"Of course, what is your mind wrestling with Cypress?"

"How long can we be this happy?"

"For forever," he answered. His answer short and sweet. But his words were too good to be true.

"It's not that simple Lucas. There is always going to be something that can happen between us. Love is hard. Do you understand that? It's not cut and dry like you want to think it is. We have to be honest about everything. And I mean we have to tell each other everything. You can't hold back from me and that goes for everything between us."

"I know. Words are valuable."

"So don't waste any."

"I would never." he playfully kissed my forehead as his arm draped over me.

"Good," I nestled closer to him. Thank God for the spring weather. The warmth kissed my cheek. I couldn't wait for the last of the winter to fade out so it would finally be comfortable enough to not have to layer ourselves. The wind ruffled my hair and my life was good.

"Are you ready for this European adventure?"

"I am ready as I will ever be." Ireland was set in motion for us. He could not wait until I met the rest of his family. He raved on and on about his cousin Callum. And then he raved about his Nan, whom we would not be able to see because he didn't want me to travel that much. He had family spread over three countries. England only held his mother's half and though he was close to them he wanted Asher and Mark to meet their grandmother and his father's side of the family.

"I want you to enjoy yourself and not think about anything. My grandmother cannot wait to meet you. I hate that you won't get to meet my other Nan. But we have plenty of time to get over there."

"What's her name?"

"My mom's mom, Nan is what I call her but her name is Natalie Alexandra Atherton," I could feel his smile. "Very English and she is Atherton all over."

"I like that name."

"It is pretty. Then there is my grandmother from Ireland. My father's mom... her name is Nadine Elledge. I call her Nadine. She would not prefer anything else. She continually states that Nadine declares her youth while grandmother defies it." He laughed. "She is one tough woman."

"Well, she sounds strong." It was quiet for a moment and his grandmother's name made me think of our child. Would he or she be a namesake? Had he even thought about it? "Have you thought of names?"

"I haven't really. I mean we really don't know what we are having... I kind of guessed that we should wait it out until we know."

"That party is in a month or so. I don't know if I can wait that long. I would rather just have a baby shower and the reveal just be intimate, between us two."

"You shouldn't have given Lydia the keys to every event concerning the baby. I mean she has revolved her final semester of High School to being the perfect auntie." He chuckled.

"Luna Alexandria Elledge?" I threw out. "It has a ring to it. We can name our first child after your family and the second after mine?"

He swallowed and sighed. His face filled with anguish and happiness. Lucas missed his mother more and more these days. He kept bringing her up. In late night conversations he pondered over rather she would be a good grandmother or not? If she would have the patience and then he missed his father. "I like it. What if we have a boy?"

"Nathaniel Declan Elledge." I had thrown the name in the air more than once before and he completely brushed me off about it.

"Declan..."

"You have the knife with your father's name engraved. I figured he was special to you." I know he was special to him. In every way he worshipped the ground that Declan walked on.

"How about Lucas Nathaniel Elledge II, he could be a namesake?"

"Your middle name is Nathaniel." I poked at him. "Why didn't you tell me?"

"I hate that name." he said. "Do I even look like a Nathaniel?"

"Well… you want to name our something you hate?" My phone vibrated in my hand and I pushed up on the ground to answer it. "Hello?"

"Hey! I found a perfect outfit for the reveal party! I don't know how big you will be and I don't know if you will like yellow but it will be perfect."

"I haven't even thought of an outfit Lydie. I've been so busy prepping for this trip that the party had been the last thing on my mind." I laughed.

"Well, I'm on it for you."

"Could we discuss it later?"

"Lydie," He took the phone. "You know this is our baby and not yours right? You have so many ideas I feel like I should make sure you and the dweeb aren't pregnant."

I pushed him and struggled to sit up. Perhaps laying on the ground was not the wisest idea that I had. He gently pushed on my back to help me sit up. "Be nice, tell her to come to your place."

"We have other things to do later on. We will see you Sunday at Brunch." He hung up the phone. "Look, we have so much other shit to worry about."

"Like drapes and apartment rentals?"

"Like passport pictures and perhaps house shopping in Ireland. We could even get a flat?"

Wow, I looked at him. "What?"

"I don't want to be here anymore. I would rather our family have a happy home. I want to live where I know we are loved. And I think that once you see Ireland or England you will be in love. Your soul isn't here."

"My soul is wherever you are." I smiled.

"So is moving okay? Is moving something that you can consider."

"I can consider it." I sipped the cool water and smiled. "I have to leave to visit my mom later on today."

"We can go together." He said.

"No, I am just going to go and spend the weekend with her." My lie sounded real. I did need to go see her, but there was more that I wanted to take care.

"No that's not an option. It's a fourteen-hour drive. You must be bloody mad if you think I am going to let you go alone? Plus, I have some things to get done on campus. Perhaps you could rake Asher with you? He has been moping nonstop about Whitney. They are the most temperamental couple I have ever seen in my life. And you have to remember to take your vitamins. Then you have to not talk about me to your mom. She really doesn't know if she like me or not. She just thinks that I knocked you up."

"You did knock me up." I added. "And why do I have to take Asher?"

"Because you can either take him or Mark. I'm not about to have you out on the highway by yourself. You can choose. I mean Asher is the best candidate. He is talkative and you love to talk on road trips, even over the music." He kissed me and stood up over me.

"Fine then Lucas. You are so controlling; every situation can't be in your hands you know that?"

"I can try to make sure I have control of them."

"I guess I should go ahead and pack up. I don't want to be on the road all day." I attempted to push myself up and he held his hand out. I grabbed it and pushed myself up from the ground.

"You know I love you and that I want you to drive safe. Every time you get on the highway, I freak out. You really can't drive. Matter of fact, Asher can drive. I'll call him and make sure he isn't busy sulking around the house like a child,"

"I know you think I can't but I have a license that proves that I can and I will continue to drive for as long as I have the license." I stuck my tongue out at him. "I don't want to burden your brother like that."

"Asher doesn't mind."

"Is it weird calling them brother and like it really means something now. The guy you tried to kill a little over six months ago is now your brother and you are being really calm about it."

"I like them both and it's comforting knowing I can have two extra sets eyes on you, clumsy."

"I am not clumsy."

"Whatever love, just make sure you call Asher and give him a heads up about everything. I know that he will be willing to do it."

Asher

For some reason the feds had slacked off of me and I could finally move without a shadow. Lucas had not been so lucky. I guessed that they had seen that Lucas was a friend now, even more he was a brother to me. He confided in me and I actually had grown to be a good friend to him. My father advised against it and I shrugged his opinion off. Margot and him had hidden enough from me. Lucas was not bad when he wasn't in lust with blood. And his recent change in his relationship brought out a side of him that I had never observed. He brought her around me and for once, was not worried that I would be interested in her. And Cypress was a good girl. She truly loved Cypress and perhaps that was the difference between her and all of the fallen women before her.

While Lucas and Cypress thrived my relationship had crumbled before me. Whitney had sensed everything off about him and demanded I end the friendship. Who was she to tell me that I could not be friends or even have a decent relationship with someone that was my brother? It was hard for her to realize that it was not the simple anymore. He was my brother and there was a bond there now that meant more than friendship. I wanted him to do well and I had to do everything I could to make sure that he was okay. I understood why Mark was frustrated. It was a full time job. Lucas had a temper out of this world and one bad remark could send him into a frenzy.

My apartment was cleaned and organized. When I returned from Ireland there would be some packing to do. I had no idea where I was going, but the option to stay here had grown to be nonexistent. I wanted a normal life and I wanted to redefine who I was in my life. And I was at the point to where a relationship was needed because it was a step in the future. I wanted someone to grow old with and this small community was full of women that wanted an education and not a boyfriend.

Whitney would not even look at me anymore. So maybe the trip to Ireland would help me find who I wanted to be. And where I belonged.

The knock on the door came to no surprise. McMillan stopped by once every two weeks to intimidate me more and I'd learned to stone face him. He had no idea that there was a common connection between Lucas and I more than friendship. And to me it was none of his business who we were. "Come in," I said as I sorted through the stack of unorganized papers on the table. All of the papers needed to be filed and thrown into storage.

"Cleaning?" McMillan closed the door behind him. He wore a gray suit and held a folder in his hand.

"Indeed." I said to the agent. "When I get back my father is going to be here for a little while. So I wanted to make sure it looked good."

"You think he will visit you in prison?"

"Sorry, what're you talking about?" The iPhone slid across the table and I answered it. "Cypress? What's up?"

"Well…" She paused. "Lucas won't let me get on the highway alone anymore. He said that I could go see my mom if and only if you come with me?"

"You didn't have to put it like that Cy." I could hear him mumbling in the background.

"How far out is it?"

"It's about fourteen hours. We can stay the night at my mom's house if you want to, no hotel."

"No, it's fine. When do you want to leave?"

"Like in an hour?"

"Perfect, I'll be there shortly." I ended the call and turned to McMillan. "What were you saying?"

"What has Lucas told you or done to you that makes you so compliant to his every whim and desire?"

"Nothing and he isn't a freak." I could feel my shoulders as they tensed up.

"We have him… It's not concrete just yet kid, but with your help we can get him off of the streets for good."

"Oh, you do. What do you have?"

"The knife marks used on our victims just happen to be the same knife marks made in England. If we had the knife or knew where it was then we would have him and so would England."

"Oh, well good luck to you." Shit, he used that knife for every kill. They could match the kill pattern and the blade of the knife to him. And he would be on death row before there was time for a trial.

"We need the knife."

"Well get a warrant." I closed my notebook. "I mean, if you have all of this evidence against him it shouldn't be so hard."

"It's the one he keeps on him. We want you to get him here and then we'll confiscate the knife. It is no telling how much blood there is on the knife. Then we will have him extradited to England and then back here. He is done."

"That's good for you. Why would you need me to get the knife for you?"

"I don't have a warrant."

"He is my friend. I am not doing anything to bring him in. You have the wrong guy anyhow. He wouldn't hurt a fly. Plus, his girl is pregnant and they are happy. Leave them be."

"He is a serial killer."

"Are we done here?"

"Why the sudden attitude change?"

"There is no sudden change, sir." I paused. "I just don't want to be involved with investigation anymore."

"Did he threaten you?"

"No," I paused. "How long is this going to go on?"

"I guess I'll dig into you some then."

"Please do, maybe I'll have time to finish up my homework and be a normal student. I have to go." I pushed passed him. "I have to go. Is there anything else that you need?"

"When we investigate him further everything will come to the light. If there is something that you are hiding I suggest that you just tell us now. This can save you a ton of time."

"Well, you should know that I found out that they are both my brothers." I looked at him. "And I don't want to have anything further dealings with your investigation. I just want to be left alone."

"Brother?"

"Mark and Lucas both... they are kin to me and I feel like this whatever partnership you think you have here..." I pointed to him and then back to me. "It can't go on. I just need to be left alone to find myself and I don't want anything else to do with it. Now if you would leave I have some packing to do."

There was another knock at my door and he flinched. "Don't fall into this trap."

"I'm not. Come in!" I yelled.

Mark entered the apartment holding three suitcases. "How much is too much? I mean I don't want to sound like a chick, but there is a chance that I might stay a little longer. Especially if there are chicks there worth seeing ag..." he paused. "Um, hi?"

"Yeah, he was just leaving. I thought you were bringing Shia?"

"I am... but she knows that we are friends. Why is he here?"

"This new brotherhood between you three is a nice twist." McMillan smirked. "I can help you both. I can make sure that when your brother fries you at most get 5 years for conspiracy. Four if you cooperate with me."

"Get out?" Mark chuckled.

"Yeah do that please."

"You are going to regret being involved with them you know that right?" McMillan opened the front door. "You are not like them. It doesn't matter if you two are brothers are not. He will drag you down. He will make your life..."

"Man get the fuck out," my voice rose higher than I expected and there was a true expression of shock on his face. "Please."

"Alright, good day."

Lucas

Cypress had left for more than an hour and I was alone for the first time in a few days. I didn't know rather to be relieved or not just yet. There was a part of me that wanted to follow her down there just to make sure that she made the trip. I lie on my bed, my eyes hooked to the ceiling I watched the smoke dissipate in front of me. This weed was comforting. It was something that I could not do when she was here. I reached inside the cabinet and felt for my knife. It had been a while since it was even in my hands. The woes of fatherhood had started and the child was not even here.

I rattled my hand around in the drawer and I could not feel it. I inhaled another drag of the blunt and sat up on the side of the bed. Where was it? I looked through the drawer. Whatever the fuck had happened to it, I didn't care. It must have been in my car.

The elevator doors opened slowly and Mark waltzed through the doors. There was no such thing as privacy with Mark. I just wanted to smoke my weed alone and in peace. "Good grief, what do you want?"

"Are you smoking?"

"Why ask if you know the answer Mark?"

"I thought you were giving up on that shit?"

"What the actual fuck do you want?" I exhaled the smoke. "Why are you here?"

"Well, I stopped by Asher's before Cypress kidnapped him and he told me some interesting news. The Agent in the case is on the hunt for your knife. "That knife... connects you to murders in England and in America."

I blinked. "England?"

"Yeah England... where is the knife you have to get rid of it."

"Absolutely not," I spat. "Declan gave me that knife."

"Why would you even want to keep it. You don't even like Declan, all you do is tell us why he was a horrible father to you." Mark said.

"What has he to do with it?" Asher was confused.

"It's his knife and it's why you are so connected to it. You can't fool me Lucas." Mark said matter of fact. It was true, I could never hold a strong face when it came to him and that was bullshit.

"Oh..."

I could feel the questions as they wandered into his mind. "Ask me Mark."

"How was he?"

"He was a cold hearted manipulative bastard that I loved." I shrugged. "I'm more like him than you know and I hate it more and more every day. But I would never allow someone else to raise my child. He was wrong for what he done to you two. And I'm sorry that he chose me at most days. But I like having you two around. You keep me level headed."

"You are high." Mark smiled.

"Ruin my speech asshole."

"Okay, I will." Mark chuckled. "Where is the knife?"

"I don't know it was in here?" I pointed to the night stand. "I'll find it later. Could you order me a pizza from downstairs?"

"Could you start paying for your food? I feel like you are destroying the cost margins for this place."

"No, Mark, are you hungry? Do you want a puff?" I held out the blunt and he surprised me as he took a deep drag from it. "Make that two pizzas."

Cypress

Asher was a talker. It was a perfect road trip for me because I did like to talk about random shit that popped into my mind when I was on the road. I sat in the passenger's seat with my seat let so far back it touched the back seat. "So how are you liking being kin to Lucas?"

"It's nice. I like having family around here." He tapped the steering wheel. "And I like the fact that they both get me free food from the restaurant. Cooking a student's worst nightmare. Especially because I suck at it."

"You can cook something."

"Not at all." He laughed. "So why are we really headed down here?"

"What do you mean?"

"I mean you said just last week that your mother was headed out of town for some kind of convention. Lucas has been so worried about your safety he kind of missed the main thing that should have tipped him off."

This smart bastard had made me two hours in. I remained quiet and looked out at the mountains in the distance. "Why are you so damn smart?"

"Well, I don't mind defying his wishes. I just hope that whatever we are doing down here doesn't bite me in the ass in a few weeks. So spill it Cypress."

Asher flashed a smile at me and then focused back on the road. I cleared my throat as I reached for the brown purse under my feet. It took a moment, but I finally had it. I felt the knife in my hand. "I don't know much about Lucas' secrecy or why he thinks he has to be secret. But this knife is the one that he keeps in his night stand. It has his father's named inscribed and I kind of guessed it had a bad air to it. I don't know if it's true."

His face was white. "Why would you think that it had a bad air to it Cy?"

"There is something about him that I have not figured out yet. And he won't let me in to see it. And since he won't I can't do what I need to in order to make sure that he is not out here making an ass of himself. And I know he talks to you and Mark here lately and he seems so much more laid back about everything. I love it about him. But I feel like hiding this knife far away from us is the best way to insure that everything is safe."

"Okay," He shook his head in agreement. "I can't say that you are wrong or right. But I agree that you are making a good decision. Just keep it to yourself."

"I can do that."

"Good and I want you to know that you can talk to me in confidence. I don't run and tell everything I know to Lucas. He doesn't need to know everything." Asher said.

CHAPTER EIGHTEEN

Lucas

I had not put thought into rather she would like Ireland or not. I just knew that the getaway was much needed for the both of us. The last month had been stressful. We were a month away from graduation and then there was the final exams that Cypress swore she wasn't prepared for but she knew every subject like the back of her hand. Being pregnant made her worry. She was a big five months. She had grown so much here recently I felt bad for her. Her feet ached constantly and she had to pee every five seconds.

Thankfully the plane ride for her was peaceful, she slept most of the time while she listened to her newest favorite band The Paper Kites. She would occasionally shift in her seat and gasped at the change views. Then every other bump she gripped my hand at the thought of a crash. Then, once we entered the country and she saw her first glimpse of Ireland, she had grown silent.

"What's wrong?" I whispered. I feared that she didn't like it and all hope that I had for us to relocate here was out of the door before we landed.

"I've never seen anything like it." Her voice was soft. "It's simply beautiful."

"And you haven't been to England yet." I chuckled.

"I know. I can't wait"

Shia was nestled into Mark. She had slept the entire flight and then there was Asher. He had come stag but he was unbothered by it. He had found himself so lost in his book that nothing else mattered at the moment. It took long enough, but I finally had gotten used to the fact that he was an older brother too. It was still weird though, and there were still questions for Tracy that lingered in the back of my mind.

"How long has been since you've seen Callum?" Asher nudged me.

"About three years," I answered.

"And he's your cousin?"

"Our cousin," I pushed Asher lightly.

Asher smiled. "Yeah, whatever," he nodded his head. "This shit is unreal."

"I know." Mark looked out at the window. His eyes mesmerized by the row of brightly colored townhouses that covered the street.

"I have some friends that live there."

"How do you know so many people?" Cypress raised her eyebrow at me. "Were you like playboy over here? Will I have to step off of the plane and start beating some European ass immediately?"

"I swear it to you that I was not a playboy over here, I just got out the house a lot sometimes. Living in three countries your entire life, you know everyone, love."

Callum's house sat in the middle of the land like a castle. The stone walls and vines grew up the home that was surrounded by a garden of flowers ranging from every color. Then there were two red head beauties. Holly, I remembered her from school, stood holding a very red head little girl. Her hair waved down her back fire red just like her mother's. I could only assume she was her mother because even from 100 feet away the similarities in the two were uncanny.

"I didn't know he was married." Mark said.

"He isn't." I chuckled. The car came to a halt at the beginning of the gravel stoned driveway. "Um driver..."

"This is as far as I go." The driver thick accent filled the car.

Cypress sighed. "Even for the obviously pregnant woman whose feet have developed a mind of their own?"

"Far as I go." He snapped. It was enough to send me into protective mode.

Mark gripped my shoulder. "Get out." He laughed.

Callum ran up the driveway playfully. "How was the journey?"

I smiled. "It was grand."

"Oh, I'm sure." Callum made it to us. His blonde hair was still short and in a disarray on top of his head. And the only obvious change was his development of some type of muscle and a few extra inches in height. "Welcome back to Ireland brother.!" He pulled me in for a hug. "Dear Jesus, it's been forever mate! Why the fuck would yah stay away for so long?"

"I know it's been way too long." I pulled back and shook his hand again. "I want you to meet some people... family really."

"Mark and Asher, the two boys me father told me about," Callum smiled at Mark. "We've met once before." He shook his hand. "Just not as cousins."

They had met once and it had been awkward. Mark had always been over protective of me and he saw Callum as a piss poor excuse for a friend. But I saw the opposite. He shook his hand sternly, "Right, how have you been?" Mark asked.

"Great, Holly and I have a child... her name is Nina."

"Nice." Mark said, in short.

"And you must be Asher, welcome to the family!"

Asher shook his hand apprehensively. "Pleasure, to meet you. You have a marvelous home." he smirked.

"And who are these lovely lasses?"

Shia climbed out of the car in a bit of a stumble and handed Mark her largest bag. Her hair was a mess and she looked like she had just woken. Her hair all mashed to the right side of her head and her shirt unfixed. "My name is Shia... girlfriend to Mark."

"Oh, he can get a girl can he?" Callum joked and Asher burst into laughter with him.

"Funny," Mark rolled his eyes.

"And this work of art here?" Callum gestured towards Cypress.

"She is my Cypress... I mean girl." I helped her out of the car and she waved politely at Callum. "She is tired from the flight."

"I assume you all are." Callum grabbed Cypress' bags and paid the cab driver. "I've cooked some bangers and mash. And then I guess you guys can rest up for tomorrow."

"What's tomorrow?"

"A big day." Callum answered.

There was something up his sleeve and I was not sure if I wanted to know what it was just yet.

His home was large and the inside looked nothing like I would have imagined. It was vast in space. The wooden beams on the ceiling were a dark hickory and the walls were a savory cream. Cypress sat down on the couch and a moan escaped her mouth. "This couch is heavenly."

"It looks nice."

"I want one."

"Your will is my command." I sat next to her. "Are you feeling alright?"

"What are Bangers and Mash?"

"They are good. Sausage and Mash potatoes."

"Wow," Cypress laid her head on my chest.

"I know. We can tour the city tomorrow if you are up to it?"

"I want to. I think tomorrow I will be well rested."

"Good," I watched as Callum lifted his little girl up and walked over to us. "Alright, now little lass, this is your Godfather Lucas..." The little girl smiled as she swirled a curl around her finger. "Say hello?"

"Hello Lucas." She grinned and squirmed her way down her father's leg.

"Tell her your name."

"My name is Nina." Her light voice floated into the room, she brought a radiance with her that I prayed my daughter had some day.

"Pleasure to meet you princess." I said.

"It's Nina." She turned and ran around the corner to her mother.

"She'll come around. Holly love come here, meet the ladies."

Holly poked her head around the corner. "Honey, let me finish cooking. We have an entire week to meet."

"Always so charming." Callum mumbled. "Tell me how you two met? I mean you must be a special girl to have snagged the attention of my cousin."

"College," Cypress didn't elaborate.

"We might have to do it tomorrow Cal, she is not friendly when she is tired. The flight kind of dragged her down."

Cypress half smiled. "I'm sorry Cal. Being pregnant and flying sucks ass."

"I can only imagine. And it's fine. No need for apologies."

"Thank you." She yawned.

"I hope Mark and Asher are comfortable here. I know not too many people are fond of staying in a castle."

"They should be."

"How did you find out about them?" He paused. "I mean I never even heard of her having any other children besides you."

"Asher has done some digging." I nodded. "But it's not bad. I actually like having two brothers."

"Yeah, mine is a pain in my arse."

"They can be," I agreed.

"Come on outside with me for a moment."

"Are you good here?"

"I'm great." Cypress rested her body back into the couch. "Go ahead."

"Okay."

Ireland, I had not stepped foot here since my father died. And it still had this grip on me. The lush green of the hills surrounded by the clearest sea that there was. The fresh air of the countryside filled my lungs and my mind saw it... I was about to have a sense of normalcy, a real family and a life.

Callum started to peel his apple and sat down next to me on the porch. "She seems like a naive girl."

"She is."

"Does she know?"

"No idea," I mumbled. I pushed my hands through my hair. "I miss this place."

"What are you doing?" Callum held his r's longer so he sounded like a pirate.

"Just taking it in."

"It's a beautiful place to do it all. What you thinking about? Perhaps moving here?"

"Is it peaceful?"

"Yeah, indeed. I live here..." He gestured towards the huge stone home. The vines grew up the side in splendor garnishing the house with a flower every now and then. It sat on a hill that was surrounded by neighboring hills and there was nothing there but nature for miles. "It doesn't have a good playground."

"You have a city though." I smiled. "I like it here Callum."

"Well move, leave America alone."

"She is from America."

"You mean your beauty in there?"

"I do."

"I can tell you love her. Your Pa used to stare at Luna that way. It's good for you."

"You sound like my brothers in there."

"What's up with the Luna look-a-like? He seems like he knows me and I have just met him."

I laughed at him, I could only assume he was talking about Asher. "He is weird. He can read and sense people and two seconds with you and he knew immediately that we shared kindred spirits."

"Yeah, I haven't retired though." Callum cut the apple and crunched into it. "Are you good?"

"I have this copper on me named McMillan and he is making my life a living hell. So do you still..."

"Kill, yes. I can't stop. I might kill her if I do. She has a bad knack for demanding dishes to be washed. I don't channel it well. I go places and do what I have to and then come home.

Speaking of which. I have to travel to Belfast this week. There I have some unfinished business. Care to join me?"

"Like old times, eh?" I pushed him. "Who?"

"Remember that prick of a teacher in boarding school that tried to rape me?"

"Carver McIntosh, how could I forget?"

"In-fucking-deed." a smile covered his face. "I've been waiting patiently for this fucker to retire for more than ten years now. And I get the chance to kill him. I have to move on it."

"I'm down." I answered. "I know you hated him. How are we going to make a four-hour trip unnoticed? My brothers in there want to keep a tight leash on me."

"Look, I am not worried about them. And Holly can keep your beauty there entertained. There are some tours she can take her on and then your brothers can hunt for daddy."

"What do you mean hunt for daddy?"

"Your father is not dead. My father killed him off, he has an alias. He's alive. He keeps tab on you and I know where he is and they will jump at a chance to meet him."

"My father? Why in the fuck have you not told me Callum?" My voice was dangerously low.

"Calm. Your. Nerve..." He said with a brief pause in between each word. "Be a lotus flower or whatever the fuck you do mate." Callum cut his eyes at me. "I don't think they can handle a brawl between us. We'll fuck each other up and you know it." He warned. "So take your seat back."

My nose flared. "You could have told me? Callum, we have always been honest with one another. I don't know what changed. But why is he alive? And why would he have not reached out to me?"

"I personally have never understood your father until I became a father. It's hard handling both sides of it. There has to be a balance. You will understand her soon. But in that house I have two people who love me with every ounce of their being and I would do anything to make sure that this whatever it is that dwells in me never touches them." His hands fell to his side. "Your father was about to be exposed. And yeah, you may have guessed what he was and Luna might have to... but he didn't want to see the hurt it caused you. If it ever boils down to it...I will leave. I will leave because I love them. And you'll get it soon enough. With that first cry you'll be sucked in and your real survival instincts will kick in. You won't need to meditate and you won't need to control yourself. You'll know what to do."

"Where is he?"

"Somewhere in Dublin," he answered.

"Look, I can get him here. Are you coming to Belfast or no mate?"

"Yes," I exhaled. "But on the way there you spill everything."

"We will see. I really like to listen music before a kill. You'll love what I have set up. Hell, your cousin might teach you a thing or two." Callum cracked his smile and pushed me playfully. "I can't believe we are a tag team again."

"Oh, shut it." I mocked. "You wouldn't come to America with me. I begged you."

"The coppers over there, are a wee too over-zealous for me." He shrugged his shoulders. "I can kind of play over here as long as I don't step on toes... plus I've become a side enforcer for the IRA. Extra money and I get to kill... sloppy or neat... It really doesn't matter. It's still money."

"Paid to kill huh?"

"Yes, it's the True IRA and I wouldn't stop for the world."

"They don't come after you?"

Callum cackled. "They wouldn't dare. I would kill them before they got through the door. You are about to have a blast. I can tell there are some things that you need to learn little cousin. I can't wait to teach you."

Cypress

The smell of the food was reassuring. I hadn't eaten a decent meal since we left and I was more than tired of the stupid Airline food. I wanted their entire home to be mine. Though it was old it was a simple marvel. The entire kitchen was marble and cherry wood. Holly moved around the kitchen like a Goddess and if it belonged to me I would too. The refrigerator even had a wooden door.

"How long have you known Lucas?"

"Oh sweetie, I have known him since boarding school. We used to get in all types of trouble."

"Like what?"

"One time we drove a teacher's car off a ravine and when asked about it, we all had an alibi." She chuckled as she placed the plates on the table. "Lucas is a good guy with some fucked up layers." Holly took down some glasses and placed them on the table. "Callum said that he was thinking of moving here."

"He's been talking about it. We are on Spring Break and pretty much once we get back we'll be graduating. He hates America now."

"Well, do you think that you would enjoy Ireland?"

"I honestly don't know."

"Well, tomorrow I can show you some reasons that you would."

"My parents live in America."

"Yeah," Holly paused. "How many months are you?"

"Five months, twenty-one weeks." I rubbed my stomach. "The baby moves now." I could feel my face turning red as I thought about the baby.

"He seems like he loves you."

"He does." I bit my lip. "Callum and him love each other."

"Lucas is Callum's best friend. They were practically raised together."

Shia pulled her a seat out next to me, "Holly your home is a beauty."

"Thank you," Holly scooped potatoes onto to the plate. "Callum spoils me."

"Mommy!" Nina handed her a flower. "I picked a flower."

"I have told you to stay out of my garden Nina." She picked her up. "Put it on the table and go get your lily behind in the living room with your pa."

Motherhood, I watched her, kiss her cheek and then continue to cook. I'd never even thought about the child being older than a newborn. I was more concerned with labor pains and Lucas. I couldn't get a grip on the future.

"It'll be easy." Holly chimed in reading my face. "Once you see that little face everything will zone out and you will defend her or him with your life."

Shia agreed, "Yes and we'll spoil her."

"I don't know what I'm having Shia."

"I told her it's a girl."

"I hope so."

Mark and Asher entered the kitchen. "Holly, thank you so much for your hospitality. I know it's a ton of people in your home."

"I love house guests. Especially family." She poured wine into all of the glasses, then placed the bottle in the bucket of ice in the middle of the table.

Asher sat on the other side of me, "The rooms are unreal. Would you mind if I snapped a few pictures?"

"Snap all you want."

"Thank you."

I was worried about Asher. He seemed like he was lost ever since he had found out who he was. Plus, from what Lucas told me he had not been able to get a hold of his mother since she gave him the news.

"You are welcome."

Shia held Mark's hand like a lost puppy. She irritated me the way she submitted to his beck and call, but he was rarely around when they weren't on their little trips. "We should come here once a year." She suggested.

"Definitely should." Mark mumbled. "Where are Callum and Luke?"

"Right here! Did you miss us?"

"Of course," Mark rolled his eyes.

"Alright Callum and Mark, it was years ago. Kiss and make up." Holly said.

"What was years ago?"

Callum grinned. "We fought one year and Mark holds grudges like his namesake and he has not yet forgiven me for it."

"I won that fight." Mark said.

"No you didn't mate."

"Whatever, I know I won that fight."

"Okay truce." Holly added. "Right now, please."

"Truce mate," Callum held his hand out and Mark shook it. "We are cousins now! We must all get along."

Lucas looked at Asher. "Is she okay?" He mouthed.

"I'm fine babe." I answered for myself.

"Okay, come on, let's get seated."

Dinner went by fast. Lucas and Callum told stories of their fathers. Asher absorbed everything in like it was the news, while Mark just chuckled at the antics and stories. They had started to actually have a brotherhood with one another and it was the most beautiful thing to me. Finally, Lucas looked like he wasn't lost and since we had been here I had never seen him smile as much as he was smiling here recently. I like to think that I had something to do with it.

The room was cozy. The California King took up most of the room and was covered with the plushest comforter I had felt since I had stayed the summer with my Grandparents. The view from the room was simply breathtaking to say the least and to wake up to it and Lucas every day would be a dream for a minute.

Lucas unpacked his bags, organizing everything in the oak chest at the bottom of the bed. "How do you feel?"

"I feel good baby." I stared at the words on the pages but there was nothing comprehended. There were just emotions seeping in and waterworks forming. "It's so pretty here." The tears rolled down my cheek and Lucas' eyes grew wide. My hormones were out of whack and he was not good at the comprehension of it.

"Why are you crying?"

"I don't know." I sniffled.

"Well stop, I don't know how to handle all of your emotions." He whispered.

"Happy tears," I gestured towards my face. "I love that this country could be our home. It seems unreal."

"I want us to be here. I love it here. The sun is nice and the scenery is grand. And you are happy here. I mean I haven't ever seen you smile as much as you have lately. I know Asher and Mark have a ton to do with it."

"They do actually. But you know this baby and you... are the main things. I have a family of my own now and I'm happy."

My hands grazed my baby bump and I exhaled. "I only have a few more months, really two and I can't travel anymore. Are we going to go ahead and buy a home over here or stay with them? We graduate here soon. I just don't want to be searching for home when the babies come. I would rather be there... I can't nest at your loft."

"Nesting... is that a real thing?"

"Yes, I have an urge to constantly clean and make everything perfect because I want everything to be right."

"Your mum would have a cow if we moved before the baby was born." He added. "Tracy would more than likely kill over and Lydia would follow soon after." Lucas rubbed his forehead. "I want to do whatever will make you happy. If that means packing up and moving time we get back... my wish is your command."

"You don't want to?"

"I don't want you to regret everything on a rash decision. There are tons of people that love how it looks here. I want you to love what you can have here. This is a fresh start. I have enough money so that work is not an option or an issue. I can work and you can do whatever you want to."

"I don't want to be like Holly." I blurted out.

"Okay, what about it don't you like? You have been here for four hours?"

I laughed. "I think she just stays around the house all day."

"You can do whatever you want to do Cypress."

"Take painting classes?"

"Please take your classes." He sat down on the bed and pulled his hair into a bun on the top of his head. "And write something and be my wife..." The word lingered in the air. Wife.

He handed a box to me, small velvet and red. I touched it and looked at him. "Lucas."

"I'm not marrying you because we're having a baby. I can be the father and not be married to you. I'm asking you to marry me because you are everything that I need. It's selfish even. I know it and I don't care. I want you to have my last name. I want you to know that no one can fuck with you because your HUSBAND, not your boyfriend will fuck them up. I want to spend forever with you."

"Lucas Elledge," I could not open the box. He had already bought me a promise ring that put my mother's wedding ring to shame.

"Please open it."

My hands were sweaty as I opened the red velvet box. The black gold ring was unlike anything I had ever seen. The diamonds were placed in the shape of a lotus flower. It simply overflowed with more beauty than I had ever seen in my life. "Oh shit," I cried. "Dear Lord, Lucas... how much did it cost?"

"It's not important. The answer is."

"Yes," I stifled.

"Was that a yes?"

"It was." I shook.

He took the box and removed the ring from it. "Thank you."

"What does this mean?"

"You have some planning to do."

"But what... I mean... yes. I am down for some planning."

"Good!" His lips crushed mine and all was right. My hands explored his body slowly. Lucas placed his hands on my stomach. "Your mum just said yes son."

"Son, we don't know yet."

"It's a boy..."

"Okay, Lucas since you are so sure."

"Thank You."

Asher

For the majority of my life there has been this sense of loneliness. My mother was not the caring kind and my father was so obsessed with his work that there was nothing that could stop him from doing it. Not even me. So the news made me happy. My brothers... they wanted to be around me, even Lucas had accepted it and there was something more than for me in the store.

My hands twiddled with the small wooden figurine. The edges smooth I played with it on the couch that seemed to engulf me with warmth.

"Ey Asher, can't sleep?"

"Not really." I smiled at Callum.

"You know your mum made that figurine you are holding. It's a soldier. She made me seven of them. I spread them throughout the house... Nina loves to play with them."

"Oh," I placed the figurine down.

"It's fine," he chuckled. "You can have it actually."

"Thanks," I looked at it. "What was my mum like? Luke hates talking about her."

"I hoped you would ask." Callum pointed to the picture of the woman on the wall. "You look so much like her it's almost eerie mate. And out of the three I think you have her heart."

"She was smart?"

"She was conserved and smart. And she did anything for her family, including giving you two up."

"Why was that important?"

"I mean I don't know. I just know my grandmother said that it was the hardest thing that she had to do and that she never wanted it."

"It has to be more to it."

"There always is more." Callum lit a cigar, filling the room with the smell and surprisingly the aroma was a delight. "How is Luke?"

"Better, I think," I paused. I don't know how much he knows granted, I am sure that he is one of the same. I can see it in his eyes. "I mean you know... what do you mean Callum?"

"I know you know." Callum inhaled a drag of the cigar and blew out the smoke. "Is he being reckless?"

"Define reckless?"

"He has always been impulsive but you'll see that is what makes Lucas, Lucas."

"Impulsive is definitely him. He seems to not think things through and everything he does is for him. He knows it and I think I am learning to get over it." I chuckled. "You can't win them all."

"Yeah, this true." Callum leaned forward, resting his elbows on his leg. "Look out for him," He asked.

"I am."

"I mean always. No matter what the situation is. He has never had a real brother. I mean I am like a brother, but there is nothing better than the real thing. Brothers always look out for one another, even when they are against each other they are for each other."

"I understand."

"Good, would you like another brew?"

"Not right now," I smirked.

"So how'd your mother take with you finding out about yourself?"

"She doesn't call me anymore." The thought of being motherless had entered my mind a few times. Margot had been distant. I had tried to reach out to her more than once and there was never a response just another voice mail left until the mailbox was full. My father even backed away from me. So there was something more and I just wanted to know what there was.

"It's her lost mate. Don't over think it. Mothers are difficult. Trust me, my mum won't even look at me sometimes because she knows what I am. It scares her and I can understand why. I am not a good guy and nor do I pretend to be. I would like her to love me though."

"I am sure she loves you."

"I don't think so mate." Callum crossed his arms and stared at the table. "I really don't think so."

We had more in common than I thought. "I'm afraid that after all of this I will be alone."

"You'll never be alone. You have more family over here than you could imagine. And we Elledges stay together and protect each other. No matter how new or old you are in the family there is always room for you here. You should probably meet our grandmother. She is going to flip when she sees you."

"I have a grandmother." I asked.

"You do, and a grandfather and some more surprises for tomorrow of course. There is a family dinner you have to be in attendance."

"Should I wear a tie?"

"Uh, be casual." He added. "I better get to bed before my lovely Holly is not so cheerful." He put out his cigar. "See you in the morning cousin."

"Goodnight Callum."

CHAPTER NINETEEN

Cypress

The world was new again. Everything I looked at and touched went from being something plain into something that could be used in my wedding or the baby's room. I spent the entire morning searching for wedding dress styles and the baby room for a cottage. I was sure we would live in a cottage somewhere here. This place was perfect. Instead of the routine of tossing and turning all night, Lucas had slept peacefully.

My phone battery was almost dead and my bladder was being danced on by some 3-pound beauty I had not seen yet. I slipped from under him and made my way to the bathroom. I stared at the diamond lotus flower on my hand and realized it was all coming together in a good way for the first time for me and him.

"You sleep well?" he moaned from the bed.

I splashed the cool water on my face and exhaled. "I slept like a baby."

"Good," He rose up. "Callum said that we were going to visit the family today. I don't know how… I doubt we can all fit in his car."

"We should have got a rental." I said.

"We'll figure something out." Lucas slid his shoes on and walked over to the small bathroom. "Mrs. Elledge has a great ring to it you know?"

"I know. I've been practicing it all morning."

"Are we going to tell them today?"

"I don't see why not." I said as my eyes looked over his body. "I think we should tell them."

"Me too." He maneuvered his way to the sink and kissed me lightly on the lips. "Have you been sick here lately? You know with the morning sickness?"

"The morning sickness is over I think, though the smell of those damn sausage about killed me yesterday. But they were so good."

"I saw you eating. Have you taken your vitamins this morning?" He sifted through his bag on the sink and took out the prenatal vitamins. "No."

"I literally just woke up before you." He was like a Nazi when it came to me or the baby and this health regiment. "Do you want to go see your father's grave today?" I wiped my face with the washcloth and then tossed it on the cabinet.

"I'd rather not." He shrugged his shoulders. "I'd rather fuck you before breakfast." A devious smile emerged on his face.

"Uh... I prefer to be made love to mister."

"You like to fuck and you know it." He pulled me into the bedroom and his hands went up my skirt. A stifled moan escaped from my mouth and Lucas smiled. His smile as normal took my breath away.

"BREAKFAST IS READY!" a small voice said as the door opened. "Godfather! Breakfast is served!" Nina jumped playfully on the bed and Lucas groaned.

"Perfect little Nina." Lucas grimaced as he held his hands above his head. "I'll go wash my hands."

"Welcome to parenthood!" Callum yelled from the end of the hall.

"Good! Come on Cypress!" She tugged my hand and moved slowly behind her.

I followed her lead downstairs and the table was completely covered by food. Tomatoes and Beans... I looked over at Asher. "Good morning Asher!"

"Morning," He answered. "How was your night?"

"Perfect," I answered. Strips of ham and a plate of eggs were in front of me. It was the weirdest breakfast; I had ever seen. "Tomatoes?"

"Yes, they are great with eggs and the beans. And I have some bangers left over from last night that are almost finished cooking." Callum said. He was serious about this meal and it looked like the nastiest feast I had ever seen.

"Great," reached for my glass of water and there was a shrill yell.

"What the actual fuck Cypress!" Shia reached for my hand and screamed again. "You're getting married! That motherfucker finally done the right thing!"

"Naughty word!" Nina said from the floor of toys.

"Thanks loud mouth." Lucas said from the top of the stairs. "We were going to announce it."

"Look at this ring. Mark, are you taking notes?" She looked over at an unamused Mark and winked.

"Yeah," he mumbled. "Congrats brother and sister-in-law. I'm happy you two are happy."

"Thanks Mark."

"I hope the wedding is soon." Shia said like it was her moment. "It would be perfect to have a summer wedding! Have you looked at venues and chose a color?"

"Shia calm down. I asked her yesterday."

"Happy to have you in the family." Asher said. "You're just gaining family every day Lucas." Asher was amused. "And I am kind of proud of you."

"Thank you Asher!" I sipped my water.

"Callum do you see it? That's what normal couples do." Holly slammed the plate on the counter and fell to the ground in several pieces. Her face had turned from cheer filled to red with heartache in a matter of ten seconds. "I am so happy for you. I'll be down in just a moment. I seemed to have forgotten my manners upstairs."

"Oh, Holly." Callum followed her.

"Great job Shia," Lucas rolled his eyes at her and sat down in the seat next to me.

"I'm sorry. She is my best friend and I got excited! You have finally done something right." She snapped.

"Oh really," Lucas grabbed a plate and put it in front of me. "Maybe you should stop being such a…" I stomped his foot causing him to grunt and stare at me with his wide eyes. "Just pass the damn hash."

"Thank you," I grabbed his hand.

Callum made his way down the stairs. "Excuse her, she's just a little moody."

"It's fine. The breakfast looks great." Mark said as he piled his plate.

"Indeed eat up," Callum sat down across from Lucas. "Congrats, cousin. I'm proud of you. Making big strides and that ring is tremendous. I have never seen anything like it."

"I know. Mark and Asher actually helped me with it. Asher has surprisingly good taste."

"Thanks, I mean you were about to get her a horrible ring."

"Yeah, it had white gold… and some kind of weird design." Mark laughed along with Asher.

"Why didn't you bring Whitney?"

"We actually decided to take a break and what better place to be single in that Ireland?"

"The best way to get over a broad is to find a new one to get under…" Callum laughed. "I know I'm not single, but there are some bars that we could get you laid in."

"Appreciate that Cal," He snickered.

"I didn't know she left you."

"We took a break Mark."

"I mean; I didn't like her honestly. I think that you can find someone a little bit better… a little less attitude." Lucas added. "She was always staring at me like a monster."

"I wonder why?" Asher tilted his head. "I get it you didn't like her and that's fine. Change the subject."

"Testy this morning little brother…"

"Luke, I'm older than you." Asher rolled his eyes.

Mark burst into laughter, "Dear Jesus, do you two have to argue every morning."

"It wouldn't be normal if we hugged."

"Baby," I snapped at Lucas. "Please be nice."

"He's fine, you guys. He doesn't bother me. I overlook half of what he says. I know it's his form of love." Asher calmed the table. "Though I appreciate you all jumping to my defense."

"Well, I'll be taking him off of your hands for a while today. We are going to go hit some old spots up in Belfast. I want to show him how everything has changed."

"I would love to see Belfast." Mark said.

"Um, maybe later this week Mark. I really just wanted to spend some time with my cousin here. We haven't had the proper chance to catch up in ages. And I know it's important to him. He can ask me to be his best man and everything." Callum winked. "And I know Holly wanted to take the ladies to some places."

"We could sight-see." Mark said to Asher.

"Perhaps."

Lucas nodded his head. "Then we can all meet at our grandmother's house around 6ish?"

Lucas had obviously made these plans without me. "So, I have to spend a whole day alone?"

"With Holly, Cypress it's not the whole day. We just really want to have some man bonding time alone."

"Fine," I smiled at Holly as she walked down the steps holding Nina in her arms. "I hear we are having a girls' day."

"Oh yeah, And I have some places to take you lovely ladies."

Lucas

Callum drove like a bat out of hell. This part of him I hadn't missed. I held on for my dear life as we traveled the curvy dirt road. "Why you look so nervous there Luke? How can you kill someone and fear death?"

"How can I not? You drive like a mad man. I'll be driving home." I shook my head. "So have you talked to this teacher?"

"I haven't... I have another to kill too. It's for half a million. Are you down?"

"I mean I guess." I looked out at the scenery that surrounded me.

"What do you mean you guess?" Callum looked over at me. "Why are you so quiet? Liven up! When was the last time you killed someone?"

"Too long... my dear friend Luther in the states."

"You'll do good. Have you thought about a career here? I mean for when you move?"

"I don't know." I knew what the entire family was over there. I remember the power my father and uncles had by just looking at someone. Though the power was an adrenaline rush I doubted Cypress wanted to put through the drama that comes with it.

"Think about it, you have to have a way to support your family. The money that you have won't last forever. I can get you a job with me. I have some people under me. I could make you my second in charge." Callum ranted about his business that was doing more than well and how he would want me to step in a run some things but organized crime was not for me. I was not a tough guy. I was just a thrill seeking killer there was a complete difference.

"I know what I have Callum and I don't bloody want it."

"Don't get snappy." He grimaced. "When are you getting married?"

"I don't know. I told her to plan everything and give me a date and I would be there."

"Smart."

"Why won't you marry Holly? You two have been together since forever."

"I know." Callum groaned. "Everything is fine and there is no ring. Rings make things so difficult. I just want to be with her and love her. I don't need to stand before the church and confess me love for her. She knows I love her and that's all I want."

"Women don't think like that Cal."

"So, I think like that."

"Alright, anyhow... I don't have my knife. I had to leave it back home."

"You use a knife?"

"What do you use?"

"Whatever is at my disposal, what knife?"

"The knife my father gave me."

"The engraved knife, that's sweet. Are you ready to see him?"

"No, the bloody bastard has some major explaining to do."

"Be nice," we finally pulled into the small town and parked. "He lives in that house." He pointed to a small cottage. "Remember it?"

"Yeah, I remember you telling me about it. What do you plan on doing?"

"Getting in unnoticed... Killing him slowly in the damned dungeon that he raped kids in. And then cutting his dick off and shoving it in his mouth. After that... I get to eat good and fuck my girlfriend senseless, so she can forget about that damned ring."

"You are such a gentleman."

"I know mate."

My instincts kicked in as we watched him water his flowers and talk to the local neighborhood kids. Callum twiddled with his knife in his pocket. He occasionally tapped the steering wheel humming some Irish tune under his breath.

"What are you the most afraid of Luke?"

"What do you mean?"

"What do you fear?"

"Death, the freaking electric chair."

"Don't fear it." Callum rested his head against his seat with his eyes closed. "When you fear something you become reckless. When you are fearless you become dangerous. I don't fear death. I don't fear the police. I don't fear anything."

"Well, lucky you." I mumbled.

"Asher said he worries that you are getting reckless."

"I did for a moment."

"That moment could have ruined your life."

"You talk to Asher about me?"

"Barely, he's a quiet guy. I like him."

"Yeah, he's different." I rolled my eyes.

"I want you to live, to grow old. I want you to see your grandchildren. And I think you need to leave America permanently to do it."

"I've thought about it and it's what I need to do. I get it." Callum always wanted to pick brains on a kill. "Why are you so nosy?"

"Why are you so content living within a place that doesn't want you there anymore?"

"You do every time."

"Do what Luke?"

"Pick my brain, make me angry and I get out of control."

"Great! Yes, you need to be ruthless. Do you still talk to the bastards?"

"What?"

"I remember you talking Lucas. You like to taunt. Kill them and leave."

"Shut up." I snapped. "Look, he's in his house. We could go around the back."

"Yeah, I see him. I'll go to the front door and you can sneak around back."

"You'll be seen."

"I have protection through the IRA. I can do whatever I want. Just go to the back door and I will let you in. Keep your hat on and glasses as well and we can go ahead and make a move." He slid his black gloves on and walked to the front door. I made my way around to the back door.

The backyard was a huge garden, completely covered by the plants and the giant trees. I walked quietly over the stones and fountains and stood on the stone steps of his backyard. I could hear Callum talking in the house.

"I know it has been forever. I heard you retired from the boarding school?"

"Yeah a few weeks back. I just want to focus on my garden and maybe travel a wee bit. Would you like some tea?"

"Oh no thank you... I hate the stuff."

"Okay, well what brings you by?"

"Just some things I wanted to get off of my chest..."

"Go ahead." The teacher said completely lost on what was about to happen.

I knocked lightly on the back door and it opened. "Mr.... How have you been?"

A loud clang from behind him and he dropped to the floor. "Come on inmate." Callum drug him to the stairs and kicked him down. The thud of his head hitting the floor made me reassured he was out like a light. Callum was nothing like me on a kill. I was quiet. I stalked and waited for an opportunity. He made opportunities occur. The house had pictures of cats everywhere. The smell of burning onions filled the air and I turned to the stove. "We interrupted his dinner. How rude?" I laughed.

"I know. He was always a good cook." Callum broke the wooden chair into pieces and handed me a leg of it. He has something that he hangs little boys up with. I figure it is best we go ahead and string him up… lend me a hand?"

"My pleasure." He was a hefty man. We lifted him up and tied his hands together and hung him by his hands on the hook that hung from the ceiling. Then Callum stripped him down to his underwear and walked around him like he had won a trophy. He stared and wiped the sweat off of his face.

"I want this fucker up!" He growled. Callum hit the man's face several times, sending the sound ringing through the room. "Wake up!"

His eyes flickered and he struggled to pull against the ropes. A yell came from his mouth and I shoved a sock in it. "Not time to yell yet. Calm yourself… a struggle is just gonna make this ugly. I want your death to beautiful…. Understood?"

Callum shook with anger. "Do you remember?"

He shook his head, his fat neck turned red and then it was there. The fear. He squirmed and a tear fell from his face. "Shall we remind him?"

"Definitely," Callum stripped him of his underwear. "You tried to fuck me. I was fifteen years old. You cold hearted manipulative bastard! How many have you fucked!" Callum drew back slapped his back with the wooden stick shattering it in pieces as the blood ran down the man's back. "How many!"

Callum's face had grown red as well. His anger had boiled over to a point of no control. I stepped back and watched him as he retrieved the knife from his pocket. The knife clicked open and Callum walked towards him.

"I should cut your eyes out." He whispered. "I should pay someone to fuck you relentlessly. But instead... I'm going to make you bleed out slowly... Lucas... here."

I held my hand out for the knife and walked towards him. "I'm a talker. I kind of want to know you. Tell me about yourself. When did you start fucking little boys for leisure?"

Callum leaned against the wall. His eyes watched everything that I have done.

"No words..." I sliced into his stomach watching the blood pool on the ground. My heart raged and finally I had this feeling again. "How does that feel?" I smiled. "I felt it and I cannot lie. It feels like heaven. You are a good kill. Ugh shit, damn it. I mean... are there other rapists like you?"

I chuckled. "I mean of course, there are... I'll find the fuckers... Callum you like this project?"

"I do." Callum nodded.

"Good, we have a new hobby..." My knife traced his face and then I applied a little more pressure and he finally started to bleed. A muffled scream filled the air and my hand slapped the sides of his face. "Shut up. Did those boys scream? How does it feel?!" I couldn't even recognize my own voice. "You sick fuck!" The growl escaped as I pushed the knife into his arms. The blood raced past his face.

"Kill him,." Callum said.

"My fucking pleasure... open those eyes." I pushed the knife into his heart and could feel the rhythm as it faded and the mess of blood splattered on the floor.

"Still a fucking messy killer." Callum laughed.

"What, I like the look of blood." I stared at his empty eyes and turned to face Callum. "How would you have done it?"

"Gun to the dome?" He snickered.

"You are a lazy killer. What's the point if you are not going to enjoy it?"

"Trust me, I do enjoy every moment of it. Let's get the fuck out of here."

Cypress

His grandmother's home was a castle. It was a literal stone castle in the middle of a plateau that had a view of the Irish Sea. This was unbelievable. I sat on the park bench by myself and stared at the view. I wanted to stay here forever. There was no such peace that could be found at home.

"Beautiful, huh?" The tall man sat beside me. His curls blowing away from his face.

"It is." I said.

"No accent, eh? Where you from?"

"America actually?"

"There is no beauty like this there." He sighed. He bit into his apple and smiled. "What brings you here?"

I looked at him. His eyes stark gray and eerie. "Who are you?"

"Just passing by," He said. "I haven't been here since I was a wee lad. My mum usually visits me."

"I asked who you were?" I looked at him. Why did he look so familiar? The way he avoided answering and the way smirked whenever I was irritated reminded me of Luke.

"Feisty, just how Luke always liked them." He tossed the remainder of the apple to the ground. "Declan Elledge... they call me, Declan Reid now. Do you know who I am?"

"Declan Elledge is dead."

"Exactly," He chuckled. "What is my mom cooking there? I smell potatoes and cabbage I just hope it's not any of that steak she does. Can I walk back in there with you? And is Lucas in there?"

"How dare you talk to me like this conversation is normal? All of your sons are in there. Every last one of them and you have some explaining to do."

"I know. It's why I came to dinner. I want to meet them and talk to them."

"Lucas might kill you."

"I might kill Lucas." he smirked. "Come on. Argue with me later, and congrats on the baby and apparent marriage. When did you get married?" He pointed to my ring.

"Dear Jesus, you are just like him. Get up and go in there right now. And don't walk in with me. You wait and then you come. I don't want him to think that I had anything to do with this."

"Yes, ma'am."

The shit was about to hit the fan and I would have to deal with it. I wanted to cry, but I couldn't. I opened the front door to the house and smiled. "Lucas!"

"Hey babe." Lucas kissed me and placed his hand on the nape of my back. "You like the view out there."

"I love it." I grabbed his hand and smiled at him.

"You okay? You seem quiet."

"I'm fine baby. Your grandmother is so sweet."

"She is a character." Lucas' arms wrapped around my waist and ran up my stomach. "How has he been?"

"The baby... is fine. Kicked the entire time we walked and continues to dance on my bladder."

"Oh good boy... I see football in his future. And I mean real football not American."

"Don't be mean."

"I'm not, love. I am just saying there are some fundamental values that are different. And I don't mind it, but we are actually going to be a European family..."

"Knock, knock." My heart pounded at the sound of his voice again. What was about to happen?

Lucas turned and his mouth fell open. "What the hell?" He growled.

"Uncle Declan, it's about time you showed your face..." Callum walked into the kitchen.

"Declan?" Asher said as he stood to his feet. "Declan is dead."

"I'm alive." Declan smiled. His arrogance infuriated me. "I can explain it all over dinner. Hi mom!"

Nadine waved from the kitchen. She too must have known. Holly never looked up and Mark just sat with his lips in a pressed line.

"We can see that." Mark stood up. "Okay, so what the fuck happened to you. And oh by the way, I'm your first born son you threw away." His eyes were red. "I mean what the fuck? Do you think that you can stroll in here and we just love you? I don't want shit to do with you."

"Take a seat." His voice roared and echoed through the house.

Lucas stepped back and there was something that had never been there, fear. "Dad, don't yell at him like that." He shook with his fist clenched. "You don't even know them and they have every right to be mad."

"I can explain." Declan's voice was still loud but it was angry. "I will explain to you all."

Asher nodded his head in frustration. His brow creased and the annoyance was written all over his face. "For us it starts with more than just your death. You gave us up. I had no one but a mom that worked too much. I wanted a father. I wanted a real father and you couldn't do it."

"Please sit down." Declan said.

"No," Asher said. "I'll just step out while you fill their heads with whatever elaborate story you can conjure up. There is nothing that you can say that will change how I feel. You're a coward." He stood up and made his way passed Declan into the kitchen.

I glanced at Lucas. His eyebrows rose in shock and smirked. He was proud of Asher. Mark stared at Declan. "You better not say shit to him."

"I won't." Declan sat down on the couch. "Lucas I left so you could have a better life." He twiddled with his fingers. "And I know that it's not a good enough..."

"You're right." He interrupted. His voice was wavering and weak. "I could have been a better person had you been there for me. I was alone." He gripped my hand. "I lost my mum. The only woman who knew me better than I knew me. All I wanted was a father that could be there for me. But you didn't even stay the whole funeral!"

"I know."

"You don't know!" I could feel the agony as it bled through in his voice. "You will never know what it was like watching her die. I have done that! I watched her wither away to nothing!" The tears streamed down his face like rain. And his voice grew louder. "You're a coward. You are..."

"I am your father and I know I fucked up, but I want to change things. Life is short."

"You will never be my father," Mark cut his eyes over to Callum. "Did you know?"

"It's none of my concern," Callum said.

"None of your concern? How can you stand him Luke?"

Lucas didn't answer, he just grabbed his jacket and made his way towards the door. It was the first time I could honestly notice that he was the youngest brother. I felt him withdraw.

"Stand me?" Callum's voice rose. "I've always been there for him Mark! I don't try to change who he is. I don't try to make him a standup guy." He stepped back. "I love my cousin for who he is. You can't it's why you constantly try to change him. You're a fucking control freak."

"Who the fuck are you talking to! He is my brother. I would die for him! I do everything that I can to make sure everything is right! I bend over backwards for him. You aren't shit."

"I'm not shite?" Callum walked over to Mark. "Who the fuck are you talking to boy?"

"You know who I'm talking to." Mark said between clenched teeth. His chest heaved and he looked dangerously furious.

"Mark," Asher said. "Come on, it's not worth it."

"Stay in your place little brother," Mark warned. Asher complied as he backed towards the kitchen.

"I'll fuck you up boy." The threat was real. Callum tilted his head at Mark. "You wanna try me ey? You think he's crazy…" He pointed at Lucas and a small gasp escaped from my mouth. "You haven't met me yet. I'll rip your tongue out and glue it to your hand so you can learn to hold it."

"Try me, you fucker. You talk a mad ass game, but I will have the last word." Mark did not back down he stepped towards Callum.

"Words don't mean shit when you're gutless on a stone floor."

"Was that a threat?"

"No, it was me predicting the future if you don't watch your fucking mouth." Callum spat.

"ENOUGH!!" Nadine yelled from the kitchen. "Everyone sit down! I mean sit down right now!"

My head spun. I had no idea what was going on. Lucas was quiet and Callum was red. "Let's just go." I whispered.

Lucas turned towards me. "This is my family and I know that they are crazy anyone can I see it." Lucas paused. "But I can't leave. I have to stay. You can go outside if you want. Get some fresh air. Don't let this stress you."

"It's not me that I am worried about, I don't want to be away from you. You need me. I can stay."

"Shia and Holly… take Nina to the backyard and pick some fresh veggies for the spread. Now." She snapped. They all disappeared and she smiled. There are some things that everyone in this room needs to know and I'm gonna tell it."

"Ma," Declan moaned. "Let me talk to my sons."

"No, shut it up Declan Marcus Elledge. When I speak you are quiet, nothing has changed." The entire room grew quiet and she started to talk. "Firstly, you owe your boys an apology. You should have been a man enough to know that you could handle raising them. Though it looks like they are more than fine without you. Mark, your father was a wild kid when Luna first got pregnant. We sent him to America to learn and be educated and every time we turned around the woman was pregnant again."

Mark scratched his head. "You didn't give us a chance."

"I wanted to but there were things going on than that you should have not been around."

"Why him?" Asher pointed to Lucas.

"Our plan was to send him away too." Declan refused to cut his eyes toward Lucas. "But he stole your mother's heart with his cry. Mark and Asher… you were two quiet babies. We took you while you were sleeping and you lived quiet lives. But this one has been acting out since he came out the wound. She never heard you cry."

"Why?"

"We were selfish." Declan admitted.

"Obviously." Mark interrupted.

"When she had Lucas, I made him cry." Nadine admitted. "She cried and then she said he was hers. Declan had no choice but to agree. And he raised Lucas."

"Barely," Lucas added.

"I'm sorry that I hurt each of you. I'm sorry that I'm selfish. Don't take it out on Callum for me being alive. Callum is a good kid and he done what I asked. He even stopped talking to Lucas so it would not be so hard to hide."

Callum nodded his head. "I'm sorry mate." he said towards Callum.

Asher looked heart broken. "I guess you don't realize how hard this has been for me." Asher looked at Declan. "Why are you here?"

"Ma told me of you boys knowing and being here. I wanted to see you myself. I wanted to tell you that I love you and even though you didn't know it, I've watched you two grow from knee high."

"Dad, I always wanted brothers. I figured they would make me normal."

"Normal is not in our family Luke." Callum chuckled. "And I understand that want, but they aren't that normal either. Asher reads people... Mark is you under control."

I looked at Lucas. What did under control mean? "What are you talking about?"

"Nothing," Lucas smirked. "Can we eat and maybe not kill each other?"

"You can and will." Nadine said.

"Good, let's eat... talk later."

Asher

I was grateful the dinner was over. Callum's house was quiet. Too quiet for me. I wanted some kind of noise to drown out this mind numbing pain that went through my whole body. I sat on the porch, it was past midnight and unlike at home, I could see every star that there was. Peace was not my friend right now.

"Asher."

I would never forget his voice. Declan stood out in the yard. "Why are you here?" I whispered.

"I wanted to talk to you alone." He held his hands up. "I really just wanted to talk."

"Talk." I said.

"Tell me about yourself. I know your stepfather researched Luna for a while. I have a feeling that it should have been me." He sat down next to me. "Tell me everything."

"I'd rather not. Tell me about my mother."

"I can do that." Declan paused. "She was the most beautiful woman I had ever laid eyes on. She had these green eyes and this long wavy blond hair that cascaded down her back like a never ending ocean. And you have her face... good features of me too. Mark is the only one with her hair."

"What was she like?"

"She was an angel. My angel mainly," he paused. "She laughed a lot and she was always trying to find the good in every single person. She was forgiving and she was perfect. There is no other way to describe her. She just was not ready to be a mother. I made that decision for her."

"Why, I mean we are good men."

"I know you are." Declan said. "But there are things about me that are just not right and they could have put our family at risk. Why do you think that she had a backup plan for Lucas? We moved his entire childhood. We kept him locked away at boarding schools. He didn't really have a good father. I was more concerned with other things to put forth effort. I had to kill myself off to avoid persecution."

"For murder?"

"How did you know?"

"I think that is hereditary." I nodded my head.

"Luna taught him survival mechanisms at such a young age. She taught him everything that she knew. Told him that if anyone ever tried to hurt him or who he loved to... kill them. And that's all he knows. He worshiped Luna."

"I can tell." I paused as my mind raced. "How did you kill yourself off?"

"I have a brother named Clyde. He is smart and he knew that my time was winding down. He found a homeless man and fixed him up for over a year. He treated him to the best of life and then when the time came we killed him. We burned him alive and the dental records proved to be me. They stopped looking for me and I hid out in Africa for a while. Then came home a few months back. I can't stay for long though. I stay for a while a disappear and my mom is happy with that."

"Nadine is a really sweet lady."

"I know she is. What I wanted to tell you is don't spend the rest of your life thinking of what could have happened."

"I know."

"You can change the future by what you do right now."

"I don't know about that Declan."

"I do want to know you. I want to know the you that is present. Not the little boy… the man."

"What do you want to know?"

"I want to know about your work. What do you do?"

"I am a psychologist. I am about to graduate with my PhD in it. And hopefully work with a university on some new study analogies."

"So you are brilliant."

"I like to think so." I said jokingly.

"What else? Are there any women in your life?"

"There is no one Declan." I paused. "Shit, I don't know where I am headed next in life. I try to think about it, but things get complicated really easily here lately."

"You'll find someone." He assured. "It's all in your DNA."

"Yeah," I looked at him. "If you are trying to be in my life there has to be some constant effort. I can't take another father that just wants to be there and then leave."

"I'll be here whenever you need me."

CHAPTER TWENTY

Cypress

I had never seen Lucas cry but that night everything changed. We slept entangled in one another and he wept. And the only comfort I could find was to say it would be alright. Comforting was not a strong suit of mine. I had to force my own tears back. He was not in the bed with me when I woke up. It was just me and the baby who was destroying my bladder. I waddled to the bathroom and finally sat down to pee.

The bedroom door opened and his cell phone was thrown on the bed. "Good Morning Cypress."

"Hey babe," I hated when he never knocked. I was not there yet. I wiped myself and turned to wash my hands. "You okay this morning?"

"I'm good." He lied. I could tell by his voice.

"You talked to him yet?"

"I'm not going to." Lucas laid back on the bed and tossed his shoes on the floor. "They cooked breakfast again."

"I don't think I can eat her eggs again. Why doesn't she just scramble them?"

"She likes poached eggs."

"Well, I say that today we talk to your father together. This is simply not something you can ignore and pray away. We are going to be living here soon and I don't want us to walk into a family mess. I would rather everything be settled."

"It's not your decision."

'Your decisions directly impact me and this baby. So you are talking to him and I am too. And you are gonna snap out of this funk. This trip was to make you happier."

"I don't think that I'll ever be happy. And I don't think it's a good idea."

"Too bad I don't care." I closed the bathroom door and listened to him fuss for about an hour.

"Open the door Cypress!"

"No!"

"Look okay! Fine. Damn it." His stream profanity continued for another minute, then I opened the door.

The yellow sundress was bright, but it was comfortable and really the only thing that I had that were not pants. It was shorter than normal because of my belly and my breast unlike usual were busting out. I could tell by his face that he was either pissed or pleased. I didn't really care to which he was. I moved passed him.

"What are you staring at?"

"Your legs." Lucas answered. "Where the hell do you think you are going with Holly today? That dress is thirty percent cloth and seventy percent air."

"Nowhere, and nothing is wrong with this dress. You're just being an asshole. I mean you bought me this dress."

"I must have been blinkered and bloody insane at the moment I made that decision. The moment you became pregnant that dress was no longer allowed." He scoffed. "You're allowing everyone to see your body. And because your body now belongs to me, I can't allow it. Take it off."

"Belongs to you? Have you lost your mind? I'm not taking this dress off Lucas. Now get your panties out of a wad and get dressed."

"Now." Lucas growled.

"You're not going to tell me what I can and cannot wear. I am wearing this dress and you are going to shut up about it." I fiddled with my hair in the mirror and looked at him. "Stop pouting."

"You are confused as to who wears the pants in this relationship." He said with an edge of playfulness to his voice.

"I'm not confused at all Lucas."

"You are."

"No, sir." I answered. "I wear the pants. I always have and you, kind sir, should know that I always will."

"You wear the skirts and too short dresses." He gestured at my dress with a wave of a hand and then turned to lock the door. "I can remind you if you truly can't remember who's the boss."

"Remind me of what?"

"Who is the boss in this relationship, it's me."

"No, come on we have breakfast and people are up."

"I don't care." His hand touched the nape of my back and crawled up to my shoulders. He pushed my strap to my dress down and turned me around. "Take it off." he whispered.

"I said no."

The sting of his hand slapping my ass sent heat to my face. A gasp escaped my mouth and he pulled the other strapped down. "I will make you change."

"You can try." I pushed him and he went nowhere. A smile came across his face. "What are you smiling for?"

"Because I'm gonna take that dress off of you and fuck you until you listen."

"So confident... what makes you think I am gonna let you."

"You are red..." He touched my face. "And though it suits you... It's a completely different color from your honey like complexion. And you are also breathing slowly, like you are trying to pace yourself and not fall into the bed with me. But it's okay. I plan to get the dress off now." He pulled the dress to my ankles and tilted his head towards me.

"Okay." I complied. "But I'm gonna switch it up."

"You are?"

"I'm going to wear this dress."

"Fool yourself if you want to."

I pushed him against the door and kissed his cheek gently scraping my tongue against his cheekbone. My hands explored his pants and stopped at his belt buckle. I pushed my hands into his boxers and gripped him. He was just about hard, but a few strokes and his dick was strained. His pants dropped to the floor and lowered myself down. My lips tasted his sweet skin and my mouth covered his dick entirely taking him to the back of my throat. I groaned a little bit and his dick flinched like he was already there. I sucked him more and his hands clasped into my hair.

"Fuck," He uttered.

I circled my tongue around him slowly, feeling every ridge. My hands explored his body and I sucked him harder than before sending him to buckle his hips into. I gagged a little and pulled back from him, but his grip on my head was strong. I could taste him coming in my mouth with a melodic sound that had me ready to fuck him senseless.

Lucas leaned against the door, breathless. "Fuck me."

"No, sir." I fixed my dress and moved him out of the way. "See you at breakfast?"

His mouth dropped as he watched me walk out of the room. "Cypress..."

"Good Bye Luke."

Lucas

I was sure that pregnancy was the best thing that happened in our relationship. I fixed my pants and walked downstairs. She wore the dress and the pants in the relationship apparently. My face still reddened from whatever had just happened up there. And words weren't exactly forming correctly.

"Morning Luke." Callum said next to Mark.

"What are you two best friends now? And who the fuck punched you?" I pointed at Callum's blue eye and then glanced at Mark.

"I did and it was wonderful." Mark said. "Good morning."

"We've made a decision to be friends." Callum laughed and then punched at Mark. Mark winced once his fist connected with his side. It was to no surprise that the fight was an even one. They were both stubborn and callous.

"Yeah, whatever," I stared at Cypress as she floated around the room with her damn yellow dress. Fuck she was radiant and that dress had my mind thinking some untamed thoughts. "Morning Cypress."

She grinned at me. She had won, my mind, body and soul had completely surrendered to her. "It is a wonderful morning isn't Lucas."

"What is wrong with you two?" Asher said.

"I don't know. She is so weird." I whispered. "Why are women so damn weird?"

Asher shrugged his shoulders. "If you find out the answer to that one, please let us all know."

"Well, it only marks the beginning cousin. When she has the baby she'll be even more weird." Callum chuckled. "She is wearing a nice dress though."

"Fuck off." I mumbled.

"You're chipper this morning." Callum nudged Mark again and caused him wince in pain. "Mark and I are going to meet your pa for brunch. You should come. Asher apparently talked to him last night."

"Why Asher?"

"Because I can. I didn't think I needed your permission to talk to my dad?"

The words my dad stung a little. I brushed his crass comment off and rolled my eyes. This little fucker had grown a small attitude. "Fuck you."

"Good answer Asher." Mark picked.

"Both of you should come. Asher I want to show you the University. Maybe you can spring a job here. I could pull some strings. My father will be there too. He never comes in from England."

"Uncle Clyde is leaving his throne? God something must be wrong."

"Actually, he wants to meet Mark. He owns a law firm in England and he wants him to open a law firm in the states. I think it's a wise business venture. Maybe he'll find you something legit as well."

"I like writing, it hasn't failed me yet." I turned to Asher. "What did he say to you last night?"

"Talk to him yourself Luke." Asher smirked. He had started to finally start acting like an older brother for once. And I must say it annoyed me more and more every day.

"I'll pass." I poured a cup of tea and my eyes were hooked on Cypress. She laughed and chatted up with Holly. I don't know what I would do without her. I don't know what I would do if she was hurt by me either. The warm liquid splashed all over the counter and I stopped pouring it.

"Prince Charming, could you pay us attention for at least five minutes?" An irritated Callum had poked his head out as wiped up the spilled tea.

"I'm listening." I lied. She was so perfect and so mine that it even hurt to think she could not be mine. "Callum where is my dad anyhow?"

"At Nadine's," he answered. "Why?"

"I probably need to talk to him before we leave." I grimaced and gulped down my tea.

My father, I had never imagined the possibility of him being alive. The pain of the final moment I saw him still tinkered around my head. He was burnt to a black, crisp with his necklace of my mom in his hand. The coroner had even identified him as my father. I grieved my mother and father so hard I had lost myself in turmoil. And there was no way to pull me out of it until I met Cypress. The fact that he was alive and well after all this time hurt more than I wanted to admit.

The plateau overlooked the Irish Sea and I hadn't been here in ages. The color of the blue was that peeked between the white puff of clouds was perfect and the sun had found its home behind a ton of clouds. All that was heard was the waves of the sea scraping the sand. This could be home in less than a few months and I was sure that I wanted it to be.

"You still love it here?" He sat beside me as he twirled a knife in between his fingers. "I'm happy that you came to see me. I was convinced that you wouldn't talk to me before you left."

"Me too for the moment." My eyes didn't move. They just stayed captivated by the sight before me. "I need to know why you done it." The silence lasted for a moment and the crash of the waves down below to fill the air.

"It was simple Lucas... I had to."

"Not good enough." My voice shook. "Why did you do it?"

"I had no choice Lucas. It's more than what you think."

"Well, I'm a grown fucking man. Explain it to me!" I yelled. "Why was it okay to leave your scared child alone with no one in this world to care for him?"

"If I didn't do it, then it was a chance I would never see you again Lucas. And the actual thought of losing you hurt more than a few years without you." He swallowed and flicked the knife into the ground. "You think it was easy to leave you alone."

"It was easy for you to disregard the fact that you had two other children out there. How could you do that? I don't even know who the fuck you are." I whispered.

"That's something that you will never understand."

"I know it. Because not having my child in this world with me would be pure hell."

Declan chuckled. "You act like you got all the answers now kid. You know that?"

"Whatever," I stood to leave.

"Sit down!" Declan's voice filled the air and I done as he told me to and sat down on the wooden bench. "I love you and them. And just so you know I was always around those two boys, even when they didn't know it. I love them too. How could I not love Mark and Asher?"

"It would have been nice to not be alone. You could have at least given me that."

"Your mother didn't want that for them. She wanted them to have completely separate lives. I honored her wishes. Asher, he's smart as hell. I was shocked that he had not figured it out sooner. But when he died, I felt like there had been a weight lifted from my shoulders. And you look like you like them well enough."

"Whatever."

"I have killed people Lucas." His admission was not new news to me. I knew everything there was to know about my father. "And at the time I was wanted for a mass murder of more than 70 people in Taiwan. They wouldn't stop until I died. So your uncle done what needed to be done."

"Killed yourself off for the sake of survival. I hope I never have to follow those footsteps."

"Is that about the las?"

"Who else?" I paused.

"Congrats on the baby. I hate that you are your father's son though. I know that you have urges and I've watched you kill a few times. You're messy."

I was horrible at this tail shit. "Bloody hell, you and Asher are fucking stalkers, I swear."

It was nice to hear a sincere laugh from him. "Well, you should probably not be so eager when you kill. What you do is not to be taken lightly and you should be more aware of your surrounding Lucas. I all but waved at you one time."

"Yeah," The words stung. "I mean..."

"It's fine, you don't have to explain to me. I am not any different. I just want you to be careful. Asher is under the impression that you are no longer careful as you once were."

"I'm fucking up because there is an agent that is on to me. He follows me and sits on me. And it's annoying. I want to kill him and I have almost killed him a few times. But I behave, but then there is something inside of me that just lashes out."

"I know the feeling."

"I can't stop it. I feel like a monster. I like to see people die." My voice was calm. "I mean it literally is no better joy for me. I can watch the blood drain over and over and there is nothing better."

"I don't know what it is."

"Is it the same for you?"

"No... I just have anger issues. I'm more along the lines of Mark. I kill only when necessary. You and Callum have that same need."

"Well, I didn't come here to compare family members." I spat. "I just want to know how you left? I need to know that if something goes down there is a possibility that I will be able to live. Even if that means leaving Cypress so that she can have a better life."

"It's harder than you think Luke."

"I know."

"You don't." Declan looked at me. "You won't even look at me. I hate knowing that I hurt you and made you into what you are."

"Oh, stop making it about you." I grumbled. "I've had whatever the bloody hell this is within me since I was younger and you had not one thing to do with it."

"It is about me. You know that you are a product of a misguided childhood."

"I'm fine. I like my life. I love my woman... my child. I love everything."

"Right." He nodded his head.

"Don't try to come at me I your fatherly woes. You are not a real father. I basically was raised by myself. I don't need your kind words. I need to know how you did it. I need to know so that if something happens, I can remove myself and she can..."

"Look," Declan paused. "I don't know what to tell you. I had to find a homeless person... Your uncle paid them to have a life. He fixed their teeth and then he put them in a real house and when the time came, he burned them alive... Told people I was in the house. I was long gone by that time. They identified him as me because your uncle paid to have his teeth done like that. No one wins in the end."

"Whatever, that takes too much time."

"If you think you are close to being turned in then you should just go ahead and turn yourself in. There is really nothing else that can save you at this point."

"You think so?"

"I know so."

"So I have to leave everything that I love behind..."

"You don't have to." Declan stood up. "I didn't leave you because I wanted a better life for you. I didn't give those boys up because they were better off without me. I did it because I was selfish. Your mother was selfless and I loved her for it. I just had a habit of doing things that ended up not being good for. I was a bad father and husband. Be there for yours. Stop the killing and move away."

"I have stopped.... After my last kill it was pretty much a wrap." I chuckled.

"What did you do?"

"Kind of wrote the detective a letter in the blood."

Declan laughed. "Bold move?"

"Too bold, he almost pegged me, but I never leave them anything to work on. I never even leave an imprint in the blood... I just maneuver around it..."

"What do you use?"

"Your knife." I smiled. "I remember when I was younger you carried that knife around like it was the bible. If someone said one-word wrong to you... your hand went to that knife and I knew that everything would be okay... you never really played too many games about the knife. And, when you died, I did my first kill... and there was no greater feeling."

"Be careful, that's all I want."

"I am careful father."

"And you can trust your brothers. I have talked to them both and they are great men. Especially Asher, who really impressed me. He is smarter than you know."

"I know I can trust them." I said.

"Tell me about this girl."

"Cypress." I added.

"Yeah her, we chatted for a minute and she seemed rather feisty over you. Does she know what you are?"

"I would rather she not."

"Your mother knew about me."

"I know she did."

"Well, I think you should tell Cypress before she finds out on her own."

"No, I've cheated on her and killed her ex-boyfriend. I don't think she wants to know that."

"You will never know."

"I don't care to know."

Cypress

Holly loved the garden and I had to admit it was a good place to escape but I didn't have the patience to actually do it. I don't think that I would ever really have the patience. I sat in the yellow chair as she pulled up weeds and Nina dug a hole in the yard.

"Tell me... what is it about Lucas that makes you love him?"

"There is a lot."

"Like what?"

"Well, he is protective of me. There is something about a man that can go to every length to make sure that you are safe. Then he is smart... he loves to read and he loves to dance with me. And then he loves me. I can truly say that never have I felt like there was someone who loved me more than me." I twiddled with my thumbs and looked at Holly. "

"The Elledge boys tend to love hard." Holly smiled. "I wish Callum would love harder though. You know I have been by his side through everything. I mean he has been arrested and damn near gunned down in the streets and I have stood there unmoving with him."

"Gunned down?"

"Callum has some bad sides. You know he can't control his mouth and so that leads to unnecessary fights with people that we don't need trouble from. You know... he hasn't asked me to marry him. I mean I have dedicated so much of my life and I can't even have the privilege of his last name."

"He'll do it on his time."

"Six years Cypress." Holly paused. "And I don't know if I can wait another one. Me mother, she shamed me from the family when I got pregnant and she hates Callum. He doesn't know how much I sacrificed just to be with him. Just to get closer to his love. And now..." Her voice broke and a stream of tears raced down her face.

"No, don't cry."

"I can't help it you know?" She tossed the gloves to the ground. "Lucas... is a good guy. And Callum can be a good guy, but what I'm saying is... I don't think that they are the same. I think there is more good in Lucas than he lets on."

"He is a good guy and Callum is like him in a ton of ways. And men are sometimes just not good with marriage. Lucas from the time we started dating... said his intention was to find the one. And little did we know... we would last. He is not perfect. Before I found out I was pregnant, he cheated on me. And I took him back, once I knew for sure. And this is a struggle for us. I have to deal with fucking cops."

"Welcome to the family." Holly laughed. "Callum is a fucking killer. I have to deal with the police every time I turn around. Luckily he has them in his hand. The IRA helps with that and..."

My mind zoned out. Callum was a killer? "What do you mean?"

"I mean... The IRA, you know, has his back. They order the kills..."

"He is a killer?"

"Yeah Callum? I thought you knew. He gets paid major money and that's why we live here. We have so much money we figured the farther away from the city the better."

"You are okay with that?"

"What do you mean?" Holly turned her head at me. "I mean he is the father of my child and he is also a very respected IRA killer. I have to accept it. I like it though. No one around here messes with me."

"How can you be okay with that?"

"When you love someone Cypress it is not about what they do."

"It's all about that. If he can kill anyone then you should turn him in. You should run. He could kill you and kill Nina. You should be glad the monster hasn't asked you to marry him yet."

She threw her head back in amusement. "Dear, are you crazy?"

"What are you two out here cackling about?" Asher said as he handed me my phone. "Your boyfriend is annoying. He keeps calling over and over like you are dead or something. I told him to shove off a few times and he threatened me. So please call him back to insure him that you are still alive."

I rolled my eyes. Typical Lucas to worry about me when there was nothing to worry over. I dialed his number and waited for him to answer, "Lucas." I said when I heard his voice on the other line.

"Where in the hell have you been and why has Asher been guarding your phone?"

"I'm in the garden. Holly is teaching me how to pick good veggies."

"Dear God, do you have a jacket on at least?"

"What do you want Lucas?"

"I miss you is all. I should be back within the hour."

"I swear sometimes you are clingy as hell."

"You made me this way." He added.

"Well, I'll see you when you get here."

CHAPTER TWENTY-ONE

Lucas

Cypress had been oddly quiet since we departed the airport and I had not asked why. A part of me was afraid to ask her what it is that had her upset. I just knew that I wanted to be home in front of my telly with beside me and the rest of the world far from view.

"Hungry, love?" I asked as I turned onto the motorway headed to the loft.

"I'm tired." She whispered.

"What's the matter?"

"Nothing," her voice was a murmur. She tussled her hair back from her face and leaned her head back against the window.

"Ever since we left you have been kind of down. I mean we will see Mark and Asher around here and Shia."

"I don't care about them Luke."

"Well, what do you care about that has your attitude in the pisser."

"I don't know; can I not be tired. I want to go home and relax in my bed."

"You don't want to go back to my place?"

"No, I want to go home. You can come with, but I want to go to my apartment."

"Alright love, can I stop by my place and toss my shit in?"

"Yeah," Her hands grazed her stomach and I noticed the small nudge push across her stomach. Feisty little guy already, that was all her.

"What the bloody hell is your problem? I mean I have tried to talk to you this whole entire time and you have been giving me nothing. We're about to be married in a few months. Better yet, we're about to be parents. I want to know what's wrong with you right now before nappies have to be changed and flower arrangements have to be made?" My voice rose and I looked at her. She had yet to stop going through the damn phone. "Hello?" I waved my hand in front of her.

"I don't know Luke. Get your hand out of my face. Drive home so I can sleep. I must just be tired."

"Tired." I moaned. It was those bloody hormones. They fucked with her too much. She would be furious, then laughing and then burst into tears all in one minute. "Well snap out of this funk. We have to talk to parents. Your parents in particular about moving and the wedding and the baby. You said your reveal is next week and you haven't said anything about it."

"I don't plan my own reveal party. I couldn't plan it. I can't know what is revealed. Lydie has all of that worked out and ready to go. So yeah, and my mom knows about the wedding and I don't know about moving just yet."

"You don't know?" I snapped. "What happened to the you that wanted to build a life there? One moment you are head over heels for me the next you are bat shit crazy. It's driving me mad!"

"I'll show you bat shit crazy Luke."

"Please don't." I rolled my eyes and we pulled into the parking lot of the loft. "Are you..." My eyes went into a frenzy. There were more than ten unmarked cars in my parking lot and they were in my apartment. "What the fucking hell?" I growled. "Stay in the bloody car!" I yelled.

"The guest of the hour is here." McMillan said as I opened the car door.

I could feel everything turning red. My hands shook as my eyes couldn't focus. "What is this?"

"Did you enjoy your getaway?"

"What is this? Why are you here?"

"For this." He handed me a sketch of the knife. My father's name engraved and it looked identical. How in the hell would he know? "You know where it is? It would save us some time and you some cleaning."

I felt my knees grow weak under me and bent over to take as much air in as I could. It was over. Everything was about to crumble before me. My chest hurt as my heart pounded against it. "Where is the warrant?"

"Do you know what it this is Luke? It's your torture piece right?"

Cypress was out of the car, she never bloody listened, even when it was for her benefit. "What's going on?"

"Glad you made it back safely Cypress." McMillan smiled at her. "You are getting out there." He gestured to her stomach. "You still look nice though. You carry the extra weight well."

"Don't fucking talk to her! Where is the warrant!" I yelled. The agents surrounded me. One, two… I inhaled and stared at him. The countdown to crazy had started less than a minute ago. I tried to relax myself and use every method that Asher had suggested and all of that shit was out of the window for the moment. "Now!"

He tossed the paper at me. It was signed and it was real. "I don't know where you got the idea that I even own a knife, but… you can't be here like this." My voice rumbled in terror.

"Your good friend helped us find it. She was so relieved that you left that she ran to us with whatever she could to lock you up. Her efforts were applauded."

Good friend, I paused. Fucking Persephone. She told. She told when I was gone. "I don't have friends."

"Well, you do now… We'll be here for a while… if you want to take a seat or help that would be great." McMillan smirked. "I know your girl here is tired. And you should enjoy the time with her while you have it. I don't think she'll let you see the kid on death row…"

I exploded. Every rational thought I had was gone out the window as my fist crashed into his face and sent a spray of blood to the ground. My body hit the pavement hard as they wrestled me to the ground. I heard her cry but I saw nothing but red. I wanted to finish him. Fuck that, I needed to finish him.

"Book him," McMillan yelled.

"Bravo fucker! Round of applause for the desperate agent! You finally got me for something!" My voice boomed as I lunged towards him. "I'll fucking end you."

"Lucas!" Mark yelled. He quickly closed his door to his car and ran over. He bypassed the officers and cars that had surrounded me. "What the hell?"

"He is under arrest for assault of a federal agent." The blood poured from his mouth like a faucet and it sparked something for me.

"Fucker," I mumbled.

"Enough Luke!" Mark made his way over. "You don't say shit and you should keep your hands to yourself. I will be down there to get you in a bit. Cypress, come with me, okay?"

Cypress looked at me. "Behave yourself, please. We'll be there shortly."

Grade A, I was about to be cuffed and tossed in jail and there was not shit that I could do about it.

Cypress

It was a good thing they would not find anything in that loft. It was 1500 miles away and safely hidden in my things. I exhaled. There was so much that ran through my mind. Had he killed Philip? Would he kill me? Were my kids safe? What the fuck had I gotten myself into and Who was Lucas?

I sat in the loft as the agents ransacked the place. My feet propped on the couch, they ached just from walking up the steps. I had bundled my legs in the cover and watched as they cut open mattresses and tore apart everything in the place. Mark continued to argue that there was no reasonable evidence to conduct the search. I was relaxed. I had to find a way to not freak out because there was a part of me that was dying inside. Who was Lucas really and why I had not figured out before the baby or the engagement? Why hadn't he told me what was really going on?

"Why are you so calm?" McMillan asked me.

I sipped my water as I glanced through the wedding catalog I had gotten from the airport. "I can't freak out... I'm pregnant and there is a high chance that I'll develop preeclampsia."

"You can still get out of this relationship unscathed, you know that? We can put you in Witpro and have you and that baby protected from him and his fucked up family."

"I hate when you talk to me like you think you know me. I love Lucas and I know for sure that he is innocent. I am not worried about a search for an item that is fake. That bitch Persephone, who I am more than sure is the reason that you are here can burn in hell. And you, sir can join her."

"We got the knife from the girl he cheated with. Do you remember that? He cheated on you and you are okay with it. The girl that was so terrified of him she almost ruined her education." He sat down on the couch.

"Do you think that I could forget it? I tried to forget it, but thanks to your little images it is permanently engraved in my head. Fuck you for that."

"What does he say to you that makes you feel safe? I mean I can look at him and with one look know that he is... insane."

"I see nothing like that."

"I can tell. What are your parents going to say when they find out that you are with a psychopath?"

"Aren't you supposed to be looking for something?"

"Right. Well... you two have a nice place here."

"I know."

They finally cleared out with nothing to take with them. And the loft was destroyed. Tables flipped as well as clothes tossed everywhere. Mark looked at me with confusion. "Why are you so calm?"

"Can you take me home?"

"Home?"

"Yeah, home to my apartment where I can sleep this jet lag off and hopefully recover from this shit Fest."

"What about Lucas?"

"One night in jail will not kill him." I rolled my eyes and walked towards the door.

He helped me down the steps and to his mini coop, which had to be the most inconvenient car for a pregnant woman. He closed the door as I adjusted myself in the seat of the small car. He pushed his hands through his short blond hair. "Why are you so calm?"

"Because I think I know the truth and it hasn't hit me yet. It hasn't hit me and I don't want it to." I smirked. "I don't want to think like that."

"They didn't find a knife."

"But they know what to look for now."

"He didn't..."

"Save that bullshit Mark!" I yelled. "What in the fuck has Lucas got you pulled into? If he has done what they say he did... there is no coming back from it. There is no way that he can be normal! How can I expect him to raise my children?"

"I know he didn't do it." Mark added. "I mean, that was a push just to get the..."

"Did you see his face when they showed him the sketch." I paused. "Right you weren't there. But I was and he went eggshell white. He was terrified. He looked like he knew it was over and I can't help but to think why would an innocent person react like that? Don't play me like I'm stupid. I know that there is no way in hell that he could be innocent. I don't want to hear your lies. I want to be alone. I want to sleep."

"Can you talk to Asher?"

"I won't. Because he's in on it too. You're all sick and the last person I want to see is you or your brothers. When you drop me off. Tell Lucas I said to stay the fuck away, please." I touched my stomach.

"You should let him talk to you. You can't judge and not know what he has to say. And I know that he loves you."

"Mark, SHUT UP! Don't you get tired of constantly cleaning up after his ass!"

The car halted and he slammed his fist against the steering wheel. "Cypress!" He said in frustration. "Don't act like this, please. This is the time that he will need someone by his side more than you know. So don't act like"

"Act like what! Act like he isn't hiding something and here I am holly, jolly and fucking pregnant. I was a fool to every god damn thing that he has going! You want me to act like he hasn't lied to me since day one about who the fuck he was! I can't. I can barely…" The tears streamed down my face I choked on my words. "I can barely breathe! I can't take it. Just take me home!"

My apartment was the kind of quiet that made me over think. There was nothing that could get my mind off of it. Maybe he did kill Philip. Maybe he has done everything that they had said. And if it was true who was I? I cleaned. Even though there was nothing to clean I wiped everything down. I played music to drown out the loud yells of my conscious. She screamed at me with anger and there was nothing that I could do about.

The night passed uneventfully. No television, no music, just silence in the darkness and everything ran through my head. Was Ireland an option to escape? Why did he want to marry me? I couldn't even look at the ring. Though my fingers were swollen, like my feet I found a way to slide the beast off and shoved it in the dresser. I needed no reminder of him. I already had a big one in front of me.

The knock at my door came to no surprise that morning. It was him. He knocked and knocked until I gave in. I waddled over to the door in my nightie and my gel house shoes. "What?" I hadn't shed a tear or bathed in my fear, yet because there was someone else I had to think about. And every decision I made at the moment impacted his or her life.

"Why did you not come with Mark? And why are you here and not at the loft?"

"Why would I come with Mark?"

"What the bloody hell do you mean? Why would you not come to get me out Cypress? I'm your fiancé." He looked weary. There had not been much effort in his outfit. His basketball shorts hung from his waist and the oversized T-shirt barely revealed his tattoos. Then his hair was down his back and his eyes were heavy.

"I know that." I paused. "Exactly who are you Lucas?"

"What?" He shifted his weight in front of me and leaned in front of the door. "What do you mean?"

"You heard me." My teeth were clenched. "The knife... what is so bad about this knife?"

"They got the information from Persephone. I know... I know it looked bad, but that was nothing. They didn't find it."

"Because I hid it." I snapped my hands crushed into his chest. "I hid it before Ireland. I wanted to know what you would do if it was gone! Good thing I did because you would be frying with no damn grease right now!"

"Shhhh!" He hissed as his eyes watched for someone surrounding him. "You don't know what you are talking about Cypress and they are watching my every move, you have to watch what you say. They can try to use anything against me." Lucas nudged me away from the door and I nodded my head and I held my ground. "What're you doing?"

"Why were you scared?" I whispered. "Tell me why you were scared."

"Where is it?"

"You don't need it. Why were you scared damn it! Answer me."

"You need to calm down before you get too upset." Lucas looked at my stomach sympathetically and nodded his head. "Just tell me where it is. I want it. It's mine." He growled.

"You gonna kill me too?" I pushed him back from me and threw my hands in the air. "I have a child coming into this world by a man I thought I knew but I don't."

"We have a child." He tried to correct.

"There is no we Lucas." The words stung as they made their way out.

"Cypress." He moaned. "Let me in and we can talk all of this out."

"I would feel safer if you made your way back home."

"You are home." He couldn't look me in the eyes. He held his head down. "We just need to talk." He mumbled in a small rant under his voice.

"I don't want to hear it. Keep your sappy love shit to yourself. I'll talk to you when I can formulate a sentence to express how pissed off I am at you. But right now... I need for you to get the fuck out of my face and don't bring your English ass over here again."

"You are assuming everything wrong. I am not a," the word sat on his tongue as if he afraid to even say it in front of me. "I'll call you later, okay? And we can talk about everything."

"Goodbye." I slammed the door in his face and closed my eyes. What the actual fuck had I gotten myself into? And why?

Lucas

There was something off. She said she knew. She said that she didn't want to see me, but I needed to see her. I needed to see her or there was a chance that I could explode. I had tried to call my father four times, but he had not called back and Callum was out of the country on some business. And everything around me had collapsed into a mess and what was formally known as my life was a disaster zone. I had just got her back and I was here in a daze as I tried to get her back.

"Persephone went and told them about what you done." Asher leaned back in his chair with his eyes pinched closed. "And now they know what the hell you use to murder people. And Cypress hid it. I was with her when she done it. She said for some reason she felt it should be moved." He sighed. "Is there anything else that I should know?"

"There is nothing else. And why would you help her behind my back?" I tried to my body from the uncontrollable shake that had taken over the past four days. It had been hell. She would not even see Lydie. And Lydie was a raving lunatic at me and Mark. "I can't get him on the phone." I said. I hated to call my father for advice, but he always knew how to solve shit with my mom and I was sure that she knew everything that there was to know about him.

"He is in Asia for a month." Asher said.

"So he can't answer the phone."

"He doesn't have it. Callum does." Mark added.

"You need to reach out to Cypress because she has the one thing that could put you away for years." Asher's apartment was almost all packed. "Where are you moving?"

"Ireland," he said. "My time is almost up here. You two are leaving and Callum said that he would pull some strings to get me a job there."

"So Ireland?" Mark nodded his head. "Why there?"

"Because," Asher could not formulate a sentence. There were several reasons that he wanted to go ahead and move to Ireland. There was the chance of being a professor. Our family had some great pull with everything in Ireland. Then there was the fact that he wanted to be around family. He was so easy to read. Asher just wanted a system of normalcy.

"He wants a change of scenery Mark." I answered simply reading every single reason that appeared on his face.

"Thanks Lucas," Asher stood up. "I can try to stop by there and talk to her. She likes me so it shouldn't be hard to get her to tell me something."

"And ask her why she thinks I did it."

"Because you did." said Mark. "Cypress is a smart woman. She isn't going to fall for your façade any longer. She hid the knife because she knew it would be a big deal. She drove it 1500 miles over to protect you."

"I have to have her back with me. I have this tendency to not think well when she is not around and it is eating me alive. Our party is tomorrow and I have to be there or Tracy and Lydie will murder me." My mind rambled. "I can't lose her! I need her. And Asher you are going to get her to see it."

"Whoa," a chuckled escaped from them both. "I can't force her to take you back baby brother." Asher shook his head.

"I'm your brother, you can."

"I can't." Asher stared at me. "I told you that there was possibility that she was going to find out what the fuck you do. You just have to stop and tell her about some, but not all. Don't you dare tell her about you playing with blood like some fucking kid. You tell her about the necessary deaths not… her ex. Her ex will hurt her."

"Fuck him."

"Brother will you listen fully for once in your life?" Mark rolled his eyes. "This is the reason that they are on you so hot right now. You don't know how to listen. You just assume that everything is going to be fine. Well, this time you could really be fucked up."

"I done it for her! I killed him so that she can have a better life without him and now you want me to feel sympathetic."

"We want you to realize that you could be on death row in the next year." Asher said.

"Fuck you." I spat.

"This is the crazy shit we mean. Calm yourself."

"Get her to love me back. Get her to take me back." The plea in my voice was sincere, for once I could feel the fear. My hands shook and I exhaled. "She'll take me back." I mumbled.

"Calm down." Asher stared. He pushed me down on the brown couch. "I'll work on it, okay?"

"What the fuck do I wear to the baby shower? We don't even know what we are having."

"It's not a baby shower. It's a reveal party."

I looked at Mark. "Reveal Party? What the hell? Whose idea was it?"

"Lydies."

"Can you go over there tonight?"

"I have plans for tonight."

"Plans?" Mark and I said at the same time.

"To read a book or end a speech?" Mark asked.

"Fuck you Mark," Asher laughed. "I have a date with a girl I met a few days ago when we got back. She was on the flight."

"Well, maybe you aren't gay after all." I tilted my head at him. "Could you talk to her before tomorrow? I don't want to be in a group of people and they all know that I am a bad guy. I would rather she love me and we just get on with the baby whatever."

"Fine. But I need you to realize something Lucas. I can't make her love you. You need to remember that. Now will you two find your way out of my apartment. I have like less than 3 hours to shower, make my future sister in law, not hate you and get on my date."

"I hope you get laid."

"I will get laid."

"You think you are gonna get laid?" I burst into laughter and hit him playfully. "If you do... I will give you one hundred dollars. The chick on the plane seemed to be out of your league."

"Have I ever told you how much I hated you Lucas?"

"Once but that was before you know... we discovered that we are kin. Now you can't hate me. You can save my relationship and hopefully get some ass."

"I am leaving." Mark hugged Asher. "I don't really care about the relationship saving part. I really need you to get her to tell you where the knife is and why she moved it. Though we appreciate it, we can't have her out there. She is pregnant and she gets really emotional really fast. She could hate him one day and we all go down the drain for some hormones."

"Thanks... do that and perhaps I will be out of one hundred dollars. And if you talk to dad... please tell him that I need to talk to him like now."

"He can't save you from everything Lucas."

"He always has." I added.

Asher

How was I always the counselor of horrible situations? Cypress had not answered one phone call from any of us and here I was standing at her door beating like Lucas. She finally opened the door, but she looked distraught and tired.

"Cypress," I smiled. "What's wrong with you?"

"What's not? I see they sent you over to talk... come in before my kindness wears off."

The apartment smelled like bleach and pine sol and my guess was had nested herself to death. I drag her bags in. "You left these at Lucas' the other night."

"Thanks."

"Are you excited about the reveal tomorrow?"

"I am. I'll know what to name him or her and then I will see Lucas for the first time."

"Lucas is torn up."

"Good." She plopped on the couch with her ice cream. "I hope he thought of some good lies to tell me."

"I came to talk to you about him a little. But that is not the only reason I am here."

"Why else would you be here Asher?"

"I have a date." A smile appeared on my face and she lit up. "She is pretty nice. We have been texting all week and for once I think that I might find happiness after Whit."

"Whitney was not polite. I hope that you like her Asher." She rubber her round stomach and smirked. "What you got planned for her?"

"I don't know. Honestly, I was thinking that we would go to a park or something and just talk."

"Get it together Asher. Take her to a park first and then tell her you are going to take her out to eat. Let her chose and make sure you tell her how good she looks."

"I promise I will."

"You will do fine."

"Thanks," I had lingered over her words. "You know I think that you can make a difference in his life."

She sighed deeply and rolled her eyes. "Here comes the don't judge my brother speech. I would rather talk about whatever else is on your mind."

"I mean it Cy, I think you can make a huge difference in his life and that's basically all that counts. You know his past is his past and I am not gonna tell you shit. I just want you to know that as far as miracles go you have made a difference. Mark knows it and I know it. Forgive him only if you want to forgive him and don't do it for any other reason."

"You are the brother that has the most sense. Mark is the protector and Lucas is the idiot."

"Oh, I love your hierarchy. It's still weird for me to call them brothers, but I like it. It makes me feel like there is finally someone in my corner you know. And it feels good. I love them no matter how asinine they tend to be."

"I have that habit as well."

"I heard about the knife."

"Yeah..." She looked away from me.

"Why did you hide it?"

"I knew that it couldn't be good and what else was I supposed to do? I mean there is this whole conspiracy with the feds that he is a killer. There couldn't be anything good about him having a knife in his night stand. I found it and hid. And thank God I did because I saw his face when they showed him the drawing. He would have fried."

"You think he is guilty?"

"I think there is something that he is hiding from me Asher. I have known it for the longest. He doesn't tell me everything and he makes everything into a lesser deal than it is. And you said it yourself... he can be dark. He just is different."

"So you did it to protect him?"

"I do everything to protect him. I don't know how much more I can take though. He just keeps hiding shit and it keeps coming back to bite me in the ass."

"Well," I paused. "I guess that means you don't hate him."

"I can't hate him Asher. I have tried and it was the most miserable month of my life. I just wanted to cry and eat."

"That was the baby." I laughed. "I know I am his brother. I get that you don't want to be around someone that is so close to him sometimes but I would love for you to talk to me. I won't go back and tell them shit. I don't have to. All they need to know is that you need your space and that you would like to be left alone. I want you to be comfortable because you are family now. And I love you like a sister. So when he fucks up lock out... him and lock out Mark but don't lock out me."

"I won't."

"Good. Now I can go on my date with peace of mind. I don't know what to bring to reveal party so I'll try something like food."

"Don't bring anything. I talked to Lydia this morning and she has everything planned out. And tell Lucas to wear the outfit that I have bagged in his closet. If he isn't dressed right, then I will flip a brick."

"I will relay the message."

"Thanks."

CHAPTER TWENTY-TWO

Cypress

I hated that the party was even scheduled for today. It was not the way to get around it though. The country club, she had chosen for the it was perfect. The high ceilings and low lights were something that I envied for myself. Then there was the fact that Lydia was a genius at extravagant parties. Plus, she had the help of her little perfect boyfriend. The color schemes had been chosen by me, green and yellow for a boy and then pink and white for a girl. Each table had just one color set, but the table for Lucas and I was split down the middle. His name on Team Boy and mine on Team Girl. There were balloons with question marks placed right behind us with a huge safety pin in front of the podium. Usually this would be too much for me to take in but the party had been a relief from the constant worrying I had put myself through. I finally had the energy to climb out of bed and try so I looked presentable. My hair for once, was not a mess. It was simply down and the curls were pulled back by a band to keep them from falling in my face. I wore no makeup just a tint of lip gloss.

Lydia moved around like it was her reveal. She fixed the table cloths and readjusted table placements. "Okay, so I have gone ahead and placed names on each table. I know that you and Lucas are at odds. Do you want him with you or do you want your mom?"

"I want him with me, Lydia." I shook my head and walked towards the table. "He should be here by now. I told him to be here an hour earlier than everyone else."

"He is still on time." Lydia moved the bouquet of diapers to the middle of the table and continued to walk around. "He just pulled up." She pointed to his jeep out in the parking lot.

Lucas hopped out. He actually for once followed instructions. He wore his white button down shirt with khakis, covered by a dress blazer that matched my outfit. His mass of brown hair was tossed in a bun on the top of his hands. A few strands hung down but he was perfect for once. Even if his hair was untamed I was happy he at least made an effort.

"Brother! You're on time! I really don't know how to feel about it!" Lydia hugged him. "You look presentable too."

"Yeah, whatever, where is she?" He asked.

"Over there, I guess looks don't change the fact you're an asshole."

"Thanks Lydie." He made eye contact with me and made his way through the array of tables and floating balloons. He smiled at me. "You look lovely."

"Thank you."

"Are you mad?"

"I'm furious. But I don't want to fight." I choked back the lump caught in my throat and stared at him. "I just want to know the complete truth and not some half lie you make up to make sure that we are in one accord. I want the truth."

Lucas looked at the ground. "I don't know how to tell you everything." He mumbled.

"The same way you lie... let the words flow." I turned away from him in avoidance of tears and shrugged my shoulders. "We can talk about it later."

"Did you talk to Asher?"

"You're wearing what I told him to tell you to wear. So you already know I talked to him."

"He is better at telling things than me."

"It's not his truth to tell." I spat. "I want to hear the truth from you Lucas. I don't want to hear your brothers make light of it with his words of wisdom. I don't want to hear Mark try and explain it to me. I want you to break everything down and you are going to tonight or you can hang this family up."

"Can you please just allow me to tell you when the time is right?"

"The feds uprooted your apartment. The time to tell me passed months back."

"I can't tell you."

"We're not arguing."

"Fine we won't argue, but you can't make me tell you something that you are not ready for. You aren't ready and I won't have you spazzing and hiding my child from."

"I would never do that!" I yelled. "How could you even let that shit come from your mouth?" I peeked at Lydia. She had made her way to the food and was sorting everything out. "You don't know me at all do you?"

"Can't the past just stay where it belongs?"

"The past, your past is fucking with my future and I can't have it."

"Give me two weeks."

"No, give you two hours."

We stared at each other until we heard the huge doors of the banquet hall open. Asher strolled into the room with a petite blonde on his arm who couldn't keep her small hands off of him. "Hey you two!" His voice was light and happy.

"Asher, right on time." Lucas walked away from me and half hugged his brother then turned to the little blonde. "Who is your lucky girl?"

"Taylor Hanson." He said. "This is my brother and his lovely bride to be... Cypress."

"Pleasure to meet you both." She said through a smile.

"Same to you," I nodded my head. "Asher you look so happy today?"

"Well, I get so what you're having. You two have been holding out long enough."

Lucas scratched his head. "If you could excuse us for a moment." His hand gripped my arm and he led me away from them. "We'll be back."

"Get your hands off me!" I growled as I snatched my arm back. He led me through the grand halls to a small room that was offset from the party. "What do you want from me Lucas?"

"I want you to stop thinking there is more to everything than there is," his voice was soft.

"I want the truth... right now."

He paced like he has always done when he was upset. His eyes were hooked to the ground. "I don't want you to run from me."

"Is there something to run from?" I asked.

"I..." Lucas exhaled. "I killed Philip..."

Everything turned into a haze. "You what?"

"I broke into his home and killed him that night." He stared at move unmoving and searched for my reaction. "I killed my ex-girlfriends."

I could feel the tingle in my legs as they tried to give out on me. "Lucas." The silence in the room made me feel as if he could hear my heart as it slowed down and then there was a sob the erupted from my chest. "Stop."

"I want you to know everything." He whispered. "I'm a killer. I don't feel anything except this..." He gestured between us. "I feel us."

"This is what Holly meant."

"What do you mean Holly?"

"Callum is a killer too." My tears were under no control. They had drenched the front of my shirt and my face was red hot. "How could you?"

"How could I what Cypress?" He growled. Lucas his hands shook a little.

And for the first time I feared him. I stepped back, inching towards the door. "Kill him." His eyes slanted towards me and it seemed that he understood who I was talking about without even saying his name.

"Would you rather I let him roam this world raping a degrading women like he had? I did this world a favor." He grumbled. "I have done, you a favor."

Lucas walked towards me. My feet shuffled as I moved back to the wall. I needed out and to be in front of someone, anyone. I felt the wall behind me to realize that the door was nowhere close to me. "Stay back."

"Stay back?" He questioned.

"You heard me."

"I can't control Callum."

"You can't control yourself." I spat.

He stepped closer to me and I stepped back from him. "Baby."

"Don't fucking touch me!" I screeched. "Don't touch me."

"This is what you wanted to hear. I gave you exactly what you wanted and you still..." He pulled at his ponytail in frustration. "What else do you want?"

"I want the father of my child to not be a killer."

"I can't help you there, love."

This was not what I wanted for today. I wanted to get over this fight, go back to his loft and be with the love of my life. It seemed that would never happen again. My heart thudded as the room started to spin before me. My eyes grew weak and everything in me was let down, humiliated even. But tears were not what I wanted him to see. My eyes stayed wide. If I even blinked for too long, there would be uncontrollable water works. "How can you do it?"

Lucas

For years I hadn't felt shit, but rage and this carnal need I could never satisfy. Then this beautiful woman entered my life unbeknownst to me and fucked everything up. I felt fear, anger, love, hell, even happiness at some point because of her. But now there was only one thing that was anchored in me and that was dread. There was nothing that could be said that could make it go down easier. I was a killer and I couldn't stop. I wouldn't stop. The hurt on her face was indescribable and there was nothing that I could do to soothe her, she didn't want me to touch her. She didn't want me to look at her.

"I don't know." I answered. "I can't help it. It's something in me that is in me."

"What?"

"A monster. And I have tried several times... over and over to quit. I even worked on it with Asher. I have started to do yoga and it does nothing. I have this need that can't be satisfied."

"So they know about you? They are just as fucked up as you."

I stepped back to allow her some room to move from the corner that she had backed herself into. I shook my head. How is it that I can slice open people, watch them drain until there is nothing left and feel nothing but emptiness, but the thought of her crying again made me feel miserable?

"Hey, you guys?" Lydia said at the door.

I snapped at her, "We're chatting, Lydia."

"Well, people are here and the party can't start without you two. So, finish this chat of yours and get out here! Oh, and Cypress, your mom just got here with your aunts and dad. And there is someone here in a suit looking for, you Lucas."

"Fuck," I hissed. The last thing I needed at this moment was that damn fed lurking around the one thing that could make her love me. "Tell him to leave it's a private affair."

"You tell him." Lydia said as she left.

Cypress navigated her way around me without touching me and she moved towards the door. "Come on." She held her hand out. "My mom is out there and she's excited. So I'm going to let them see us happy, even if it's fake."

"We can talk later." I whispered. Her hand in mine felt like maybe she could get over the fact that the love of her life was a raging serial killer.

"Baby... there might not be a later." The threat was in her voice. We walked into the overly decorated party. I had waited long enough as far as knowing what we are having, not to mention I hated parties. She smiled and waved at everyone. "Hey! Sorry we're late!"

I was quiet. I watched as the guests clapped as we walked out and we took our seats at the front of the room surrounded by the black balloons with the white question marks. There were several faces in the crowd that had traveled great lengths to get her. Her sister and her mom sat beside her father at the table in front of mine. Then there was Tracy, Mark and Asher. Nothing worse than being the center of attention.

Lydia took the podium. "I am so excited that you all could be here. We are here to celebrate the new arrival in our family. It's easy to say that I love these two guys more than anything and the thought of the perfect couple bringing a child into the world just amazes me. I'm also honored that they let me plan out this event. Before we get started with the big reveal, would the lovely couple like to say something."

"No," I said through my teeth. I grinned and Cypress gripped my hands under the table. She was nervous about the gender and I was dying because she was so close, but she was unreachable at the moment.

Cypress stood up. "Like she said, we are so happy that you could be here with us for this reveal." She glanced at me. "Lucas had decided months ago that I was having a boy and I can't wait for the moment to prove him wrong." The crowd snickered. She covered her eyes. "I'm just so excited you guys. This changes our lives forever."

I could feel the double meaning to her words. I shifted in my seat and smirked. "Change means we're growing love." I leaned into her. "Right?"

"Right."

"See why I love these guys!" Lydia smiled once more and she continued her speech. "Before you two are two safety pins and one balloon. We are going to count to three and then you guys pop the balloons and set baby Elledge free!"

"I'll let you do the honors." I handed her the small safety pin and the crowd began to count. On three there was a loud pop that rang in our ears. The pink and blue confetti sprinkled all over the ground. "What the bloody hell?"

Cypress looked at Lydia for some sort of explanation and so did I. "It's both colors here." She was confused and I was not too far behind her.

"Well, the doctor didn't tell you because I asked her not to! There are two bundles of joy in there, boy and girl."

Cypress touched her stomach and the tears started to flow from her eyes like a faucet. "Lu..."

"Well, damn." Declan stood at the back of the room with Mark beside him. I had never imagined that the man in the suit was him. He nodded at me and I smiled.

The drive to my loft was silent. She no longer feared me, or she didn't act like she did. Her hands just continued to rub her stomach like she was comforting them. It even half shocked me that she came home with me. I opened the door for her and helped her waddle up the stairs to the loft.

"Are you tired?" I asked.

"My feet hurt." She whispered. Cypress sat down on the couch and tossed her head back on the couch.

"What can I do for you?" A foot massage was out of the answer, they could trigger early later and that was the last thing that we needed.

"You can start explaining to me who the hell you are." She said.

"I'm Lucas. The man that you fell in love with nine months ago, I'm…"

"That Lucas would…"

"I'm the same person Cypress." I snapped.

"I don't want to talk." She exhaled. "I don't want to think about it."

"We can't avoid it." I said.

"I don't want to talk about it!" She yelled. Cypress was up on her swollen feet. "I can't even have a damn foot massage." She made her way upstairs to the bed and I could hear the springs on the bed as she sat down. Her shoes hit the floor with a loud thump and then she sobbed.

Fuck. I inched up the steps. "Cypress." I said.

"It's like I don't fucking know you! And that scares me Lucas because stupidly I entered this relationship one person and now I'm someone else completely. If I don't know you then who the fuck am I?" The mascara bled down her face and I sat next to her. "I don't know what to do."

"I can't tell you what to do." I grimaced.

"I know." She wiped her face.

I touched her shoulder lightly and she didn't pull away from me. Instead, she came closer to me. Her hands Pulled at my hair and her lips grazed mine. There was nothing more than I wanted than this moment, it was like she forgot everything that had been said to her and she wanted me. I kissed her back and I could taste her tears they didn't stop; I wasn't sure how to feel. She tossed her clothes on the floor and she sat in my lap. Her baby bump in front of us. It was more than me and her now, she had said it several times, but it had never clicked until now. I touched her stomach lightly and leaned into her chest. I wanted nothing more than I wanted her. Cypress' hands ran down my chest and she pushed me back onto the bed. She stripped my shirt off and then unbuckled my pants.

"Fuck me?" She pleaded.

She had no reason to plead. I would do whatever she asked me and this was one request I had no problem doing. I kicked my pants to the floor and gripped her breasts. Her head fell back in pleasure as a moan escaped her mouth. I touched her folds, separating them and kneading at her clit. She was eager. I lifted her up slowly and slid into her.

My eyes closed and I growled. It felt like it had been so long since I had her like this, she was so warm. Cypress wound herself against me. The friction she created gave her everything that she craved, but it only teased me. I wanted more, I wanted to be deep inside of her. I twisted her nipple between my fingers and she stifled profanities under her breath. And her stifled moan sent me into a frenzy as I pounded my dick into her at a relentless pace. Her hips met mine until all of the energy was drained from her and she fell breathlessly on my chest. Her pussy clenched me so tight I could come just from one more touch. I couldn't breathe. She slowed the pace and planted her hands on my chest to anchor herself. "You're so perfect." I mumbled.

Cypress' tears fell onto my chest. She had continued to weep, but she never lost her focus. She hated herself for being with me and I couldn't say I blamed her. I lifted her off of me and she lay on the bed beside me. Her back against my chest, I entered her once more, her clit pulsed. She was almost there. I rubbed her clit and her legs shook slightly and a scream followed. I dove back into her finding my release shortly after her. "I'm so sorry."

"I love you." She whispered as she nestled into me.

"I love you."

I slept until I realized that she was gone... My eyes opened with a folded letter on her pillow. *Good Morning,*. I wiped my eyes and slid my glasses onto my face. I pulled apart the folded letter and begun to read.

Good Morning.

       I've been here before; some call it a crossroad, but I call it a devastation. Lucas to say that I love you would be an understatement. The love that you and I share is more than a simple notion or declaration. It's who I am and who I thought you were. I don't know who or what you are anymore. I only know the image of you that I have gathered in my mind. I only know the Lucas that you wanted me to know. And from what I can tell that version of you was far from who you are. I thought I would live my life out with you. I thought that I would spend every morning and night with you. Live with you and die with you. Be with you forever.

       How stupid can I be to think that I could do this with someone that I barely know? Someone that lived his life like I was never in it behind closed doors. I would rather not know what you have done. The torment of the real I've envisioned in my dreams has already started to haunt me. The thought that I was the reason some people have died sickens me. It sickens me to my core. I gave you everything that I had and you single handedly destroyed everything that I am... I can't just think about me anymore. There are two very important people coming into this world that I have to consider. I don't know if I can be with you and I don't know if I can even love you anymore. But there is too much love manifested among us bot that, I don't even know if I can leave you alone. I want you to stay away from me. I need this time away from you Lucas. Please give it to me. Please.

                           Cypress

CHAPTER
TWENTY-THREE

Asher

The new chick was no comparison to Whitney. Whitney had her damn hooks in me and letting go was the last thing that I wanted to do. I just wanted to go back to her and talk through everything because starting over was new. I lie in the bed with my eyes close, but my mind raced. How in the hell could I get her out of here without rude or crude? I wasn't Mark I couldn't just say what I wanted to women, rather it be rude or nice. I had a heart, just my heart wasn't into her.

She curled into me and I exhaled. Fuck. It was morning. There were some things that I had to do, mainly concerning graduating. I shifted out of bed and covered her back up. There had to be some easy way to this dating thing. I moved to the bathroom and started to brush my teeth and wash my face. I heard her stirring in the sheets, so I moved out of the cold room to the living room.

The fumbled knock at my door startled me at first. I walked over to it and to no surprise it was Lucas. He was for once a savior. Whatever story he had brought would be a good enough reason for her to leave and for me to be alone. "What are you doing out this early?"

"It's ten." He whispered. "Can I come in?"

Lucas looked miserable. His eyes were red and he had his pajamas on. "Come on," I closed the door behind him and watched as he slumped over in my favorite recliner. "What's wrong?"

"She left me." He stated.

"Cypress?"

"No, who the fuck else?" His voice broke.

I could hear her footsteps as she hopped out of bed. She stumbled into the living room, holding her purse and keys. Great. She would just leave and we could talk about whatever was bugged Lucas and then I would get back to Whitney. "Asher," She moaned.

"Good Morning." I smiled. "You met my brother yesterday?"

"Oh, hi, congrats again on the two babies."

"Thanks."

"I have to go. Could we do coffee sometime later this week?"

"Certainly, just give me a ring or text and I'll be there."

She kissed my cheek and then made a run for the door. "Bye!"

"Bye." I said. I waited for her to leave and then turned towards Lucas. "What happen?"

"She bloody fucked me and then wrote a note. This note proclaiming, she doesn't know if she can love me. She doesn't know if she can be with me because she hates what I am and I lied to her and..." His hand collided with his face in anger and kept my distance. His anger was nothing to kid about. I watched as his face redden and he pushed his hair back from his face. "What do I do?"

He hit himself once more and I nodded my head. Lucas loved her with every ounce of him and at first I was genuinely scared that she would end up like some of the other women in his life but I knew there was nothing that he would do to her. "First, stop hitting yourself." I hesitantly pulled his hands down from his now red and almost bruised face. "Second, let me see the note." I held my hand out and I glanced over the letter. She had done what any sane person would do. She had distanced herself from a bad situation. "Fuck."

326 | LR Johnson

"Yeah, fuck. She's my fiancé."

"She has the right to feel this way Lucas. You can't expect her to be okay with all the fucked up shit that you have done. And you can't expect her to willingly just go back to you. Give her what she wants and if she comes back to you then don't fuck it up."

"What do you mean if she comes back. You have to talk to her."

"I can't clean up all of your messes Lucas. I talked to her last time. I gave her every bit of advice that I could give her. The fact of the matter is that you can't make a decision for a person. You have to accept that she doesn't want you or give her more of a reason to want you."

"I've never felt this way before in my life, about anyone. I mean anyone." He paused. "I fancied her so much in the beginning that I knew that everything that I felt for her would fade. She was like a toy that I had to have and that I wanted to be mine. But instead of faded feelings I swear they grew stronger. It went from not being able to sleep without her to now... I can't breathe or think when she is not around. I want her back."

"Well, give her space and when she comes around... like she always done... tell her all the shit that you just told me and I swear that she'll be yours." I ran my fingers through my hair. "But, the real question that she will ask you is if you can stop and will you stop?"

"I can't answer that."

"Then you don't need to talk to her. You need to give her space and perhaps use this time to figure out if you're willing to stop something for someone that you love."

Cypress

Lana had made my new couch a bed and she splayed out on it like she lived here. I hated to sleep alone. I hated to be alone, period. I was surrounded by an array of food. Pickles, Nutella and pretzels. My food cravings had been so thrown off here lately I could hardly eat a regular meal. What I needed most was real food. I wobbled out of bed and into the kitchen.

"About time you woke up! How my babies doing?"

I appreciated the fact that Lana stayed with me and let mom take her baby back to Tennessee. She had no idea what was happening between Lucas and me. She only knew what I told her which was a fabricated story about Persephone. "They're sleeping on my bladder like it's a freaking pillow." I moaned. I got up like seven times and struggled to make it to the bathroom. Then there was the struggle of heat and the air conditioning.

"I'm sorry babe!" She giggled. "Have you heard from him?"

It had only been one day since I left the note on his bed and snuck out in the night. It was the only way I knew that I could make a clean break because it was always hard for me to leave him, especially when I looked into those emerald eyes. "I told him to leave me alone for a while." I nodded. "I just want some time to be alone." I wanted some time to figure out if he was what I needed in my life.

I had heard of serial killers before. I mean, who hadn't, but the fact that I was sleeping with one, damn near living with one for half a year was scary. Lucas seemed to be the same normal person to me. He seemed to be the same guy that held my hand, held doors opened for me, cried to me about his father... he was a serial killer. I closed my eyes and pushed the thought back out of my mind.

"Well, are you going to take him back?"

"I think I'm going to pray about it."

"I mean he was just texting her and you said it wasn't bad things." Lana rolled her eyes. "Is a text really worth ruining a family."

"Whose side are you on?"

"Those babies?" She snapped. She sat back up on the couch and nodded her head, "But it's not my life so my opinion doesn't matter."

"Are you hungry?"

"You shouldn't be."

"Thanks." I rolled my eyes at her and then grabbed my keys. "I'm about to go out and get something to cook. I would kill for some egg rolls and some pizza."

"That's takeout."

"Perfect!" I smirked. "I'll be back and we can share some food together and talk about some girly shit."

"Yeah, like your wedding."

"Or how pastels are so in right now." I laughed and opened the front door.

"Cypress," I heard a thick Irish accent. Declan. He stood before me in a gray suit and a fedora hat. Always dapper and handsome, yet here every time he's not needed. "How are you?"

"Perfect..." I paused. "Why are you here?"

"Well, Lucas said that we would have dinner before I left town and I haven't heard from him. Then Asher calls me and tells me what's truly going on and I just wanted to see you and make sure you were okay."

Declan, was not my favorite person. He had walked out on his child willingly just so that he could live a separate life. And I didn't want to know why. I wanted him to go back to Ireland. "I was just leaving."

"Oh pity," He paused. "Would you mind if I joined you then?"

"I can go." Lana volunteered. "I've really wanted to see the city anyhow."

Way to fucking go Lana. I shrugged my shoulders. "Be my guest." I turned back into the apartment and Lana made her swift exit. She just wanted to go to the damn mall. I wasn't able to walk far anymore and the mall was my least favorite place at the moment.

Once she was gone Declan took a seat. "I won't keep you long." He shrugged out of his jacket and smiled at me. "It's safe to talk in here?"

"What do you mean?"

"There are no wires or bugs here, eh?"

"No," I nodded my head.

"Perfect." He cleared his throat. "I know he told you the truth. It amazes me that he's finally become man enough to let you see every piece of him. It's a tremendous feat. I have been in his place before with Luna it happened right before the birth of Mark."

"The same place..."

"I'm a killer Cypress."

"Fuck, what is it hereditary," I groaned as my eyes started to sting.

"Luna was not as strong willed as you. She just blocked it out and whenever she knew something had happened, she made herself disappear. We didn't have this perfect marriage. We didn't even have a good relationship at the start of it all. You know... but we made it into something."

"Are you here to guide me to Lucas?"

"I can't do that and wouldn't if I could. I want you to make the best decision for you and those babies. And if it's not Lucas then I cannot blame you. I can't sit here and say you should love him and here is why. The only thing I can say is that you make him a better person. I've seen him calm himself and slow down here lately."

"Calm down."

"My son has been a killer since he was sixteen years old. I've covered tracks for him longer than I can remember. He once was insatiable and we had to move all around every year to keep people from noticing the increase of the deaths. I knew he was a killer. I knew he was a killer from the moment he opened those green eyes."

"You cleaned up after him."

"I did."

"You might as well have put the knife in his hand." I shifted in my seat and readjusted my pillows. "You're worse than him."

"I can't disagree with you, but don't act like you haven't cleaned up after him, even if it was unknowingly."

The knife. I paused to gather myself before speaking to him again. Declan knew more than I thought he knew about us. "I... don't know why I did that."

"Because you knew already." He said. "Luna knew already. She just followed her intuition, that damn woman knew everything about me before I could tell her anything and you know you are not much different from her. And that's a good thing because she knew how to call bullshit on him, she knew how to control him and you can do the same thing. I can teach you if you want."

"You mean have him kill for me."

"I mean stop him from killing." Declan crossed his legs and nodded his head. "I can't say it will work, but it could save some people." The silence hung there for a moment and then he sighed. "But then I have to say that he killed some people that needed to be killed."

"He has not right to kill anyone."

"Not even the bastard that raped his wife and child before killing them in cold blood? Or the porn star that passed HIV on to over thirty men and women through carelessness. Or how about the woman who beat children because they asked for bread and then slammed one to the ground so hard a bone cracked?"

I couldn't tell which was more sickening, their acts of cruelty or the fact that Lucas had more than likely enjoyed putting them down. "None of it is right."

"I feel like had he not killed any of them… they would have killed more. They would have killed more than he was ever capable of and the fact that he killed them doesn't bother me."

"Of course not you kill too."

"I'm a hired assassin." He corrected. "And yes, I kill. I kill when it is necessary by my job and I kill when I have to… we're alike but different."

"Okay."

"He should explain everything to you himself, but he's so afraid that you are going to say no to him that he can't function right. I can't stay long. I have a few places to be tonight but I would love to see you again before I leave the country."

"Certainly." Thank heavens he was leaving.

"Think things through thoroughly before you make a decision. I want the best for you and him and if that means that you can't be with him than it is fine. Just take care of yourself."

"Will do. Are you leaving?"

"Yes, Cypress."

Lucas

"You have so much to do before next week. Number one they want you to go under psychiatric evaluation." Mark went through his folder. His apartment was so white it made my head hurt. "Then there is the meeting with the defense lawyer, she wants to set up some things that can help you. She said something about it being your first offense and…"

My eyes were held on the all-white table and the only person that ran through my head was Cypress. All the banter he had over the past few minutes had gone over my head.

"Lucas!" He said.

"What?" I snapped.

"You have some big shit in front of you! You need to snap out of it and focus for a few minutes so that I can get you back straight."

"I can't be back to normal. Normal is Cypress and she isn't here and I don't feel like talking or being around you honestly."

Mark pushed me back on the couch and nodded his head. "Man the fuck up dude? I mean I'm not Asher I don't give a damn about your feeling right now. I care about you serving up to ten years in prison for hitting some dumb ass cop."

"The pig had it coming."

"Because he was right about you? Are you not the one person that needs to be caring about your freedom. What if you are in prison when those babies are born?"

"Continue," I rasped.

"You need to exhibit miraculous behavior when being observed. I'll have Asher bring you something to read up on and keep you occupied while I talk to Cypress."

"You're going to talk to her."

"I have to, so you can shut up and get the fuck out of America." He smiled at me. "I have some things that I want to talk to her anyhow. And I know that you need the help."

"Thank you, I swear you are a godsend."

"I know. Now give me your journal."

"NO."

"No, it's the only way I see her coming back to you, sir. Break out that damn journal and let me work, please."

"Fuck."

"I know what is in it. It's how I know that she'll choose you, but you have some explaining to do once she does."

My journal held my deepest and darkest secrets. It held everything about me that people had no idea about... like the rage and the fear of being alone. If she saw it, she would think, I was weak. "It's upstairs..." I paused. "Is she going to read everything?"

"That's what I hope."

CHAPTER
TWENTY-FOUR

Lucas

For some reason Mark's plan worked and reluctantly she came back to my loft so that someone would be there for her besides her sister who needed to go home to her own child. I didn't know if she would heal from the truth. Cypress barely talked to me. And the move to Ireland was for now was on an indefinite hold. The only real hope I could hold onto was the fact that she still wore the ring, swollen fingers and all.

"Are you comfortable?" I asked. Patience was something that I lacked. I wanted us to be back to normal.

Cypress sat propped up in my bed, the covers engulfed her and she held my journal in her hand like it was her bible. "I'll live." Her eyes skimmed the pages like it was the best book she had ever read and I didn't know if I should even be around her.

"How long are we going to be like this? You really don't talk to me anymore and..."

"You kill people. I mean am I supposed to just go on with my life like everything is normal. The agent is on to you and there are fifty million things that are flowing through my mind. What if you get caught?"

"I…"

"Have you ever thought about what it would do to your entire family. And then you have your brothers sucked into this like it is normal. None of this is normal. I don't know if I should be scared for my life or not. I don't know you."

"You know me."

"I don't." She yelled. "I know who I thought you were but there is so much that I don't know it's safe to say that there is no chance that I know the real you."

I tried to conjure up words to say, but there were none there. She knew that I loved her and that nothing would ever happen to her while I was around, but I couldn't make her believe it." I touched her arm and she flinched like it hurt her. "I have court…" I nodded.

"Like I could forget." She paused and exhaled once she realized how mean she sounded and rolled her eyes. "Go to court and bring some food back Lucas. I want some cream cheese wontons and a jar of Nutella."

"Anything else?"

"There is nothing else." She answered.

The drive to the store was uncomfortably silent and the radio was more of a drag to listen to so I just watched everything around me. I had court in less than an hour. That punch to the agent had been so exhilarating that the threat of jail time was really not an issue. Perhaps some time away from me was what she needed.

Downtown was abandoned, it looked like. There were a few cars at the courthouse, but not much. Hopefully it would be quick. Mark was already parked and inside. He did not agree with the fact that I had told her. It wasn't his choice though. I walked into the courthouse and sat next to him on the bench.   "You do realize that you could face some jail time." Mark said.

"Nice to see you too."

"I am serious Lucas. You could be in jail when the babies are born."

"I don't think I will be."

"Well, happy to know that you have good faith." He pulled out a leather folder and shuffled through the pages. "I have substantial proof that the agent has been harassing you and you met your boiling point."

"Okay... I can get you to plead guilty to misconduct and they'll throw a light community service at you and anger management?"

"Anger management?"

"Yes, it's something that you need anyway Lucas. If we don't take the plea, he will nail you for assault of a federal employee. And that means you can serve ten years. Lower your pride and take the plea."

The plea was basically a get out of jail free card. I would be dumb to go to court and face the prick. "Yeah, alright."

"Good come on," He stood up, walked to the Judge's chambers.

McMillan stood there with a smirk on his face. "Good evening Elledge Boys."

"Afternoon," Mark answered. "Is your lawyer in there or..."

"Elledge, McMillan I will see you now." The judge said as she opened her doors.

His lawyer stepped in front of me and walked in the door. "Good to see you Judge Patterson."

"Same to you Patrick." She sat down. "You are a new lawyer?" She said to Mark.

Mark cleared his throat and nodded. "Yes, ma'am."

"Well, welcome to the wonderful world of law. All of you take a seat." We done as directed and she flipped through the pages on her desk. "You hit a federal officer Mr. Elledge."

"Yes, ma'am." I said.

Judge Patterson stared at me. "Your lawyer here gave me some interesting things. Agent McMillan has been on you for months about a series of murders."

Mark spoke up. "Harassing him mainly."

"Investigating doing my job." McMillan added.

"I see here that you have no viable evidence that ties Lucas Elledge to the crimes? This case has been open almost an entire five years. Just speculation after speculation?"

"Yes, ma'am but there are some developments that we are looking into."

"I will be talking to your superior officers." She nodded her head. "Lucas, I hear that they have put a plea for misconduct. I hereby order that you pay a fine, $10,000 and that you receive the psychiatric evaluation asked by the prosecution."

"Evaluation?" I knew it already. Mark had said that they were going to ask me to do it. Asher had even trained me on the correct answers.

"Yes, we would like to run a series of evaluations on you."

"Why?"

"Lucas, enough. He will submit to the testing. What are they?"

"Psychopathy test... personality disorder."

"How is this related to the offense that the defendant committed?" Judge Patterson asked.

"It isn't." Mark spat.

She grimaced. "Pay the fine and seek out anger management. Mandatory."

"Yes, ma'am."

Cypress

The journal had opened the door for insight for me. I understood now that Lucas kept tons locked inside of him. Mainly things concerning about how he felt inside. He had rage issues, and anger issues when it came to certain types of people and he had changed when he met me. The journal went from angry prose to almost angelic poems of love. It was perfect for me to see what an impact I made. But I still needed answers.

"Stay there," Lucas said as he walked through the front door.

"Okay," I lay back on the bed and roll my eyes. It had become basically uncontrollable to not roll my eyes at Lucas here lately. If he wasn't irritating me by smothering me, it was by annoying me to death. "How did court go?"

"I got a fine and anger management and she is talking McMillan's superior about having the case closed."

"Really?"

"Yeah, Mark brought up the fact that they have not got one piece of evidence on me and blah. And he said that it was basically harassment. The best thing for them to do would be to find another suspect. The Judge said that she would see what she could do."

"Your father called." Declan had called me more than three times and each time we talked the conversation got longer and longer. I hated to say it, but he knew more about my situation than I did. He knew what to do and how to handle it so for once I just started to listen. And listening has me almost loving him like I had before this whole bomb was dropped.

"Oh, he did."

"Yes, he is coming over here, he said that he wanted to see us both before he went back."

"Great," Lucas said as he shifted through the living room below me. "Do you want to talk now?"

"Yeah, come up here and tell me everything." I laid the journal down on the bed and waited for him to make his way up the stairs.

"Everything, you don't want to know everything."

"Okay, look I have been sitting here all day staring at this book." I gestured towards the journal and exhaled. "It tells me so much about you. And then I stared at the ceiling for an entire hour trying to see how Holly doesn't kill herself with what she goes through? I want to know everything."

"Holly is different than you think. She has known about Callum since the beginning."

"Lucky her," I mumbled.

He walked up the steps with two Subs and bottles of water. "Here, take this and I guess I should tell you everything. And at the need of the conversation I want to know what you are thinking."

"I'll see what I can do." I mumbled.

He tossed me the sandwich and I stared at him. "I killed first when I was younger. There was a woman that lived next door to us that was a bitch. She hated the world and I could understand that to some extent, but keep it to yourself."

"You hate the world."

"I hate some things, yes." There was a pause and then he started back. "Her name was Delphine and she was a bitch. She owned the bakery. One day I saw her beat these kids from my neighborhood. They were bad children because they had to scrounge up food. Their mom was poor. And she worked to survive, but it was never enough. She always was suffering basically and her oldest children were like eight or nine. They would hang around the bakery. Then one day they stole some bread from her and she beat them with a damn broom. It had been a bad day already. I was home for the summer and my father had disappeared on us like always. I was angry and I hated her so I killed her. I slit her throat."

My eyes were hooked on him. There was nothing there. He didn't flinch. He just sat there. "How did you feel?"

"It was amazing. I needed that first kill more than I needed anything else. It was like a release... a climax, I had been fighting to get to since I was born."

"That's not normal Lucas."

"It's what I feel every single time I slice into someone."

"Why?"

"I don't know. It's always been there. I mean ever since I was younger and I can't stop it."

"Have you ever killed a family member?"

"I thought about killing my dad." He laughed. "But I couldn't do it and I won't do it. I'm a monster, but I could never kill the man that raised me." Lucas cuts his eyes at me. "I won't give you the details to every single person I have killed and I won't give you a number."

"I don't think you are a monster."

"You don't think so?" Lucas rubbed his chin. "Your view is tainted love..."

"Tainted."

"Yeah tainted."

"The first thing you ever said to me was, It's okay if it's tainted."

"I wasn't talking about me."

"Perhaps you were and you didn't know it."

"I don't think I was. But I know that if you walk down this road with me... you can't look back. You can't run from me and you can't hate. I just have to be me and you have to accept it."

"I have to accept a monster?"

"It's a sacrifice and I can't force you to make it. I don't want to force you to. I want you to know that I have issues. I get mad and when I get mad there is something that brews and brews and then finally it reaches a boiling point and I have to do something about it and it may be something that you don't like."

"What about our kids can you stop for them?"

"Don't do that Cy." His voice was low.

"It's more than just you now Lucas!" My voice rang throughout the apartment and his eyes melted. "You have to realize that you can't do everything that you used to. This could be a way for you to start over. This could be your escape route."

"There is no escape Cypress. You can't run from this. That you have to realize. It can't be roses and sunshine and birds chirping every morning with me. You'll wake up one day and see a storm brewing that you can't control."

"Let me help you. I can try to help you."

"Help me by being there oblivious to everything that is happening. That is how you can help me."

The elevator door opened and Declan walked into the loft. "You two here?"

"Up here, we'll be down in a few. Sit down and don't break shit." Lucas growled.

"Remember who your father is," He warned from below.

"How could I forget? You want to eat and then go down there?"

"We can go now." I held my hand out as I waited for him to help me up. The stairs had become a tedious chore. I missed my place, but he wouldn't let me out of his sight. Declan was handsome, he carried himself so well. I had never seen him in anything other than a tailored suit. His curls were always neatly gelled back though they waved up.

"You look good, Declan." I said.

"I can say the same thing about you." He helped me to the couch. "What are you two doing still in the bed?"

"Relationship talks." Lucas said. "What are you doing here?"

"I wanted to talk to you two."

"Well, talk." Lucas mood had changed. His father was so much like him that it scared me and gave me hope. Maybe he would grow up one of these days and we could be happy. "And hurry it along."

"Calm yourself, boy," Declan sat next to me. "I won't be here for the birth. I don't like to stay in the states too long. I would rather not... so I wanted to uhm... tell you Cypress that I am happy to be a part of a family that has a strong woman like you. We need a woman besides my mom to grab the reigns and you have everything in you that can get you there. I know he can be a pain. But you are a wonderful woman who can change him..."

"Like mom changed you?"

"I didn't come to argue with you. I came to say goodbye until we see each other again. I would rather it be a joyous occasion rather than a fight."

"Joy on then," Lucas watched from the table.

"Have you two thought of names?"

"Luna Elledge and Nathaniel Elledge." I said.

"Beautiful." He chuckled. "Those names are beautiful."

"Those names are preliminary."

"Those names are permanent." I snapped.

"Yes, ma'am."

"Thank you." I rolled my eyes at Lucas. "Please be safe and let us know when you are there."

"And tell Callum to give me a call." Lucas added.

"I'll do all of the above. You take care."

When he left it Lucas looked angry. "You said that we were discussing names Cypress."

"I'm naming them what I want them to be named. Nathaniel was your idea a month back. I like it. And you can calm down." I couldn't reach the damn remote and my show was two minutes away from starting.

"I don't think I can call another person Luna, Cypress. She was my mother."

It hadn't crossed my mind that it would be painful for him. "I understand. Think of a first name and Luna can be the middle." I pointed to the remote. "Please get the remote before I roll off of the couch.

"How about Meagan?"

"No." I took the remote from his hands and flipped the TV on.

"Willow?"

"That's pretty… Willow Luna," I toyed with the name silently. "I mean I am named Cypress."

"Good. I like it better than just Luna."

"Swear to me that you won't kill again while I'm pregnant?"

"I swear to it. I won't."

"Good."

"Unless provoked."

"No, even provoked Lucas."

Lucas

I had basically been placed on probation by Cypress. I could tell one wrong move would infuriate her to the point of not seeing my children until they were grown. So I played it cool. I let her have some space and shopped with Lydia, who was more excited than I was about the baby shopping.

"Is there a limit for car seats?"

"No," I said. "We probably shouldn't spend much based on the fact that I feel like we won't be in the states long."

"So Europe. Why there?"

"I have more family there and she wants to start over completely."

She picked up a ton of towels. "So you mean that I won't really be seeing my niece and nephew grow old."

"No, I mean you can come visit any time you like."

"Trey and I are moving to Texas for college, so I'll be busy and mom will more than likely want me there at Christmas."

"Tracy understands," I hadn't really talked to her since the news broke about my brothers and she understood. I felt like she had lied to me and in every way she really had lied to me.

"You will be a good father. I just hope that you can be a better boyfriend or whatever the hell you two are."

"Yeah, whatever."

"I'm serious. She loves you and I know you love her. You are so stubborn."

"Love is stubborn Lydia. When you find your soul mate, you will see that it is not as easy as you want it to be."

"Mom told me about Mark."

"Yep," I tossed some bottles in the cart.

"You two alike and the other guy looks like Mark. So it's good that you are not alone in the world anymore. Now you'll be surrounded by more family than you could have ever dreamed of. You will have babies and a wife."

"I know this."

"Well, do me a favor and smile." She snapped. "You could have nothing!"

"Alright, damn sister."

"I'm serious. You sit here and you scowl your life away and there are so many reasons for you to smile and enjoy life."

"Okay. I will enjoy life." I grabbed a few pink blankets. "I don't know the first thing about babies."

"They are not hard to deal with and you will be great."

"I'm scared of it you know. This is about to be one of the most difficult times of my life. I'll have to change everything about me to fit them."

"That's what parenthood is, add in some throw up and shit and there you have it."

Such a comfort she was. I rolled my eyes and continued to walk down the aisle. "If we move this summer will you spend the summer in Ireland with us. You can help her adjust to the house we get and motherhood. The only girl she will have over there will be Holly and I can tell that they are not fond of one another. I doubt the friendship would last more than a month."

"I can't. I have already registered for summer classes. And I have to get a dorm room and find my life there. She will be fine."

"I hope so."

"Spend time with her. Smile at her and make her realize that you love her and you will be fine."

"Always chalked full of advice."

"I know. Mom taught me how to be considerate. It didn't rub off on Mark."

"He's more considerate than you will know."

"Then why did he end things with Shia?"

"Shia was a means to an end. Mark is not ready for love and she was trying to push him there. And if you back a dog into a corner you are gonna get bit. She should have known. Hell everyone else around her knew that it was not real."

"Trey isn't that way."

"Good, because I would kill him if he was."

"So sweet!" she laughed.

"I was so serious. He has one time to screw up and it is over."

CHAPTER TWENTY-FIVE

Lucas

She'd been in labor for seven hours. "Alright sis, I need you to breathe because it's a big one coming." Asher held her hand as she pushed air out slowly. I watched from across the white room. She didn't want me to help her because I wasn't the best person to give words of encouragement while in pain. She had the grip of a grown man and I would pass this time. There was nothing that I could do about her pain at this point. She had three more centimeters and the babies would make their grand entrance into a world I didn't know was made for me.

"Breathe babe." I watched her and pushed the mess of hair out of my face. It was about to happen. I had created life rather than take it. I watched her as she sweated and panted to stay calm. "Can I do anything Asher?"

"You're fine brother."

"Am I? You're doing all the work."

"Take over if you want to Luke." He stood up and Cypress pulled him back down.

"He stays. You grab the other hand, if you want to help!"

"Yes, ma'am." I paced the room. "There's a head there." I stared at the crowning head of hair. "Should I call the nurse?"

"Call them Luke."

I hit the red button. "There is a head down here, we need a nurse."

Asher stared at me. "Could you not say she was crowning?"

"I don't know. Look, I'm scared. I don't know what the hell is going on. I just really want a drink."

"Go wait with Mark and send Lydia in."

"I want to be here when they are born." I said.

"Well, you need to be here in my place. Grab her hand and I'll go."

"Where is my mom?"

"She is outside love." I answered.

"Send her in..." She cried.

"Okay, make sure you tell her mom and not her crazy auntie with the bad attitude." I held her hand and she started to grip it. I exhaled breathing just as she was. "You're doing great, you know?"

"I hate you." She spat.

"Good to know." I counted with her and the nurse walked in.

"It's time! Are you ready?" She was a super thin perky woman.

She shook her head and smiled at her mom walked into the room. "Mom, make sure he does right."

Her mom laughed. "Luke, you okay?"

"I don't know." I chuckled and stepped back.

"The doctor will be in. No matter how bad you feel you need to push... don't."

The doctor made his entrance and the actual births started. She pushed for ten minutes for the first one. The cry filled the room and I felt everything go white... a girl. Baby Willow. Her head full of sandy curls like her mum.

"Sir... would you like to cut the cord?" The nurse smiled at me.

Slicing just happened to be my specialty. I snipped the cord and they wrapped the baby in a blanket. Then there was another shrill cry in the room and the second... my son came.

They were both here. My eyes stung from the oncoming rush. They placed the babies on her chest and she sobbed.

"They are precious!"

There were no words. I watched them as they cried in her arms and she cried as she held them. My tears could not be stopped. Happiness had found me at last. I touched their tiny fingers and kissed Cypress. "I love you and them. Look at them wee people."

She laughed. "Oh my god stop it." She looked at me. "Nathaniel and Willow... say hi to daddy."

Daddy, I exhaled. "Hi, loves."

Cypress

He was drained. He had to be tired because he paced the entire time I was in labor like he gave birth. Lucas was sound asleep in the chair like he was home. The babies were beside the bed as well. Sound asleep and then we had grown by two.

"They are beautiful." Asher whispered.

"They are." I wiped my face.

"Are you moving?"

"I think it's best."

"I think you're right. There is something in Ireland that soothes him and makes him feel like he can do better. So you should do it. Those babies will have an amazing life."

"Thank you for always being that voice of reason."

"You're welcome."

"So Cali?"

"Maybe, dad has something that he wants me to be a part of, so who knows we might be neighbors here soon. I just have to tie up so many loose ends here."

"Loose ends..."

"Yeah, for some reason Whitney wanted to talk to me about something and then I have to pack all of that shit in my apartment. I don't know if I will move to Ireland yet so I need storage and blah." Asher looked at Lucas. "Look at him."

"I know he is tired like he went through labor."

"He was freaking me out. I almost hit him, but my conscious told me that the results would not be good." Asher stood up. "I have to leave sis. Keep him straight and I'll stop by tomorrow."

"Good, we will see you tomorrow."

When he left the room was filled of the babies' occasional coos and Lucas' light snores. There was so much to do and no time to really get anything done. We had nowhere to live over there and something kept urging the move. There had to be something there I could do that could bring in money. I had my degree now. Just needed to get everything together.

"What are you thinking about?" Lucas stretched in the chair.

"Everything."

"Get some sleep."

"I can't sleep."

"Well, try to."

"So we are moving. I have decided that if we truly want and need to get a fresh start this is what we need to do. What do I need to?"

"Find a house." He said simply.

"I want to live in a place that is not so secluded from people. I want some neighbors and I would rather not be around Holly and Callum."

"Callum is not bad."

"Yeah, whatever."

"I'll find somewhere that is in a good spot."

"I want to choose it."

"Okay, well get to looking." Lucas eyes were glued to the babies. "I can't stop looking at them. They are everything I could have imagined and if anything comes between us and them... I won't hesitate to destroy it. I want you to know that. I don't care who it is and I don't care how it ends. I will destroy it. Do you understand?"

"Okay."

"I mean it. I will."

"I understand Luke. It's the reason I want us to move."

"We'll wait until you are healed completely."

"And you better stay out of trouble. Please," I begged. "I haven't asked about anything else because I decided that I don't want to know. I would rather be oblivious to some things."

"That works for me."

"Good."

Asher

It was safe to say that it had been a long day. The dramatics of Lucas combined with the unsteady feeling of the end. Everything that had been the norm was now about to be the uncommon. My apartment was packed and ready to go. Home was somewhere and I didn't necessarily know where. I just knew that I had planned to be moving on.

I closed the door behind me and placed my keys on the counter.

"Where have you been?" her voice was familiar.

"Whit?"

"Yeah, I came by here three times and you've been gone the entire day."

"Well Cypress had her babies and I was there for Lucas."

"Playing big brother now?"

"I'm not playing anything." I shrugged my shoulders. "Why are you here?"

"Well, I know that he has done something for sure now. And I know you know where the weapon is." She paused. "You took a picture of it. I need the picture so they can lock him up. It won't have anything to do with you. It'll just be a me thing."

"Fuck off Whit." I shook my head. "Why do you hate him so much?"

"Just give me the picture."

"I never took a picture."

"Oh come on. I know you did."

"No, I didn't." The picture had been destroyed long ago and there was no chance that I was about to tell her it was one.

"You love him so much. Why?"

"Why the hell are you here?"

She threw her head back in laughter and pushed over the picture of me and my father. "They can't repair you. You're broken."

"Get out."

"Make me." She snapped. Whitney stood in front of the couch. Her arms crossed and her stupid grin infuriated me. "You are a coward and I'm embarrassed to ever say that I loved you. You made my life a miserable hell."

"The feeling is mutual."

"I'm going to the agents with everything that I know. And I'm doing it to save your mother's grief. You want to know why she hadn't called you in months. She knows who his father was."

"My father was a great man."

"Your father beat the shit out of her until she couldn't walk. DO you want that to happen to Cypress? I am going to help everyone out and let this fucker fry."

"Come on," I moved past her and she snatched my phone. "Give it back."

"Does he tell you everything now?"

"Stop!" I snatched the phone back.

"Pussy." She grumbled.

Something clicked inside of me. My heart pounded against my chest and I took everything I had and shoved her into the fireplace. Her head swung over and hit the corner of the stone and she fell to the ground with one quick thud. I could feel the sweat of my palms. I stood over her and she was lifeless. It happened too quick. I'd turned into my brother with less than a blink of an eye.

I paced the room, shoving my hands through my short brown hair. What the fuck had just happened? I grabbed my phone, sending a text I knew would get a response. 911 to Lucas and Mark and waited.

It felt like forever, but in reality only 7 minutes had passed before there was a knock at my door. I opened it frantically. Mark sat there with his arms crossed. "What did he do?"

"He done nothing." I pulled him into the apartment and wiped my face. "She came here... and she threatened me." I pointed to her body. I hadn't touched anything on her. She lay just as she had landed.

"Asher... is she dead?"

"I think so." I shook my head as my voice cracked. "I think she died."

"What happened? I mean, why is she dead."

"It happened too fast I can't remember. I don't know what to do."

"We can make it a break in if we do it fast." Mark drew back and his fist crashed into my cheek. Sending a flare through my body.

"Wait!" I yelled.

"I need to beat the shit out of you Asher." Mark looked at me. "I'll break the door in and everything but you have to be injured or they are gonna know that you done it."

I closed my eyes. His punch had already triggered a headache and it had been a mere second. Time passed. Moments. "Do it."

The beat down that he gave me was deserving. My chest ached and my rib was sure enough broken. He flung me into walls and destroyed what was left in my apartment. I was so weak. I could barely move from the ground.

He looked at me. "Are you okay?"

"No," I whispered.

"Good." He smiled. "Hello, operator. I'm in the Pine Haven Apartments on Park Street... my brother is beaten badly and his friend is unconscious. I need help!" he cried.

I ended up in the hospital sooner than I thought that I would be, my ribs broken and face pounded. And my mom made her way to the hospital because when I finally was stable enough to stay awake she was the first person I saw.

"You're up."

"I am," I could barely recognize my own voice. The raspy voice filled the room enough for everyone around me to stand up. They were all there and it felt good. Though the whole thing was a hoax. "Where is Whitney?"

"Honey, we can talk about her later." My mom ran her fingers through my hair and kissed my forehead. I winced and she grabbed my hand. "Do you know who did this?"

"Mom where is Whitney?"

"I said not right now, babe. Let's just get you stable."

"Mark," I whined. "Where is she?"

"She didn't make it." He whispered. "She bled out." Mark closed his eyes. "Lucas stopped by for a moment. He had to be back in time to feed the babies."

"She died?" My voice cracked. I was officially a killer

"Yeah, look don't bother with that right now. You just need to do what your mom said and don't think about it. We can sort everything out in a few okay?" Mark stood next to the bed.

The tear escaped and I wiped it quickly. She was dead. "Yeah."

"Take care of him." He touched Margot lightly on the shoulder. "I have to run upstairs and check on the other brother and then I will be back before I leave. Shia has been bugging the mess out of me."

The medicine had me numb. I stared at the ceiling. "There is an agent here to talk to you. Please work with him so they can figure out who done this to you okay?"

"I promise mom."

"Good."

To no surprise McMillan made his grand entrance into the room. "Asher, you look beat up."

"Yeah, someone fucked me over."

"So you know how it feels." He chuckled. "I just want to know what happened."

"A guy bashed in my door and he slammed her into the fireplace. I lunged at him and he beat the shit out of me." I squinted as I tried to sit up slowly. The fluids from the IV had me ready to piss on myself."

"I saw his kids upstairs."

"Yeah, they are some lookers." I hit the button for the nurse.

"Too bad they won't know their father that long, huh?"

"Did you come to find out who killed my ex or do you want to play cops and robbers with my brother again? He's in room 405b if you are looking for him." I coughed and a pain shot up through my body. I winced at the pain and hit the button once more for the nurse.

"Whitney died and you are still here, why is that?"

"I saw here hit the fireplace."

"Where were you when this happened."

"In the back room. I wanted to change shirts before we sat down and talked. She said wanted to talk to me before I left." I clenched my fist.

"So you were in the backroom?"

"My bedroom, I heard the door shatter and I ran into the living room. I saw him there as he pushed her into the fireplace. I ran towards him and he commenced to beat my ass around the room. I sent a text to my brother... 911."

"To Lucas?"

"To both of them... Mark called the cops and I was passed out before he even got there."

"So why not call the police yourself?"

"I barely had the energy," I inhaled slowly and then pushed out the air. "He beat the shit out of me."

"Okay. Well get some rest."

"I will."

The nurse entered the room, followed by Lucas. "You bloody bastard? What the hell happened?" He ran to the bed. "You can't fucking almost die on me when I need you the most. I don't even know how to change their knickers." His rant continued until he noticed McMillan.

"I'm not going anywhere." I smiled.

"Neither am I." McMillan added.

"Good, I like having you around." He ignored the agent and touched my shoulder. "Whoever this fucker was beat the shit out of you." Lucas laughed. "No traveling for you anytime soon."

"I know. My apartment has to be cleared, but now it's a crime scene."

"Well, good thing it was just you." Lucas looked at McMillan. "Can we have a moment?"

"It was not just him."

"What do you mean?"

"Whitney Sanders died."

"Whit?" Lucas stared at me. "Are you okay? I mean I know you loved her?"

"I don't think it's hit me yet." I grimaced.

"Whatever you do, keep this shit away from Cypress. She has cried three times in the last ten minutes and I don't know why. I don't want to know why. And she wants to see you. So you need to get better by tomorrow."

"Impossible. I have like three ribs broken and my face looks like..."

"You lost the worst fight of your life." McMillan nodded his head. "I will be checking back in with you once we have evaluated the crime scene. Please stay available."

"I have no choice. I'll be here." I watched him as he left. "You should be with those kids."

"I know what you done." Lucas said. "And I can't go into it because I have to feed those babies when I get there, but I appreciate it and I will be back down here shortly."

"Who?"

"Mark." He smiled. "I know you loved her."

"I can't talk about it."

"Don't talk about it." Lucas advised. "It's better when you don't."

Lucas

I couldn't help but think that I had turned everyone around me into some kind of monster. Asher, the one brother that had nothing tied to him was a murderer now. Cypress even turned a blind eye to everything that I had done, granted she didn't know much.

The babies slept. And my eyes were glued to them like they were going to get up and walk away. I just wanted to make sure that they were never touched, but whatever was in me.

"You should go home and shower?"

"I wouldn't dream of it." I said with a smile.

"You can't be smelling up the place Lucas." Cypress was playful. I shook my head. "I think that she can survive you showering."

Willow had a mess of blonde curls piled on her head, but her skin was already the most beautiful shade of tan I'd ever seen. She had yet to open her eyes and I just wanted to be there for it. "I can't leave. What if she opens her eyes while I'm gone?"

"She'll open them again."

"I don't want to miss it." I touched the Nathaniel's hand. He'd opened his eyes and gripped my finger already. He had stolen my heart with just the first cry and Willow just first sight.

"How is Asher?"

"What do you mean?"

"I overheard the entire conversation with Mark." She added. "Don't try to hide shit from me. It won't work."

"He is okay."

"Well, I hope he gets better soon... I want him to be Willow's godfather and it really can't work if he is crippled."

"You want that?"

"Yes and Mark the godfather for Nathaniel. They have to have some good male role models in their life besides you. And Callum definitely didn't have a chance in the running."

"You hate him and he really is not a bad guy."

"I don't hate him."

"You do too babe." I nodded my head.

"It's because he won't even marry that poor girl. Holly has been there for him for the long run and he can't even give her a ring and some stability."

"My cousin is a thinker. He doesn't love with his heart. He loves with his mind and that is why he hasn't even thought about asking her. He wants to make sure that if he makes this commitment that it will be a wise commitment. He isn't like me. I love with everything he loves with one step at a time and it works for him."

"Whatever, I call him a coward. You made the choice and yeah, we are not perfect by any means, but we are both on the same page or at least in the same chapter. We want something more. I couldn't be your girlfriend for more than two years."

"I know."

"You know me well."

"This is true." I sat down on the bed with her.

"Should we get married before we leave?"

"We can get married in a courthouse and I would be happy Cypress."

CHAPTER TWENTY-SIX

Cypress

The days seemed to fly pass us now that there was a deadline. Lucas had found a home on the Ireland Sea Shore and it sat alone on a plot of land that gazed into the most beautiful view in all of Ireland. He had closed on it with the help of his father and Callum. We just had to move everything which was not as simple. Especially because at only 3 weeks old the babies had developed their little personalities. Nathaniel was a screamer. He screamed when he needed to be changed. He cried when he wanted to be fed and then he sat quietly in his swing. He rarely wanted to be held though Mark held him enough for everyone.

Then there was Willow. She was always with Lucas. She was his princess. It even hurt me because she would cry for him. Daddy's little girl was picky. He sang to her an Irish song he said his mom used to sing and it lulled her to sleep every time. I didn't even know he could sing but his voice was like an angel. The Parting Glass seemed to me and her away when he sang it.

"This milk makes her gassy." Lucas laid her in the bassinet and walked over to Nathaniel who was quiet. "Little fella you are like me. Change it."

"How is he like you?"

"I hated to be held. I found more comfort in my solace. My mum said I even cried sometimes when she held me."

"Well, that just means you liked your independence." My heart raced. If whatever Lucas was burdened with I didn't want the burden on my baby. "How many people in your family are like you?"

"Like me?"

"Killers Luke."

"Declan, Callum, me... maybe another one, two or five." His eyes wandered. "He won't end up on that path okay. He has a mother that loves him beyond his wildest dreams."

"You had a great mom, Lucas."

"I know."

"So it didn't help you."

"It did more than you can know."

"Have you told the painters what color to paint their rooms?"

"I don't even know why are we painting their room. We know that they will be with us for some years to come."

"Yeah, well they still have a room and I want it painted." Lucas chuckled. "The house is a beauty I can't stop staring it."

"Your father did well."

"Yeah, he said that it was secluded and not far from everyone that we will need."

"Well, good."

"And I've been thinking. You could be a teacher..."

"A teacher?"

"Yeah, you love English... they speak it in most areas. There are some that don't but the area we are going to be in you could thrive. Just put in your application and I can have some strings pulled."

"What about my babies?"

"Nadine is great with children of all ages. You said you wanted to work. I just wanted to make sure you have something to do over."

"I will. I can be a mom for a while and then maybe I'll go ahead and jump into the job world of Ireland." The thought of leaving the babies with Nadine had not seemed pleasant though she was a great woman. I just wanted them to myself for a while… some years probably. "What are you going to do over there?"

"Uhm, actually I was going to be a professor over there at the local Uni."

"Teach college?"

"Yeah, my uncle is a professor over there and he said with my credentials, I could teach basic English and a writing class or two. It's good money. It's a good little job. It'll keep me close to home and I'll have a flexible schedule."

"I like it… Professor Elledge."

Lucas smirked. "They said that Persephone is talking to the FBI about me."

"Bitch," I murmured under my breath. "Well, you shouldn't have fucked her."

"I know."

"Once we leave, she'll be a pigment of our imagination."

"I can be extradited love. It's not that simple." Lucas poured a glass of juice for himself. "I need to know that if I can't be with you that you can survive without me?"

"Without you?" My voice cracked. "Why would I have to?"

"You know now love. There is always gonna be this chance that something could go wrong and someone could tell. Hell, Persephone is a perfect example."

"Your past is done now."

"No, ma'am. Everything that I have done is under a microscope and they are digging. I'm always careful. I always think. But a moment of weakness, one simple drop of DNA and I am a dead man walking."

"Stop talking like this."

"Listen to me Cypress." His voice raised and his eyes pierced into me. "I need to know that you are strong enough to be alone."

"I can't think about that. I just had a set of twins for God sake. You don't come with a warning sign you know that? Like a hey, don't fuck with him… I fell for you and you got to fix everything that is wrong and do it now. I can't be a single mother in Ireland."

"Fix it?" The anger lingered between us.

"Yeah." The wooden stool had grown uncomfortable. "I told you before it was more than just now and you have to be here. I don't want to be like Luna... I don't want you to be like Declan. I want you here and I want you to stay here. This is us. So you have to fix it."

"Think rationally. Step out of that fantasy world Cypress. Shit could go downhill tomorrow and you wouldn't have a clue of what you are going to do. First don't grieve me. I deserve whatever the fuck is coming to me. I know it. I know that there is too much bloody wrong that I have done to be living this great. I want you to listen."

"Shut up." I snapped.

"Don't listen then."

"I won't." I heard the small cry of Willow and turned to get her pushing pass Lucas.

"Stop!" The boom of his voice filled the room. His grip on my arms was tight. I squirmed. "Please listen to me. I don't want you to be like my mum. She grieved him, and he was still alive. Promise me that you'll move on. I'm not worth grieving."

"Do you plan on dying?" I pushed him and was still hooked to him,

"Does anyone?"

"I don't have to think about a world without you. That's not what normal couples do. They plan their future together and then they think of death 70 years later when the great grandchildren have children." My eyes ached from the pressure of holding back tears. "It's not fair to," I paused. "I'm not gonna do it."

Lucas shook his head. "Go get her," He whispered.

"Thank you."

"You're welcome." I heard the rattle of his keys.

"Where are you going?"

"Out baby, I won't be long. I swear to it."

Lucas

There had always been a plan for the end. There was always an end and from a young age, I knew that mine would not be a good one. Good things don't happen to horrible people. I couldn't force her to understand, but McMillan had me backed into a corner. The feds were known for not losing and McMillan had gathered enough evidence to make it stick. If he hadn't he would have backed off by now. Persephone, she was a link and there had to be someone else but I couldn't think of anyone else to link the shit together.

The whiskey burned the back of my throat. The chatter of the bar was a dull roar. My mind raced constantly. I knocked back the rest of the drink and my eyes stung. I cleared my throat and realized that there were tears. What was I here for? To kill? To love? To be loved? To love to kill? I wiped my face and slid the cup towards the bartender.

"You okay?"

"I'm fine sir," I pointed at the cup. "Another round?"

"Yes, sir," The old man poured the glass full. "It's on the house okay?"

"Deal," I must look horrible. "I sipped it slowly and felt the tingle of the alcohol fill my body.

"Lucas, just who I was looking for." The stool beside me was now filled with Shia. She pushed me lightly. "Fatherhood not so good?"

"Perfect actually," I shook my head. "What can I do for you?"

"Well, I have a dilemma on my hands and I know that you are the one person that can help me." She smiled. "I found out I was pregnant last week."

"Congrats," my mumble escaped. "You'll love it."

"Well, Mark said that he didn't want it. And that he didn't want me either."

"That's unfortunate."

"It's devastating. I want to be with him."

"You can't force someone to do something." I answered.

"Could you talk to him?"

"I'd rather not. I have enough shit on my plate. Convincing my brother to be a man is not one of them." I sniffled. I stared at my pitiful reflection in the mirror. My eyes were red as wine. "Sorry."

"What's got you hot and bothered?"

"Shit."

"I know about you. I mean Ireland was enough to know. They all but blurted it out and you have fed on your tail."

I blocked her words out and cleared my throat. The walls tilted in and everything felt light. "Shia... fight your own battles."

"Tell him to stay with me... or I'll talk to the agents myself. I mean... then me and my baby could be under Witpro... and maybe have a normal life. That would eliminate everything..."

"You must not understand who you are fucking with..."

"Perhaps I could tell Cypress a little about you and then your mom and sister." She kept her voice down to a whisper and then touched my arm. "I know exactly who you are and I don't want much."

"Fuck you." I growled. I stood to leave my legs wobbled. I gripped the wooden bar beneath my fingers to keep from falling to the ground.

"Sir, if you're leaving I'll have to call someone for you."

"Perfect, call this normal..." I slid my phone across the counter and stared at her. "Get the fuck out of my face bitch."

"I'll talk to you when you're sober."

"It'd be safer if you didn't."

"You'd be safer if you knew everything I did. You know where to find me... Congrats again daddy."

"Bitch." I stuttered.

"Yeah, he is hammered out of his mind. I can't let him leave like this." The bartender said. "Yeah, I mean he seems cool with waiting. We're on the corner of 8th and Anderson. It's called Stoners. Yeah, no thank you. I'll keep an eye out for him." He clicked the red button on the screen and handed me my phone. "You want something while you wait?"

"No, I'll just wait."

Ten minutes seemed to drag by before Asher and Mark walked into the bar. They both had this fucking grin on their face. Everything was fine for them. Persephone's death had been ruled a homicide, but they were looking for an unidentified robber and then there was Mark. He never worried and he was never bothered.

"What the hell are you doing here?" Mark looked around. The bar was a quiet place. No one came here except for loners.

"Drinking." I nodded my head. "You two are always here to save me."

"That's what brother's do most of the time." Mark sat down on the stool to my right. "What's the matter?"

"I can't do it anymore." I whispered.

Asher looked. "Do what? Fatherhood, you just started. And you seem great. There is nothing to worry about."

"Not about fatherhood." My words slurred.

"Then what?"

"Nothing."

"Tell me, damn it." Asher turned his head to me once he understood me. "You here drinking yourself into a mess. It has your mind all fucked up and you can't think like this alright. Come on."

"Yeah."

"Don't."

"Don't what? Why are you crying?"

I felt the tears fall onto my shirt. "Get me out of here, please."

"No, tell me what's wrong." Mark pulled my face up and I shook uncontrollably.

"Get me the fuck out of here! Right fucking now!" I yelled.

"Come on, we can go somewhere and talk for a while."

I didn't answer them. I followed them out to the car and lay in the back seat. I could kill dozens of people, but myself... I felt shattered. I had no idea where the car was headed. I just knew that the sky was no longer blue. It rained oranges and yellows with clouds that hypnotized me. My eyes hooked to them like there was nothing left.

"What was he talking about?" Mark whispered.

"Nothing," Asher lied. I wiped my face.

He knew. He looked terrified. "Tell me," Mark growled.

"Let him tell you." He spat.

"Lucas wake your ass up." The car stopped and they opened their doors.

"I'd rather not."

"Come on." Asher opened the back door and held his hand out.

We were at the ravine and it was peaceful. So peaceful. I climbed out of the back seat. "Thank you." My head pounded from the combination of drinking and the tears.

"Spit it out. Why are you down? I mean you are about to leave."

"Mark, I guess... I should tell you."

"Tell me please." Mark opened a bottle of the beer.

"I don't believe in angels." I smirked. "I don't believe in miracles and I don't believe in fate. I do believe in karma and it's coming full circle. I've killed so many people. And I don't know why I do it. I wish I knew why. I would stop it. I would be a soccer dad who has sleep overs and lets my wife have book club at our house. I don't want to anymore, but I can't stop. I've tried and it's all catching up to me..."

"You're leaving."

"It doesn't matter." Mark's words were rushed. "It's about to be a brand new start for you."

"Yeah, it does. I can't just start over. It's not that simple. It's not fair to everyone else around me."

"Oh chill out Lucas!"

"Take me seriously please." I paused. "I want her taken care of. I want my children to receive the best education that they can have. I don't want her to struggle. I need her to know that I love her and you have to make sure she does. You are good with her. She likes you. Please." I had both hands gripped at Asher's shoulders.

"I will."

"Don't fall into this shit. You are drunk. Everything will be fine and you will go home to those babies and,"

I interrupted him. "I'm going to kill Shia." I stared. My words lingered in the air. "The little bitch came up to me and she basically tried to black male and I don't have time for that shit... nor do I have the patience for her to threaten me. I can only juggle so much."

"I'll talk to her. Stay away." Mark exhaled. "Don't change subjects."

"There is not a reason to stay on it. Let's drink."

Asher patted my back. "Now you're talking."

Cypress

The door to the loft opened. Asher carried Lucas on his arm and Mark was on the other side. "Uhm, for some reason he seems a tad bit emotional..." Asher smiled. "And he should be treated with care."

There was a sight that I had never seen. Lucas lay on the couch moaning something under his breath, then he chuckled. "Where are my babies?"

"Shhhh," I hissed. "You guys couldn't have taken him to your place for the night? I can't care for three babies at once.

"We actually had plans to take the twins." Mark smiled. "We would rather have them and you need the night off."

Asher scooped up baby supplies that were scattered across the apartment. "And we will be right downstairs if you have any concerns. But he is yours for the night. We'll go get his car in the morning."

They left out of the loft quick and I could hear him moaning. "Cypress..."

"Lucas..." I whispered.

"I love you." He laughed. "I love you so much."

"I know."

"How can you be with me? I don't even deserve you..." The slur in his voice made me smile.

"What do you mean?" I walked over to him spread out on the couch and sat at his head. He perched his head in my lap and played with strands of my hair. "How can you love me knowing I'm a monster?" He looked at me with slanted eyes and his hands grazed my face lightly.

"I don't see a monster."

"I see him every day."

"You need to clean your mirror." I ran my fingers through his curls and exhaled. "I see a wonderful man whenever I look at you. I see Lucas Elledge the writer, the lover, the fighter, the avenger, the father, the brother and the friend."

"You see shit differently don't you." His words slurred.

"I do. It's why you love me."

"I can think of more reasons." Lucas' eyes met mine and he turned his head. "But that's a good one."

The smell of the whiskey was strong. "Why'd you leave and go drinking? You could have drunk here?"

"I'd rather not be sloshed with the kids here." He paused. "Next week… I want us to go on a date. I mean a legit date. When can you have sex again?"

"Not next week." I laughed.

"Why?"

"They said 6 weeks."

"A month is good time."

I burst into laughter. "No, sir."

"Damn, well, we shall see."

"This real date…"

"What about it love?"

"Where to?"

"Everywhere."

CHAPTER TWENTY- SEVEN

Asher

Mark's loft was dirty, mainly because two grown men lived there at the moment and he was depressed over Shia. Everything pointed to him loving her, but there was nothing there for him. Every time he thought of her he changed subjects, he pushed things around and acted like I had mentioned the devil and in my eyes I had. She had sown discontent among us. Lucas was on edge. Everything set him off and he was simply a deteriorated mess.

He was in the stages of grief. I clearly understood where all this shit was headed.

I remembered what he had said a few months ago about offing himself. I paraded around the subject, it was harder to talk to someone that you were kin to than it was to counsel strangers. Strangers I give this generic line and they might not do it. But with Lucas I couldn't be generic. I had to be completely honest with him. He had too much to live for and it wasn't fair to everyone around him. Yes, he'd done so pretty fucked up shit.

He had done some pretty horrid things to some people that deserved it. But who was he to judge?

"Where are you going?" I asked Mark.

"Didn't know I needed to tell you whenever I was leaving." He rolled his eyes and reached for his keys on the table. He looked worried, his brow creased and eyes weary. "I have to finish some work at the school. Then I was going to ask you to talk to Shia for me." He mumbled.

"Why do I have to talk to her?"

"Because you are understanding and right now she needs to hear understanding and not mean." He paused. "I want to talk to her, but everything I say to her leads to tears. I can't take tears right now. There is too much that must be done."

"What should I tell her? Sorry you got pregnant by my brother that no longer wants you. Please stop blackmailing Lucas and if you do so kindly… we can sponsor the abortion?" The sarcasm poured from my mouth. "Why am I always the person that ends up having to deal with this shit?"

"Yeah, something along those lines." He ignored my question and smirked at me.

"Why don't you just step up? You see how it worked for dad? Three completely fucked up kids. Just talk to her and maybe you'll see that you want…"

"Let's just clear this up, I am not Declan." He rarely called him dad. He rarely spoke to him. They were not on good terms in his book. But it didn't bother me like it bothered Mark. "And the next thing is I don't want any kids. The thought that I could raise a little me is highly intimidating and frustrating. What I want is for her to have an abortion and find someone who truly loves her. I don't love her. I don't even like her most of the time. When Lucas said that he would kill her I almost felt some relief." Mark spun around. "But he doesn't need another death on his shoulders. So please just talk to her."

"No just let him kill her." I snapped.

"Don't be an asshole." Mark took his keys. She's at the elevator downstairs so I am just gonna go ahead and leave. Try to make her see reason, please."

Reason. They had a knack for forcing me to be the bad guy. I understood Shia. Hell, to a certain extent I honestly felt sorry for her. She had one brother that wanted nothing to do with her literally and then she had one that wanted nothing more than to see lying a pool of her own blood. Then there was me who didn't want to touch this subject with a ten-foot pole.

I picked up the clothes that were thrown around the apartment and then plopped down on the couch. What the hell was I about to say to her? I know you might love him but... he doesn't love you. *Sorry for the misunderstanding, the family trip to Ireland was just a show and the fact that he is pleading basically for you not to die is a coincidence.*

The elevator doors opened and she stepped out of the elevator. Shia was a beautiful woman and I really was not clear on why Mark didn't want her. He was harder to figure out than Lucas. Lucas wore his emotions on his sleeves like a dark reminder to stay the hell back. While Mark was unreadable. "Where is he?"

"Who?" I shrugged.

"Mark, he said that he wanted me to talk."

"He wanted me to talk to you, you want to sit down, I can get us something to drink before we get into everything."

"No, you know I have gone over this one hundred times in my head. This baby is mine and I am not going to listen to none of your shit. I told him already. I'm not getting rid of this baby. If he doesn't want to be a father, he doesn't have to be. I'll just make sure that none of you see daylight again." Her head rolled and she smacked her lips. "I know that this family is fucked up and I would rather my child not be a part of it anyhow." Her eyes cut at me and she smiled.

The nerve of her. "What good would that do you or the child?"

"I don't want to hear this Asher!"

"I just want to know what your logic is?" I folded my arms and watched her as she strutted around the loft.

"I get what I want Asher, there is no other logic." She smiled.

"I heard you threaten Luke. He has nothing to do with you or Mark."

"He has a problem. I can tell it by looking at him. I told Cypress to leave him. And I wish she would have never gone back to him. It's pretty much part of the reason I have not been around. I hate that she settled for that piece of shit. I figured out everything out once we went to Ireland everything made sense. And your father is wanted for like ten murders. I could just imply tip some people off."

"Maybe Lucas was right." I mumbled. "I want to help you. But I can't if you are gonna make some crazy accusations. I need you to sit..."

"Fuck you, fuck Lucas and fuck Mark. You might have her in some choke hold, but I am not the one. I don't understand why he won't even talk to me. We were together for almost a damned year and now he wants to just kick me to the curb. I will fuck his life up."

"Just get out."

"Oh, so now you're mad."

"No!" I yelled. "I'm tired of your shit. Get the fuck out. You act like you can't comprehend common sense. If this was about the welfare of the baby, you wouldn't have threats. You would just want him to help. You're mad that he doesn't want you and that doesn't make sense in my book. You should know better. You aren't shit."

"Perfect..." She rolled her eyes. "So they ruled Whit's death an accident?"

"What?" I turned my head.

"I heard the conversation when you called Mark... he thought I was sleep. I heard every damn thing..."

"Get the fuck out."

"I'll take you down too... all three of you boys can have matching white jumpsuits on death row... The Elledge Boys..."

"Yeah just leave..." I stood up. "Be careful on those steps..." I said as she walked out of the back door. I wouldn't want you to fall."

Now there was a real threat and if she didn't calm down there would not be any other answer to the problem. I just knew it wouldn't be me. I hadn't even gotten the image of Whitney out of my head.

Lucas

They were sleeping in their beds. Willow had developed the habit of sucking her entire finger to lure her to sleep and Nathaniel slept with no worries. I looked at myself in the mirror and searched to find what she saw. I splashed water on my face, then turned to her in the shower.

"Shame about the sex." I winked at her as she wiped her body down with the wash cloth. My eyes looked over each curve. She swatted at me. "You are beautiful."

Cypress dropped the towel and smirked. "You hate waiting don't you?"

"More than anything else in this world."

"Too bad, get out. Check on the twins and I'll slip into my dress."

My eyes were hooked on her curves and the small things. She had battle wounds now. It was evident that she had a baby, but that was what made her more perfect to me. Her scars were perfect, stretch marks even seemed to make her prettier by the second.

"Lucas."

"Come on..." I winked.

"Go check on the kids please!" She giggled.

"Fine."

To no surprise they were still asleep. The loft was silent and virtually all packed up. There were several things that I was giving away to Lydia. She had gotten an apartment with her boyfriend and Tracey didn't care. I figured it had something to do with the fact that there were no more children besides grandchildren that she had to see.

I actually put on a decent outfit. The white shirt hung loose on my body covering the top of my jeans and my hair was in a bun on the top of my head. She loved when I wore my hair up and I figured that I should do everything that I could to make sure that this date was a good one. I wore my black square framed glasses. There was no telling what she would come out wearing. She had said that she wanted to dress up as much as she could because she hadn't been close to her probably weight in a while.

I lingered around the apartment cleaning and checking on my babies until she finally stepped out of the bathroom. The yellow dress clung to her body and accented her every curve. Yes, she was thicker in places that had simply been nonexistent before, but now they were there and perfect. Her legs were accented by the stark white heels; they lead straight to her hips that were slowly but surely driving me mad. Her hair was tamed. It was straight. I had never seen it flow so far down her back. My eyes danced with amusement.

"I am ready whenever..."

"You look so damn perfect." I couldn't think straight. My eyes were hooked on hers and it might have been a miracle if we made it out of the apartment."

"Sorry I'm late! Mark didn't give the damn code before he left and I had no way in hell to get here except the steps." Asher walked through the side door. "Damn, you look good." Asher tossed his phone on the couch and smiled. "Where are you going?"

"He won't tell me."

I nodded my head. "We have reservations so it's probably best that we head out. What time did Lydia say she would be here?"

"Later, stop worrying. I got them. And Mark said that he would stop by after he finished doing whatever he was doing. I have no clue what."

"Perfect," I grabbed my keys. "We will be back around midnight. Don't call us fifty million times. Everything is where it always is and please take care of our kids. I hate to throw death threats around loosely, but I will kill you brother or not."

"Stop being an ass and take her out." Asher clicked on the television and nodded his head.

"Have you talked to Shia yet?"

"I have no plans to. She is not my girlfriend. She is with Mark, so he should be the one that handles that. And don't ask me again, you two head out so you can get back by curfew."

Dates had never been my specialty. We took her car, the feds rarely followed her car and for once we wanted some privacy. No matter how limited it was. We hopped in her car and I started the engine. "Are you going to sell it?"

"I technically don't own Luke." She chuckled. "I'll just take it back to the dealership and then maybe get one in Ireland."

"I bought this car the day you said you were pregnant." I admitted.

"You what!"

I cut my eyes over to here and gripped her thigh. "Calm yourself. Why do you think they keep returning your money back to your bank account? You shouldn't have to worry about bills like that. I take care of you and you should let it happen."

"Fine." She submitted to me finally. Her fingers laced with mine and she kissed the back of my hand. Her fingers were so soft. "What do you have up your sleeve?"

"Something nice." I answered.

"Like what?"

"Are you down for food? No soup... just a really good meal." I pulled into the parking lot of the steakhouse. "I know you will probably eat a salad, but I wanted us to have a real date."

"Lucas, I am about to destroy a steak." She smirked.

I opened the door for her and extended my hand out to her. "The entire restaurant is empty." It had been a small task to rent out the place but the owner was fine with it. I paid him enough to cover the entire night anyhow. We made our way into the restaurant and she exhaled.

"Wow... It's so beautiful in here." The candle light filled the room with a dim glow and the soft whites were splashed all over the room. The violin started and she gasped. "You went all out." She laughed.

"I did." I placed her purse on the table and extended my hand. "We should dance."

"I don't..."

"You have and you can... come on. I will guide you."

"You always do." Her hand was in mine and spun her out to the dance floor in one swift move and then pulled her back to my chest. Cypress swayed with me. Her feet barely moving just placed on mine so I could glide her across the floor. "This is perfect."

"I know... thank god we have someone like Asher to keep those babies."

"Yeah, what is he going to do when everyone moves?"

"Believe it or not he plans to go to spend some time traveling with our dad. He said that he wanted to know more about him and that he doesn't have a girlfriend so it should be fun. Dad is excited... granted, I don't know. I don't want Asher to lose who he is."

"He won't." She assured me.

"Yeah, well they have our food almost done... do you want to freshen up before they come or no?"

"Yes, I'll run to the bathroom." She kissed my cheek and she disappeared around the corner.

I followed her to the bathroom and closed the door behind me. "Public sex is the best way to step back into things..." I smiled.

"No, sir..." She could not hide the smile.

"Please..."

"No..."

"Okay." I walked towards her slowly and lifted her skirt up. "I just want a minute... maybe two... probably more." My hands crawled up her body pinching at her nipples. She gasped a little and fell onto the wall behind her. "This place is mine for the evening... No one is going to walk in that door..." The bathroom was just as classy as the restaurant. "Say yes."

"Yes." She said.

"I can make it quick. Hard..." I pushed her panties aside and pushed my middle finger into her. She clenched around me and her eyes rolled to the back of her head. I needed to be inside her. I wouldn't last long anyhow. My eyes closed as her warmth surrounded my finger. "That feel good?" I groaned.

"Oh..." She bit her lip at the punishing rhythm I had started with her. She rotated her hips as her head laid back in pleasure. Her hands wrapped around my neck and she dug into me with her nails. "Lucas... harder."

"I missed the way you said my name the most..." I added another finger and pumped it into her. "Almost like a plea to get you there. No need to beg." I unbuckled my pants and my dick was hard as a rock. My lips kissed her cheek and move slowly over to her lips. Her hands cupped my dick and everything went still for a moment and I pushed her panties to the ground. There was no more patience. I lifted her off of the ground and wrapped her legs around me and slammed into her. She trembled as something that resembled a moan and a yell escaped her body. I went into her again, this time I guided her down on me and she bounced to make it better. I drove into her panting for dear life. Everything around us was gone and she was my light. I slammed into her faster until the friction of my friends brought her there.

Her clit twitched and she was in bliss. Her legs melted around me as she bit down on my shoulder. I sat down on the couch still inside of her and she ground her hips into me at an unbearable speed. My mouth was open in the shape of an O as I tried to hold onto the last bit of pleasure. But I was done. Her body had me above the clouds. I gripped her hips and thrust into her two more times, losing everything that I had to give. "Fuck…"

She smiled and ran her fingers through my hair. "God, I missed that."

"I can't believe I trusted those bloody doctors and waited that long."

Cypress laughed and laid her head on my chest. "Finally checked that, from my bucket list…"

"Stop moving." My eyes closed. "One wrong movement and I could die from too much." I smiled at her and she moved her hips around again.

"Woman." I said as I kissed her. "Have mercy," I pleaded.

There was so much up my sleeve for tonight and I didn't know how to let her know. We drove for an hour. And she filled my head with her wonderful ideas for our life. How she wanted nothing more than to be with me and the kids. Then we were finally there at the ravine. This place meant everything to me.

"Oh, I love this place." She smiled. Her eyes widened as she noticed all of the cars. "Why is everyone here?"

Cypress

My mom's car was parked next to Tracey's. And then there was Lydia, Lana, Mark, Asher and even some friends I'd made from class. I looked at him. "What are you doing? How did my babies get here so fast?"

"I wanted to surprise you." Lucas smirked.

My father opened the car door. "Come on," He held his hand out and smiled at me. "Before the moment is over… let's get you down that alter." He gestured behind him.

My eyes met the alter where Asher stood holding Nathaniel and beside him was Mark. Lydia stood across from them and her arms was Willow, my sleeping beauty. Lucas walked over to the alter and finally it all clicked. It was a wedding. A simple wedding.

"Oh. My. God!"

A smiled stretched across his face and he waved.

The walk down the aisle seemed unreal. The strumming of the guitar filled the air and I tried to keep a straight face and not cry. Finally, we were there and he couldn't stop smiling. Everything seemed surreal.

"Ladies and Gentlemen, we are gathered here today... to demonstrate the meaning of love with this wonderful couple Lucas and Cypress."

He touched my hand and smiled. "Are you okay?"

"I'm fine..." My tears, said otherwise. His hand wiped my face and stopped on my cheek.

"You wouldn't be lying to me, would you?"

"Never," I sniffled.

"Lucas... you can start with your vows..."

Lucas cleared his throat. "It is extremely weird how life happens. I don't know why, but I have loved you from the moment our eyes met in that classroom." Lucas paused. "And that's a feat for me because I didn't know what love was..." "But I have come to realize that it's not just one reason that I love you, Cypress. There are several. I love you for the fact that you snore in your sleep, but you think you are sleeping beauty. And no matter what state your hair is in... a curly disarray or a bun on your head, Cypress you're perfect. We argue like an old married couple. I swear that it will never stop. I swear to fight for you until my last breath." He shook his head. "I thank you so much for the life you have given me. Before I was colorless and moody."

"Not too much has changed." Mark whispered.

I laughed. "Shut it."

"And I know that I have not been the most honest. I have made mistake after mistake... but here today I swear to you that I cannot live without you. You are my forever. And living in a world where you are not my wife is no longer possible. I know that for the rest of my life I will cherish every moment we have. I promise that I will honor you with my entire self. And those babies are just half of what I want with you."

"You want two more?" I jumped.

"Shhhh woman." He kissed my hand. "I love you. I vow that that will never change." He held my hand. "The end."

"I have never been great at freestyle." I stuttered. "I love you Lucas and whatever you promise to give me, I plan to give you tenfold. I don't want to spend a moment of the future with the same last name. So my vow is that I will forever be Mrs. Elledge no matter what happens." My heart thumped as he shed tears. "I mean no matter what... we are a part of you..." I wiped his tear. "You don't have to worry... and I love you. I vow that I will never stop."

"You mean that."

"No matter what." I whispered.

"Do you take her to be your lawfully wedded wife...?" The minister asked.

"I do." Lucas smiled.

"And Cypress..."

"I do."

"Ladies and Gentleman, I now present to you... MR. and MRS. Elledge."

His lips crashed into mine and my hands went to his neck. "I love that name... on you."

"I love it on me too."

CHAPTER
TWENTY-EIGHT

Lucas

We left in four days, in the green world of Ireland and there had been some peace. There had been no more Persephone and though Shia still had idle threats in the background, I pressed to leave her be.

"Okay, almost everything besides like pots and pans are packed. I figured we could give those to my mom. I still have to find somewhere to put my furniture and then Willow has an appointment. I don't want Nathaniel around sick children."

"Fine, I can watch him baby." I continued to jot down notes in my notebook. "Is there anything else love?"

"Act excited," She said.

"I am excited. It's just nostalgia. I have been here for three years, basically and now tenant number one will be taking over and potentially destroying it."

"Well, our home on the Ireland Sea is going to be much better. I even have an interview for a preschool position at a daycare there."

"Good, let life continue."

"And you have your book you have been working on nonstop these days. I am disappointed that you won't allow me to get a glimpse. I am your biggest fan."

"You will wait with everyone else." I bit the top of the pen. "What time is the appointment?"

"Four," She walked around the place like the busy body, she was now that her energy was back and threw things where they belonged. I was thinking that I would go ahead and get a car. I don't like being car less. What are some good cars?"

"I don't know what's hot at the moment."

"Of course you don't... your jeep is like 30."

"Classic," I mumbled.

"Right," She laughed.

"I am going to do some running around until three gets here." I put the pen in my pocket and then closed the notebook. "Can you handle the two until I get back?"

"I can handle whatever comes my way." She beamed. Cypress continued to throw everything around the loft and make it tidier for the moment. "Make sure you are back before I leave because I can't afford to take them both with me. Nathaniel always cries when I hold her."

"I would be jealous of the little man." My arms wrapped around her waist and I kissed her lips softly. "Make sure that you call me and remind me. I tend to forget a lot."

"You better remember."

I made my way into town and there was not a sign of any agents around me. I finally had a breath of fresh air. The park close to downtown was practically empty. It was just me and nature. Birds chirped and the wind rustled through the leaves all while Radiohead played in my head. I needed quiet.

My feet moved quickly as I jogged through the park. My eyes locked in on Shia. It was in her routine to be here every day around this time. Fucking Shia had finally been caught alone. I sat down on the park bench and watched her as she stretched her legs on the lawn. I deserved one kill... just one to take the never ending edge off. I pulled my shades down and walked slowly over to her. "Shia, wanna talk? I'm not drunk now." I chuckled.

"Yes, finally one brother has sense." She rolled her eyes. "Why did you send Asher?"

"I didn't send Asher." I answered. "I stretched with her. "Why would I send Asher; I think he is more a female than you."

"Well are you going to talk to Mark."

"I will."

"Well, jog with me." Shia jogged towards the trail and I followed by closely.

Cypress had taken my knife. Said it was best that I didn't have it. It was fine to me... though it felt weird holding a different knife in my pocket.

"You are nicer when you are sober..."

"I think everyone is." I laughed. The trail was long. The woods had engulfed pavement and their hills and it was perfect, my heart raced as I caught up to her. I paced myself and looked around. There was no one in sight. No one even close by. I gripped the knife in my hand and snatched Shia by her arm. "Now we can really talk." I growled. My hand covered her mouth. Her shrill scream muted immediately. "Who the fuck did you think you were dealing with?" I ran the knife down her body slowly. "I should let you know... I'm not normal... you were so right."

"Please," she muffled through my hand. "Please! I swear..."

"The last woman that swore to me broke her vow... you women have a reputation of lying to me. I'd rather watch you bleed."

I could feel her heart throbbing. "Lucas..." she wept.

"What? Not so tough now, huh??" I pushed the knife into her heart slowly. Her blood gushed from her mouth and ran down my hand. I nodded my head. "Fuck!" I pushed her down the hill towards the small creek and took my shirt off. The red stained it brightly. So I jammed it in the pocket hiding the blood. My eyes locked on Shia's dead body and I exhaled. "One problem down. Persephone to go."

Asher

There was no telling what was so urgent from Lucas, but I waited at the restaurant patiently as he walked in shirtless. "Why are you in here flaunt your muscles man put on a damned shirt."

The women stared and he winked at them. "What have you been doing?"

"I have actually been trying to sort out my life. What about you?" I looked over the menu and debated over what to eat.

"I handled Shia," he whispered.

"By handled, I hope you mean gave her a ticket and made her leave."

"I gave her peace." He was joyous. He grinned and tossed the menu on the table. "They have the best burgers in the city."

"You are happy as shit. Mark loves her you know?"

"Whatever, look I leave in a few days. It'll all be fine."

"Are you trying to convince yourself of that? We told you no. We told you that there were agents hot on your trail and you went."

"I'm a grown fucking man Asher. I don't need babysitters."

"Don't call us when this bites you in the ass."

"Whatever." He rolled his eyes.

"How can you be so happy?" I whispered.

"I'm not happy." Lucas' grin was unstoppable. "I just feel lighter and that feels good."

"I couldn't even think after Whitney." I murmured.

"Glad you have a conscious. I don't." He was blunt. "I just know that there is no greater feeling than being light."

"Sick."

"I'm sick, yeah."

I nodded my head. "What if you get caught man? I mean damn she said she had ways to make us pay. What if she talked to someone about everything?"

"I'm on it."

"Okay, explain."

"I think she was in cahoots with Persephone. I'll handle her tonight and then when I leave there will not be a trace..."

"Don't touch her." I snapped. "Just leave damn it Luke. Must you make everything in your life dramatic. Pack up and leave tonight actually. I'll join Cypress on the trip over. But you are out of control."

"Shut up. You are dramatic."

"You tell Mark."

"The news can tell Mark."

"You are a trip. "I closed the menu and sipped my water. "I don't want to eat now. I would rather just go home and read. Maybe I can make him not kill you."

"When you tried to talk to her what did she say?"

"She said a lot of shit. I didn't take it seriously. She was a woman scorned. A woman scorned..."

"Is dangerous as shit. She could have ruined everything that I have and I would not let that happen for nothing. So fuck her and fuck everyone else that thinks that they are gonna mess up my life. "

"You are the ultimate destroyer of your own life. You make things hard. You make things harder for everyone. You need to think about someone else besides yourself for one fucking moment in your life. You cause so much grief. You can't comprehend that this earth doesn't revolve around you. And I'm pissed right now so the best thing for me to do is to leave. I have to go. See you later." I snatched the keys from the table and left the small restaurant.

"Fuck it leave then!" Lucas yelled like a five-year-old throwing a tantrum.

I rolled my eyes and made my way towards the door. "Shut up."

Cypress

He was late, which had not surprised me at all. I packed the diaper bag for two and placed Nathaniel and Willow in their stroller.

"Sorry love," Lucas walked through the door, his shirt hanging from his pocket. "I took longer than expected."

"What errands have you ran undressed?"

"I went on a run."

I snatched the shirt from his pocket and it was drenched with blood. "What the fuck!" I yelled.

"I got cut."

"Where?" I stared at him. "Where did you get cut? Why?"

"You're lying to me. Who the fuck did you kill? My heart raced. "I told you to come to me whenever you felt like you couldn't control yourself. And you what? Who was it?"

"No one!" He yelled.

"Ugh, you're lying to me? You said you would never lie to me." a small cry escaped from Willow and he walked towards the stroller. "Don't touch my kids." I growled.

"Your kids?" He yelled.

"Yes, my fucking kids. You're drenched in blood, Lucas... your pants... your fucking hands are tinted. Go clean yourself up!"

"Lower your voice."

"Or what?" I stared at him and he shrugged his shoulders. "Go clean yourself up right now. And you better not get blood on any of my linens." I rolled my eyes. The thought of him actually killing someone had made me sick to my stomach. "Who was it?"

"It doesn't matter."

"It matters." I yelled. "Who was it!"

"Shia!"

My heart stopped. Shia, one of the only people in this world that I had developed a friendship. My hands shook and I felt my knees grow weak. "What the fuck?"

"She said she was going to turn me in... if I didn't convince Mark to stay with her." He whispered. "I couldn't and I didn't want her to ruin everything that we had together. She compromised."

"Don't talk to me right now."

"Baby."

"I mean it." I wiped my face. "Is this going to happen every time we get close to someone. You killed a friend. Is Asher next? What about Mark or Lydia? Once they get fed up with all the shit that you are playing and they say he has to be stopped."

"They wouldn't do that."

"Are you sure?" I whispered.

"Yes."

"I feel like I would." I added.

"You don't."

"I do Lucas. I can't even have a life in America with you. My family is here. Everything that I love is here, but I am moving so you can be comfortable and we can raise our babies together."

"Love is about sacrifice."

"You don't sacrifice enough for me."

"What does that mean?"

"Figure it out." I snapped.

Lucas

The kill from Shia was still fresh. My adrenaline still pumped and I couldn't think of anything else, including the fact that Cypress was once again mad. The shower, washed off anything that still lingered and the hunger would not die down. I shook with it. I paced around the room and my mind rummaged through my thoughts. Persephone, she wanted a death wish and she knew that it could be given. I should give it to her. I pondered with the fact, as I laid out my black outfit. Cypress in anger took the kids both with her and I was free for a moment to lie in the fucking moment. I dressed quickly burning the gloves in the fireplace. I grabbed my keys and made my way to the car.

Cypress would never know if we left quickly enough. My car roared to life and I made my way into town and sure enough, there she was wasting her limited life on shit she didn't need.

Persephone spent more time worried about her appearance than anyone else I had ever known in my life. She was manicured and pedicured. Her time in the tanning bed done nothing but make her look even more natural. It was like she totally unhappy with whom she was. I would be doing her a favor. I would set her self-loathing free.

She bounced around the city buying more than she afford in purses and makeup. There was a need for all of that shit. She was a pretty girl once upon a time. Before she was so envious of everything that she could not see straight.

I headed to her home and canvassed the place. There were some older neighbors and there was no roommate, she had left when the semester ended like Persephone was supposed to do but didn't. Stupid bitch should have followed directions; she would have lived longer.

The bricked home in its secluded area was perfect. Surrounded by trees and her neighbors, elder had made their way to bed. There were no signs of an FBI car. I had not been tracked and it had immediately turned into the most perfect kill. The outsides were dimmed enough for me to see the door and let myself in by quickly picking the lock. The door opened and I walked into the home, the smell of pumpkin hit my nose and it hit me she was one of those women that loved everything pumpkin. It irritated me more than anything. I rolled my eyes and made my way through the pastel themed home. The darkest item in her home was the black television screen. I entered her room. Her bed made and her shoes lined the side of the wall. It was full of material items that would do her no damn good after tonight. I sat on her bed, my gloves on and knife in hand. Not the knife I wanted it to be but it would do. It was perhaps better that it wasn't my knife. My alibi was tight. And this kill would be final. Then it was goodbye to the Americas.

I waited for her patiently. I read through her diary, a few lines about me and the fear of me. She was right to be scared, but she caused this herself. The instructions given to her had been simple really. I just wanted her to leave fucking town and leave Cypress and I the fuck alone.

The door clicked open and my heart raced. She was here.

"No mom, I am almost done packing. I can give you a call back here shortly okay. I love you too." she threw her bags on the couch. "Bye babe." She placed her phone down on the counter and made her way to her bedroom. She clicked the light on and the bright yellow just about hurt my eyes.

"Turn the light back off will you?" A smile appeared on my face. "Hello Persephone."

Her feet hit the ground quickly as she turned to escape. I scooped her up in my arms and restrained her arms to her chest. "Let me go!" She squirmed.

"Don't make me, make this quick." I held the knife to her neck and she went still. "Good girl. Sit down." I said.

"Lucas, don't do this." she shrugged. "I can recant everything."

"You'll do no such thing." The smile on my face could not be hidden. She fell back on the bed. "You don't know how to keep your mouth shut." Persephone opened her mouth to speak again and I placed my finger over her mouth. "You should just shut."

"I swear!"

"You lie." A growl escaped my chest and I clenched my fist. "I'm leaving for Ireland in a few days and I have to tie up every loose end and you my dear are extremely loose." I slashed into her arm lightly and watched the blood spatter hit the wall.

She screamed and I pushed her on her back. "Please," She held her wound and plead to me.

I could feel nothing. There was no remorse, I could see her fear and it ignited something more from me. My knife pierced into her leg it pushed past the bone and the blood gushed from her. Her scream was like a nail on a chalkboard, but it did not phase me. I twisted until my hand could not turn anymore.

I stuffed a one of colorful socks from the night stand in her mouth. She fell to the floor not knowing what to clench her leg or her arm. She made a half effort getaway and a chuckle escaped. "Where are you going?"

Her cries were muffled, I snatched her back towards me and her nails clawed into my arms taking blood. Everything went dark as I kicked her to the ground and removed the sock. "Help please!" Persephone cried as she wept.

I snatched her by the hair. "I gave you simple instructions and you could not even follow those!" I growled. "Shut your fucking mouth!" I yelled. "No one can hear you and no one cares! I have learned that here recently. The only person that truly loves you is yourself. Do you love yourself?"

Her tears flowed from her face and I nodded my head. "People always waste their tears. For what? It is not going to change anything. I am going to kill you. Today was your last day on earth and how did you spend it?" I nodded my head and restrained her arms. I pushed the black sock into her mouth. "You fucking scratched the shit out of my arm. I don't understand why you don't take hints well. I told you that I would end you and you talked to the feds anyway. And you see where that got you? Where the fuck are they anyway?"

Her eyes closed.

"Exactly nowhere to be found. They are fucking useless. Probably off somewhere looking for me. But they can no longer save you. Plus, I don't think you want to be saved." The sliced into her neck with one quick thrash and her blood hit my face.

I could hear her screams as if she was still making them. They replayed in my head over and over and there was no silence. I stared at the red splashed on the walls. Her blood was everywhere. I closed my eyes and then reopened them. Monster. Something inside of me grew to life. It made an appearance for the first time in a while. It was the real me, a fucking monster.

CHAPTER TWENTY-NINE

Asher

Dare I ask what was going on with Lucas? No, I had no words or no way to make this catastrophe disappear that lay before me. Mark had no idea yet, but when he did there was little that I could do to prevent the fight from happening. I sat in the bedroom I had claimed as mine for the past month and exhaled. Too much shit had happened and it needed to process.

Cypress paced in front of me. "Has he lost it?"

"I don't know."

"He has," She answered. "He's been gone for hours. I have not heard from him in hours?" Cypress had worried herself into a frenzy and had drug me down with her. "Why does he do it?"

"Cypress," I paused. There were several clinical reasons that I could give her, but she didn't want to hear those. There was no way to help him and I didn't want her to hear that either. I just wanted her to calm down so I could calm down. "He is bored. He has to have something to take the edge off of being him. Lucas… is selfish. You should just leave him to deal with this mess and stop worrying yourself. Please?"

"How am I not supposed to worry when he came home with blood on his body." She shook from anger or nerves. I could not tell the difference between the two. "We should have just left weeks ago. He has an anger problem."

"It's not just anger." I added. "When Mark finds out I don't know what his reaction will be. She was pregnant and I felt like he wanted to be with her, but he doesn't know how to cope. Something that he has in common with Luke." My hair fell on my glasses. It was beyond time for a cut, but these past few months had me everywhere but in my element.

I switched on the television. "The University is mourning this morning as it remembers two fallen students. Persephone..." The words hit me like a wall. Fuck. Fuck. FUCK.

Cypress turned toward the screen. "What the fuck!" She stared at me. "Did you know about this? Asher, please tell me you didn't know about this?"

"I have been here with you since yesterday!" I said. My hands trembled at the mere thought of what was to come. "Dear fucking God. The entire FBI is about drop down on him." Was he insane? I shook my head. Who was I kidding, I knew he was insane. I exhaled and grabbed my phone. Cypress didn't need this to be on her at this time. "Stay here, okay, don't talk to anyone and don't answer the door. If he comes by let him know I'm looking for him. And he better call me." I took my keys and turned towards the television. "And if Mark calls tell him I said that we need to speak like...now."

"The main suspect in this case is twenty-six-year-old Lucas Elledge. Police are warning the public that at this moment that he is considered armed and dangerous to not approach him but to contact the authorities immediately."

Perfect, I didn't even turn around to see Cypress' reaction, I could hear it as the sob filled the room. There was no time to try to deal with her. The police would be here in a few minutes to destroy her apartment and take us both down for questioning. "Is there anything upstairs that could harm this case?"

"Gloves, but he took them with him."

"Alright, hang tight." I slipped my hat on and walked towards the elevator. The doors of elevator opened and a very disarrayed Mark stood before me. "Please, tell me what the fuck is going on?"

"I don't know." I shrugged my shoulders.

A crackling sound pierced throughout the room and we turned to the side door as it was busted open. An army of suits stormed into the apartment with their guns aimed at us. "Hands in the air right now!"

Nathaniel's cry filled the white halls behind us. "Shit!" I lifted my hands in the air. "They're up."

Mark dropped his briefcase to the ground and held his hands up above his head. "What the fuck? I hope they'll replace that fucking door." He grumbled.

Our world had crumbled in front of us and the only damn thing that lingered in his mind was the door being replaced. A laugh escaped from my mouth. "Dumbass."

"Well, boys we meet again as promised. I had hoped it would be a friendlier way though. Sorry about the door." McMillan smiled at us both. "Where's your brother?"

"He's right there?" I pointed to Mark with a small grin on my face.

"You think this a fucking game! Where is Lucas? Where the fuck is he?" He lifted me by the collar and then tossed me to the ground with one swift movement.

"We haven't talked to him." Mark spat. "Now get your hands off of him officer."

McMillan stepped back. "I can't wait to see him go down."

"What is he wanted for, speaking as his lawyer?"

"Capitol murder." He paused. "But you knew that already didn't you Mark? Always playing guardian even when it's at your demise? You let him kill Shia?"

"Excuse me?" Mark's look of terror was a clear indicator that he knew nothing about it. "What did you say?"

"Aw, this is perfect." McMillan paused and fixed his jacket. "Your brother is suspected to be the murderer of your girlfriend. He was last seen at the park, she was murdered at... Sweep the entire place. Leave nothing untouched. You two remain on the ground." He started pulling the cushions off of the couch and sifting through things.

Mark's face was red with fear and regret. The pain flushed to his face. And I couldn't blame him. I actually felt sorry for him. "You okay?" I asked.

"I'm fine." He spat.

"Cypress how great it is for you to join us. And you brought the kids." McMillan paused as he looked Cypress over. "Is there not anywhere you can put them?"

"You are not taking my kids." Cypress cradled them both in her arms.

"Of course not." He nodded his head. "But the state can and more than likely will take them once they figure out what kind of environment they have been living in… You know where he is don't you?"

"I don't know where Lucas is and I wish I did." She paused. "He could clear this whole story up and we could get away from here. Ever since I came here, there has been nothing but complete drama all because some over worked Agent has a hard on for my husband." A smirk appeared across her face and she nodded her head. "But to answer your question… No, I haven't heard from him."

"You really love this sick son of a bitch don't you."

"As his wife… I don't have to say shit to you. That was actually just a courtesy to tell you that I don't know where he is… And I want to see your warrant for searching a place that he doesn't even live in!" Willow cooed quietly and Cypress rolled her eyes.

"Stop talking Cypress." Mark barked. "I want to request a lawyer for us three. We don't know what the fuck is going on."

"So to the station?"

"No!" I said. "Can we not take care of this now? We don't know, honestly."

"Asher, shut up!" Mark snapped.

Cypress handed me Willow. "Check his mom's house. If I were in trouble, I would be there with my mom." She said.

"He isn't there."

"Well, that's the only other place he could hide."
Cypress shrugged her shoulders at McMillan. "So I guess you are
out of luck... huh?"

Lucas

What the fuck had this word come to? I was a suspect
and they had no evidence. What was this? I watched from across
the street as they walked back and forth from my loft. Cypress
and my children were there and I was here in this cafe, wearing a
fucking hoodie and a pair of glasses. I was fucked. I retraced my
steps. Persephone had scratched. I cut off her fingertips and
soaked them in fucking bleach in the sink. There was nothing
else that tied me to her rather than the damn tip she gave.
I sipped my coffee and the patrons looked at me.
"Pardon me, is there a fucking problem?" I tossed
money down on the table and nodded my head as I left the
building. I would have to be on foot there was no way in hell
that they would not notice the jeep. I clinched the letter in my
pocket and slid it in the post office box.
Now where in the fuck could I go? I clenched my eyes.
There was a warehouse downtown that I had considered buying
not too long ago. I kept walking and turned onto an alley. The
cool breeze hit my face and I realized that if I was to hide there,
Cypress would never find me. I knew that it was only a matter of
time before she found a way to get to me. The fucking ravine. I
smirked. That place meant the world to us both now and it was
secluded. She would know to go there. Hell, I went there so
much it could be a second home. There was a cabin there a mile
passed my normal hang out spot. It was generally empty during
this time of the year. The owners only spent holidays there. I
could easily slip inside and hide.
I whistled for a cab, it screeched to a halt and I hopped
inside. "Lights Ravine, please?"
"That's thirty minutes out."
"I know that." I snapped.
"Alright, hop in," The Hispanic started his timer. "I
used to go there as a kid. I didn't know that people still went."
"Yeah, I like it." I tried not to roll my eyes, I slid the
glasses back on and slid down in the seat. There was a small
chance that I would even make it out of here alive. They had

check points all over the city and then there was the agent that wanted my head on a splint.

"Hold the cab!" I heard from behind me.

"Please don't..." My heart raced as my palms became sweaty.

"Special Agent McDonald." Declan flashed a shiny badge. "I'll be joining you."

"Dear God..."

"Exactly..." Declan slid into the vehicle and closed the door behind him. "Carry on."

Cypress

They questioned me for what seemed like hours about things that I was clueless about thankfully. The less I knew, the less there was to hide. The marriage had worked in our favor because they wanted to know everything about him and there was nothing that I could offer them. The only thing that I was certain of was that I needed to find him before they did. Mark held Nathaniel in his arms. A smile over his face that almost hid his tears. Perhaps Asher was right about everything. He might have wanted Shia. I hadn't really thought about his feelings in this matter and neither had Lucas.

"Do you know where he could be?" Mark whispered, his voice was small and there was pain behind his words. The lobby of the club held only us three and the kids. His voice echoed.

"I'm sorry." He knew what my apology was for, my voice shook as it broke and I exhaled. "I really am so sorry."

"I knew he would do it. I just didn't want to be a part of it." Mark wiped his face.

He was just as cold hearted as Lucas he just never went through with it, for him to overcome whatever lived inside him made him a bigger person than Lucas. It made him human. It was something in Mark that I feared no longer lived with Lucas, a sense of humanity. "It doesn't mean that you don't hurt."

Asher shook his head. "You should leave Cy."

"I am. I'm going to get him. But I know that they are going to follow my every move." I laughed. "Could you keep them?" I pointed to my children and regretted the fact that I had to leave instantly.

"I can." Mark said. "If you promise to punch him for me?"

"That promise I can keep."

"What're you going to do?" Asher asked. "I mean what are you going to say to him to make him come home. Because at this level of a break, I don't think he can be reached, even by you Cypress."

"I can perhaps ask him to turn himself in." Shit, I didn't know what I was about to do. I just knew that I had to do something.

"He will never do that. He sees that he has done nothing wrong? That's what a psychopath is Cypress. Do you get that? That is the most dangerous thing about him. He shows no remorse in anything that he does. He is a killer."

I looked at Asher. "He feels something Asher, so I don't really give a damn at whatever your psych babble is. He might be unhinged and that's fine." I rolled my eyes. "But he shows remorse for certain things Asher! He grieved his father and his mother. He loves me and these kids. He even fucking loves you." I snapped and the room grew silent. Perhaps I was too harsh, but there were a million and one negative thoughts racing through my head. I didn't need Asher adding fuel to the fire. "I'm sorry." I paused. "I know where he could be and more than likely where he is. I just don't know how to get away from the agents without them trailing my ass. They will follow my every move and I'll lead them to him..."

"There is a side exit no one is guarding. You could take the company van."

"Thanks Mark," I said.

"There are road blocks everywhere." Asher added. "So take the county road out to the ravine." He smiled at me. Asher knew him so well. "And hit that bastard for me too."

I chuckled. "Thank you... and I will."

I hated sneaking anywhere and out of the city was a hard one. They had surrounded the city with blocks. The county road was unscathed and the extra time it took to get there gave me time to think about whatever the fuck I was going to say to Lucas if he was even there.

It took forty-five minutes. I had tossed my cell phone out the window out of fear that they could be tracking me through it. I looked a horrible mess. My eyes were red from tears, the reality of everything. It had been a year and my life was completely different from what it had been. It now was a perfectly sculptured mess.

I parked the car and there was no sign that anyone was here at all. There was not a car in sight. I hopped out of the car and looked all around. "LUCAS!!" I yelled. My voice echoed. "Lucas!"

There was nothing except nature. I could hear nothing but the stupid fucking birds chirping and the water crashing on the rocks below me. I wept, my tears streamed down my face. I sat down on the damp floor and screamed. All of my anger and grief poured out and it was what I needed. There was too much bottled in me.

"Now what are you crying for love?" I heard his stupid accent behind me and my heart skipped a beat or two. "There are wild animals out here love."

"Baby!" My arms wrapped around his neck and I exhaled. "I thought..." I wiped my face. "What the fuck happened?"

"Such dirty words, I love the influence I've had on you." He kissed my cheek. "Come on, I can't stand out here." He whispered. "There is a house unoccupied about a half mile out... can you walk that far?"

"Yeah..."

"Good come on, no one followed you out here right?"

I nodded and gripped his hand. "We have to talk."

"In the house please."

The small white house was comfy and apparently belonged to a family that never spent time here. It was spotless and barely furnished. I sat down on the only couch in it and looked at Lucas. "What happened?"

"There is something in me that no one can understand Cypress."

"I get it."

"You don't and you never will." He snapped. "I can't stop myself sometimes and it has become my downfall. I couldn't leave America with Persephone still alive. I felt like if I did… I would have come back to finish. So I offed her."

The remorse was not there. His eyes were cold. "Why?"

"I can't explain. I don't know how to explain it to you. Perhaps this is why my father never got too close to my mom. I can't stop. It's addicting and like an addict was feening for that feeling…"

"We can still leave."

"Interpol would be on me before I made it anywhere. I'm done."

"Done?"

"Dead, might as well be." He shrugged. "I wanted to talk to you before talking to you alone is not a privilege."

"What do you mean?"

"Just listen…"

I could hear the sirens as they whaled somewhere nearby. There was something in his eyes that I had not yet seen before. It was fear. He was terrified. He stared at me. "What is it?"

He slid against the wall. "I never wanted any of this shit to happen the way it did. I would have never planned a future for us elsewhere if I had not been wanting to include myself."

"Then why did you do it?"

"I'm a monster." He mumbled. "You…" his word lingered in the air and the room filled with sirens. "When my mom died…" He paused. "I felt for the first time in years. Have you ever heard of asperatus clouds?"

I paused. "No Luke, I haven't. What do they have to do with anything?"

"The clouds filled the skies in Cumbria and the welled up like waves in the sky and the skies began to cry. This woman was so loved that even the earth literally wept for her." the streams of tears swam down his face. "They mourned her death and she was remembered as the flower lady on the corner of Magna Avenue."

"Luke."

"Shut it for one bloody moment Cypress." His face was red. "I won't be remembered as the man you loved. I won't be remembered for being Nathaniel and Willow's father or the guy who wrote a best seller. I killed 54 people."

My spine grew rigid. "Don't tell me anymore."

"I love you and I don't want Nathaniel to remember me as the man that was a monster that you see in movies. So do me a favor, Forget me." Tears streamed from his face and I jumped at his words. "I'm so sorry that you had to find out who I was. I'm sorry that there was something for you to find out."

"I don't... I will mourn you Lucas... but you aren't dying."

"I want you to go before they get here. If you are caught with me then they'll count you as an accessory. You need to be a mother to our kids. And not associated with any of this shit. So get out."

"No."

"I didn't ask you Cypress! Get the fuck out of here!" He grabbed me by my arm. "Leave, before your fate is worse than mine." His lips crashed into mine and their desperation that bled through. "Please, don't make it hard."

I clung to him. "Don't be mean to me. Just let me stay."

"Listen to reason. Get out!" He yelled.

I stepped towards the door. "Okay, I love you."

"I love you." He shook his head. "Go to the right and circle around to your car. Get out of here and don't look back."

"Tell me you won't do anything stupid?"

"I won't."

I ran through the forest blindly to the right coming out beside my car and my hands shook. I could hear the cops as they closed on the house, pangs of gunfire everywhere and then there was silence, followed by a loud explosion as the yellow flames appeared in my rear view window.

EPILOGUE

Cypress

Ireland was a good idea. The lush green and water surrounding us was what I needed. Because there was no peace for me in America. They'd found his body burned to a crisp by an explosion that was still being investigated and I wanted nothing to do with it anymore. Five agonizing months had passed and Nathaniel had learned to crawl successfully. He had now started the terror on the house. He destroyed everything in his path much like his father and Willow, well Ashe rarely let her out of his sights. He'd found a university to teach at and had an apartment in town. I think for once he had found some kind of happiness.

I doubted that I would ever find happiness again. The words of the letter that Lucas had mailed prior to his death had lingered over and over in my head.

My Love,
It's funny how the mind works. Everyone thinks differently. And my mind tends to think so differently that it poses as a danger to us both. There are things that I can never tell you. I guess it's true the only emotions that linger in me are those regarding you. There is love, hope, joy, trust, friendship, but mostly there is fear. I fear that you cannot accept me for who I am and who would. I am bat shit crazy, perhaps more than you tend to believe. So I have to leave you and I know that this will make you incomplete, and love that is not my intentions. I

searched my whole entire life to feel something rather than the monster that dwells inside. And you have given me the ability to feel and for that I am forever grateful. The monster, which is me, tends to be selfish, but this I am doing for you is selfless. I love you forever and always and there is not one thing that can change it. Promise to keep me in your heart and I swear to leave you with a slice of mine.

Yours Truly, Lucas.

He was truly mine and it made getting over it impossible. Especially when Nathaniel was his look-a-alike in more ways than one. The waves of the sea crashed on the beach nearby, but were not close enough for me to worry about the kids. Willow rolled around on her blanket, her tight sandy blonde hair was untamed like mine and they were starting to take their true forms.

"It still amazes me that the sound of the beach is like music to your ears." Declan's voice said from behind me.

"What are you doing here?" I hugged his neck and closed the book that was clasped in my hand.

"I was in the country for a while. Looks like I'll be here with Nadine. That fall, she took a few weeks back has her worried out of her mind."

"Yeah, we go there every morning. I've gotten quite good at Chess. I hate the game, but anything to keep her from killing me." The ritual was one she had with Callum but Callum was always on the go. He had taken Lucas death extremely hard. As did Mark, who disappeared right after the funeral. He sent letters and video messaged Nathaniel and Willow quite often.

"How are you?"

"Uhm, well as I can be. The family loves me which is good because I think mine hates me."

"I doubt it." He sat down on the towel next to me and watched as the kids played. "I hate I missed most of my kids growing up." He touched Willow's hand and w3iped the sand from her palm.

"Well, they turned out good."

"All but one," He shook his head. "You got some mail in the house. I can keep an eye on these two if you want me to?"

"Perfect, I was expecting some books to arrive today." I hustled to the cottage and tossed my old book to the table. There was no mail here at all. But I could easily see that the place needed a little tender love and care. The toys covered most of the floor and the clothes were mixed in there occasionally. I picked up a few of the toys and prayed that Declan had not seen any of the shit tossed on the floor.

"I love the way you look when you are cleaning love..."

It almost sounded like Lucas, the British accent was thick and perfect alot like his. But I was sure there was more of an Irish accent shooting out. I turned around, expecting Callum but it wasn't. His hair was all gone. There was just a short sex hair look. And his eyes were bright. It was Lucas.

AUTHOR'S NOTES

Thank you so much for the taking the time out of your life to read my book! I am so thrilled to finally be able to share my story with someone other myself! Your support means everything to me and I honestly cannot thank you enough! If you are interested in more of this family's story, there will be more from this series released very soon! I've actually added a playlist of the songs that truly inspired me to write! In order to keep up with news about the release dates and other works, please add me as a friend on Facebook! My name is LR Johnson on there as well! Not to mention you can go like my Author page on Facebook and add me on Goodreads to keep yourself updated as well! Thanks once again for all your support!

Happy Reading!!

<u>Music to Read By Playlist:</u>

Monster: Mumford and Sons
Not About Angels: Birdy
I Found: Amber Run
Work Song: Hozier
Make it Rain: Ed Sheeran
If I Could Fly: One Direction
Can't Let Go: Adele
Let it Go: James Bay
Move Together: James Bay
Little Things: James Bay
My Love Will Never Die: Hozier
Gravity: Sara Bareilles
The Words: Christina Perri
A Message: Coldplay
Unsteady: X Ambassadors
Resolution: Matt Corby
This Time: Jarryd James
Bloom: The Paper Kites
Only Love: Mumford and Sons
The Parting Glass: Ed Sheeran
Meet Me in the Middle: Jessi Ware
Little Things: One Direction
Brother: Matt Corby

Here is a Sneak Peek from:

HAVOC

Promise to keep me in your heart and I swear to leave you with a slice of mine. The last line of his letter loomed in my memory over and over. I could hear those words on in my mind even though he never said to me. I was haunted by Lucas daily by my children. They grew more and more like Lucas each and every day. I wanted to scream. I needed to break free, but there was nothing that I could do besides grieve silently. His family had already decided that I was fragile. His grandmother, Nadine had made it her goal in life to keep me busy. She planned something every day and if I wasn't busy she would stop and talk.

It was too no surprise that she knew so much about life and there was enough wisdom in her to teach classes. She had a rough life and had raised a family with someone so similar to Lucas it scared me. George Elledge was a force to be reckoned with even in his old age he demanded respect. The fear the town had for him showed when his name was mentioned. He was more domineering than his grandson, but I could see the inner workings.

Wicklow, Ireland was the most beautiful place I had ever seen. The house on the beach had been Lucas' idea. He wanted to be close to his family, but far off enough to feel distant. The view of the Atlantic Ocean done it. The waters were a dazzling blue year round and though they were colder in the incoming winter months. It's what I looked forward to the most. Freezing waters and silent nights. The children were dressed and loaded in Nadine's car. I had convinced myself that I could go out for a night on the town. The town was small but the pubs were plenty. It was all I needed. I hadn't had a drink since I had gotten here. One drink, by myself in my best dress. That's all I wanted.

Nadine kissed my cheek, leaving a faint smudge mark on my less than perfect makeup and took the kids with her and Asher. They said that they would be back tomorrow afternoon to give me the morning to myself. Asher had been the glue that held me together. He didn't have to come to Ireland with us. He had a job offer to teach at several American Universities but he took the one in Ireland. He said that he couldn't watch me try to merge with the family without some assistance. He was new to the family too. I think it was because he wanted to feel like he belonged somewhere. And he had found a home. His grandparents welcomed him and he had a flock of cousins, uncles and aunts. People I had yet to meet myself. They never all came to dinner. They were engrossed with their own lives. They made time when they had it. They were not like me and constantly looking for an escape from the annoying silence in my head.

I had felt empty ever since he died. No matter how much I loved my kids, I still felt like there was something wrong with me, to the point that I forced his cousin, Callum, to sleep on my couch for a few days. Just to make sure that I was fine. I didn't want to harm my children, but it seemed possible with my distraught mind frame.

My outfit was less than perfect. The slim cut blue jeans hugged my hips, but they disagreed with the remnants of pregnancy. My stomach had not yet snapped back to that perfect size waist. I was never a skinny girl, but my curves used to be all in the right places. Now I felt like they just got in wherever they fit. I tossed on a flimsy black shirt and some black heels. Ireland was a festive place. The people were always down for a party. This could be a way to escape it.

I drove into town and spotted a few familiar faces from the church Nadine had me join with her. The girls were pretty, young and free. They had no children or no dead husband, just ambition, hopes and time.

I waved to them as I stepped out of the car and freaked out as they saw me approach them. They were one year younger than me, but it seemed like I was the old lady out of the group. I was the only one clothed and not already half wasted upon arrival. The blaring of music shot the speakers on the streets and the three girls started to dance. I hadn't bothered to ask their names. I just know that they loved my kids and they worshipped Nadine and George like everyone else in this town. So I followed with them and once we entered the bar I watched the people.

The smell of ale filled the air. The beer here was to die for. It was not like American Bud Light or Michelob, I was accustomed to, this beer was smoother and it was fresh, straight from the tap. I ordered a pint and sat down on the wooden stool of the sidebar. The men here were older and heavy set, all full of laughter and good times apparently. The bar filled with old Irish tunes and it felt warm. My eyes glanced around the green walls of the bar. Pictures of old customers and their wives and the most alluring item was the wooden plaque. EST. 1859. The bar was antique but it was still a really well known spot.

I sipped my beer in the corner and from nowhere a guy slides in. His eyes are familiar, but there is nothing else that I can recognize.

"What's the craic?"

Damn Irish slang. I roll my eyes. "Hi."

"What're you doin' here alone?"

His cologne filled the air that surrounded me and I was allured. It was hypnotizing. The smell of the sandalwood and the amber mixed. Then there was his perfectly parted hair that was brushed back and his beard. I was never one for beards, but on a face like that I could get used to one. "I don't know anyone really."

"You're American... tourist?"

"No... I live in Wicklow?"

"Wicklow, I haven't been that way in ages... headed there in a wee bit though."

"Wow, what a coincidence. Why are you headed that way?"

"Family business," He gulped down the remainder of his beer and slid it to the bartender. "'Nother?"

"I haven't finished this one."

"You can never have enough to drink... I mean at least get bolloxed with me." He winked and the bartender refilled both of our glasses. "So you're a culchie huh?"

"Pardon me?"

"Country girl..."

"Yes." In only the American sense, Tennessee was the heart of the south for me.

The bartender smiled. "Kage, glad to see you back eh? I haven't seen you in donkey ears?"

"I'm only back for a minute... family concerns are driving me mad? You know how they can be. Tiring and worrisome, but they are family and you have got to take care of them."

"Of course they are and of course you will." He nodded his head. "Your drinks are on the house. You and the lass. Let me know you what want eh?"

"Aye." He smirked and looked back at me. His name was Kage. "So pardon me manners, I'm Kage love… who are yah?"

His shoulders were broad and masculine and that damn jaw line would make a model look like shit. "I'm Cypress."

"Perfect name, beautiful just like you."

"Good one…" I chuckled.

"So why is a lass as fair as you here alone?"

"Drinking my sorrows?" I smiled half-heartedly.

"And what are your sorrows?"

"Dead husband?"

"Oh," He grew quiet. Way to kill the conversation before it can start. His finger swirled around the rim of the glass. "That's sad."

"I know. I'm sorry. I don't even know why I came out. My brother in law took the kids and I was thinking that I could feel alive again if I came out, but I think it's draining what little life I have in me out." Shut up, Cypress. Jesus.

"Well, look, I would like to offer you so relief by being the one that makes you smile tonight. We can sing bar songs… or we could dance around under the stars. Whatever, your wish is my command." He flourished himself and cracked a smile.

"Could we get out of here?"

"I would love to but I didn't drive. I rode into town with a cousin."

"Leave him, I can drive you." The impulse was something I was not used to but it had been such a while since I had even reacted to a man. Sure, I got hit on all the time but I blocked the out for good reason. But now I wanted to feel something… not emotions. No, this was all physical.

"Where are we going?"

"Anywhere?" I swallowed down the remnants of my beer and shrugged my shoulders.

"Are you looking to shag?"

"Shag?"

"Pardon me, you American women are so crude." His smile brightened and he leaned closer to me. "Are you looking to fucked senseless?"

My chest ached from the beat of my heart pounding on it. "Yes, I whispered.

"Perfect, lead the way."

www.ingramcontent.com/pod-product-compliance
Lightning Source LLC
Chambersburg PA
CBHW030620250626
47154CB00006B/1862